The adventure continues with tales from the Battle Frontier, where new enemies and new Pokémon await Hareta! Plus, Hareta's egg finally hatches! I've also included another bonus episode! I hope you enjoy reading this volume as much as I enjoyed creating it!

– *Shigekatsu Ihara*

Shigekatsu Ihara's other manga titles include *Pokémon: Lucario and the Mystery of Mew, Pokémon Emerald Challenge!!* and *Battle Frontier, Dual Jack!!*

Pokémon DIAMOND AND PEARL ADVENTURE!

Vol. 7
VIZ Kids Edition

Story & Art by SHIGEKATSU IHARA

© 2010 Pokémon.
© 1995–2010 Nintendo/Creatures Inc./GAME FREAK inc.
TM & ® are trademarks of Nintendo.
© 2007 Shigekatsu IHARA/Shogakukan
All rights reserved.
Original Japanese edition
"Pokémon D•P POCKET MONSTER DIAMOND PEARL MONOGATARI"
published by SHOGAKUKAN Inc.

Translation/Kaori Inoue
English Adaptation/Stan! Brown
Touch-up Art & Lettering/Eric Erbes
Graphics & Cover Design/Hitomi Yokoyama Ross
Editor/Annette Roman

VP, Production/Alvin Lu
VP, Sales & Product Marketing/Gonzalo Ferreyra
VP, Creative/Linda Espinosa
Publisher/Hyoe Narita

Printed in the U.S.A.

Published by VIZ Media, LLC
P.O. Box 77010
San Francisco, CA 94107

10 9 8 7 6 5 4 3 2 1
First printing, July 2010

www.vizkids.com

POKÉMON®

DIAMOND AND PEARL ADVENTURE!

Volume 7

Story & Art by
Shigekatsu Ihara

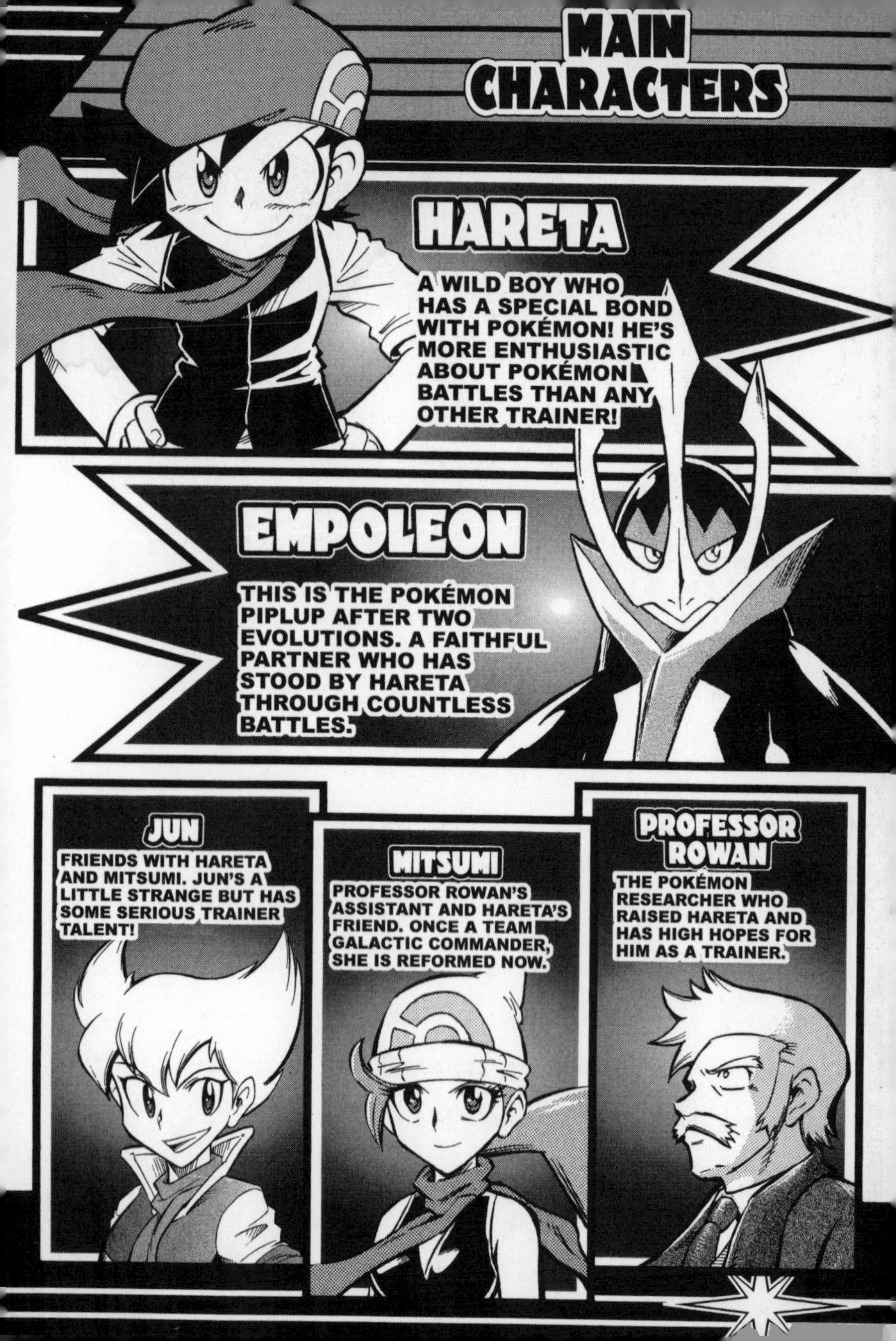
MAIN CHARACTERS
HARETA
A WILD BOY WHO HAS A SPECIAL BOND WITH POKÉMON! HE'S MORE ENTHUSIASTIC ABOUT POKÉMON BATTLES THAN ANY OTHER TRAINER!
EMPOLEON
THIS IS THE POKÉMON PIPLUP AFTER TWO EVOLUTIONS. A FAITHFUL PARTNER WHO HAS STOOD BY HARETA THROUGH COUNTLESS BATTLES.
PROFESSOR ROWAN
THE POKÉMON RESEARCHER WHO RAISED HARETA AND HAS HIGH HOPES FOR HIM AS A TRAINER.
MITSUMI
PROFESSOR ROWAN'S ASSISTANT AND HARETA'S FRIEND. ONCE A TEAM GALACTIC COMMANDER, SHE IS REFORMED NOW.
JUN
FRIENDS WITH HARETA AND MITSUMI. JUN'S A LITTLE STRANGE BUT HAS SOME SERIOUS TRAINER TALENT!

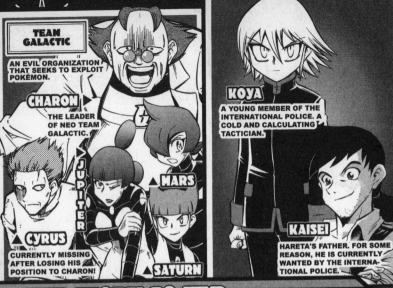

KOYA
A YOUNG MEMBER OF THE INTERNATIONAL POLICE. A COLD AND CALCULATING TACTICIAN.
KAISEI
HARETA'S FATHER. FOR SOME REASON, HE IS CURRENTLY WANTED BY THE INTERNATIONAL POLICE.
TEAM GALACTIC
AN EVIL ORGANIZATION THAT SEEKS TO EXPLOIT POKÉMON.
CHARON
THE LEADER OF NEO TEAM GALACTIC.
JUPITER
MARS
CYRUS
CURRENTLY MISSING AFTER LOSING HIS POSITION TO CHARON!
SATURN

THE STORY SO FAR

In the Sinnoh Battle Tournament, Hareta faces a cold-as-ice boy named Koya. But the tournament is disrupted when Neo Team Galactic attacks! What is Neo Team Galactic after? Hareta is briefly reunited with his missing father, Kaisei, who gives him a Pokémon Egg and immediately runs off again. A new set of enemies stands in Hareta's way as he tries to track his father down!

TABLE OF CONTENTS

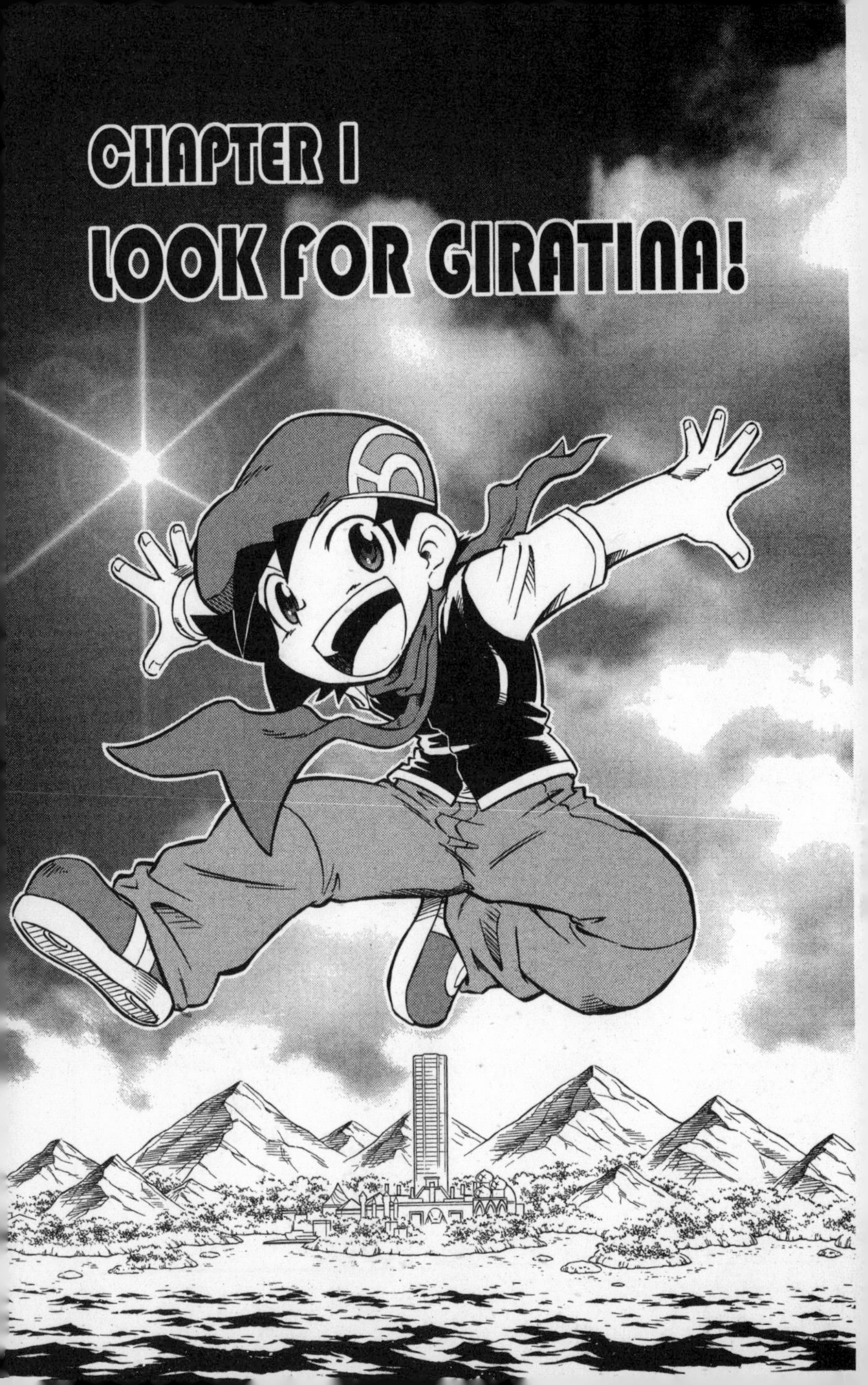
CHAPTER 1
LOOK FOR GIRATINA!

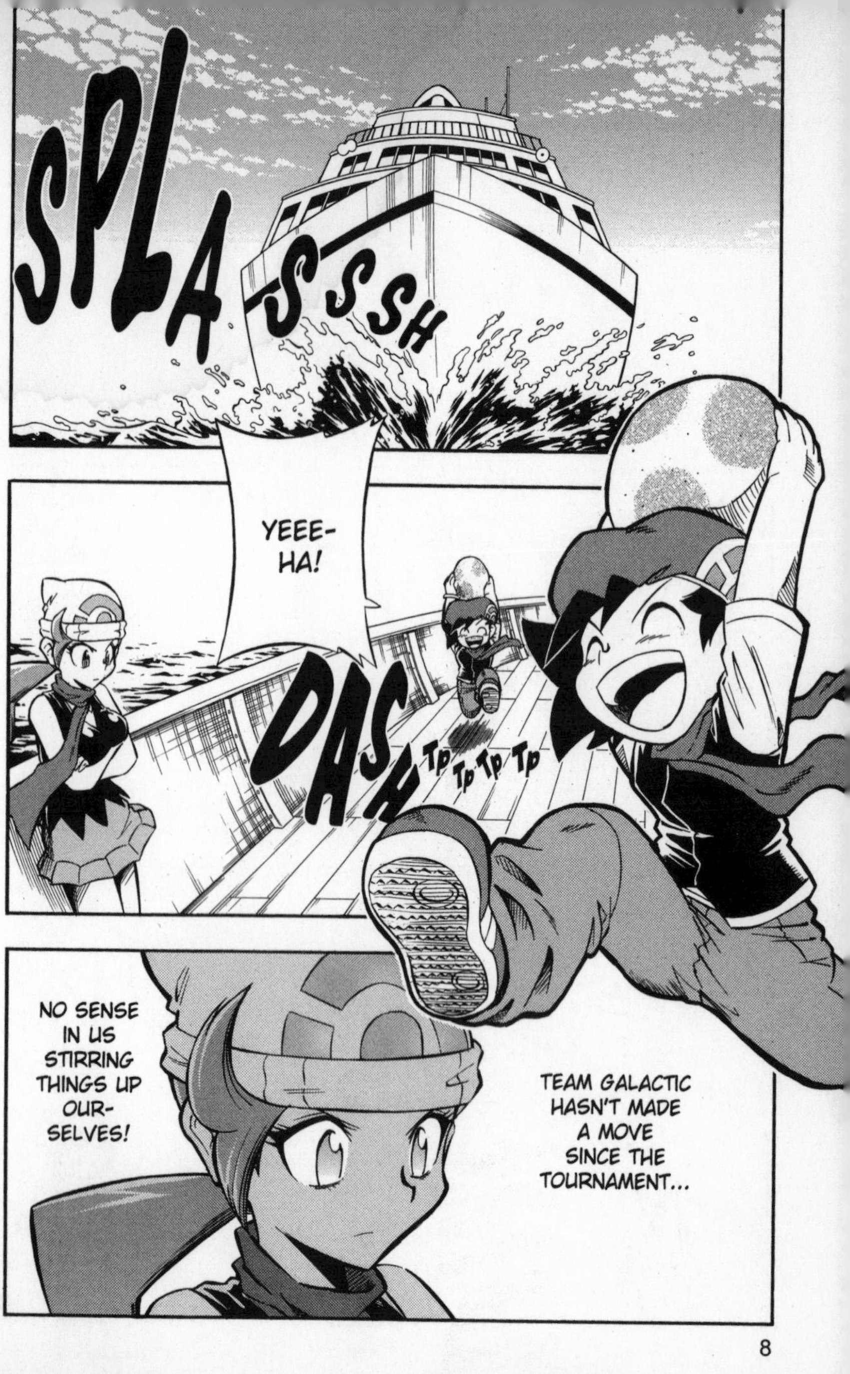
SPLASSSH
YEEE-HA!
DASH
Tp Tp Tp Tp
TEAM GALACTIC HASN'T MADE A MOVE SINCE THE TOURNAMENT...
NO SENSE IN US STIRRING THINGS UP OUR-SELVES!

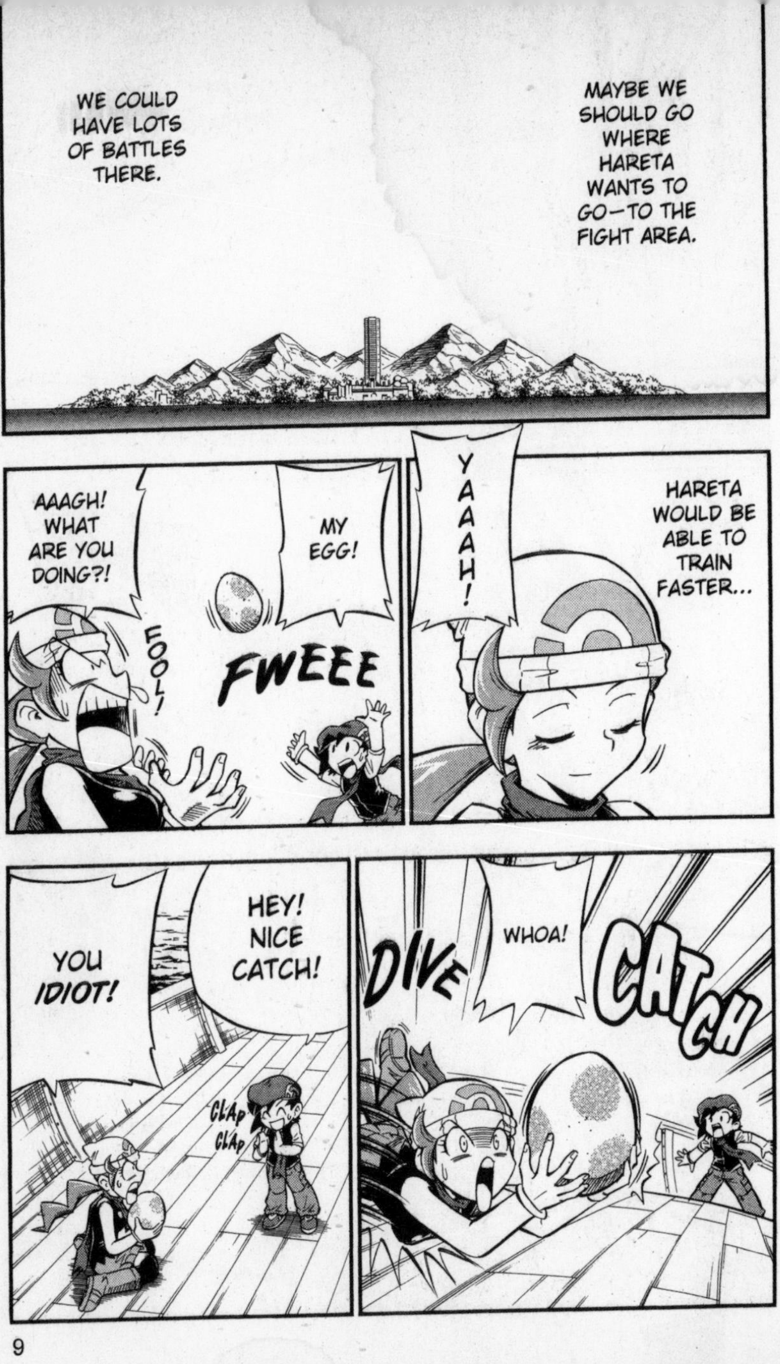
MAYBE WE SHOULD GO WHERE HARETA WANTS TO GO—TO THE FIGHT AREA.
WE COULD HAVE LOTS OF BATTLES THERE.
HARETA WOULD BE ABLE TO TRAIN FASTER...
YAAAAH!
MY EGG!
FWEEE
AAAGH! WHAT ARE YOU DOING?!
FOOL!
WHOA!
CATCH
DIVE
HEY! NICE CATCH!
YOU IDIOT!
CLAP CLAP

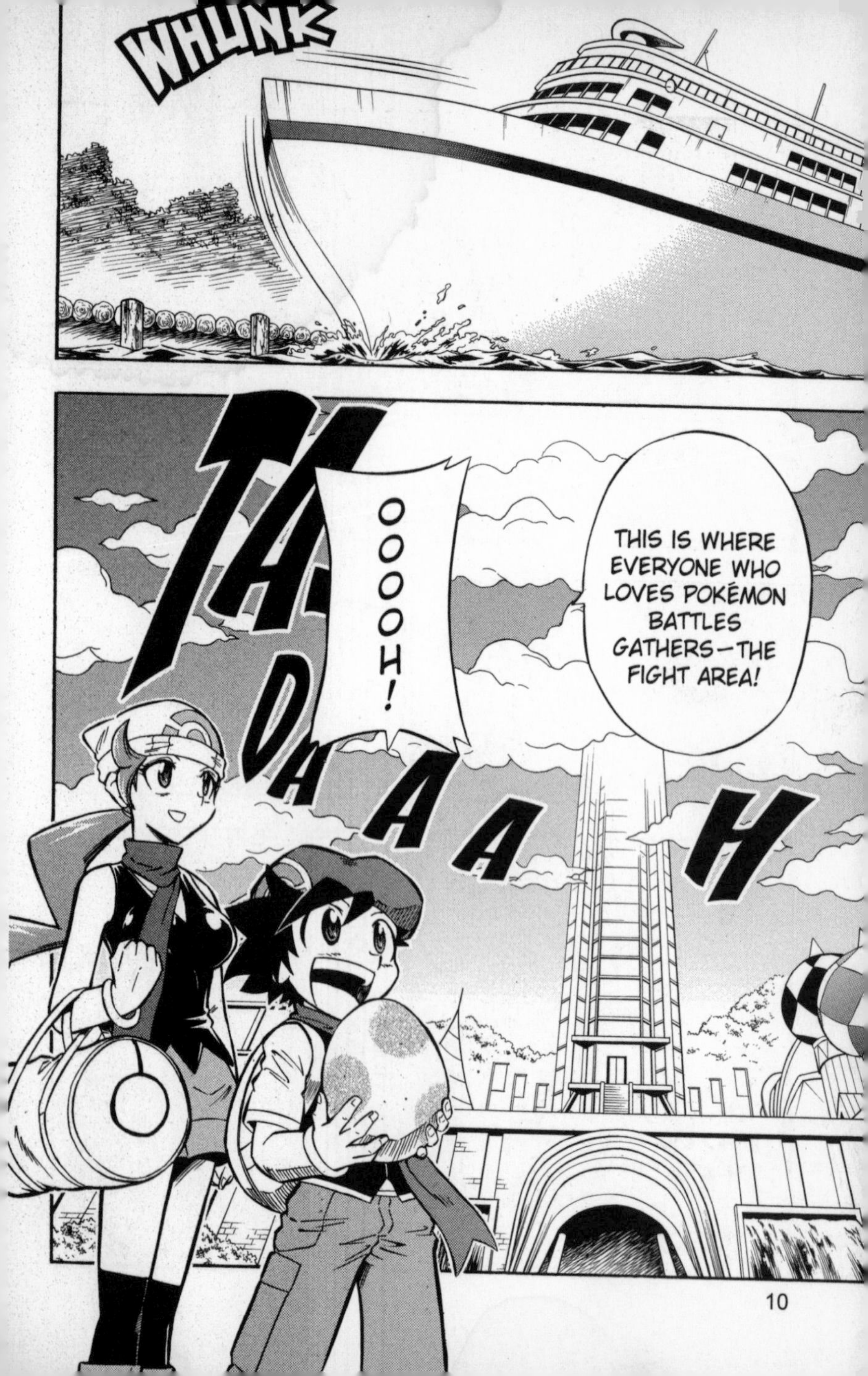
WHUNK
THIS IS WHERE EVERYONE WHO LOVES POKÉMON BATTLES GATHERS—THE FIGHT AREA!
OOOOH!
TA-DAAAAH

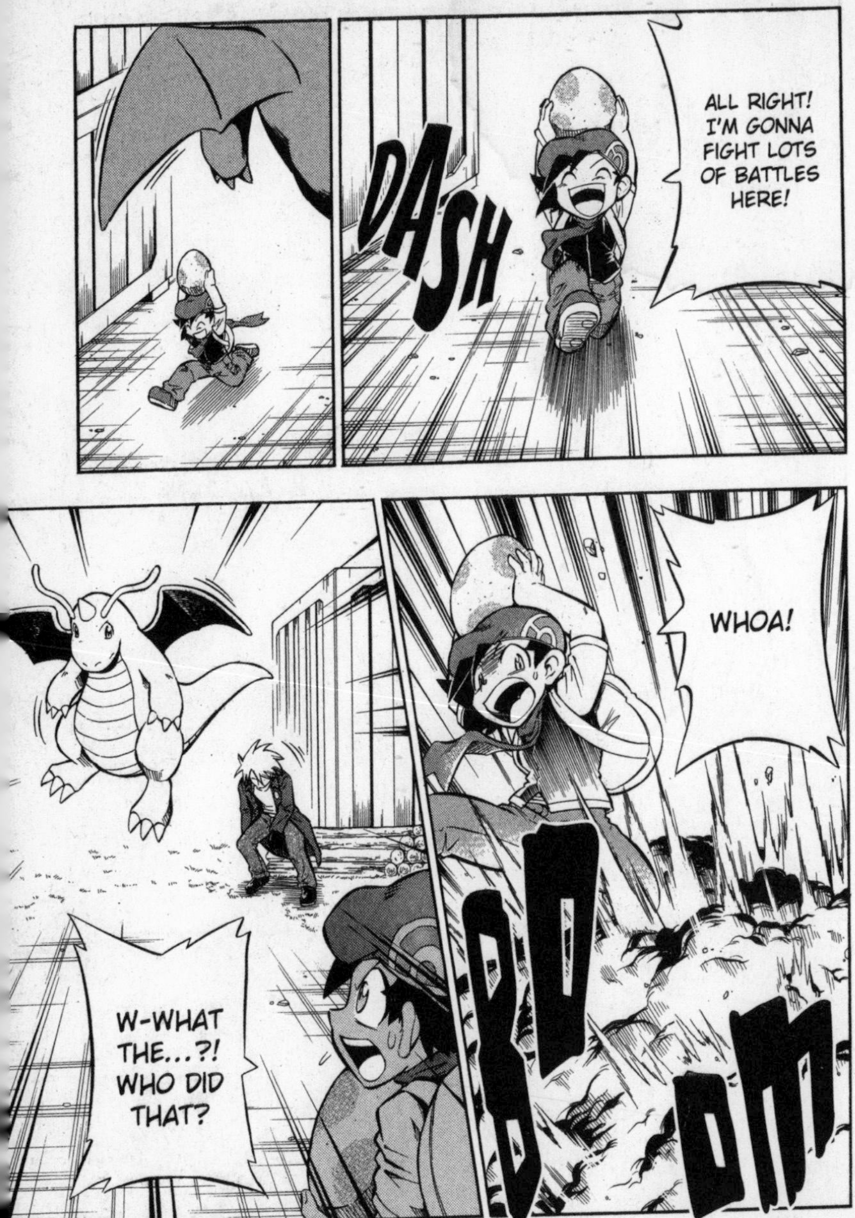
ALL RIGHT! I'M GONNA FIGHT LOTS OF BATTLES HERE!
DASH
WHOA!
BOOM
W-WHAT THE...?! WHO DID THAT?

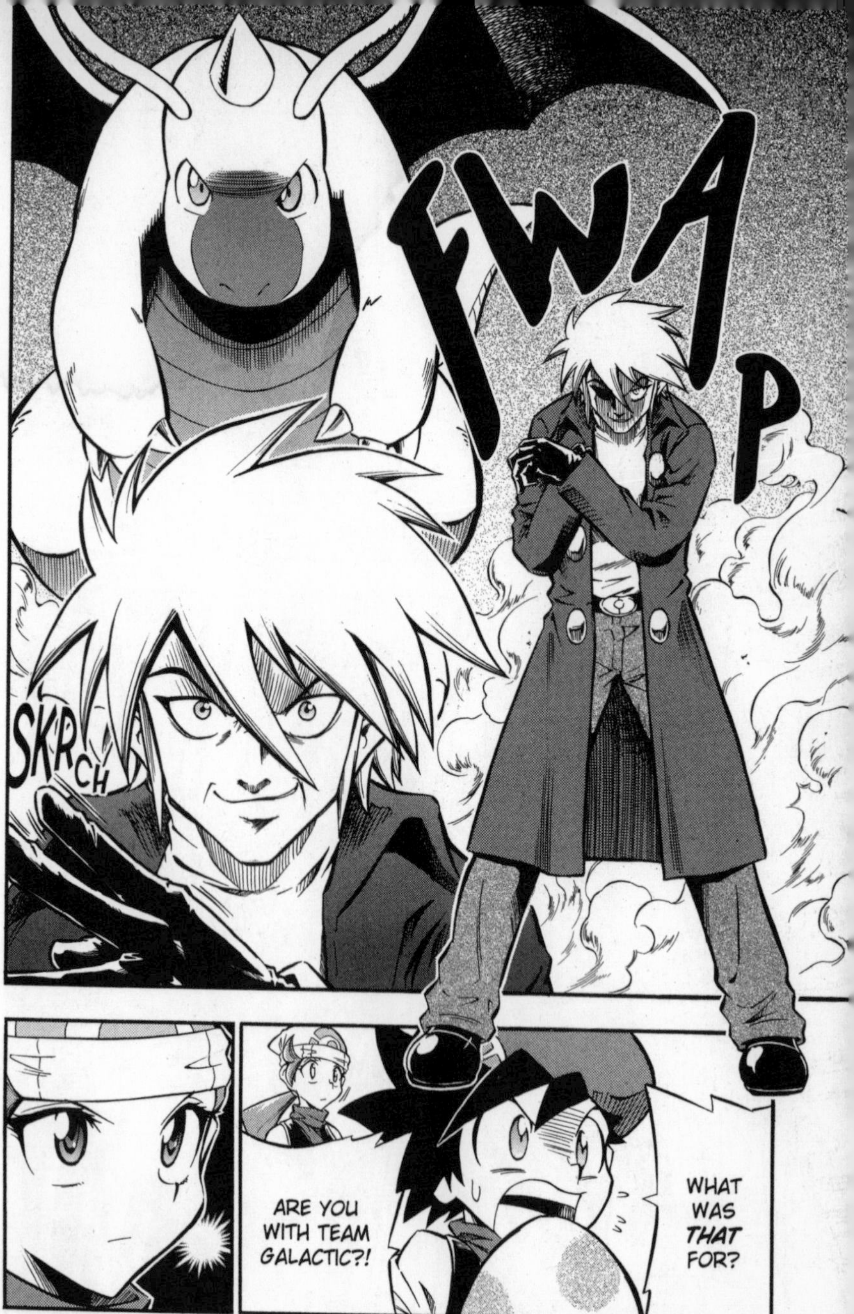
FWAP
SKRCH
WHAT WAS *THAT* FOR?
ARE YOU WITH TEAM GALACTIC?!

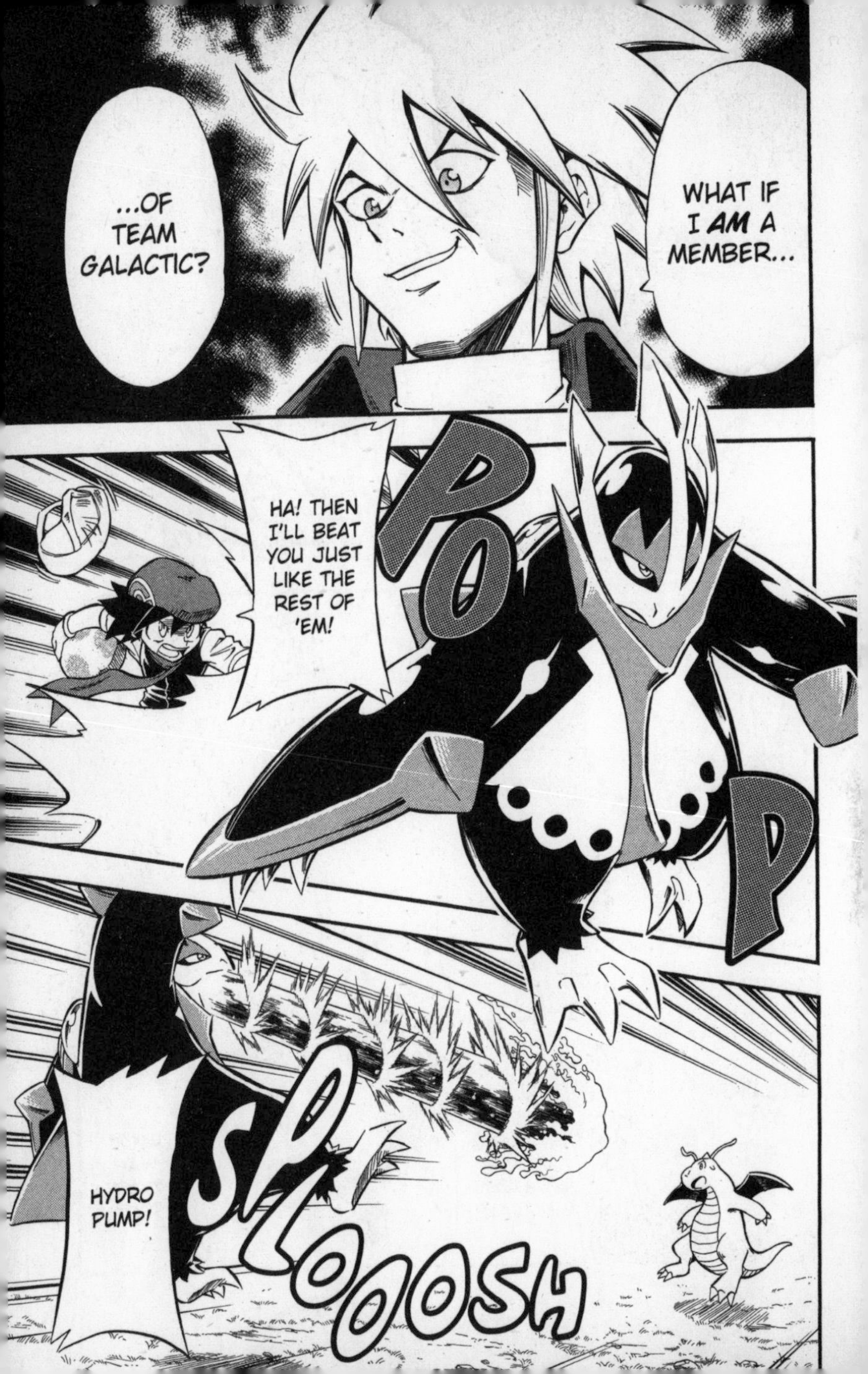
WHAT IF I *AM* A MEMBER...
...OF TEAM GALACTIC?
POP
HA! THEN I'LL BEAT YOU JUST LIKE THE REST OF 'EM!
SPLOOOSH
HYDRO PUMP!

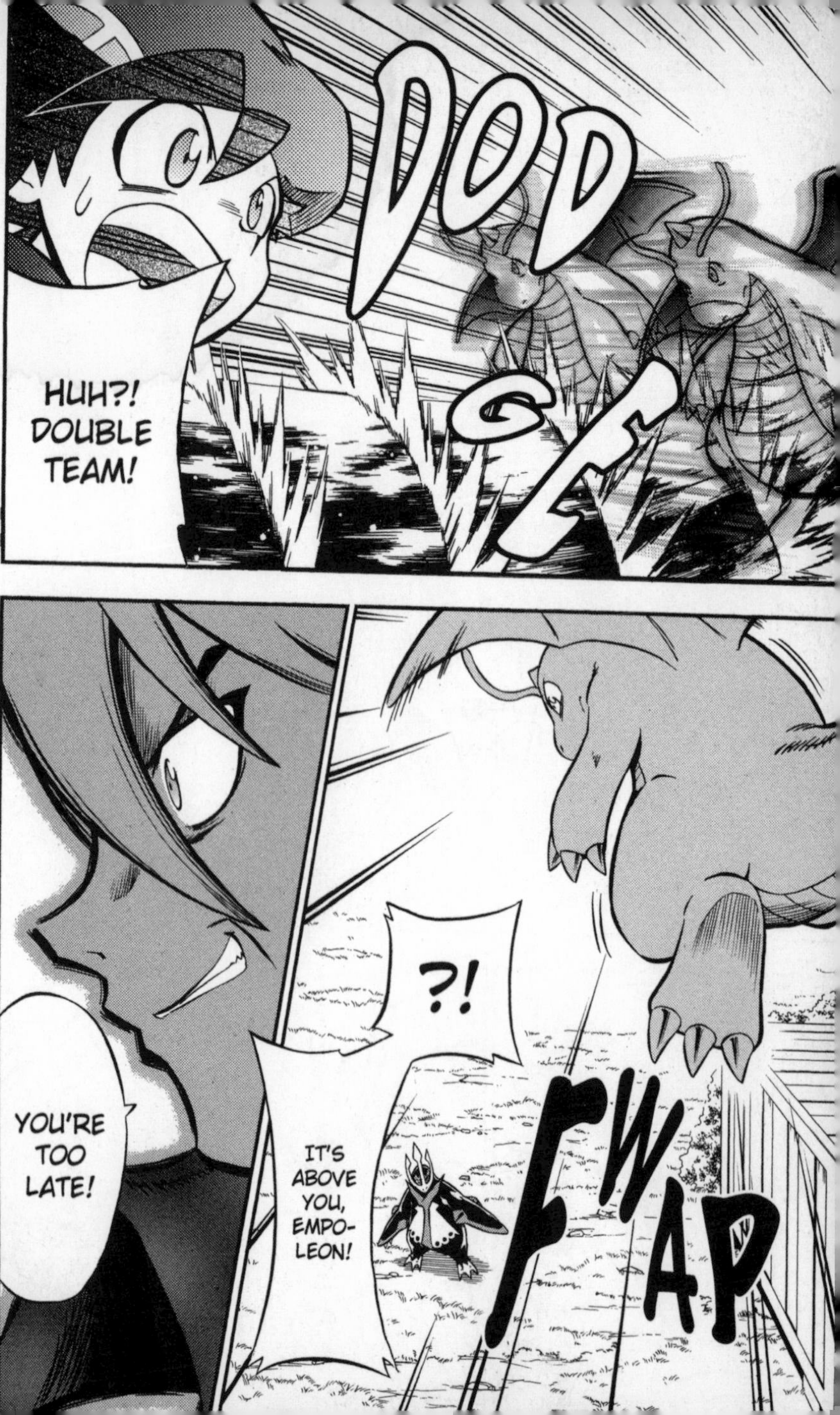
DOD
GF
HUH?! DOUBLE TEAM!
?!
FWAP
IT'S ABOVE YOU, EMPO-LEON!
YOU'RE TOO LATE!

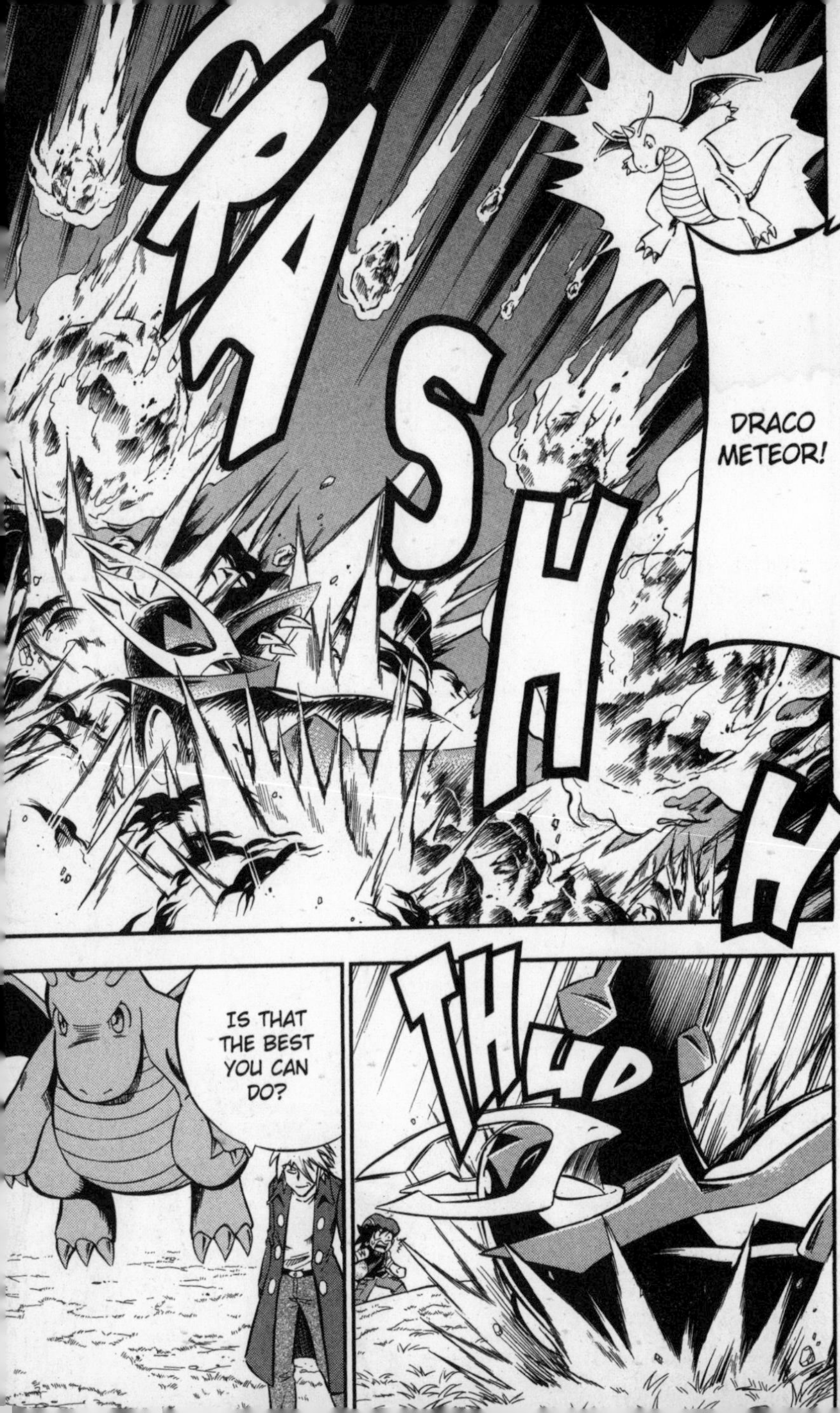
DRACO METEOR!
CRASHHH
THUD
IS THAT THE BEST YOU CAN DO?

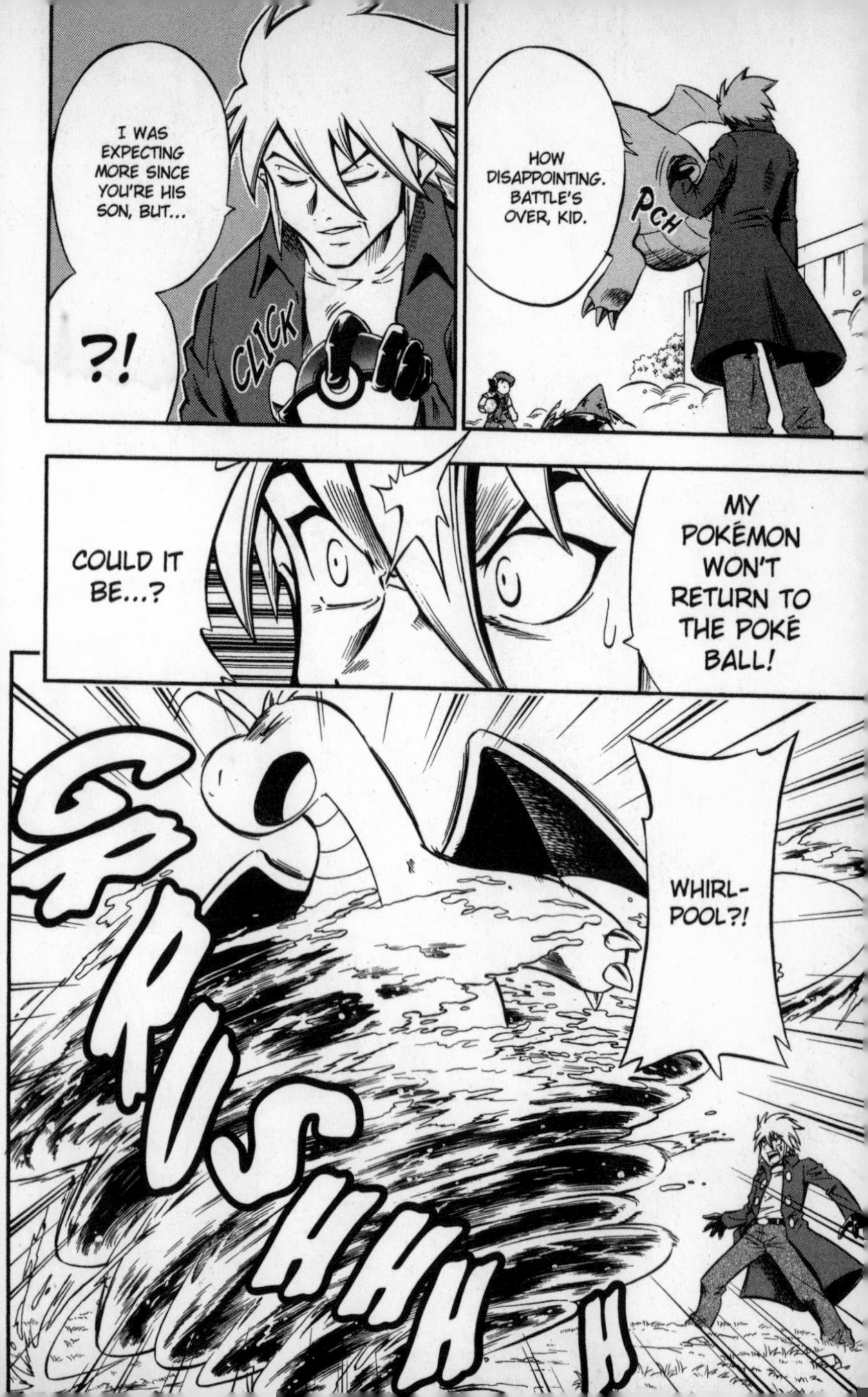
HOW DISAPPOINTING. BATTLE'S OVER, KID.
PCH
I WAS EXPECTING MORE SINCE YOU'RE HIS SON, BUT...
CLICK
?!
MY POKÉMON WON'T RETURN TO THE POKÉ BALL!
COULD IT BE...?
WHIRL-POOL?!

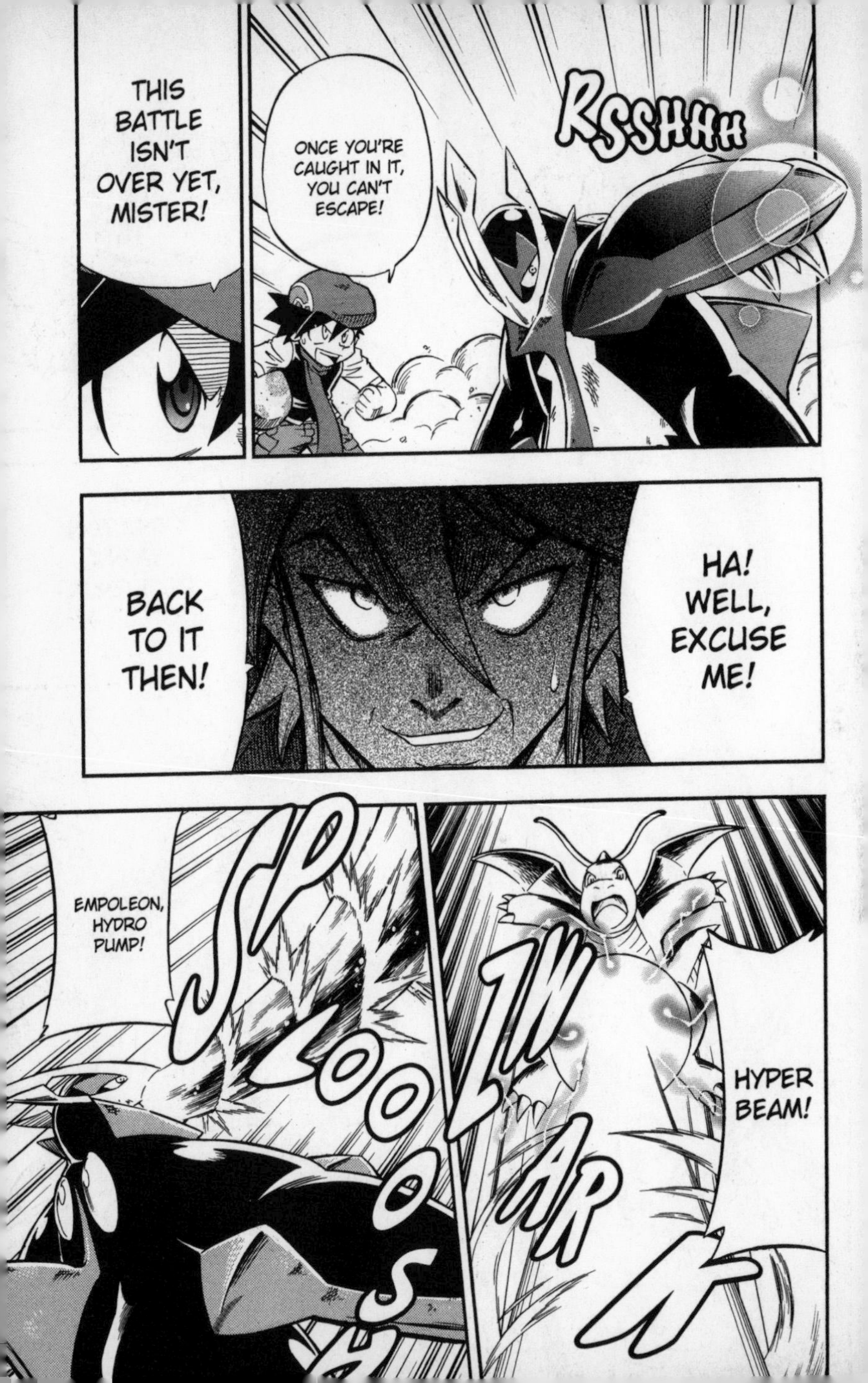
RSSHHH
ONCE YOU'RE CAUGHT IN IT, YOU CAN'T ESCAPE!
THIS BATTLE ISN'T OVER YET, MISTER!
HA! WELL, EXCUSE ME!
BACK TO IT THEN!
HYPER BEAM!
ZWARK
EMPOLEON, HYDRO PUMP!
SPLOOOOSH

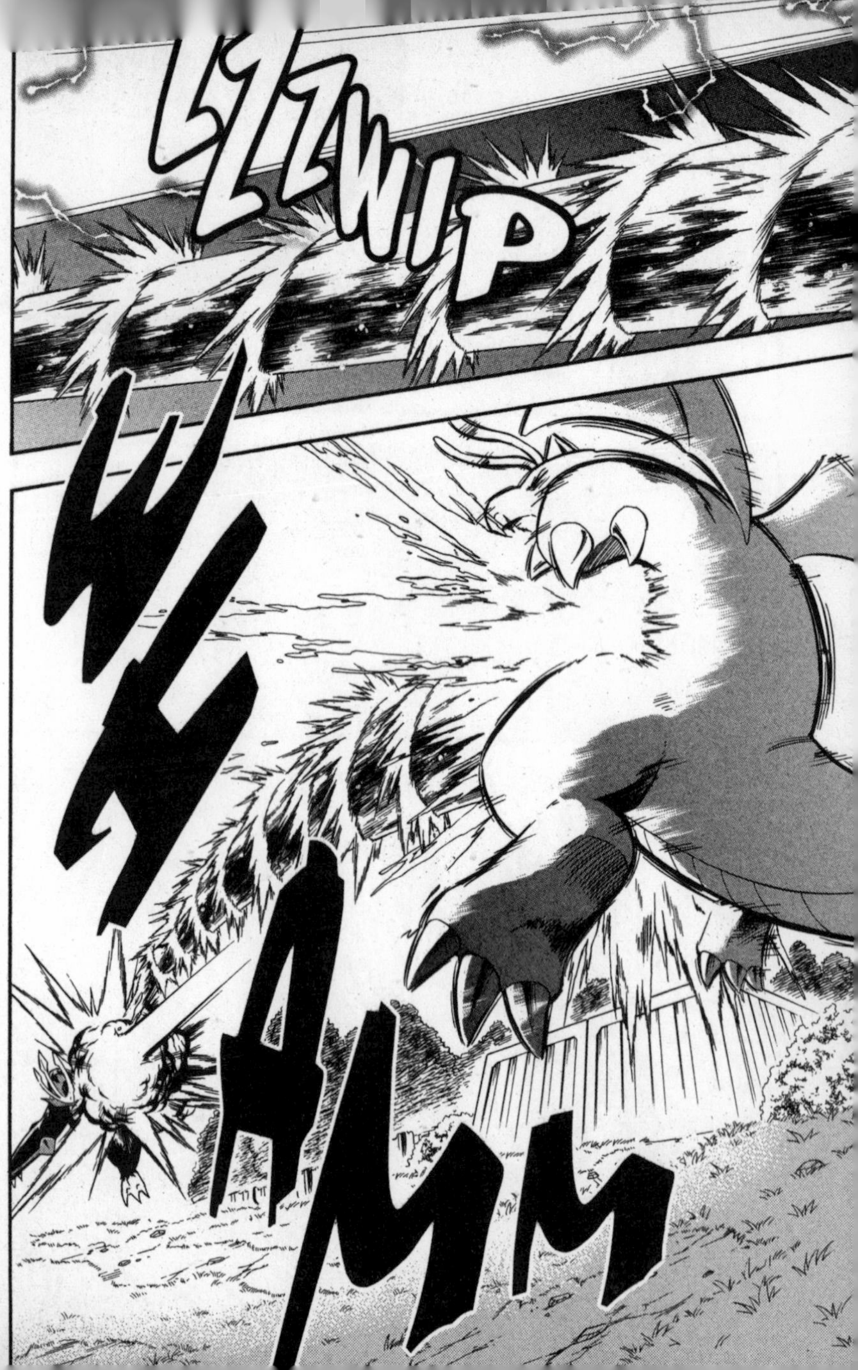
LZZWIP
SHAMM

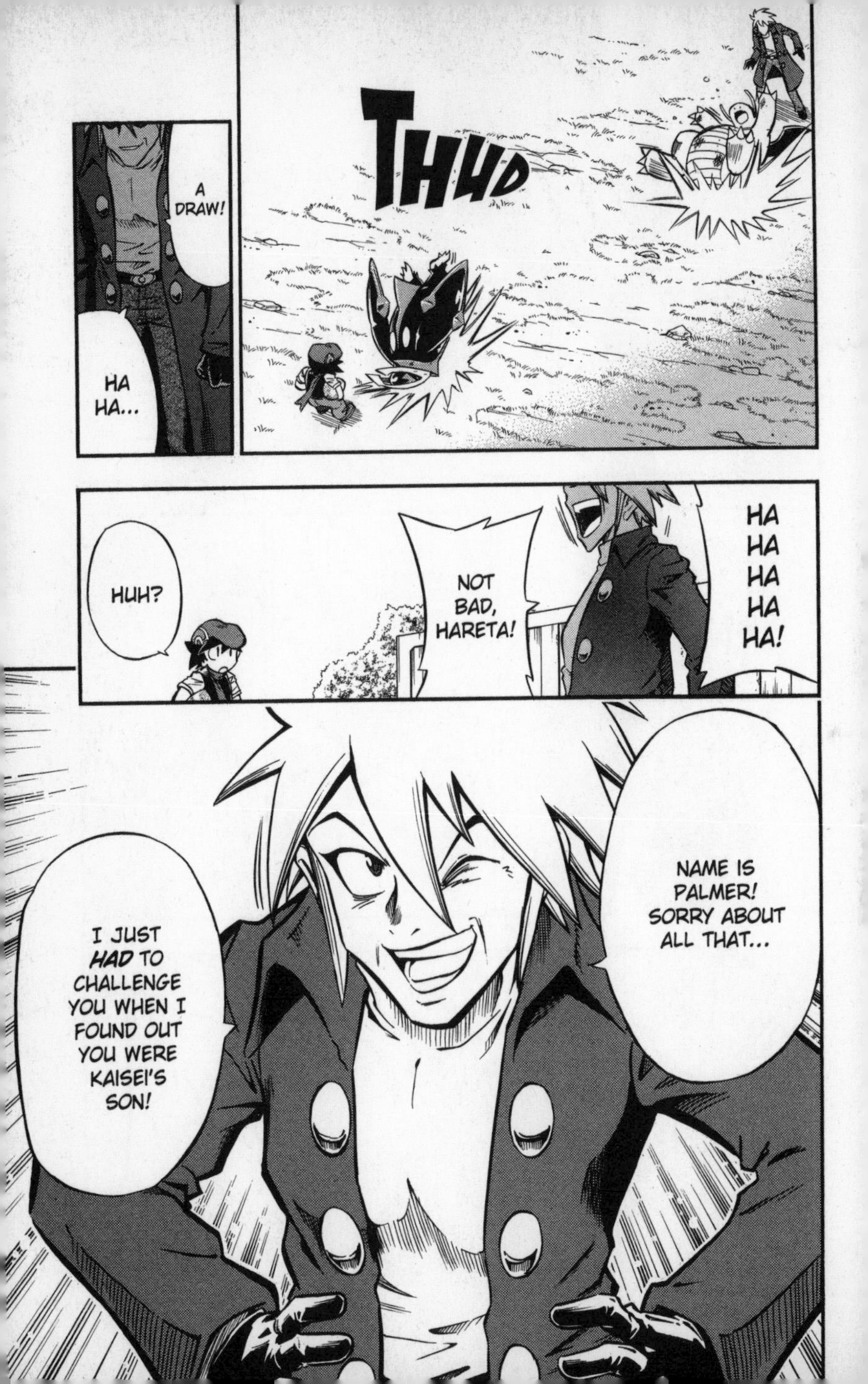
THUD
A DRAW!
HA HA...
HA HA HA HA HA!
NOT BAD, HARETA!
HUH?
NAME IS PALMER! SORRY ABOUT ALL THAT...
I JUST *HAD* TO CHALLENGE YOU WHEN I FOUND OUT YOU WERE KAISEI'S SON!

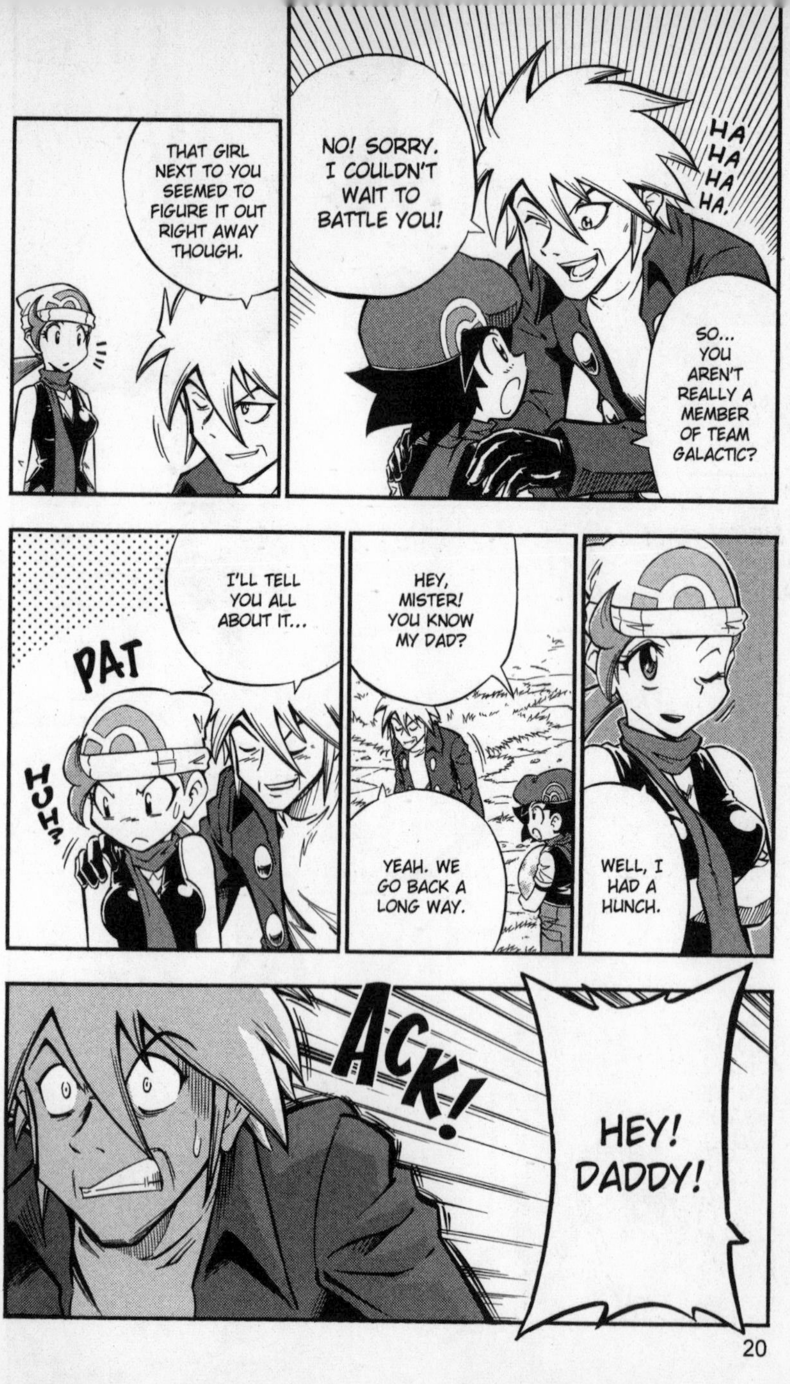
SO... YOU AREN'T REALLY A MEMBER OF TEAM GALACTIC?
HA HA HA HA.
NO! SORRY. I COULDN'T WAIT TO BATTLE YOU!
THAT GIRL NEXT TO YOU SEEMED TO FIGURE IT OUT RIGHT AWAY THOUGH.
WELL, I HAD A HUNCH.
HEY, MISTER! YOU KNOW MY DAD?
YEAH. WE GO BACK A LONG WAY.
I'LL TELL YOU ALL ABOUT IT...
PAT
HUH?
HEY! DADDY!
ACK!

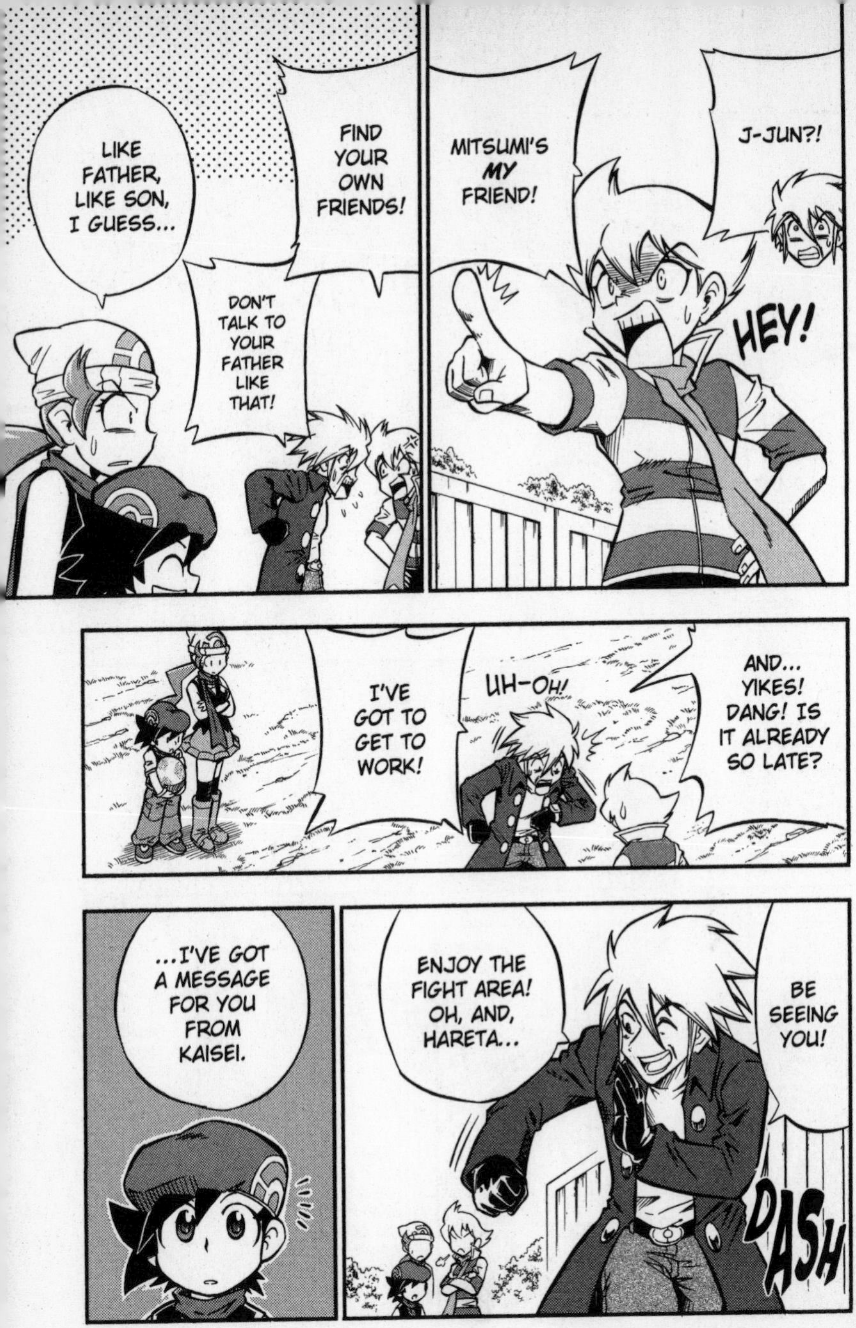
J-JUN?!
MITSUMI'S *MY* FRIEND!
HEY!
FIND YOUR OWN FRIENDS!
LIKE FATHER, LIKE SON, I GUESS...
DON'T TALK TO YOUR FATHER LIKE THAT!
AND... YIKES! DANG! IS IT ALREADY SO LATE?
UH-OH!
I'VE GOT TO GET TO WORK!
BE SEEING YOU!
ENJOY THE FIGHT AREA! OH, AND, HARETA...
DASH
...I'VE GOT A MESSAGE FOR YOU FROM KAISEI.

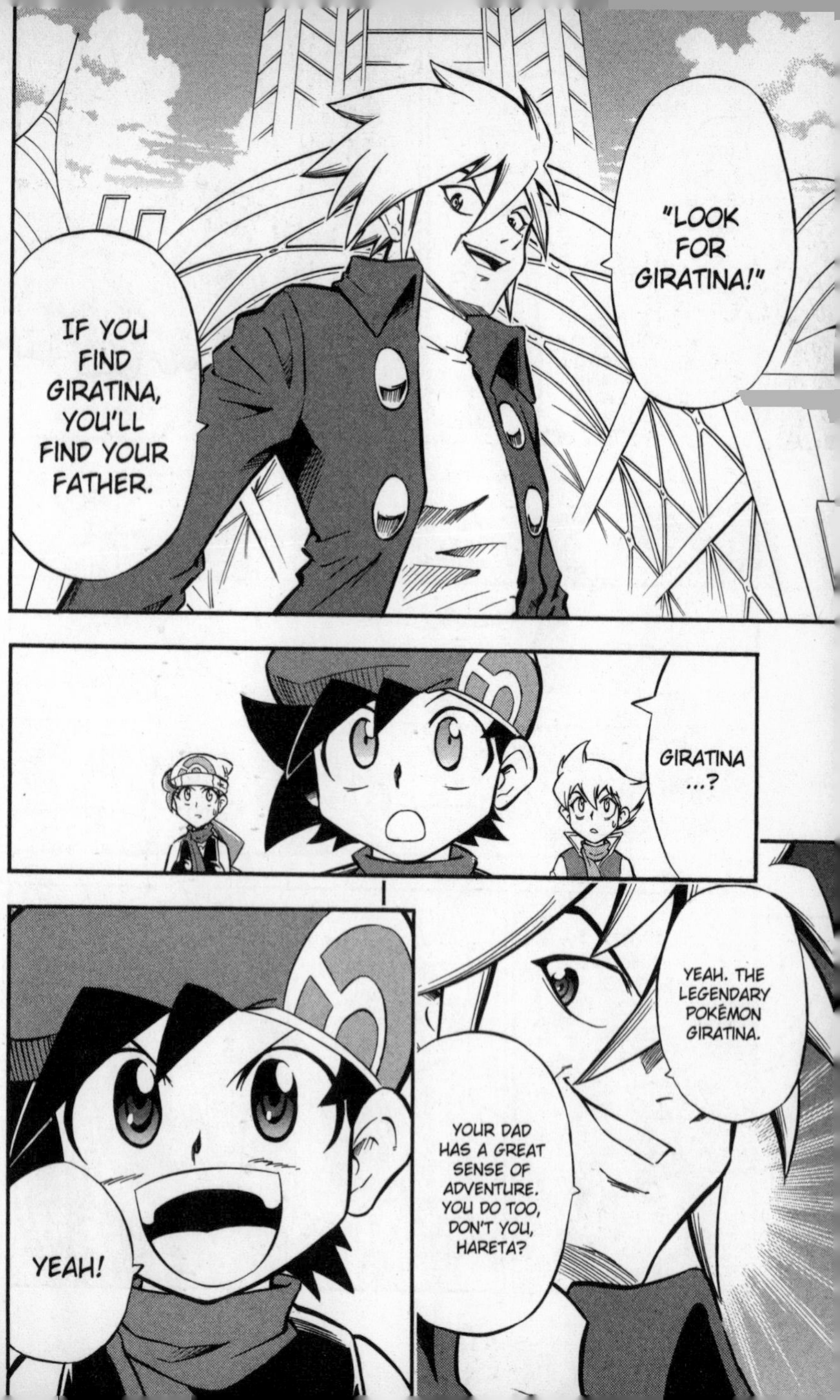
"LOOK FOR GIRATINA!"
IF YOU FIND GIRATINA, YOU'LL FIND YOUR FATHER.
GIRATINA ...?
YEAH. THE LEGENDARY POKÉMON GIRATINA.
YOUR DAD HAS A GREAT SENSE OF ADVENTURE. YOU DO TOO, DON'T YOU, HARETA?
YEAH!

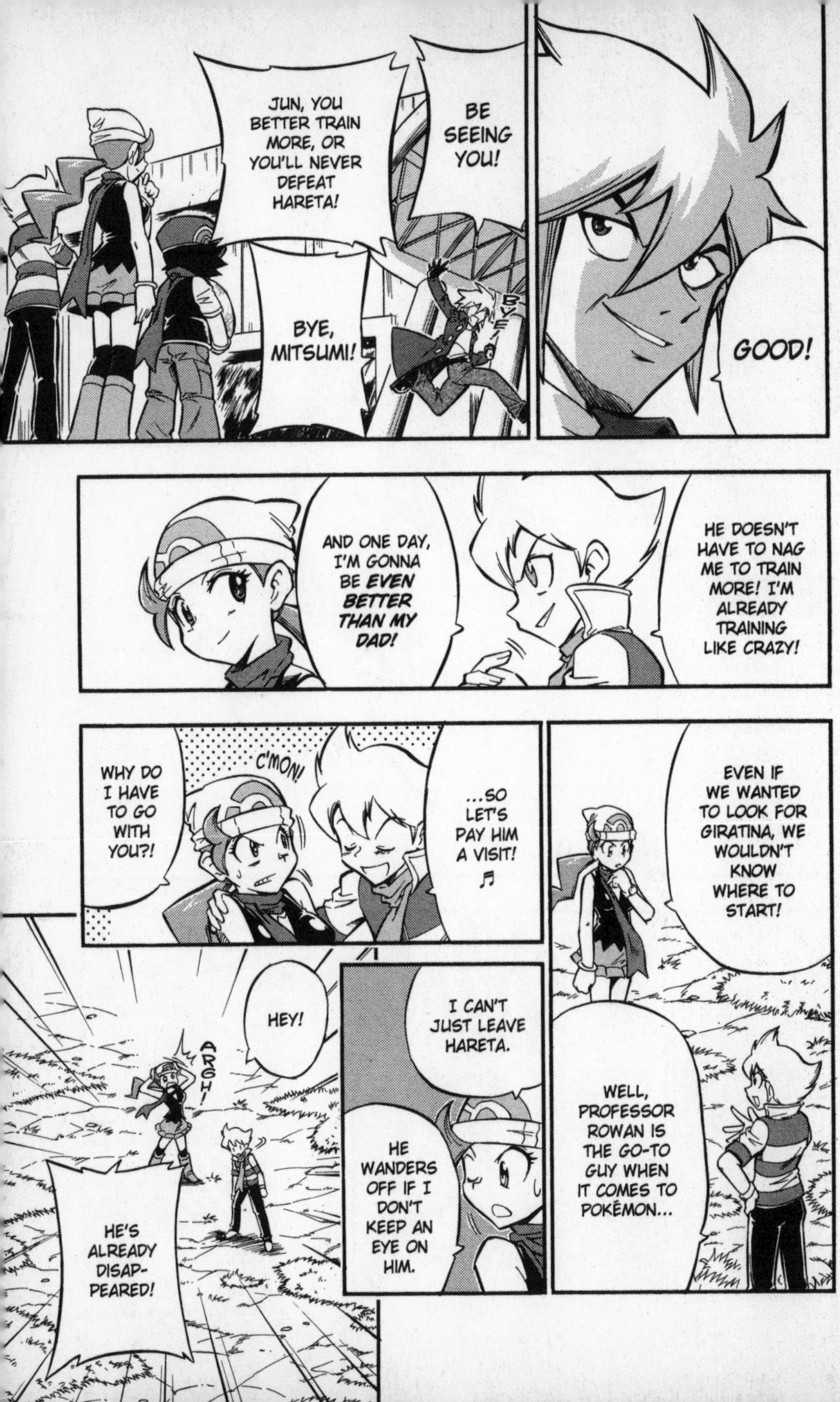
GOOD!
BE SEEING YOU!
JUN, YOU BETTER TRAIN MORE, OR YOU'LL NEVER DEFEAT HARETA!
BYE!
BYE, MITSUMI!
HE DOESN'T HAVE TO NAG ME TO TRAIN MORE! I'M ALREADY TRAINING LIKE CRAZY!
AND ONE DAY, I'M GONNA BE *EVEN BETTER THAN MY DAD!*
EVEN IF WE WANTED TO LOOK FOR GIRATINA, WE WOULDN'T KNOW WHERE TO START!
WELL, PROFESSOR ROWAN IS THE GO-TO GUY WHEN IT COMES TO POKÉMON...
...SO LET'S PAY HIM A VISIT! ♬
C'MON!
WHY DO I HAVE TO GO WITH YOU?!
I CAN'T JUST LEAVE HARETA.
HE WANDERS OFF IF I DON'T KEEP AN EYE ON HIM.
HEY!
ARGH!
HE'S ALREADY DISAP-PEARED!

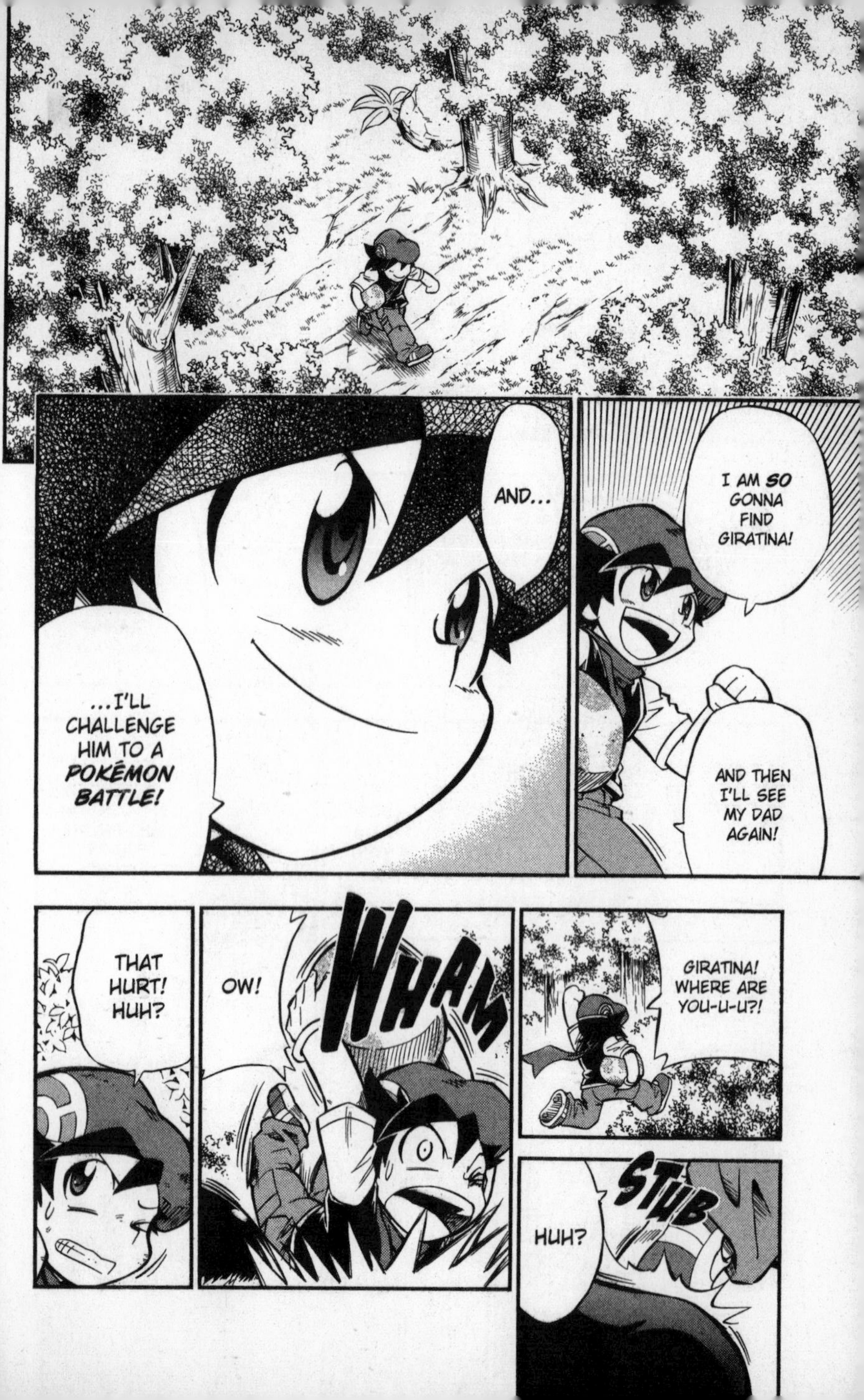
I AM SO GONNA FIND GIRATINA!
AND THEN I'LL SEE MY DAD AGAIN!
AND...
...I'LL CHALLENGE HIM TO A POKÉMON BATTLE!
GIRATINA! WHERE ARE YOU-U-U?!
STUB
HUH?
WHAM
OW!
THAT HURT! HUH?

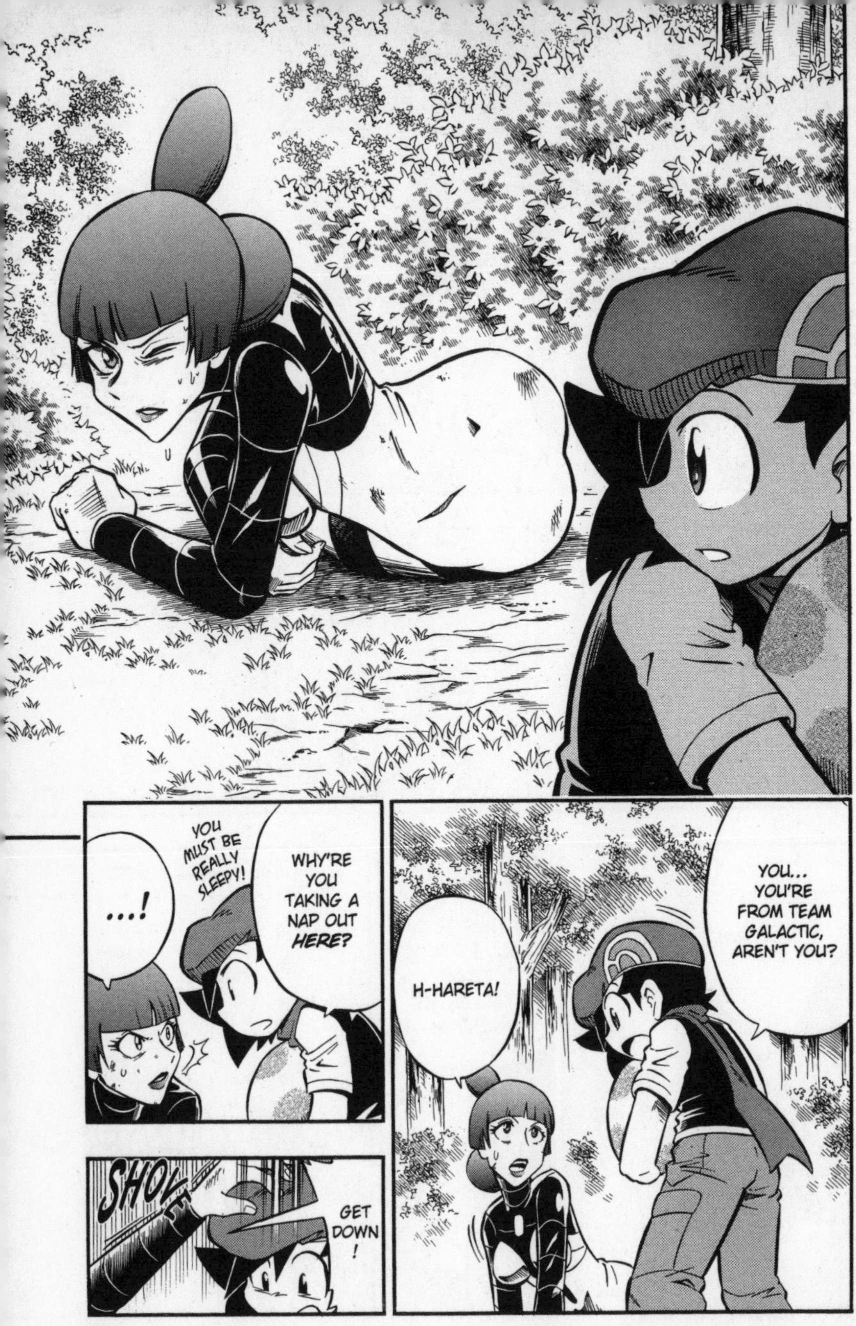
YOU... YOU'RE FROM TEAM GALACTIC, AREN'T YOU?
H-HARETA!
WHY'RE YOU TAKING A NAP OUT *HERE?*
YOU MUST BE REALLY SLEEPY!
...!
GET DOWN!
SHOVE

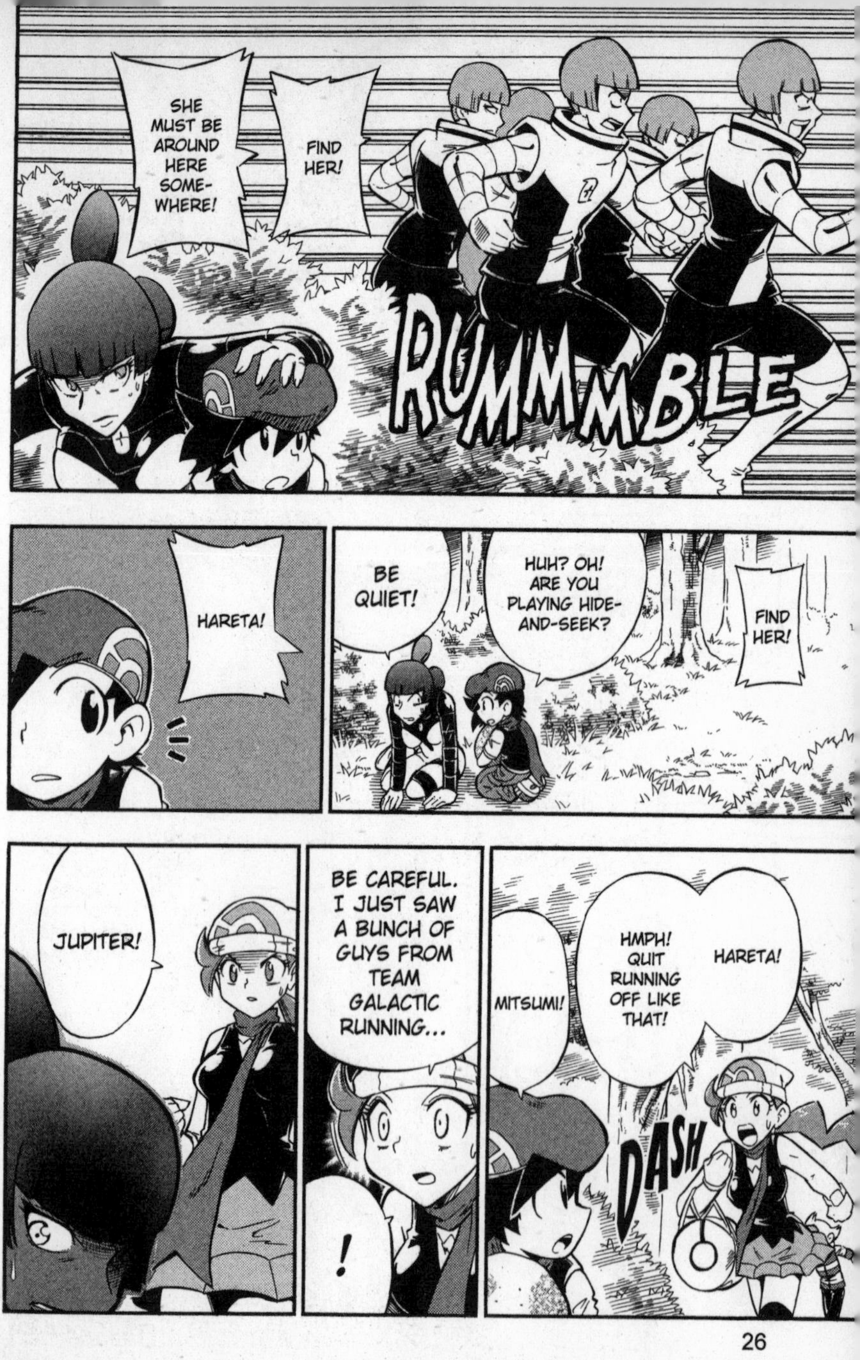
FIND HER!
SHE MUST BE AROUND HERE SOME-WHERE!
RUMMMBLE
FIND HER!
HUH? OH! ARE YOU PLAYING HIDE-AND-SEEK?
BE QUIET!
HARETA!
HARETA!
HMPH! QUIT RUNNING OFF LIKE THAT!
MITSUMI!
DASH
BE CAREFUL. I JUST SAW A BUNCH OF GUYS FROM TEAM GALACTIC RUNNING...
!
JUPITER!

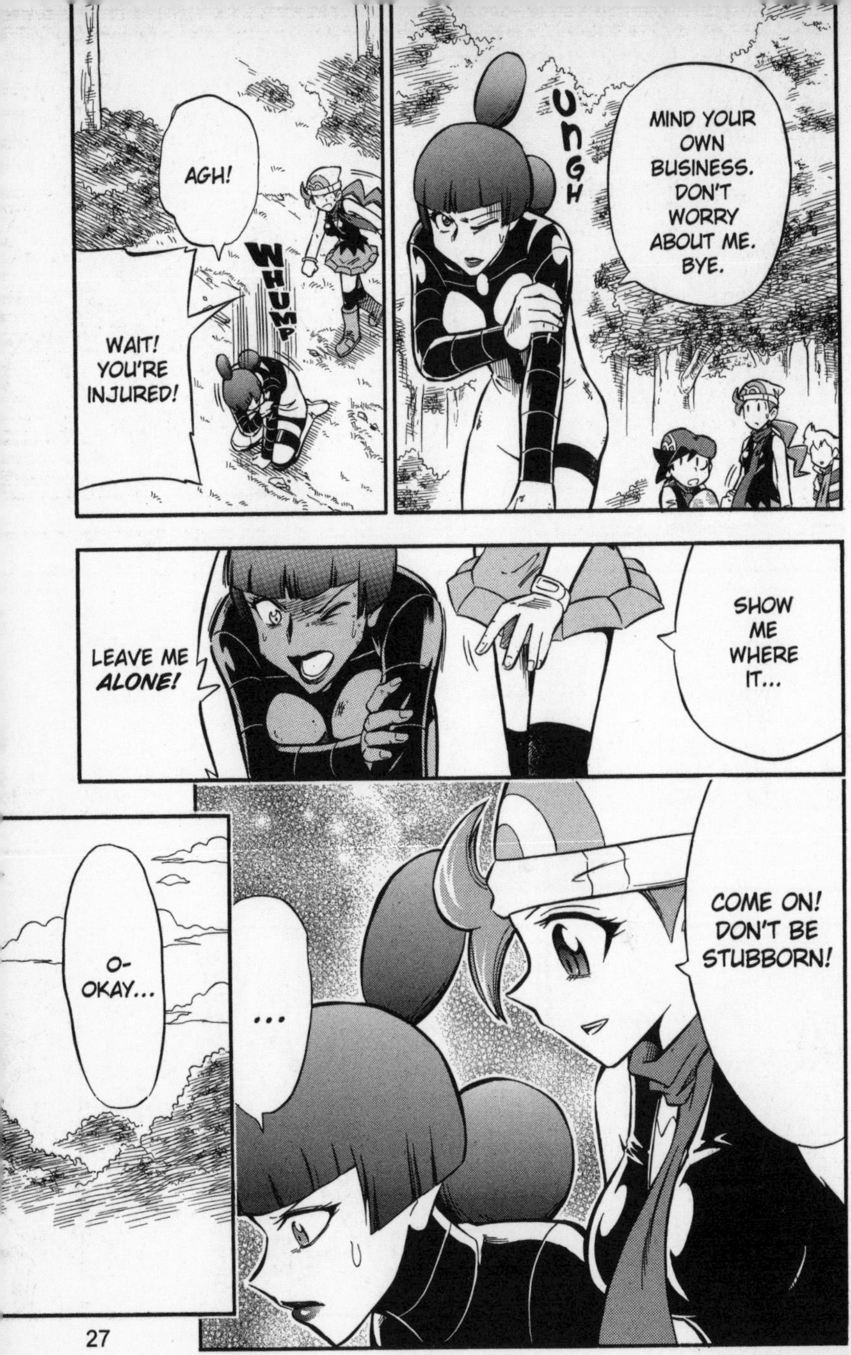
UNGH
MIND YOUR OWN BUSINESS. DON'T WORRY ABOUT ME. BYE.
AGH!
WHUMP
WAIT! YOU'RE INJURED!
SHOW ME WHERE IT...
LEAVE ME *ALONE!*
COME ON! DON'T BE STUBBORN!
...
O-OKAY...

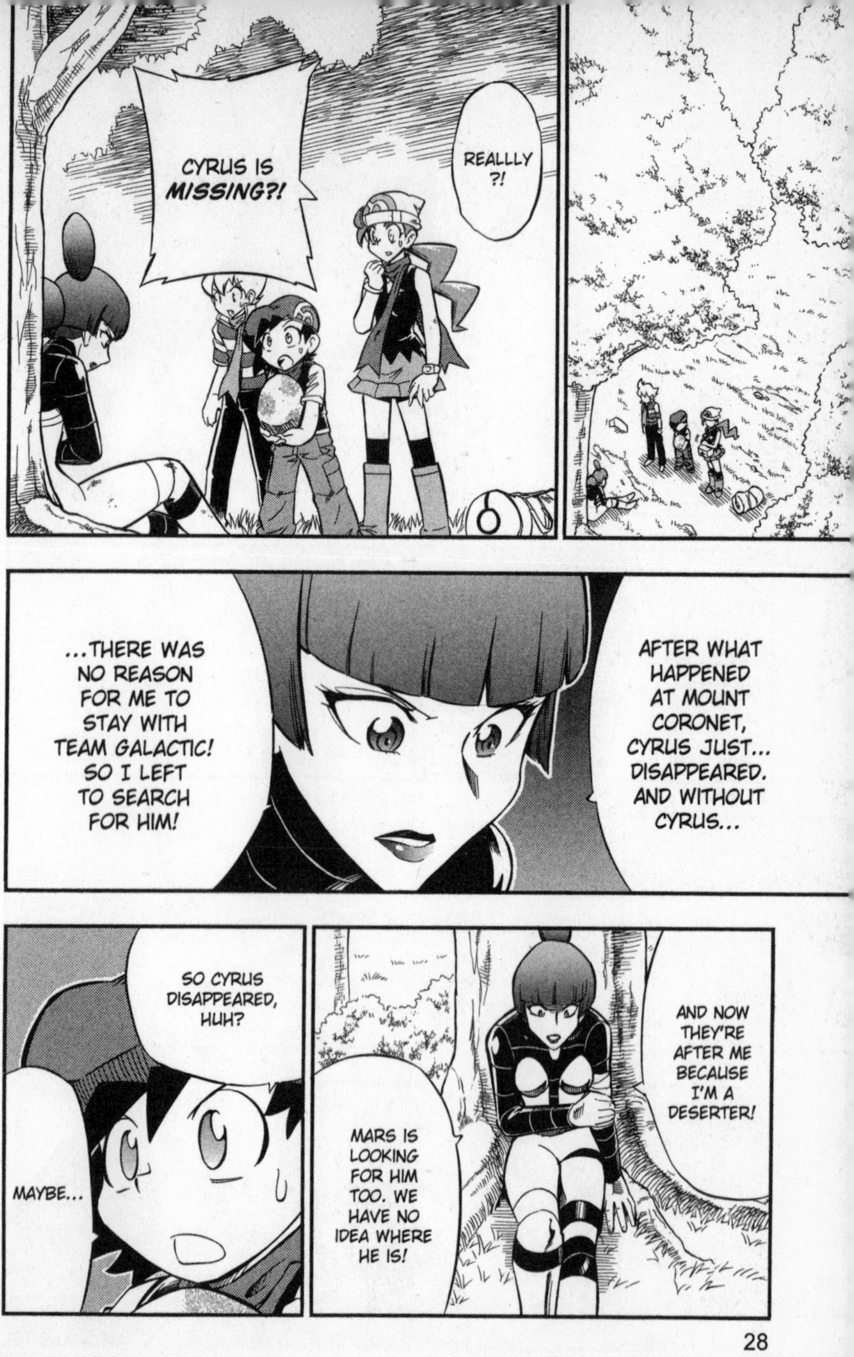
REALLLY ?!
CYRUS IS *MISSING?!*
AFTER WHAT HAPPENED AT MOUNT CORONET, CYRUS JUST... DISAPPEARED. AND WITHOUT CYRUS...
...THERE WAS NO REASON FOR ME TO STAY WITH TEAM GALACTIC! SO I LEFT TO SEARCH FOR HIM!
AND NOW THEY'RE AFTER ME BECAUSE I'M A DESERTER!
MARS IS LOOKING FOR HIM TOO. WE HAVE NO IDEA WHERE HE IS!
SO CYRUS DISAPPEARED, HUH?
MAYBE...

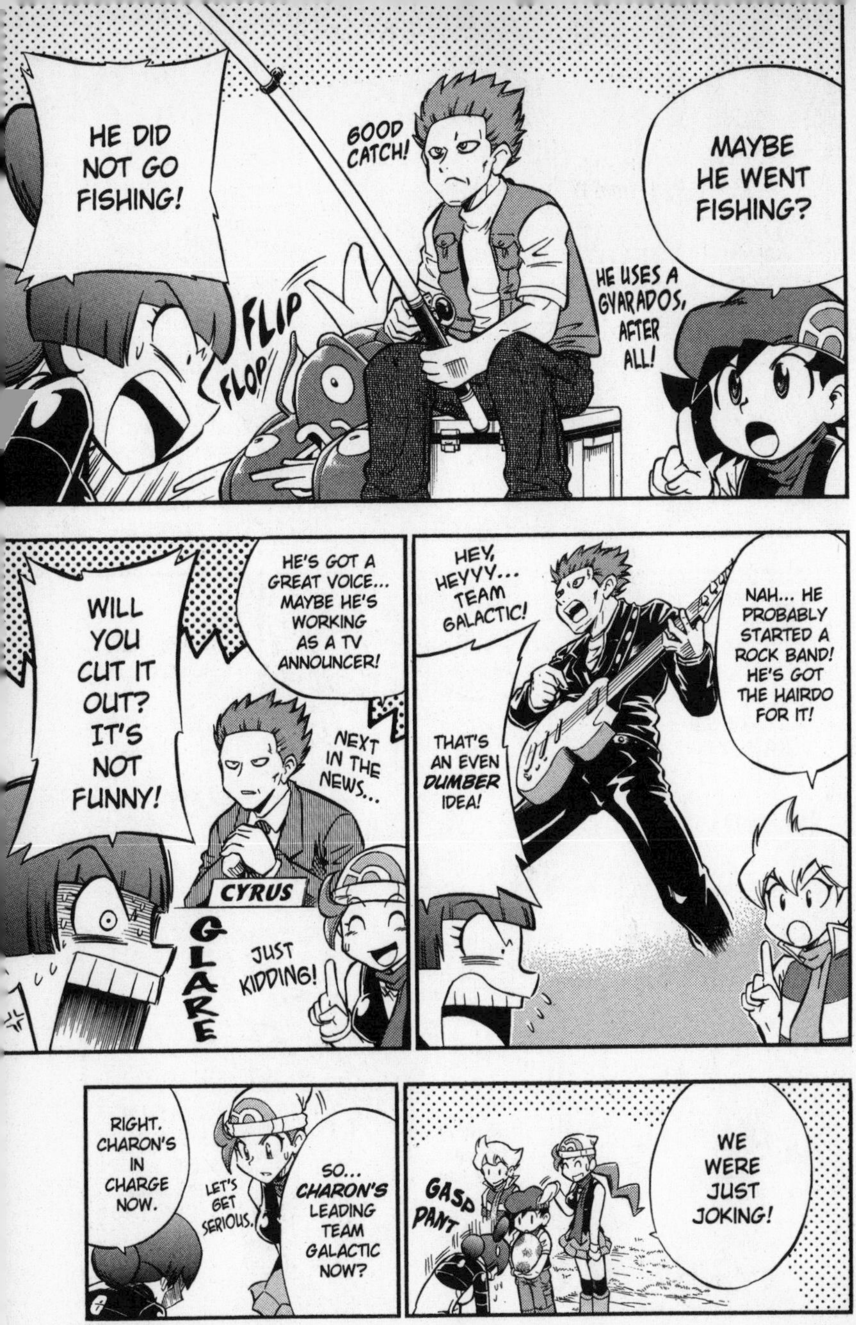
MAYBE HE WENT FISHING?
HE USES A GYARADOS, AFTER ALL!
GOOD CATCH!
HE DID NOT GO FISHING!
FLIP
FLOP
NAH... HE PROBABLY STARTED A ROCK BAND! HE'S GOT THE HAIRDO FOR IT!
HEY, HEYYY... TEAM GALACTIC!
THAT'S AN EVEN DUMBER IDEA!
HE'S GOT A GREAT VOICE... MAYBE HE'S WORKING AS A TV ANNOUNCER!
NEXT IN THE NEWS...
WILL YOU CUT IT OUT? IT'S NOT FUNNY!
CYRUS
JUST KIDDING!
GLARE
WE WERE JUST JOKING!
GASP
PANT
SO... CHARON'S LEADING TEAM GALACTIC NOW?
LET'S GET SERIOUS.
RIGHT. CHARON'S IN CHARGE NOW.

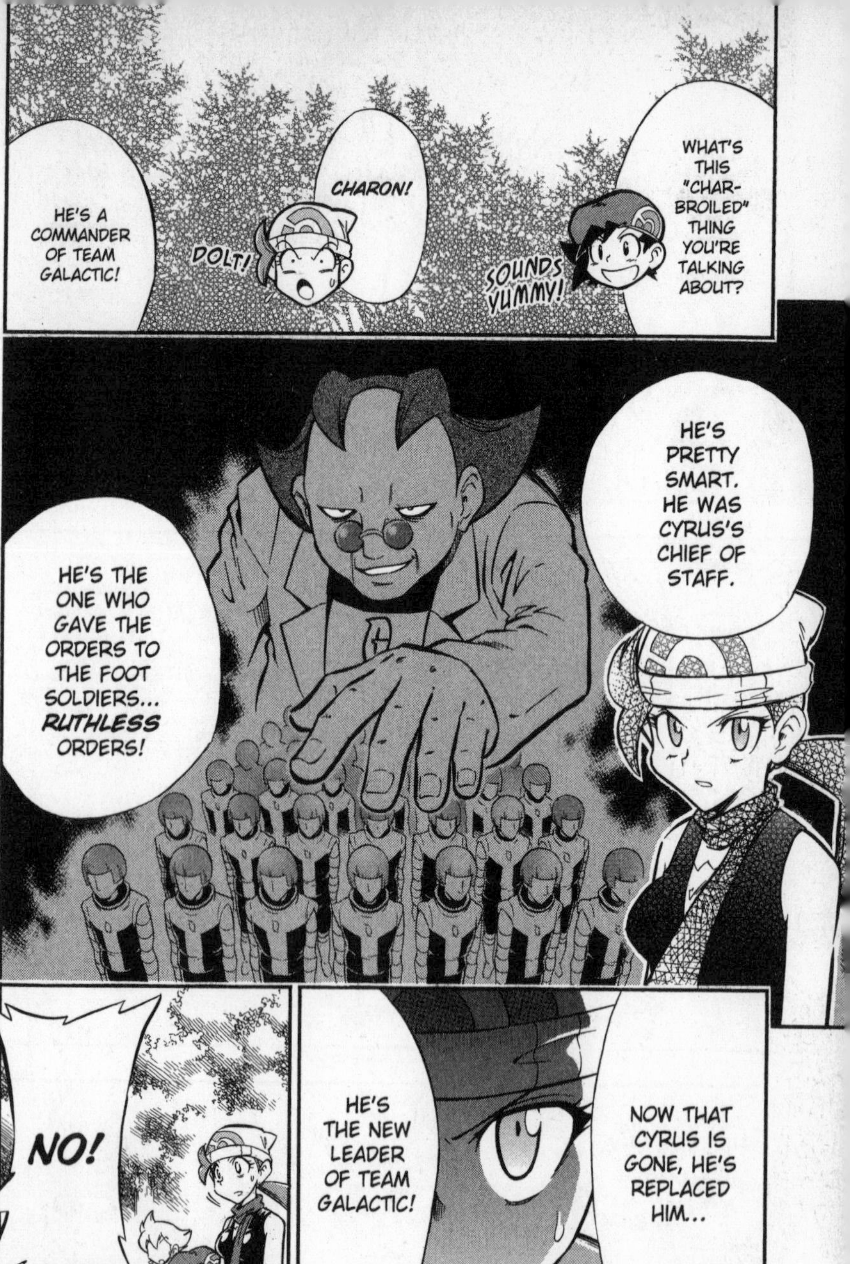
WHAT'S THIS "CHAR-BROILED" THING YOU'RE TALKING ABOUT?
SOUNDS YUMMY!
CHARON!
DOLT!
HE'S A COMMANDER OF TEAM GALACTIC!
HE'S PRETTY SMART. HE WAS CYRUS'S CHIEF OF STAFF.
HE'S THE ONE WHO GAVE THE ORDERS TO THE FOOT SOLDIERS... RUTHLESS ORDERS!
NOW THAT CYRUS IS GONE, HE'S REPLACED HIM...
HE'S THE NEW LEADER OF TEAM GALACTIC!
NO!

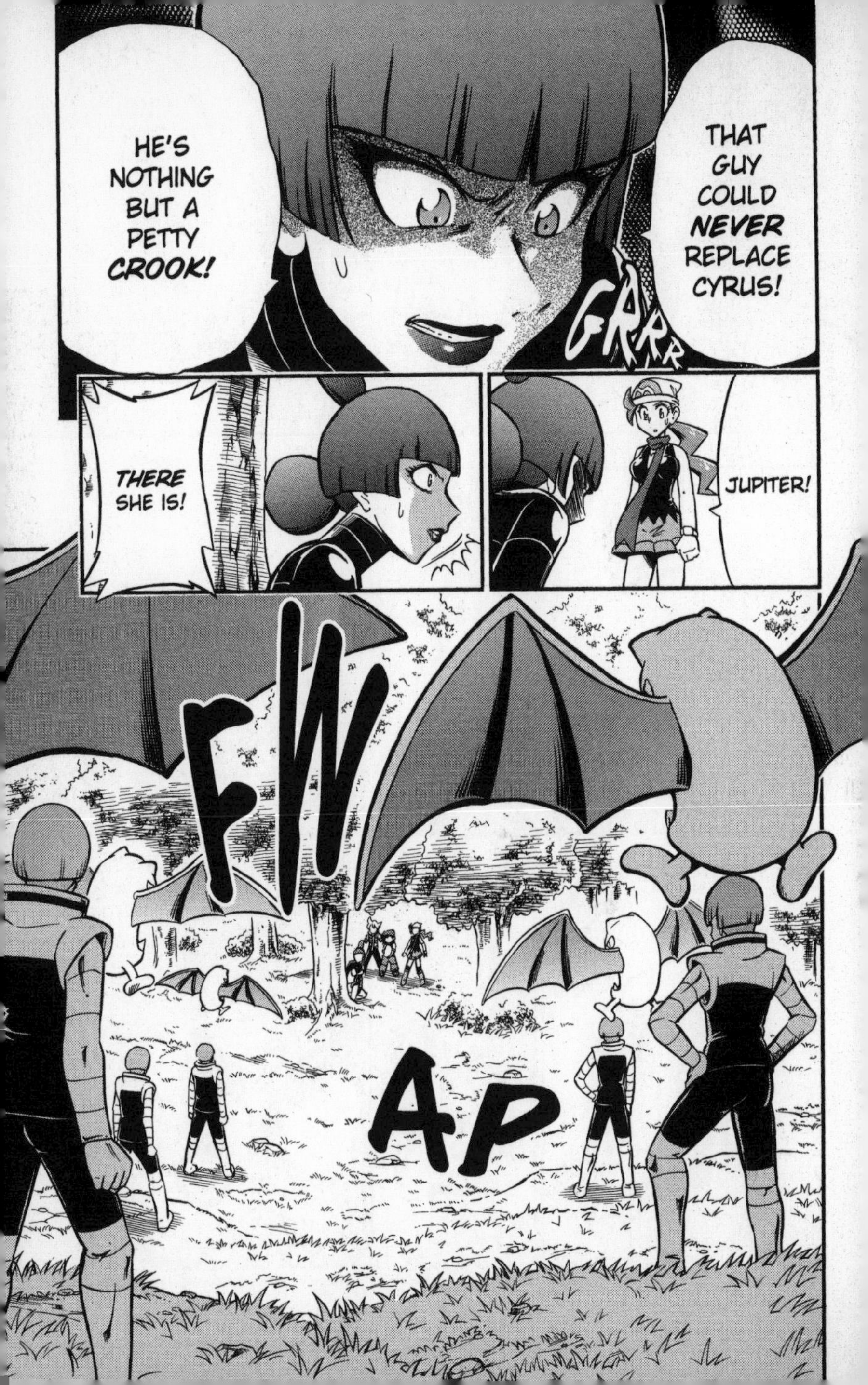
THAT GUY COULD NEVER REPLACE CYRUS!
GRRR
HE'S NOTHING BUT A PETTY CROOK!
JUPITER!
THERE SHE IS!
FWAP

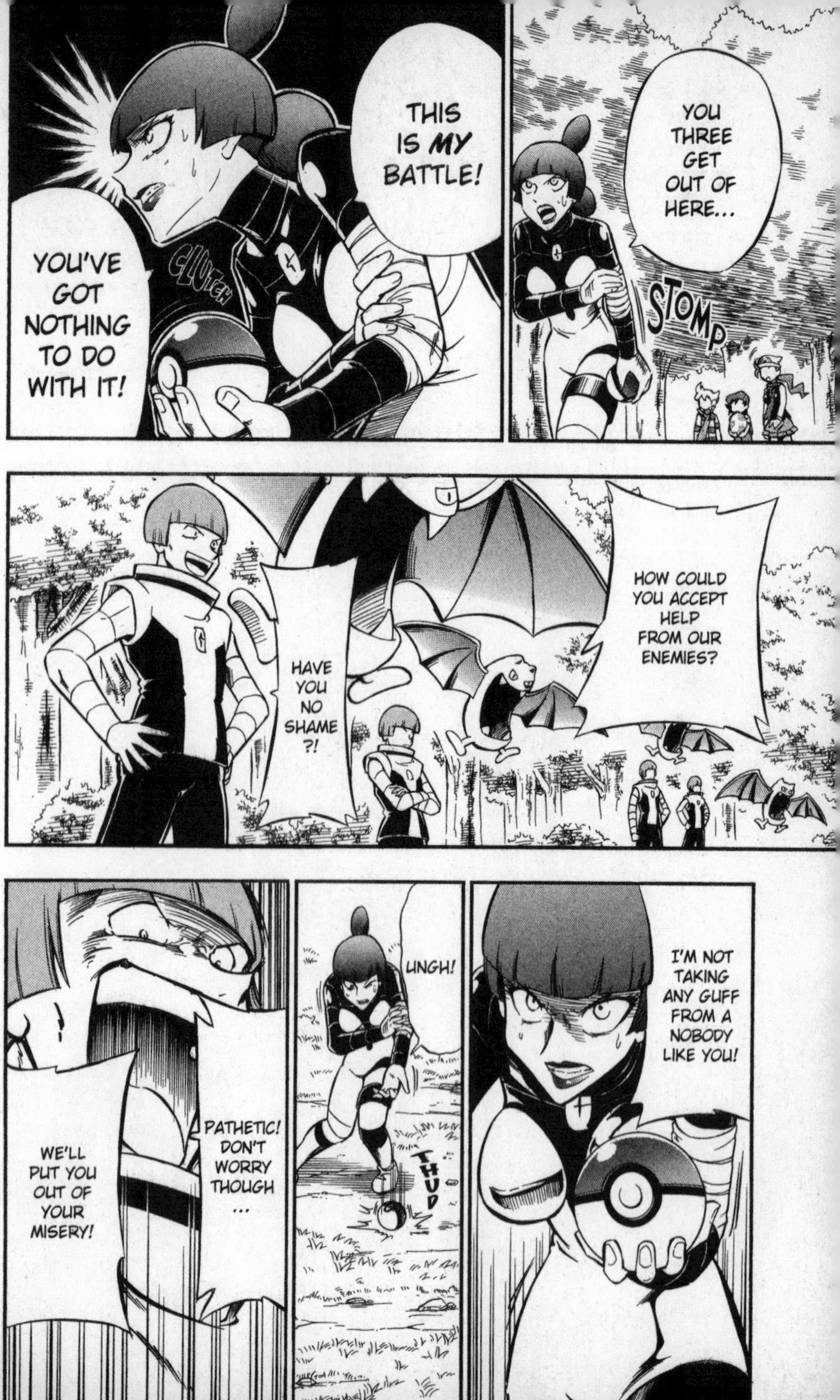
YOU THREE GET OUT OF HERE...
STOMP
THIS IS MY BATTLE!
YOU'VE GOT NOTHING TO DO WITH IT!
HOW COULD YOU ACCEPT HELP FROM OUR ENEMIES?
HAVE YOU NO SHAME ?!
I'M NOT TAKING ANY GUFF FROM A NOBODY LIKE YOU!
UNGH!
THUD
PATHETIC! DON'T WORRY THOUGH ...
WE'LL PUT YOU OUT OF YOUR MISERY!

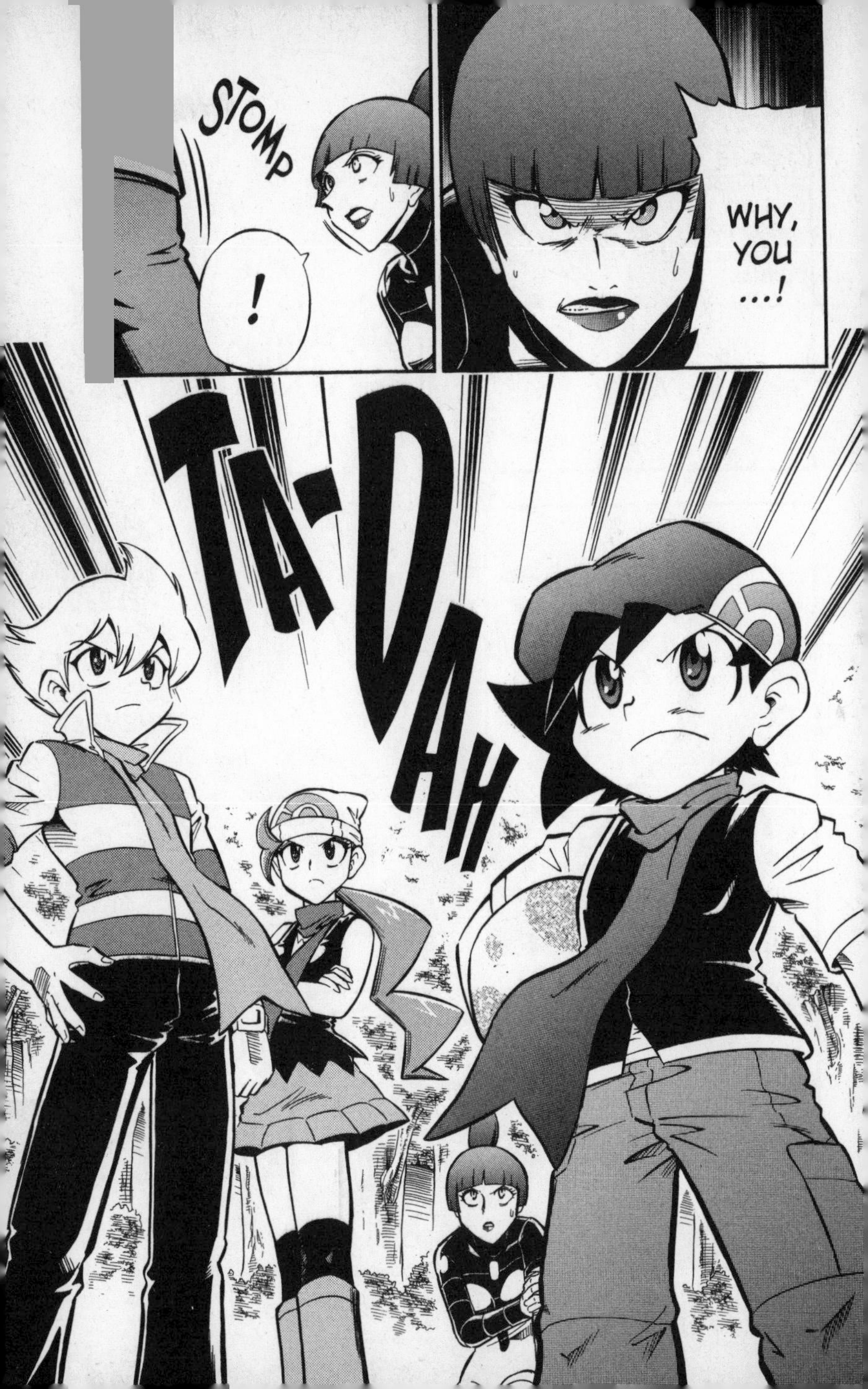
WHY, YOU ...!
STOMP
!
TA-DAH

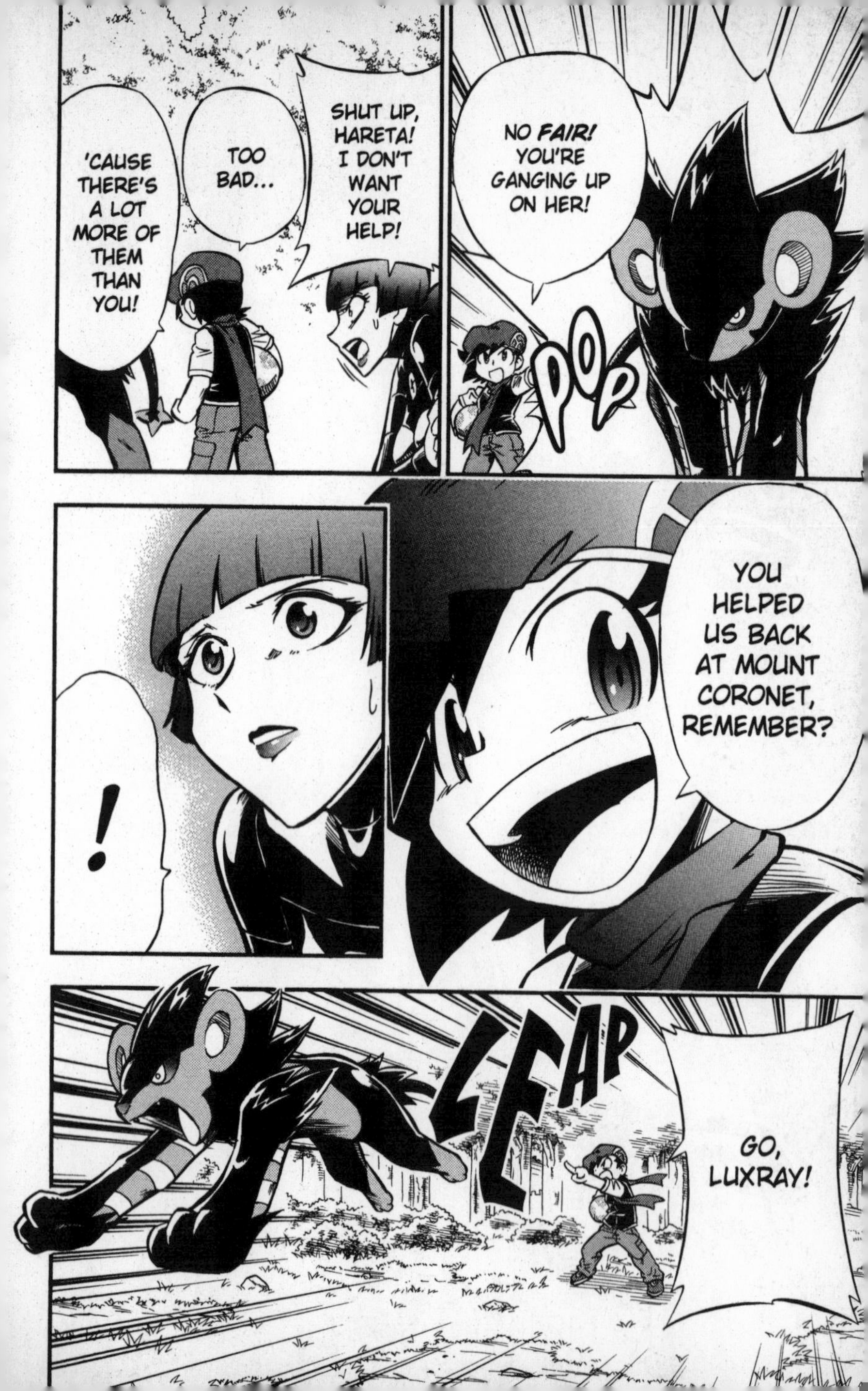
NO FAIR! YOU'RE GANGING UP ON HER!
POP
SHUT UP, HARETA! I DON'T WANT YOUR HELP!
TOO BAD...
'CAUSE THERE'S A LOT MORE OF THEM THAN YOU!
YOU HELPED US BACK AT MOUNT CORONET, REMEMBER?
!
GO, LUXRAY!
LEAP

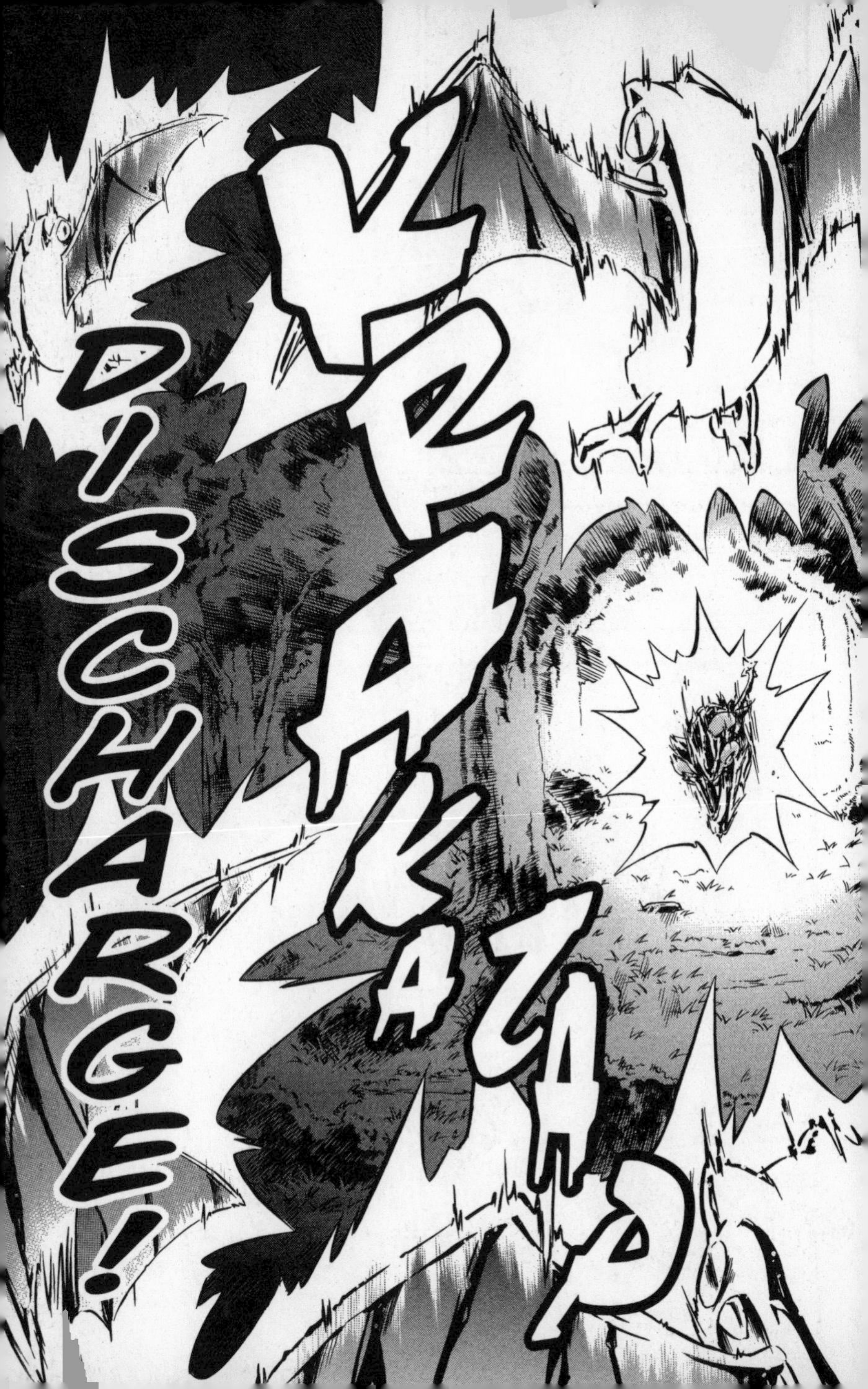
KRAKAZAP
DISCHARGE!

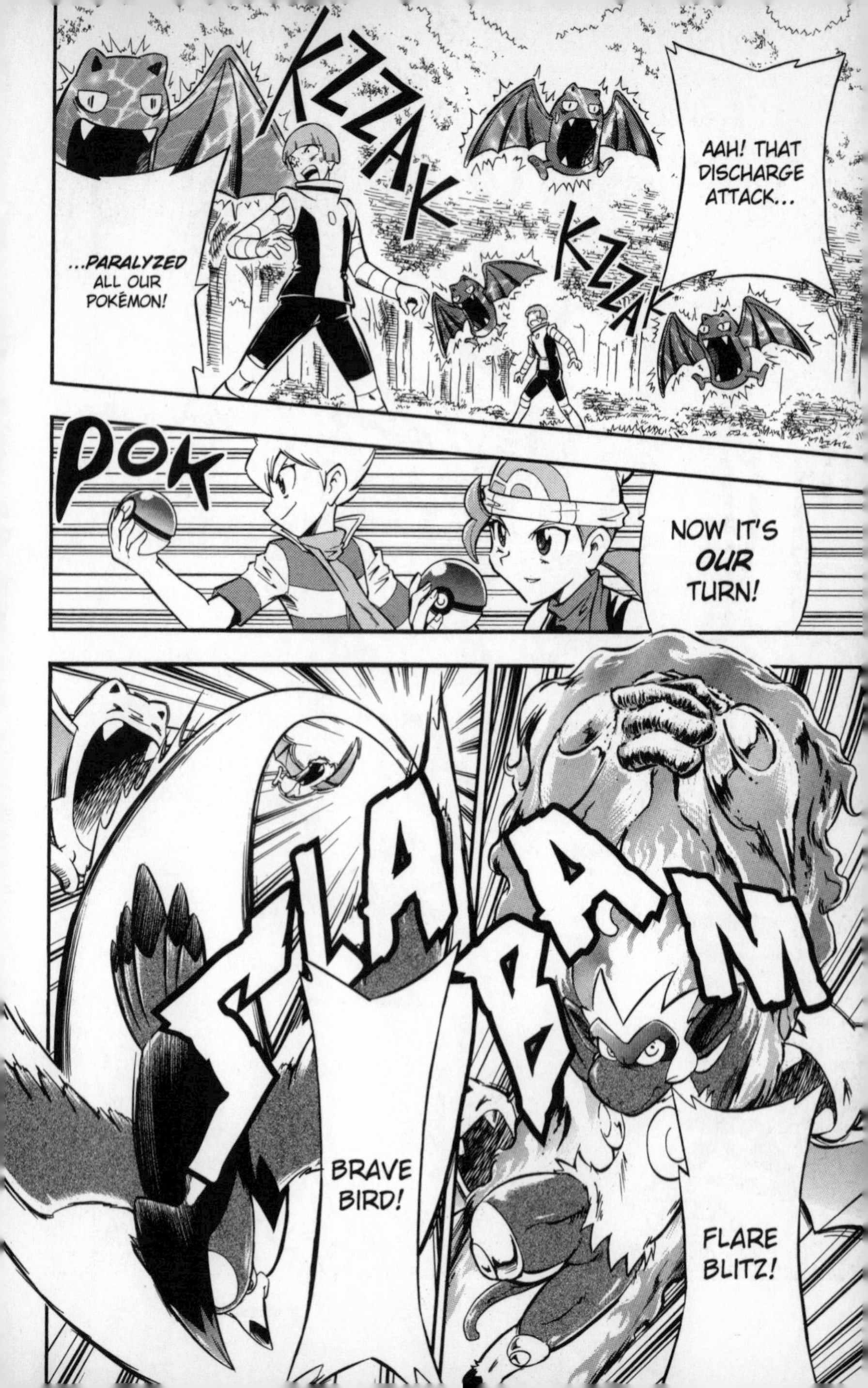
AAH! THAT DISCHARGE ATTACK...
KZZAK
KZZAK
...PARALYZED ALL OUR POKÉMON!
NOW IT'S OUR TURN!
POK
FLARE BLITZ!
BRAVE BIRD!
FLABAM

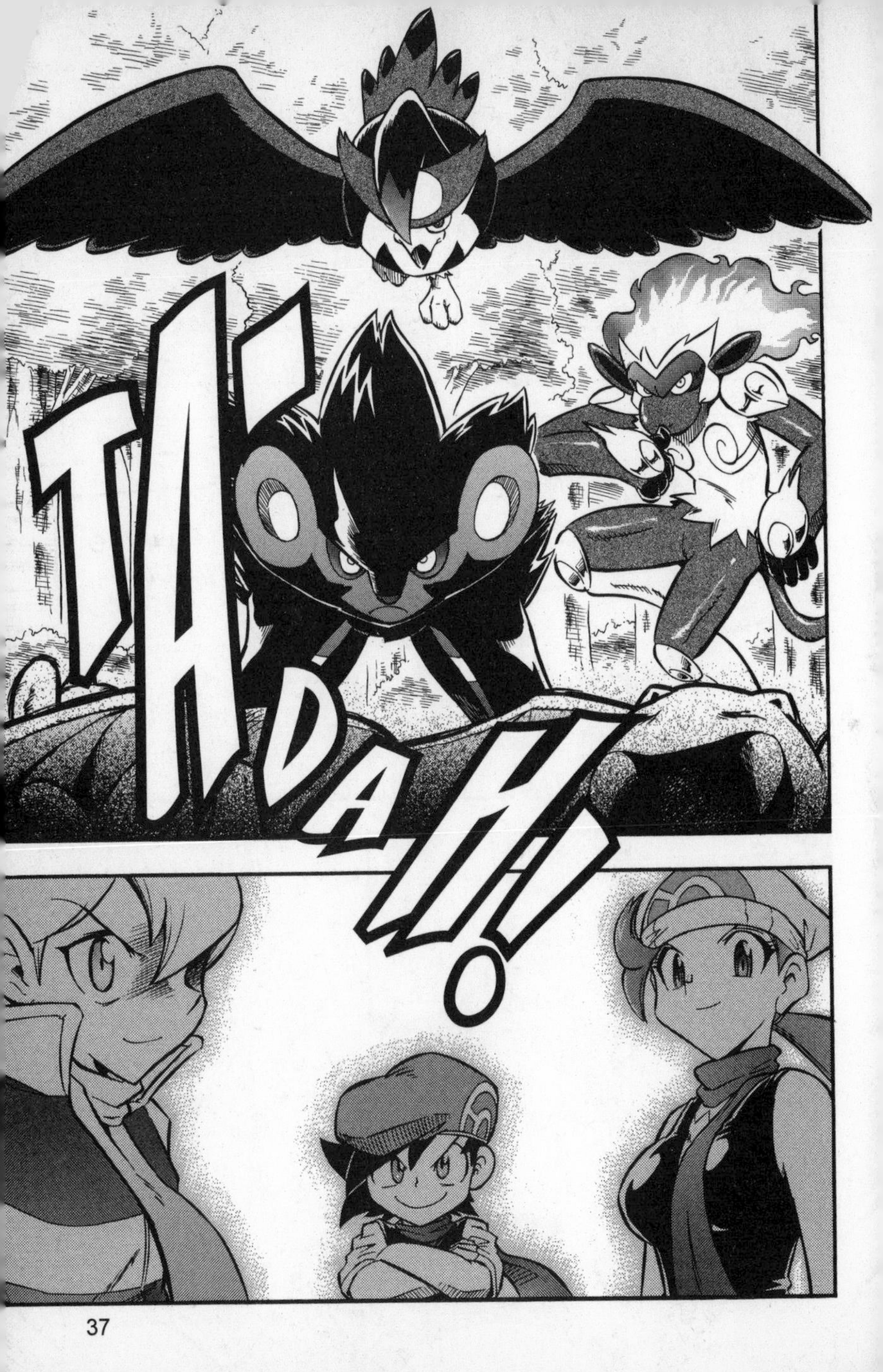
TA DAH!

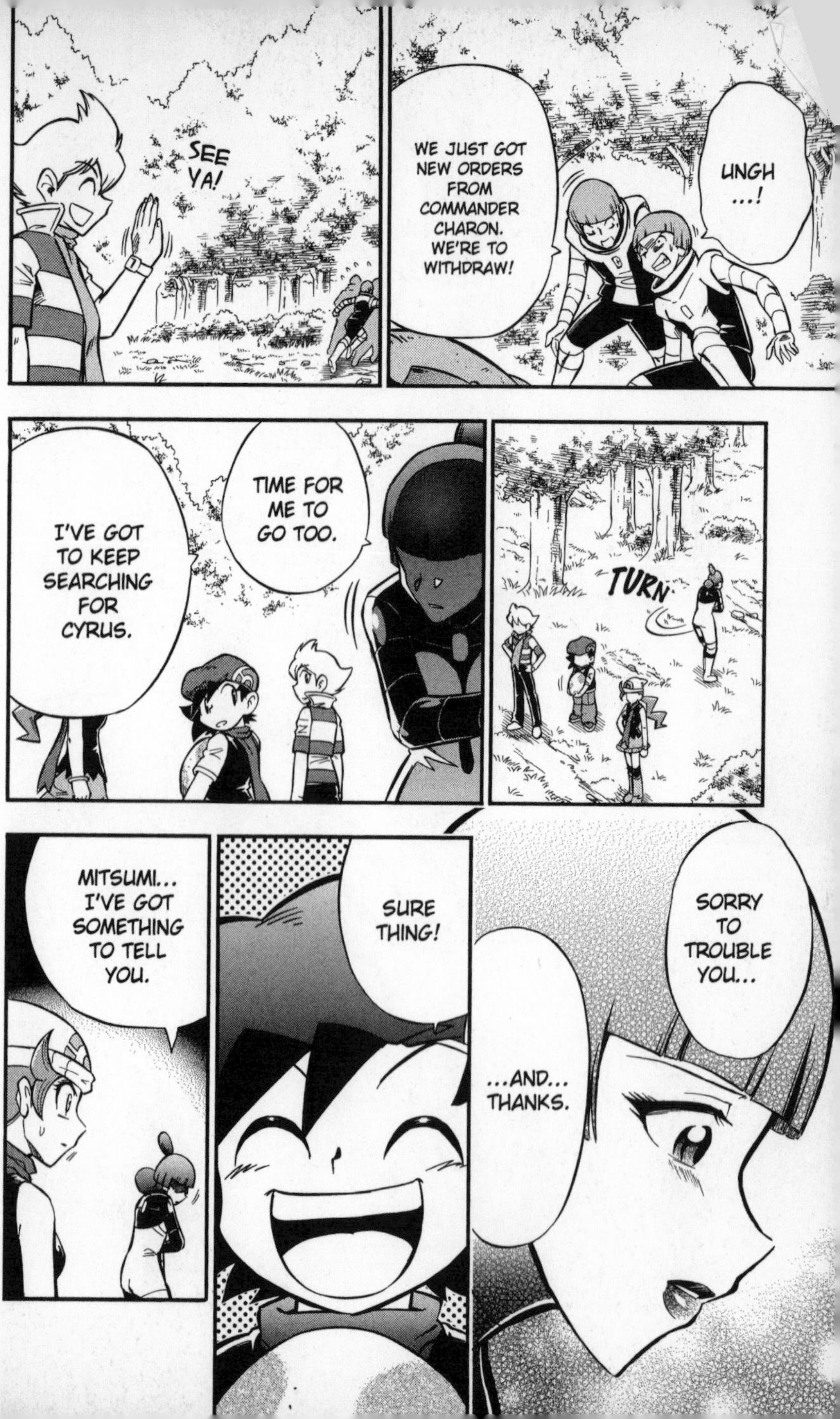
UNGH ...!
WE JUST GOT NEW ORDERS FROM COMMANDER CHARON. WE'RE TO WITHDRAW!
SEE YA!
TURN
TIME FOR ME TO GO TOO.
I'VE GOT TO KEEP SEARCHING FOR CYRUS.
SORRY TO TROUBLE YOU...
...AND... THANKS.
SURE THING!
MITSUMI... I'VE GOT SOMETHING TO TELL YOU.

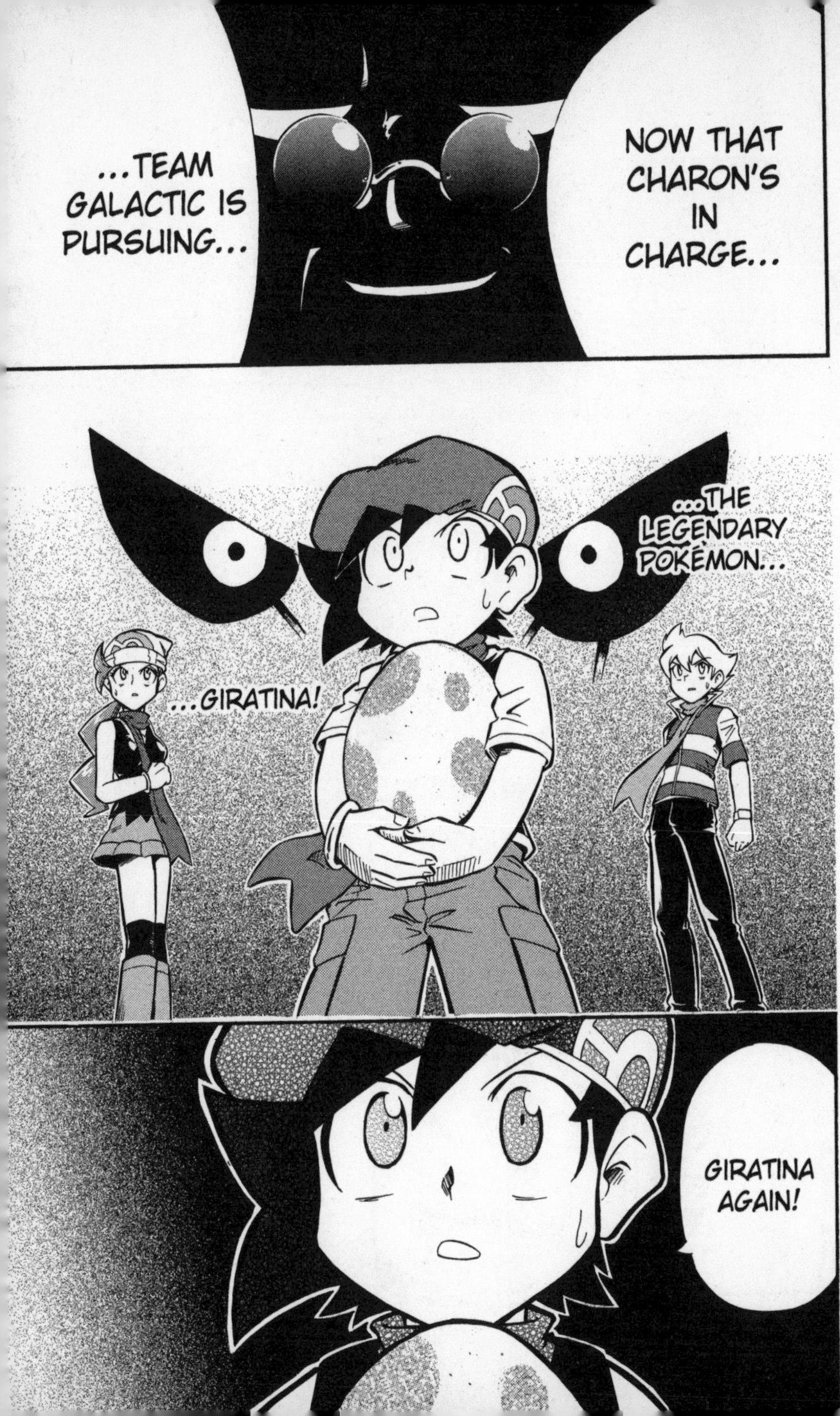
NOW THAT CHARON'S IN CHARGE...
...TEAM GALACTIC IS PURSUING...
...THE LEGENDARY POKÉMON...
...GIRATINA!
GIRATINA AGAIN!

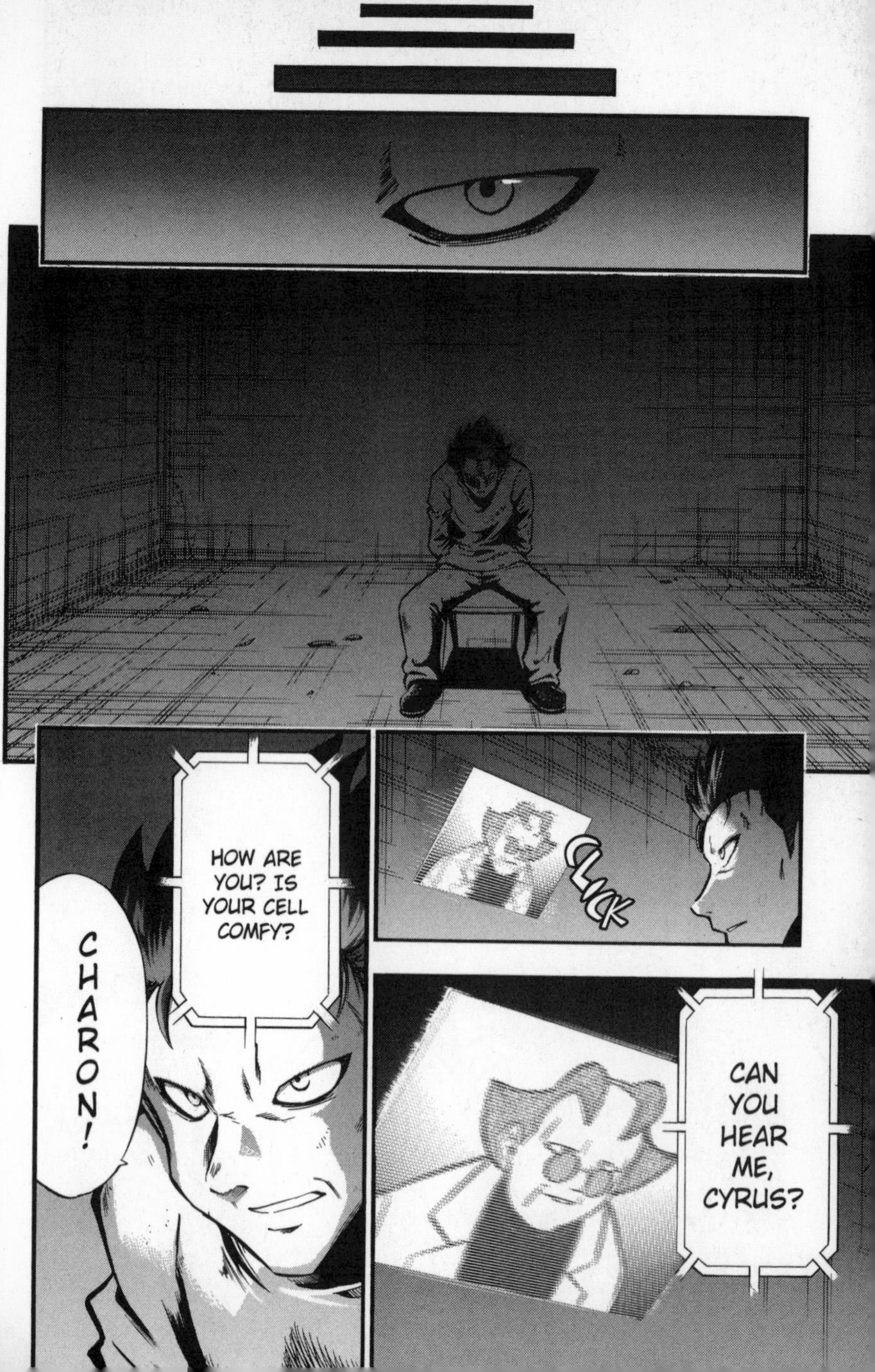
CLICK
CAN YOU HEAR ME, CYRUS?
HOW ARE YOU? IS YOUR CELL COMFY?
CHARON!

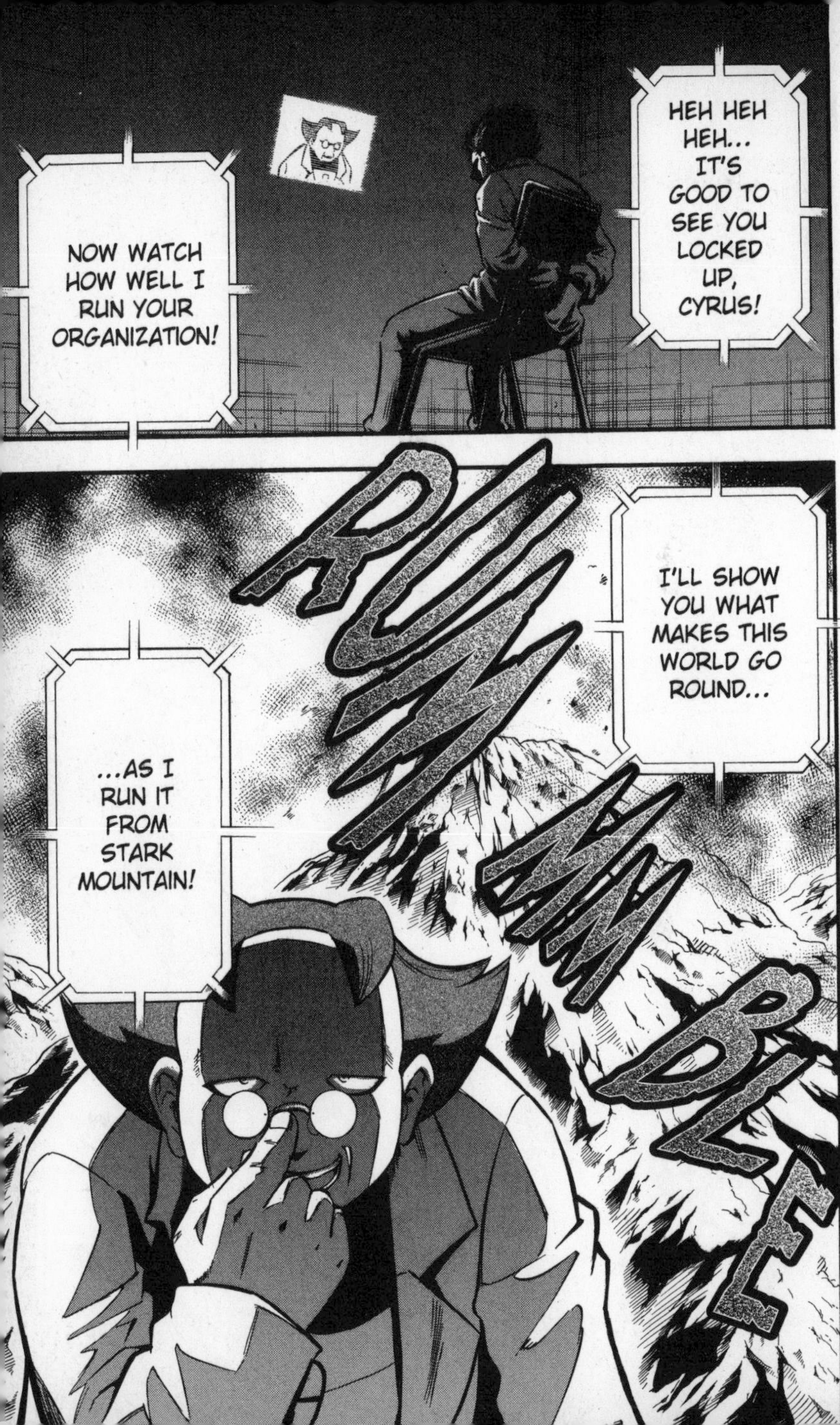
HEH HEH HEH... IT'S GOOD TO SEE YOU LOCKED UP, CYRUS!
NOW WATCH HOW WELL I RUN YOUR ORGANIZATION!
I'LL SHOW YOU WHAT MAKES THIS WORLD GO ROUND...
RUMMMMBLE
...AS I RUN IT FROM STARK MOUNTAIN!

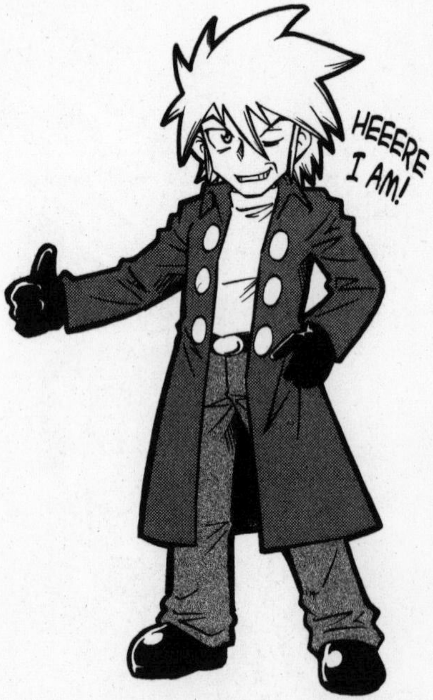
HEEEERE I AM!

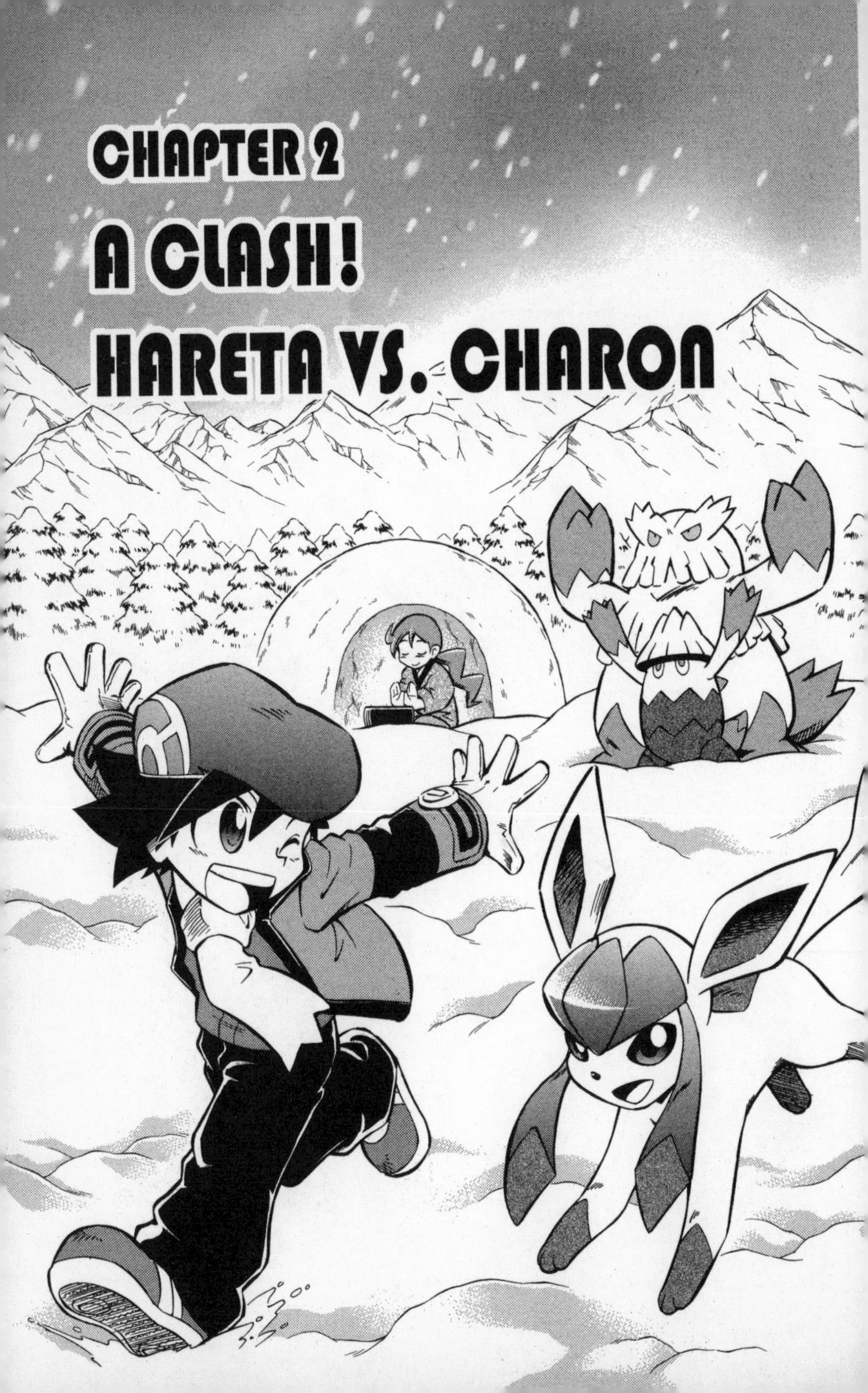
CHAPTER 2
A CLASH!
HARETA VS. CHARON

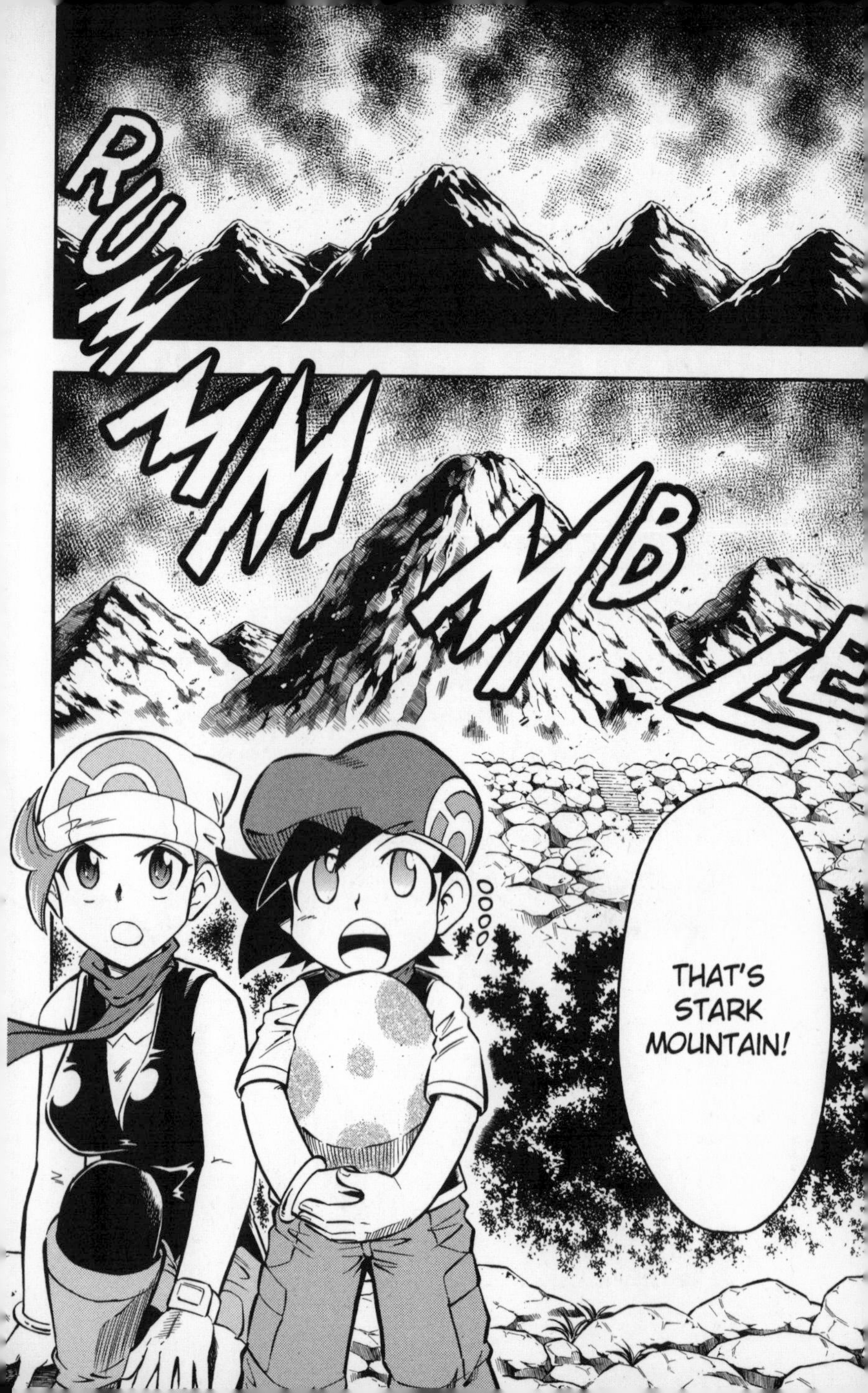
RUMMMMBLE
OOOOO!
THAT'S STARK MOUNTAIN!

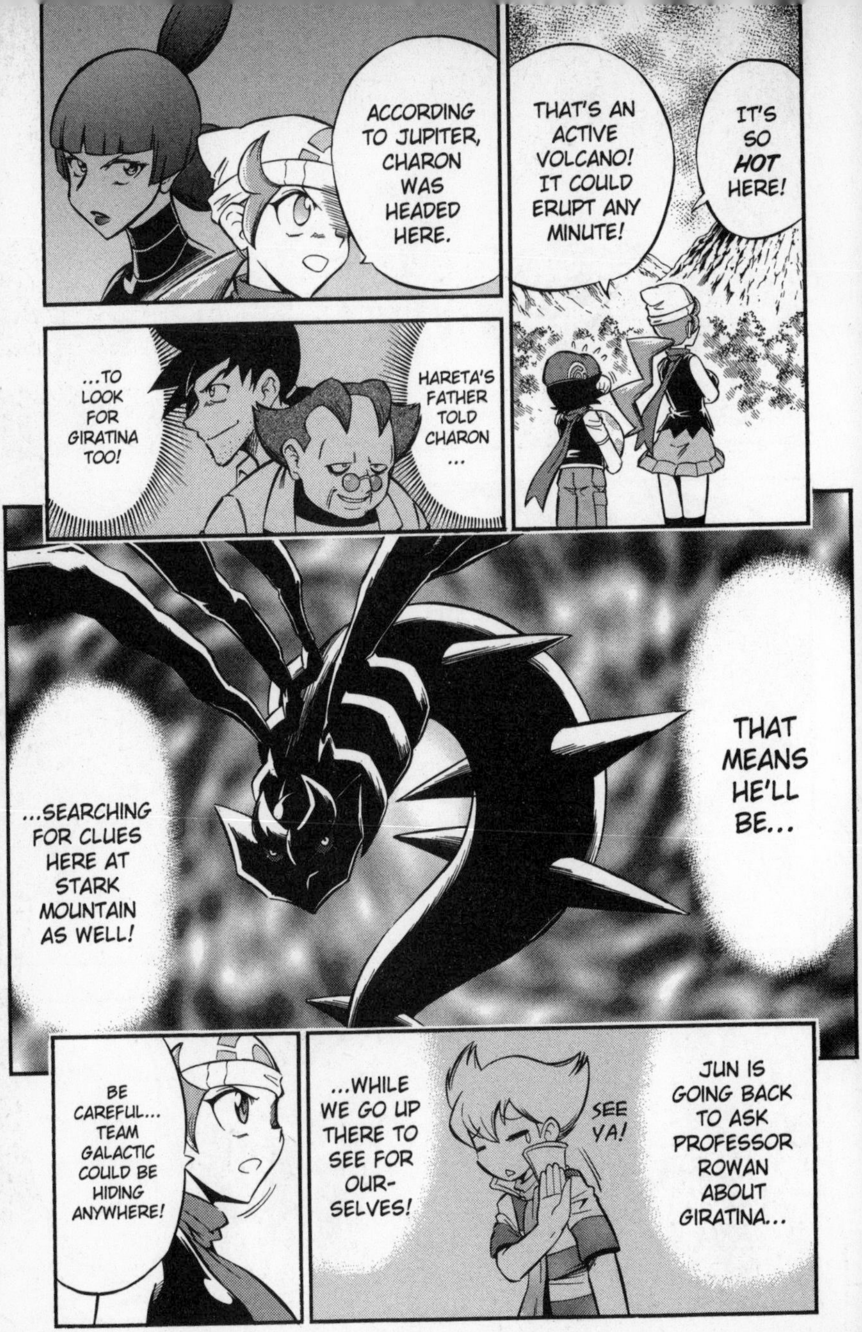
IT'S SO *HOT* HERE!
THAT'S AN ACTIVE VOLCANO! IT COULD ERUPT ANY MINUTE!
ACCORDING TO JUPITER, CHARON WAS HEADED HERE.
HARETA'S FATHER TOLD CHARON ...
...TO LOOK FOR GIRATINA TOO!
THAT MEANS HE'LL BE...
...SEARCHING FOR CLUES HERE AT STARK MOUNTAIN AS WELL!
JUN IS GOING BACK TO ASK PROFESSOR ROWAN ABOUT GIRATINA...
SEE YA!
...WHILE WE GO UP THERE TO SEE FOR OUR-SELVES!
BE CAREFUL... TEAM GALACTIC COULD BE HIDING ANYWHERE!

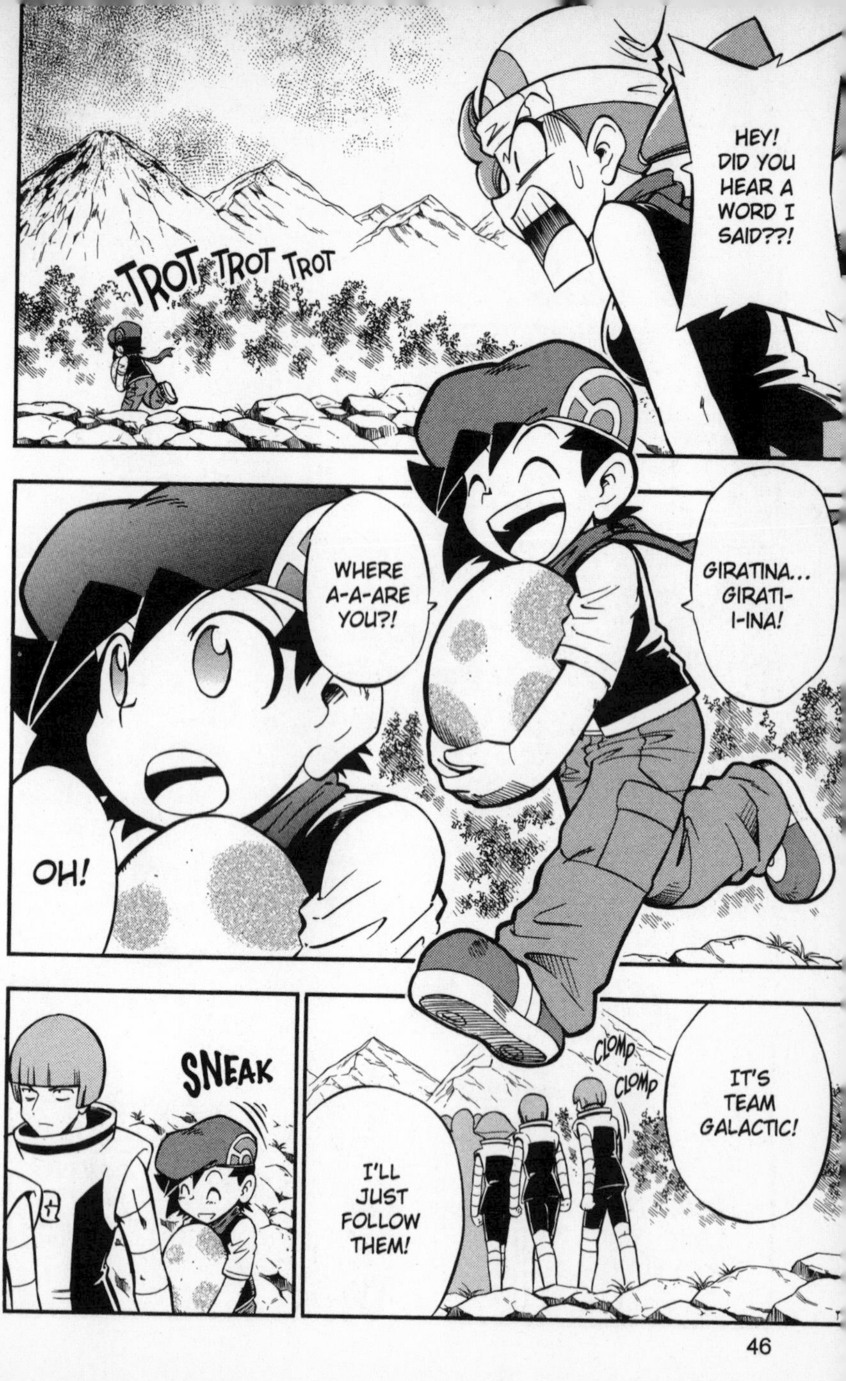
HEY! DID YOU HEAR A WORD I SAID??!
TROT TROT TROT
GIRATINA... GIRATI-I-INA!
WHERE A-A-ARE YOU?!
OH!
IT'S TEAM GALACTIC!
CLOMP CLOMP
I'LL JUST FOLLOW THEM!
SNEAK

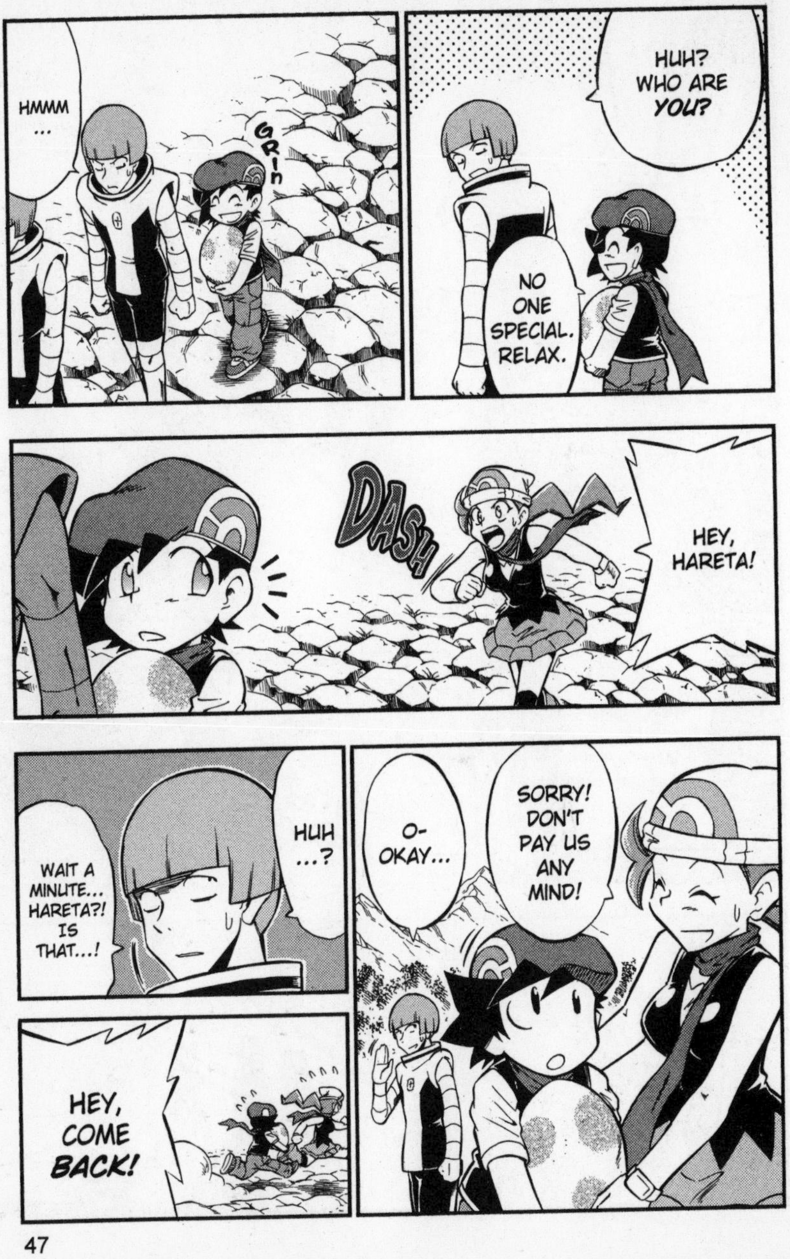
HUH? WHO ARE YOU?
NO ONE SPECIAL. RELAX.
HMMM ...
GRin
HEY, HARETA!
DASH
SORRY! DON'T PAY US ANY MIND!
O-OKAY...
HUH ...?
WAIT A MINUTE... HARETA?! IS THAT...!
HEY, COME BACK!

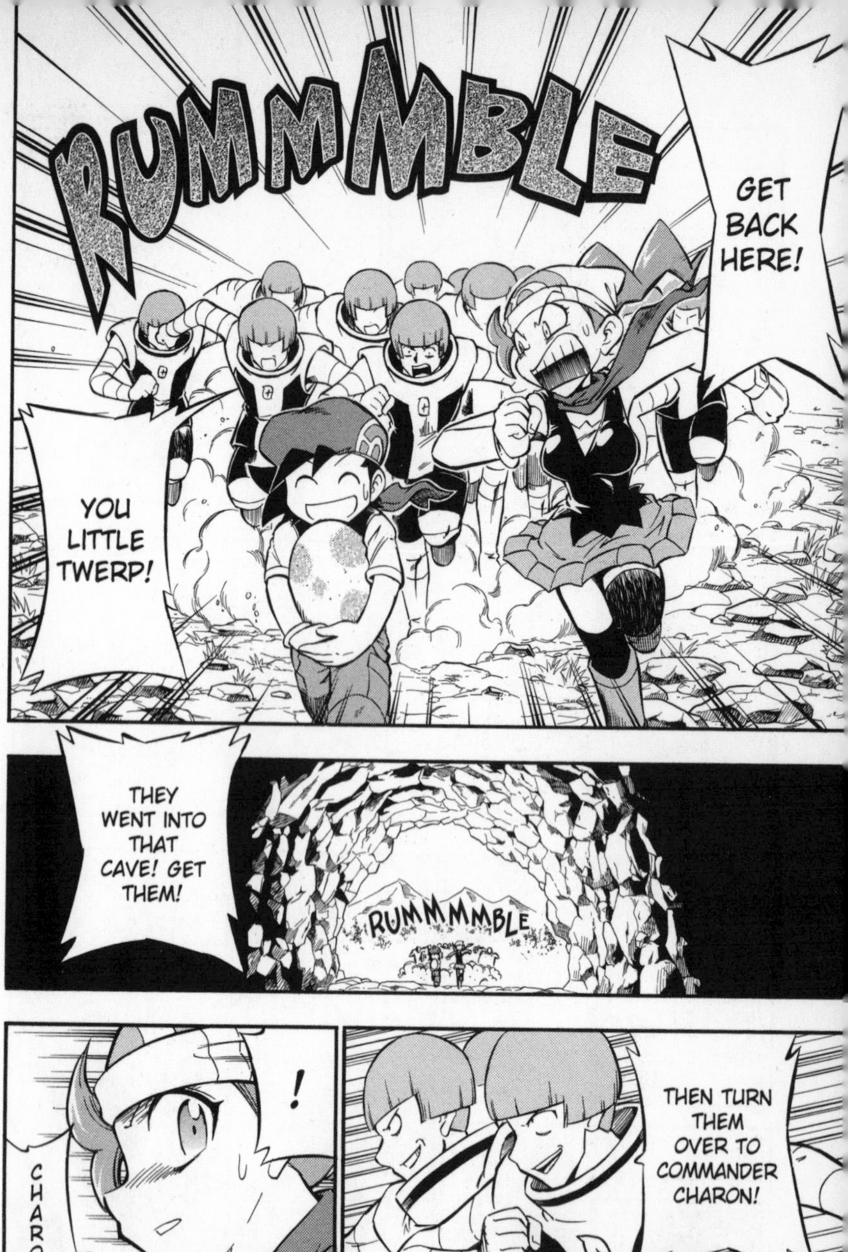
RUMMMBLE
GET BACK HERE!
YOU LITTLE TWERP!
THEY WENT INTO THAT CAVE! GET THEM!
RUMMMMBLE
THEN TURN THEM OVER TO COMMANDER CHARON!
!
CHARON!

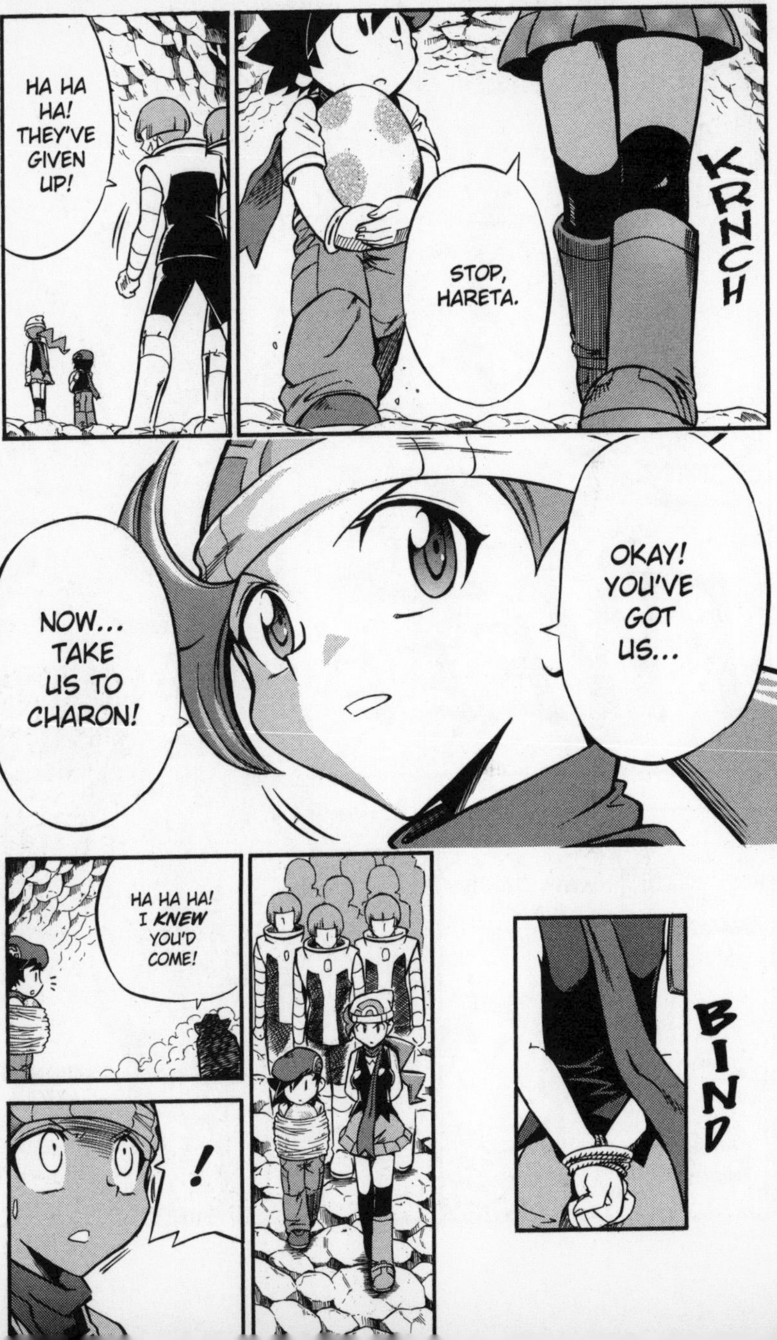
KRNCH
STOP, HARETA.
HA HA HA! THEY'VE GIVEN UP!
OKAY! YOU'VE GOT US...
NOW... TAKE US TO CHARON!
BIND
HA HA HA! I KNEW YOU'D COME!
!

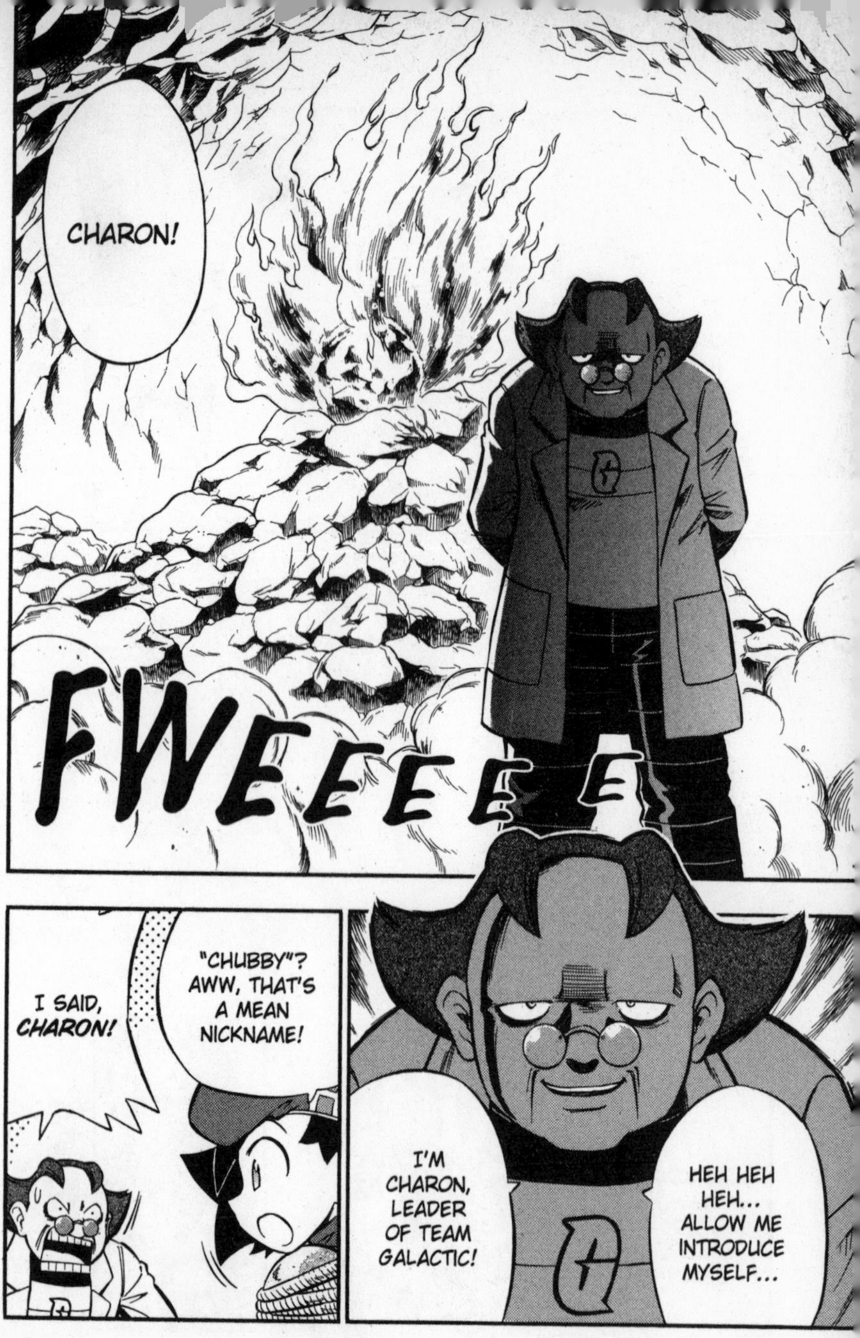
CHARON!
FWEEEEE
HEH HEH HEH... ALLOW ME INTRODUCE MYSELF...
I'M CHARON, LEADER OF TEAM GALACTIC!
"CHUBBY"? AWW, THAT'S A MEAN NICKNAME!
I SAID, **CHARON!**

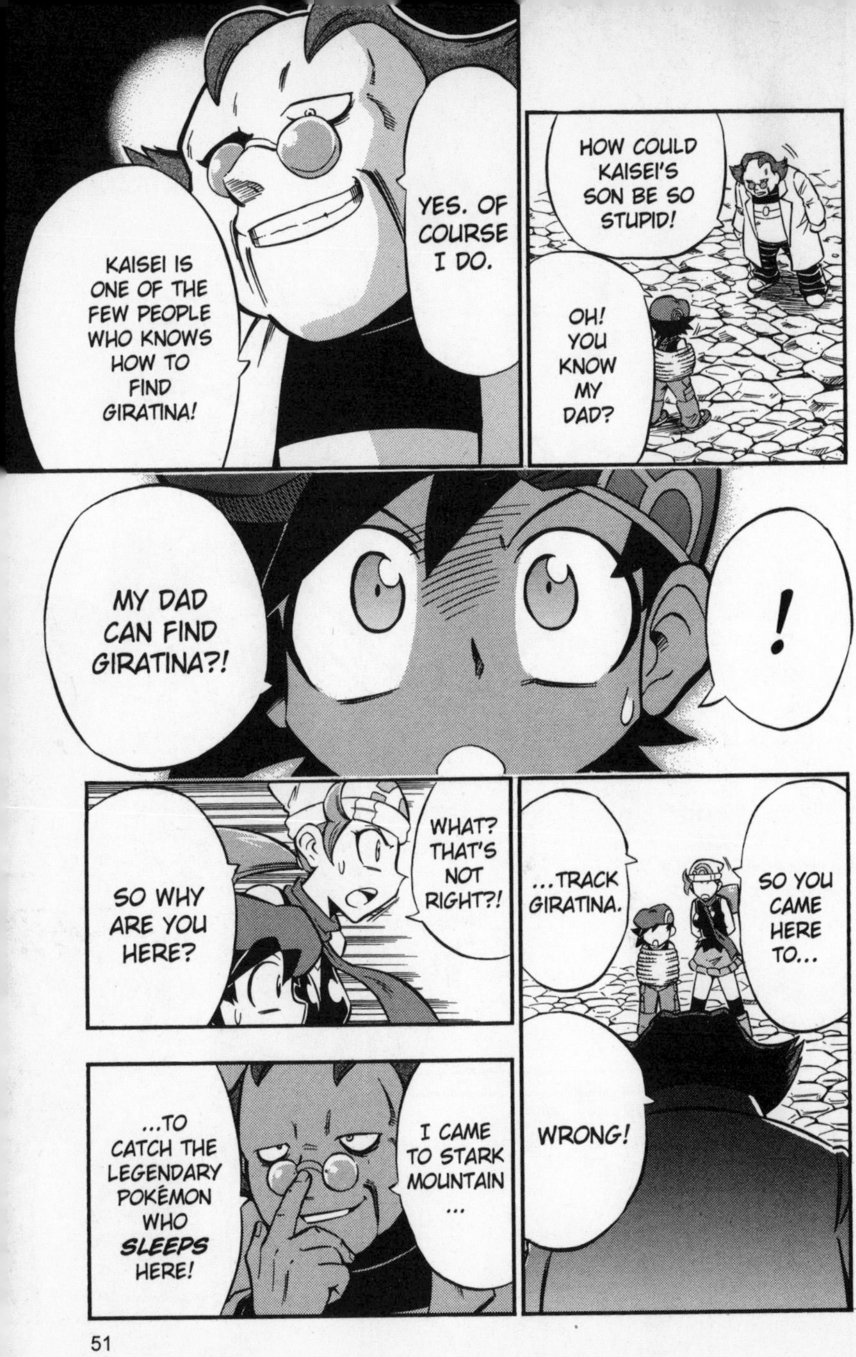
HOW COULD KAISEI'S SON BE SO STUPID!
OH! YOU KNOW MY DAD?
YES. OF COURSE I DO.
KAISEI IS ONE OF THE FEW PEOPLE WHO KNOWS HOW TO FIND GIRATINA!
!
MY DAD CAN FIND GIRATINA?!
SO YOU CAME HERE TO...
...TRACK GIRATINA.
WRONG!
WHAT? THAT'S NOT RIGHT?!
SO WHY ARE YOU HERE?
I CAME TO STARK MOUNTAIN ...
...TO CATCH THE LEGENDARY POKéMON WHO *SLEEPS* HERE!

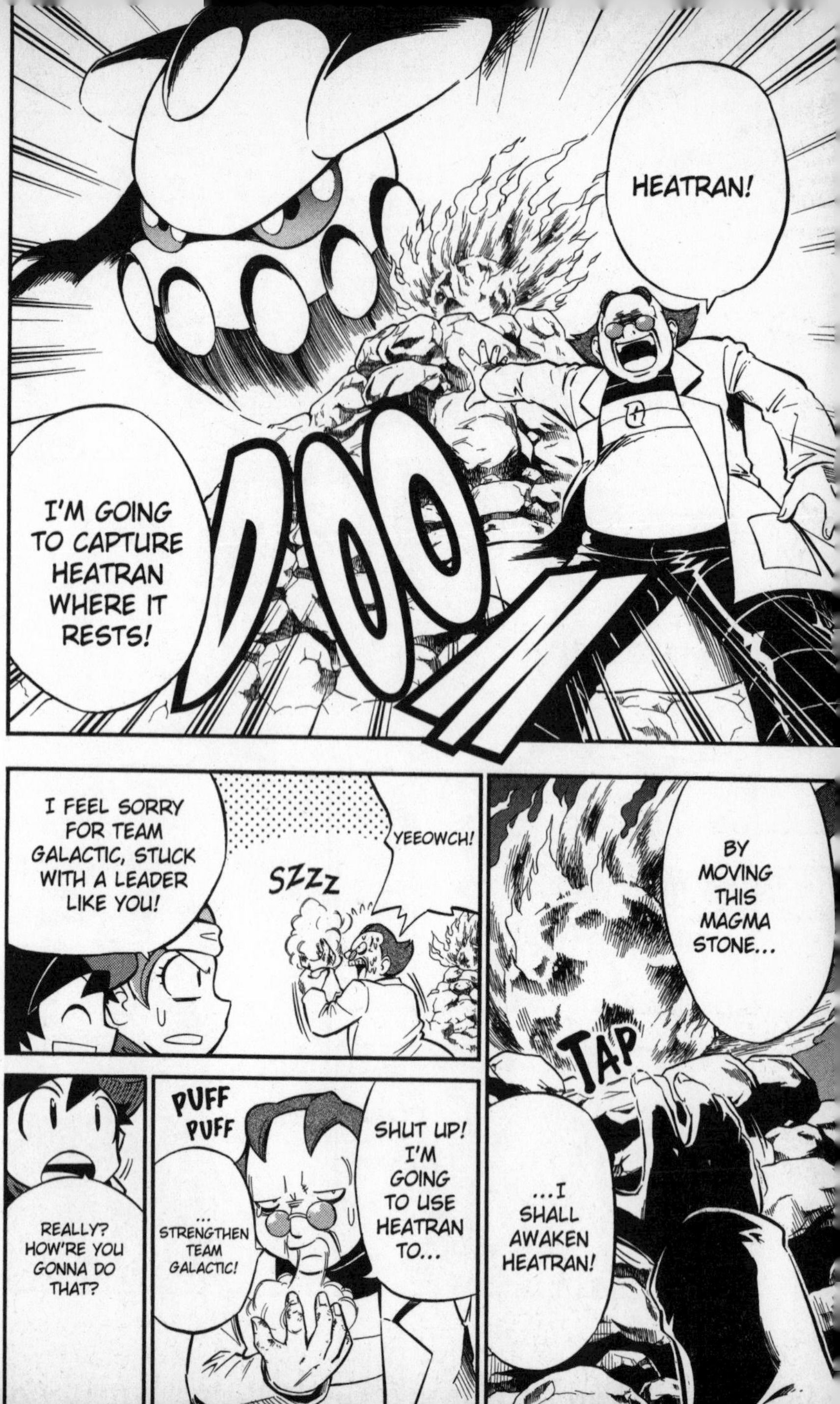
HEATRAN!
I'M GOING TO CAPTURE HEATRAN WHERE IT RESTS!
DOO
BY MOVING THIS MAGMA STONE...
TAP
...I SHALL AWAKEN HEATRAN!
YEEOWCH!
SZZZ
I FEEL SORRY FOR TEAM GALACTIC, STUCK WITH A LEADER LIKE YOU!
SHUT UP! I'M GOING TO USE HEATRAN TO...
PUFF PUFF
...STRENGTHEN TEAM GALACTIC!
REALLY? HOW'RE YOU GONNA DO THAT?

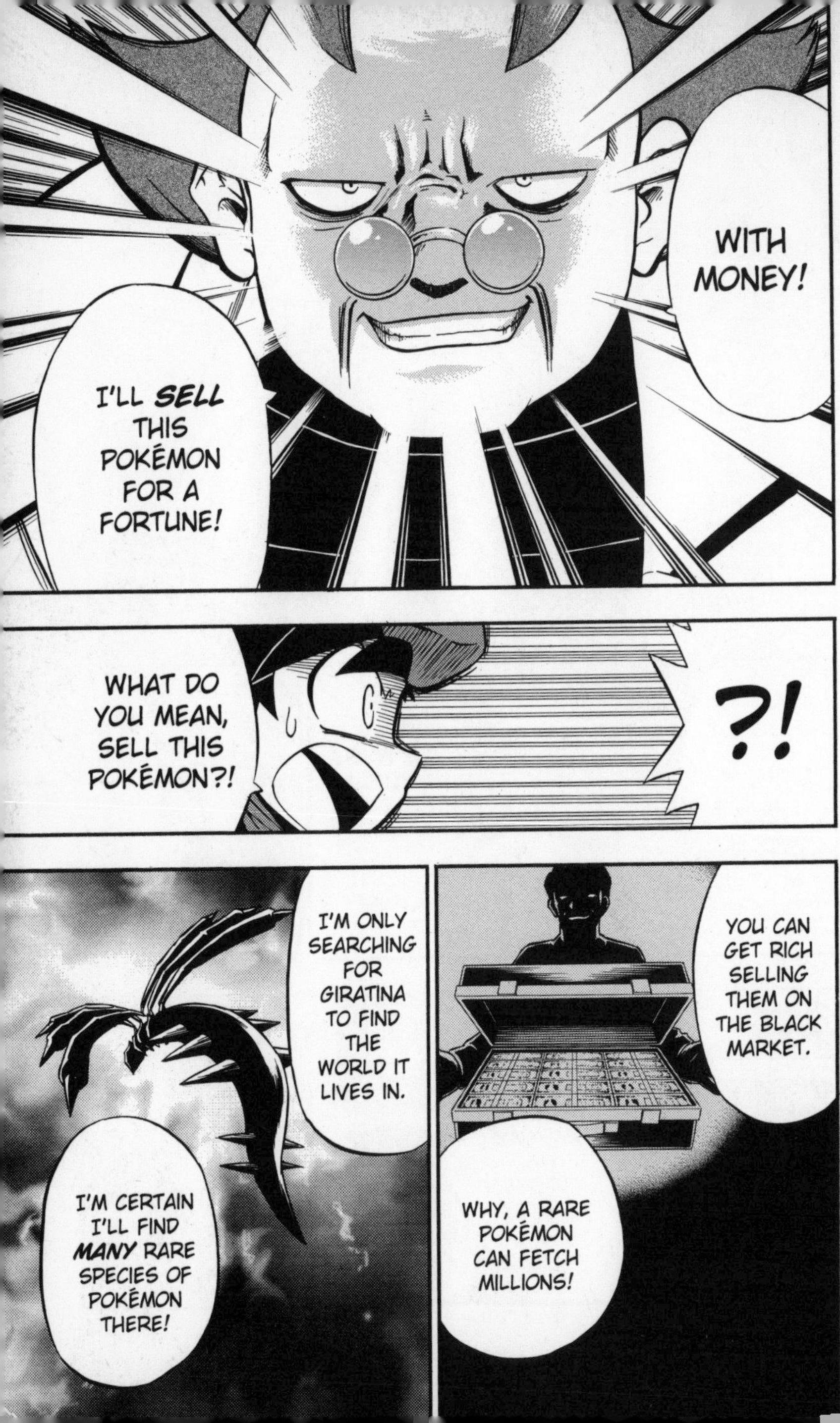
WITH MONEY!
I'LL **SELL** THIS POKÉMON FOR A FORTUNE!
?!
WHAT DO YOU MEAN, SELL THIS POKÉMON?!
YOU CAN GET RICH SELLING THEM ON THE BLACK MARKET.
WHY, A RARE POKÉMON CAN FETCH MILLIONS!
I'M ONLY SEARCHING FOR GIRATINA TO FIND THE WORLD IT LIVES IN.
I'M CERTAIN I'LL FIND **MANY** RARE SPECIES OF POKÉMON THERE!

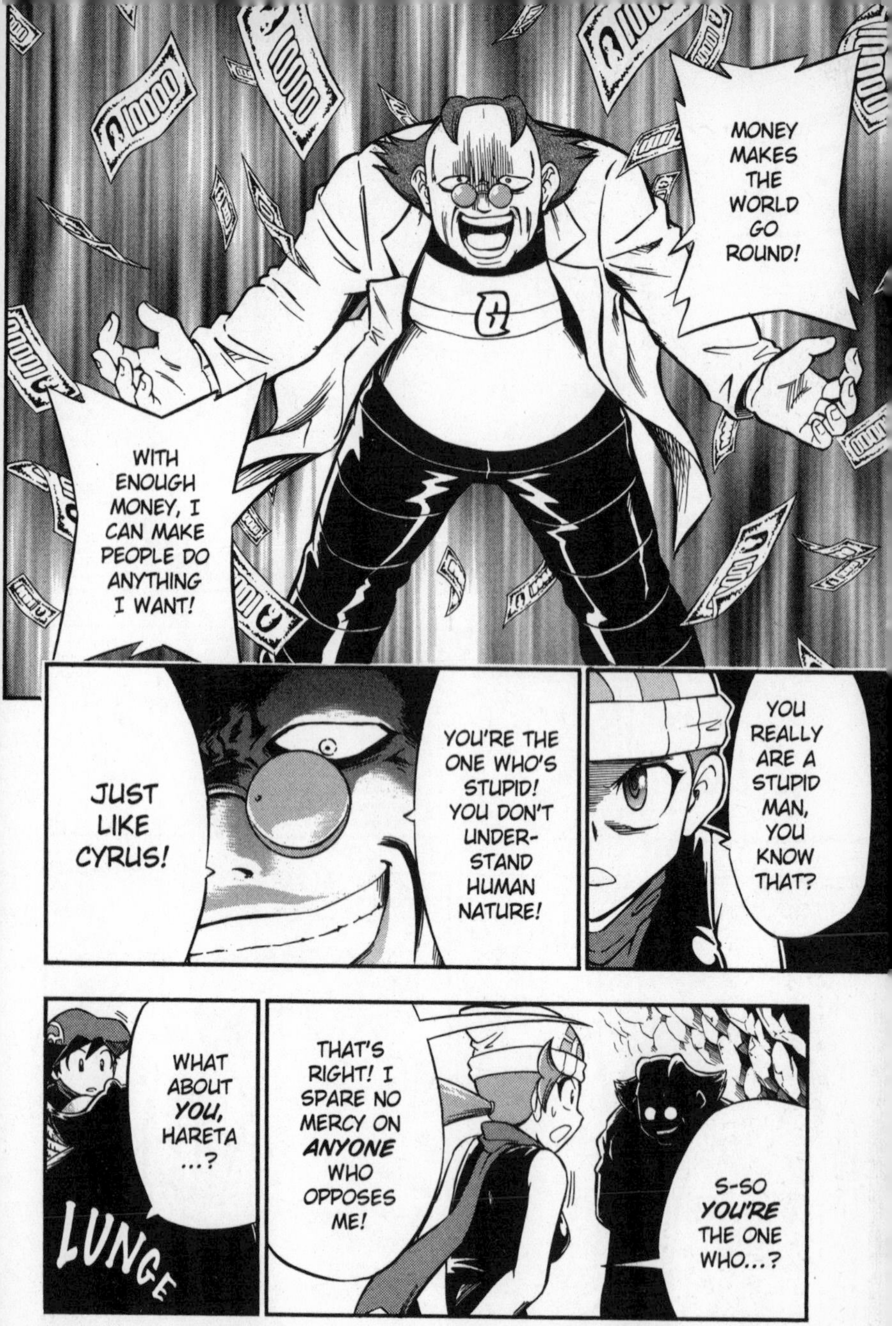
MONEY MAKES THE WORLD GO ROUND!
WITH ENOUGH MONEY, I CAN MAKE PEOPLE DO ANYTHING I WANT!
YOU REALLY ARE A STUPID MAN, YOU KNOW THAT?
YOU'RE THE ONE WHO'S STUPID! YOU DON'T UNDER-STAND HUMAN NATURE!
JUST LIKE CYRUS!
S-SO *YOU'RE* THE ONE WHO...?
THAT'S RIGHT! I SPARE NO MERCY ON *ANYONE* WHO OPPOSES ME!
WHAT ABOUT *YOU*, HARETA...?
LUNGE

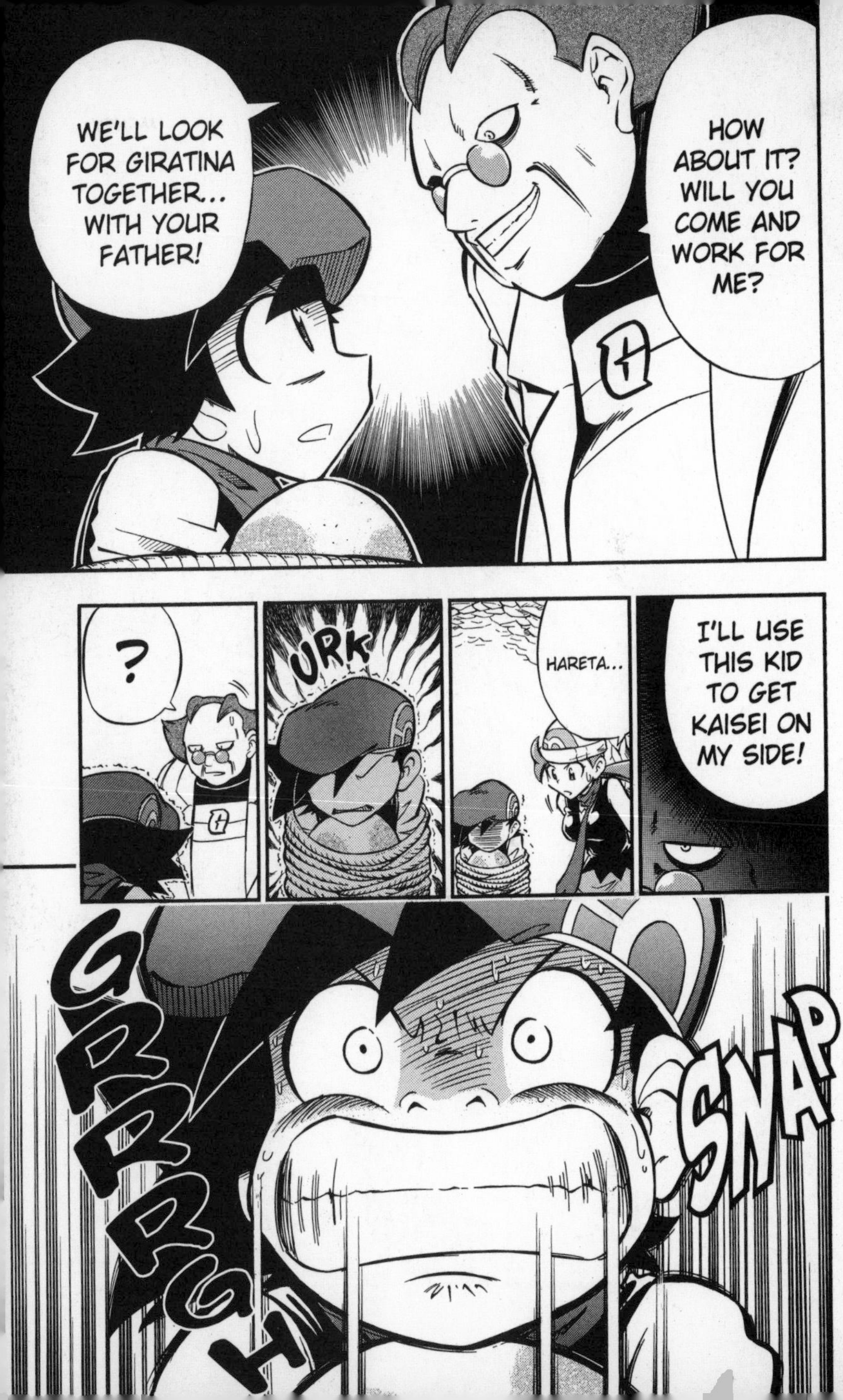
HOW ABOUT IT? WILL YOU COME AND WORK FOR ME?
WE'LL LOOK FOR GIRATINA TOGETHER... WITH YOUR FATHER!
I'LL USE THIS KID TO GET KAISEI ON MY SIDE!
HARETA...
URK
?
SNAP
GRRRRGH

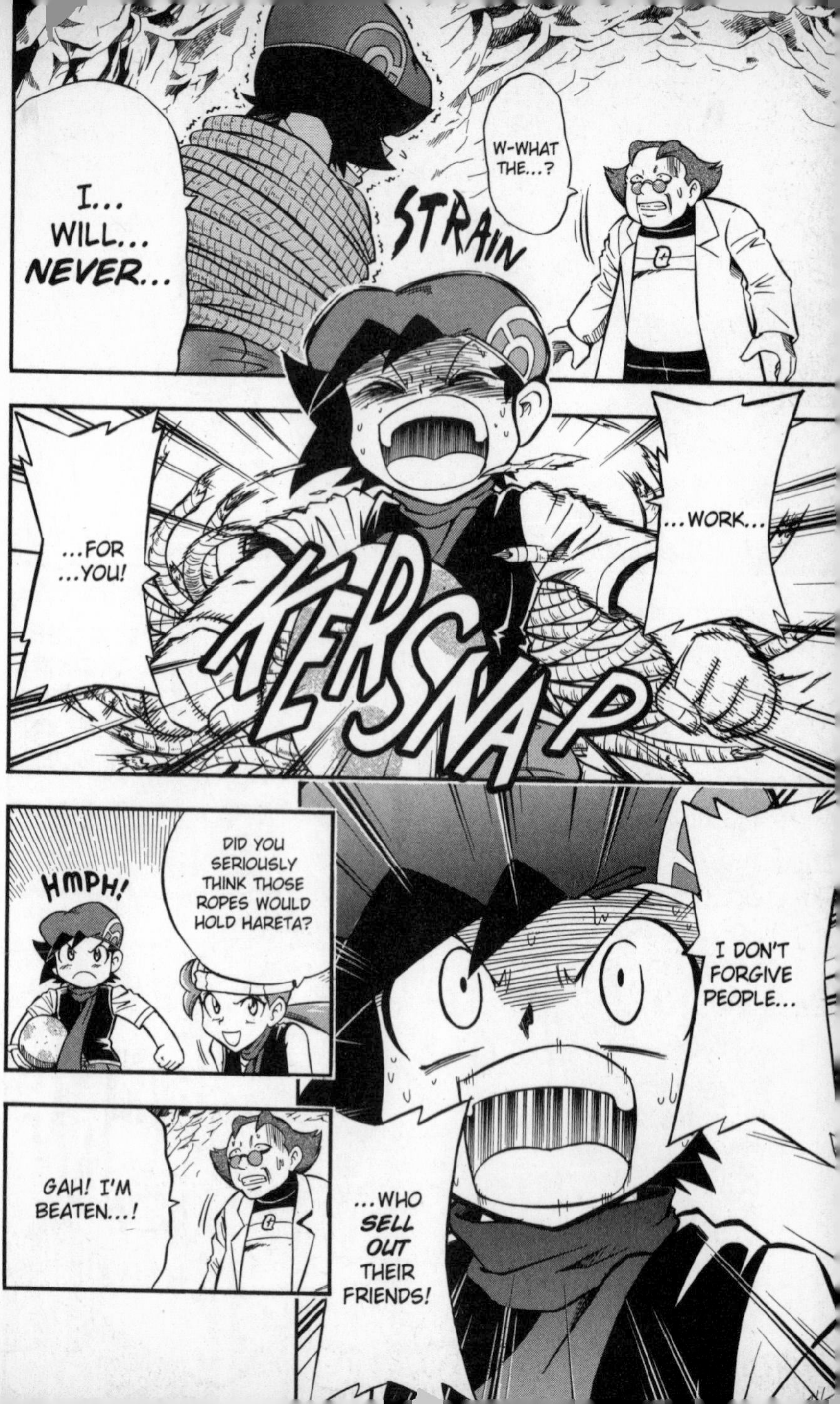
W-WHAT THE...?
STRAIN
I... WILL... NEVER...
...WORK...
KERSNAP
...FOR ...YOU!
I DON'T FORGIVE PEOPLE...
...WHO SELL OUT THEIR FRIENDS!
DID YOU SERIOUSLY THINK THOSE ROPES WOULD HOLD HARETA?
HMPH!
GAH! I'M BEATEN...!

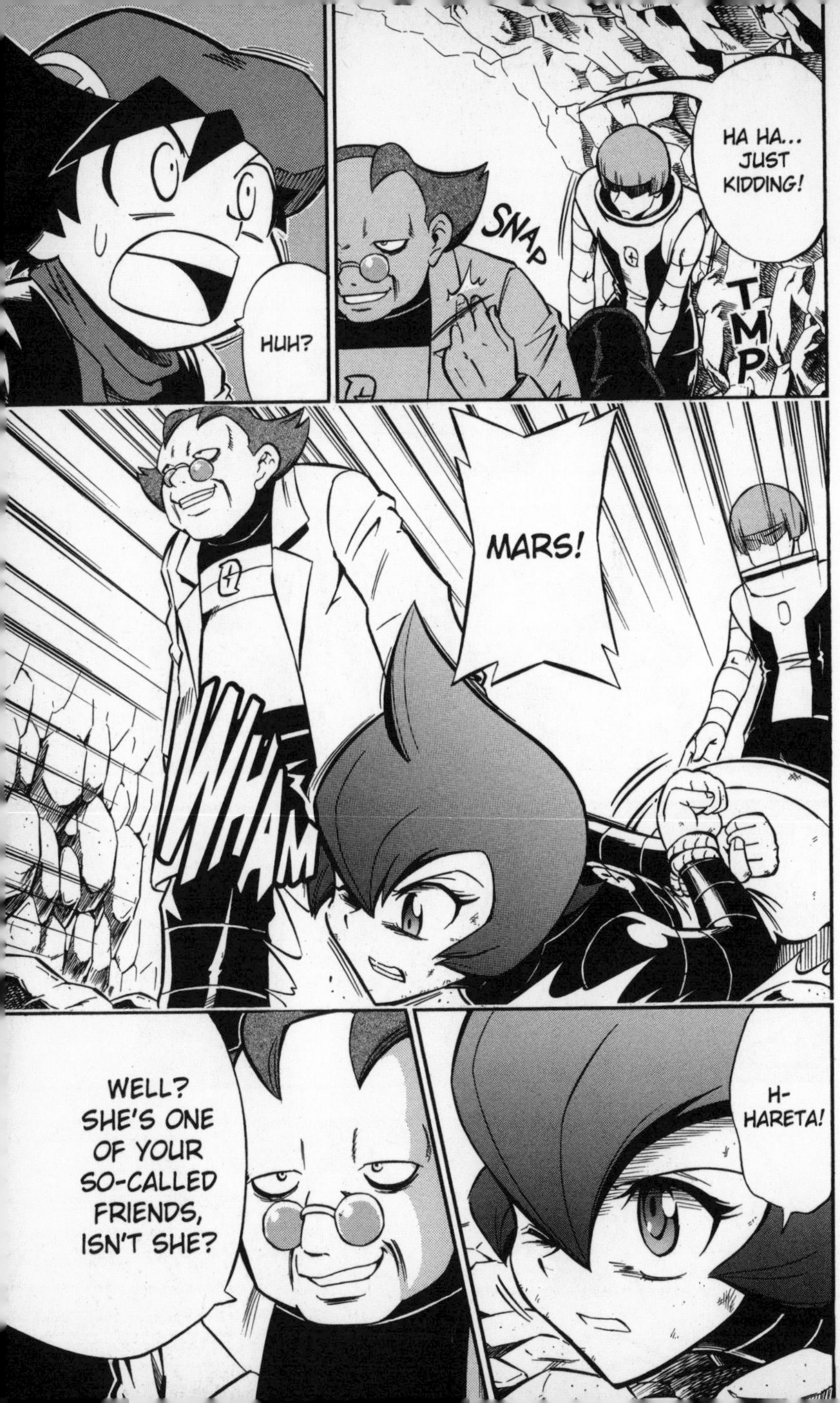
HA HA... JUST KIDDING!
TMP
SNAP
HUH?
MARS!
WHAM
H-HARETA!
WELL? SHE'S ONE OF YOUR SO-CALLED FRIENDS, ISN'T SHE?

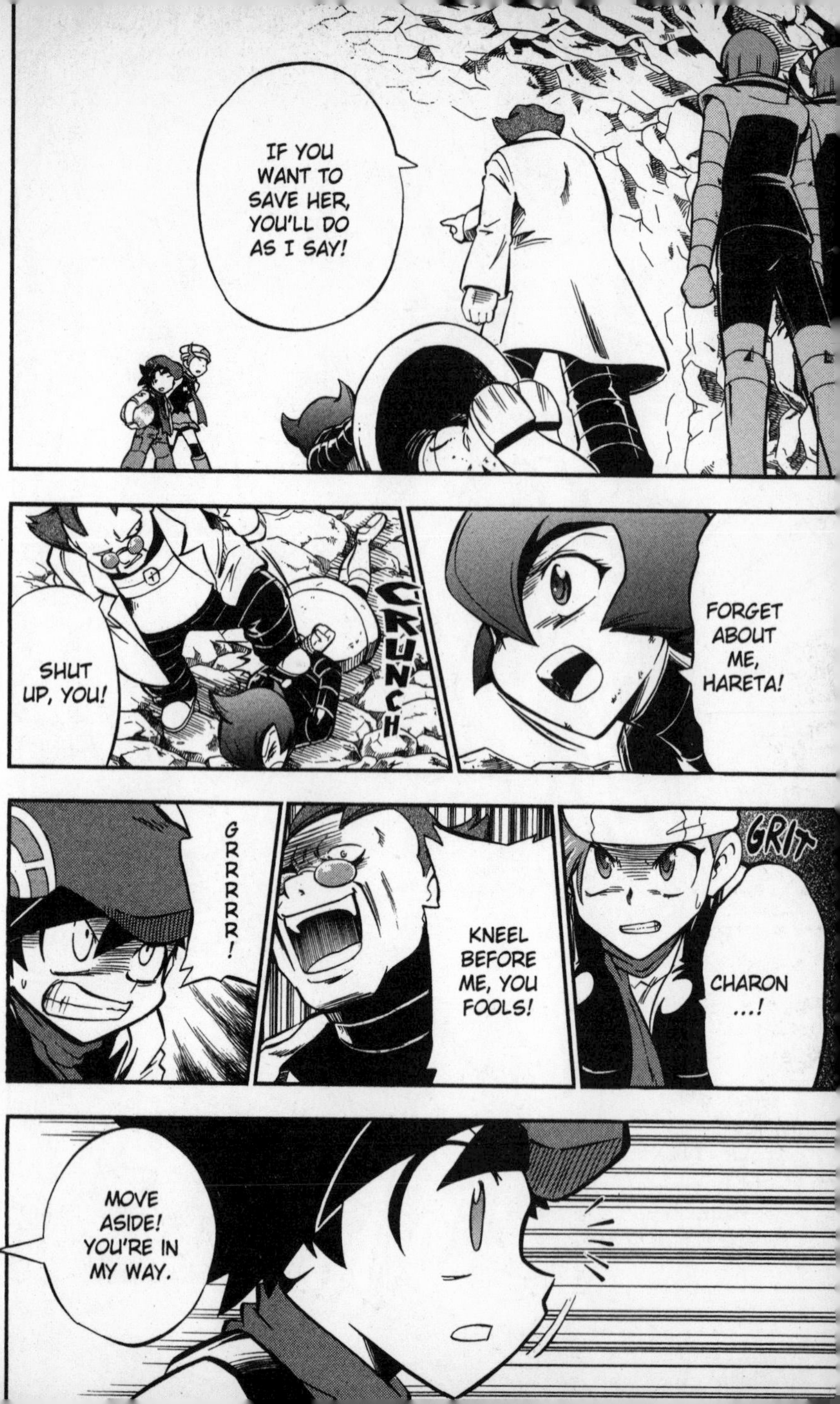
IF YOU WANT TO SAVE HER, YOU'LL DO AS I SAY!
FORGET ABOUT ME, HARETA!
CRUNCH
SHUT UP, YOU!
GRIT
CHARON ...!
KNEEL BEFORE ME, YOU FOOLS!
GRRRRR!
MOVE ASIDE! YOU'RE IN MY WAY.

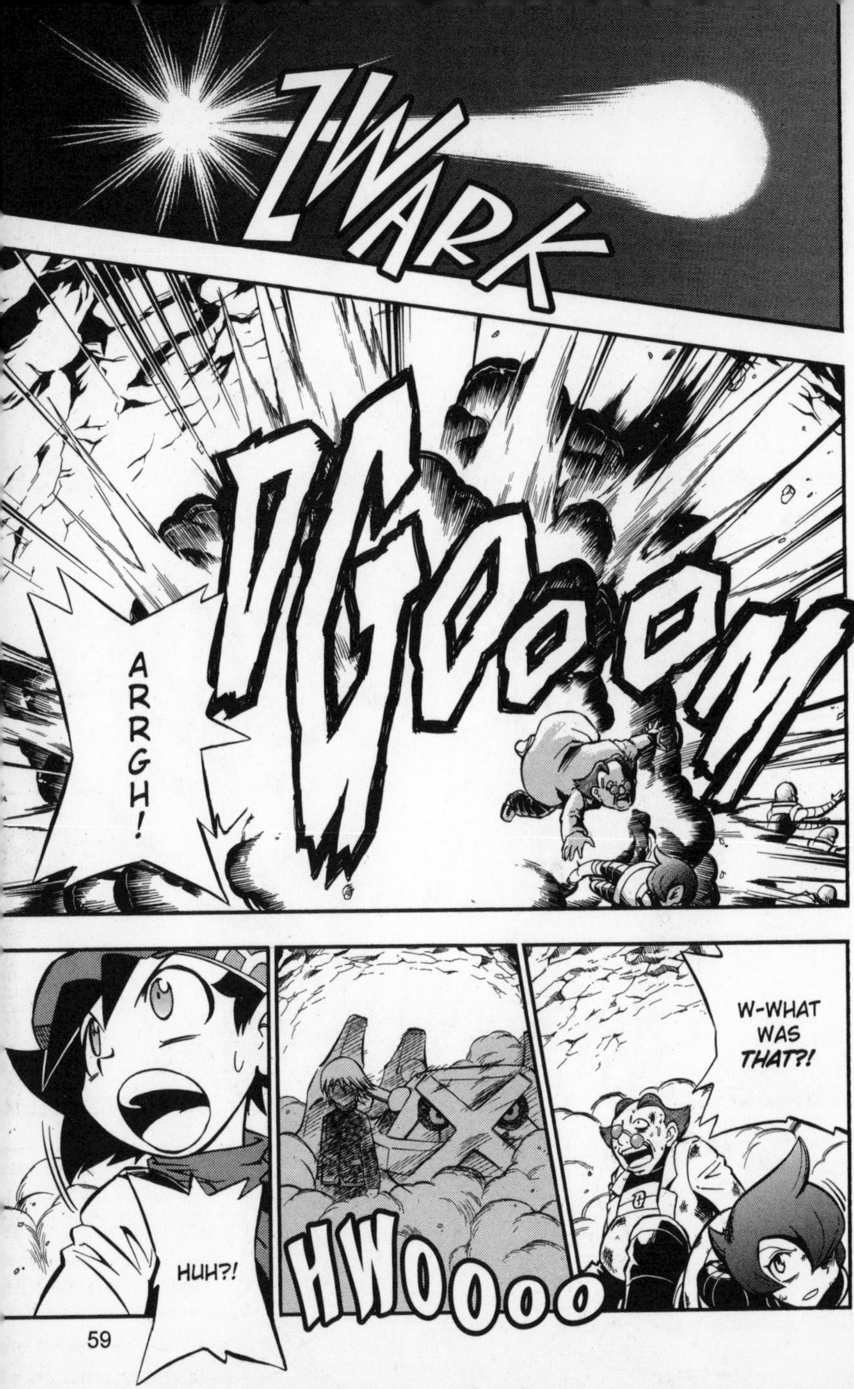
ZWARK
ARRGH!
W-WHAT WAS THAT?!
HWOOOO
HUH?!

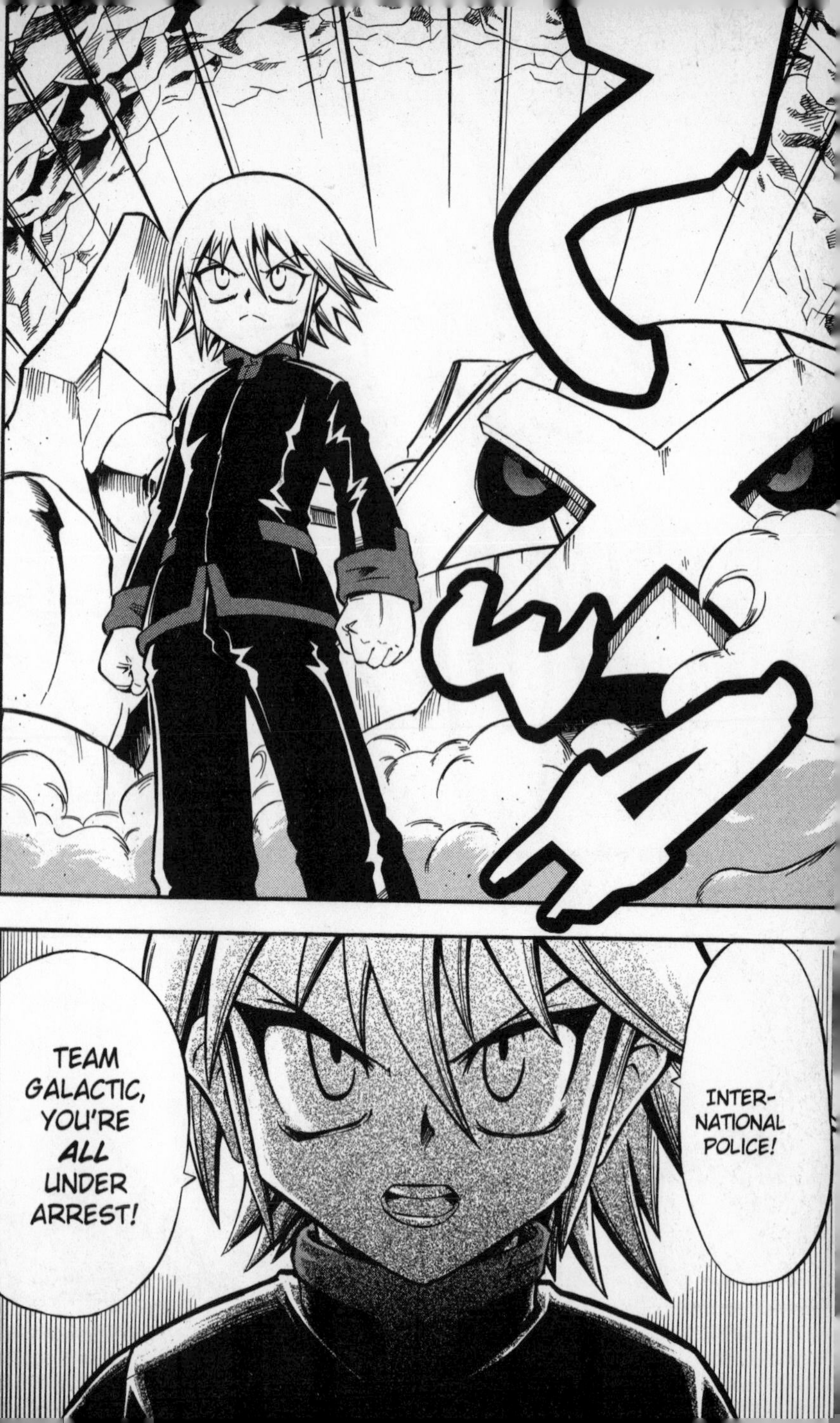
INTER-NATIONAL POLICE!
TEAM GALACTIC, YOU'RE *ALL* UNDER ARREST!

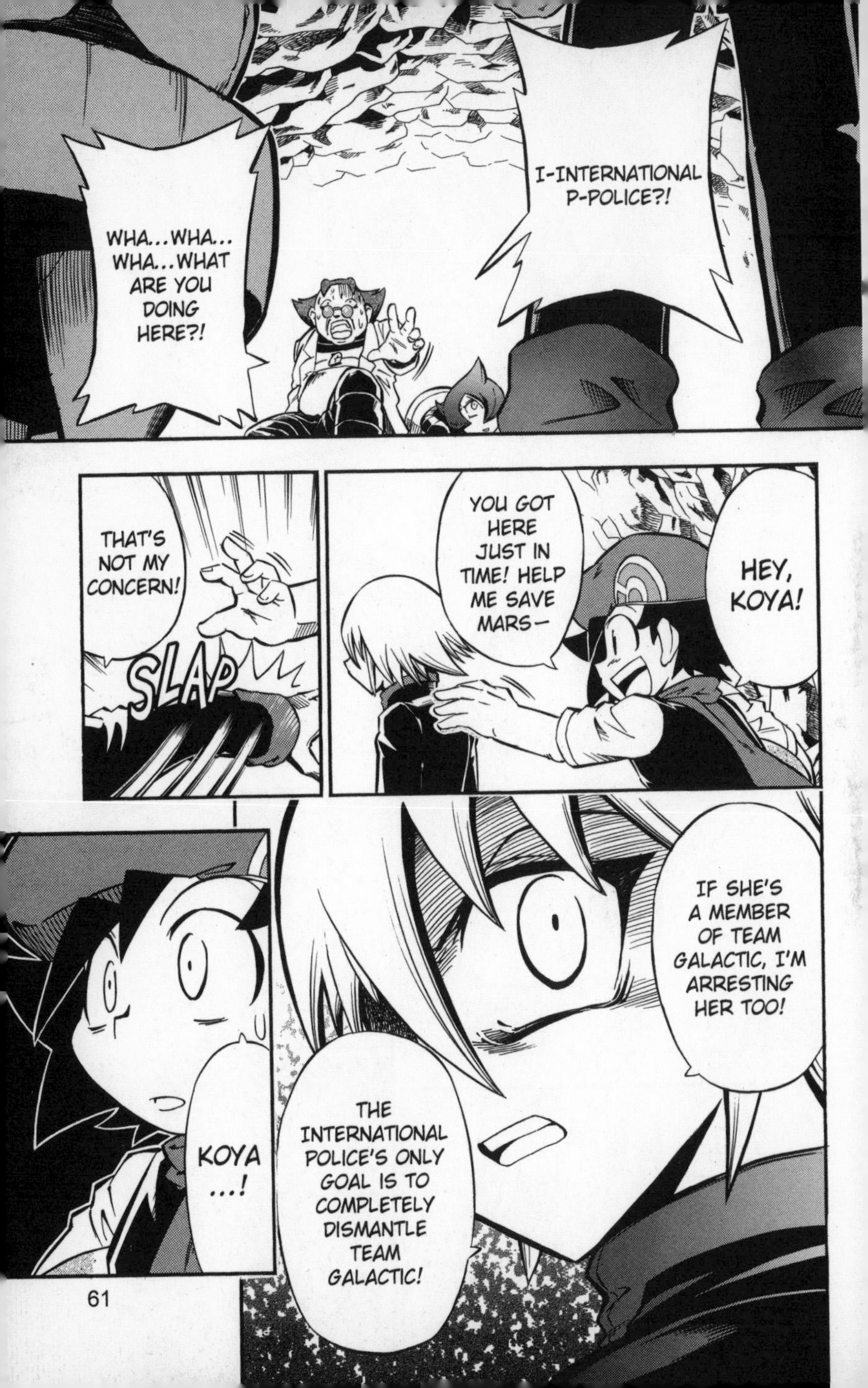
I-INTERNATIONAL P-POLICE?!
WHA...WHA... WHA...WHAT ARE YOU DOING HERE?!
HEY, KOYA!
YOU GOT HERE JUST IN TIME! HELP ME SAVE MARS—
THAT'S NOT MY CONCERN!
SLAP
IF SHE'S A MEMBER OF TEAM GALACTIC, I'M ARRESTING HER TOO!
THE INTERNATIONAL POLICE'S ONLY GOAL IS TO COMPLETELY DISMANTLE TEAM GALACTIC!
KOYA ...!

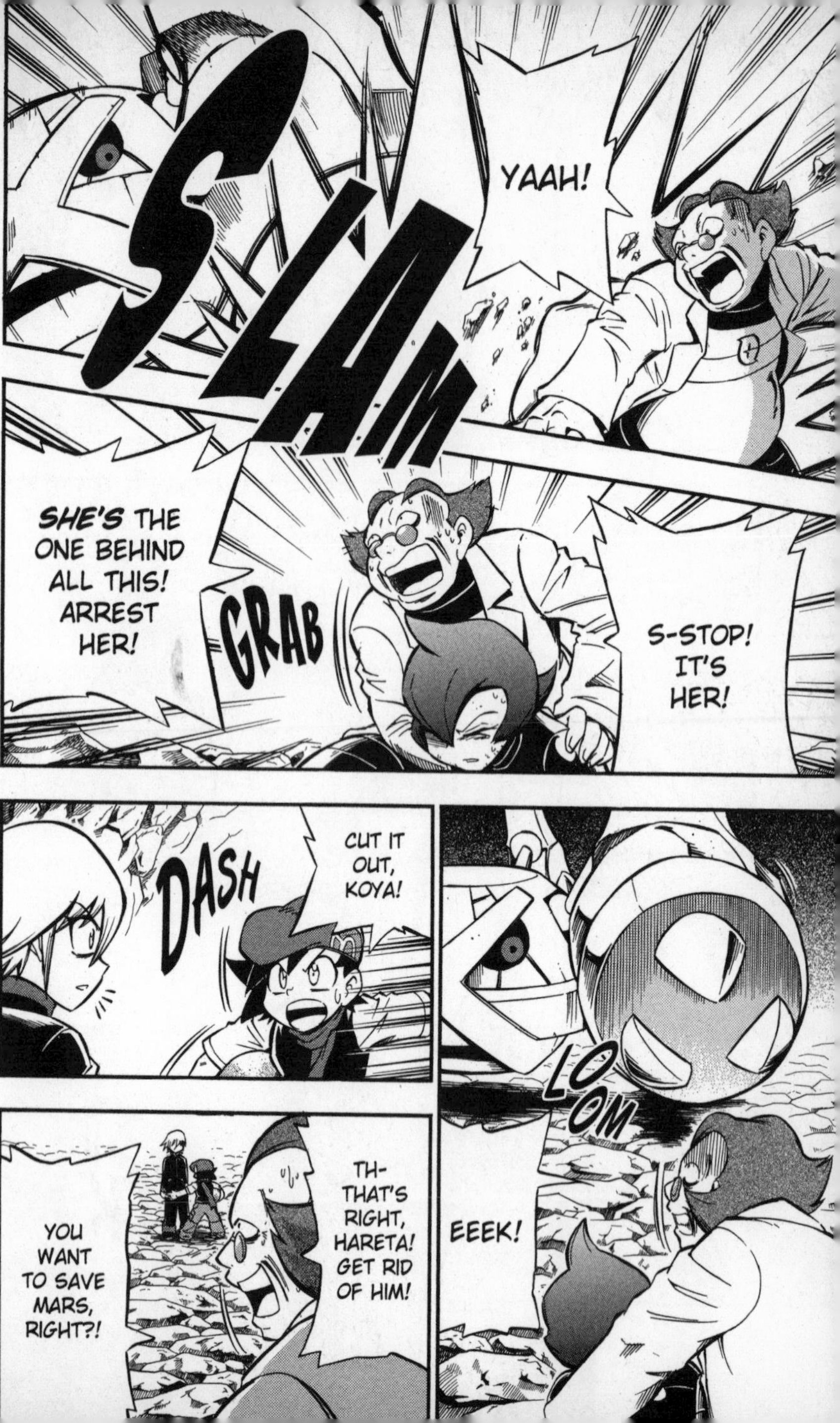
YAAH!
SLAM
S-STOP! IT'S HER!
GRAB
SHE'S THE ONE BEHIND ALL THIS! ARREST HER!
LOOM
CUT IT OUT, KOYA!
DASH
EEEK!
TH-THAT'S RIGHT, HARETA! GET RID OF HIM!
YOU WANT TO SAVE MARS, RIGHT?!

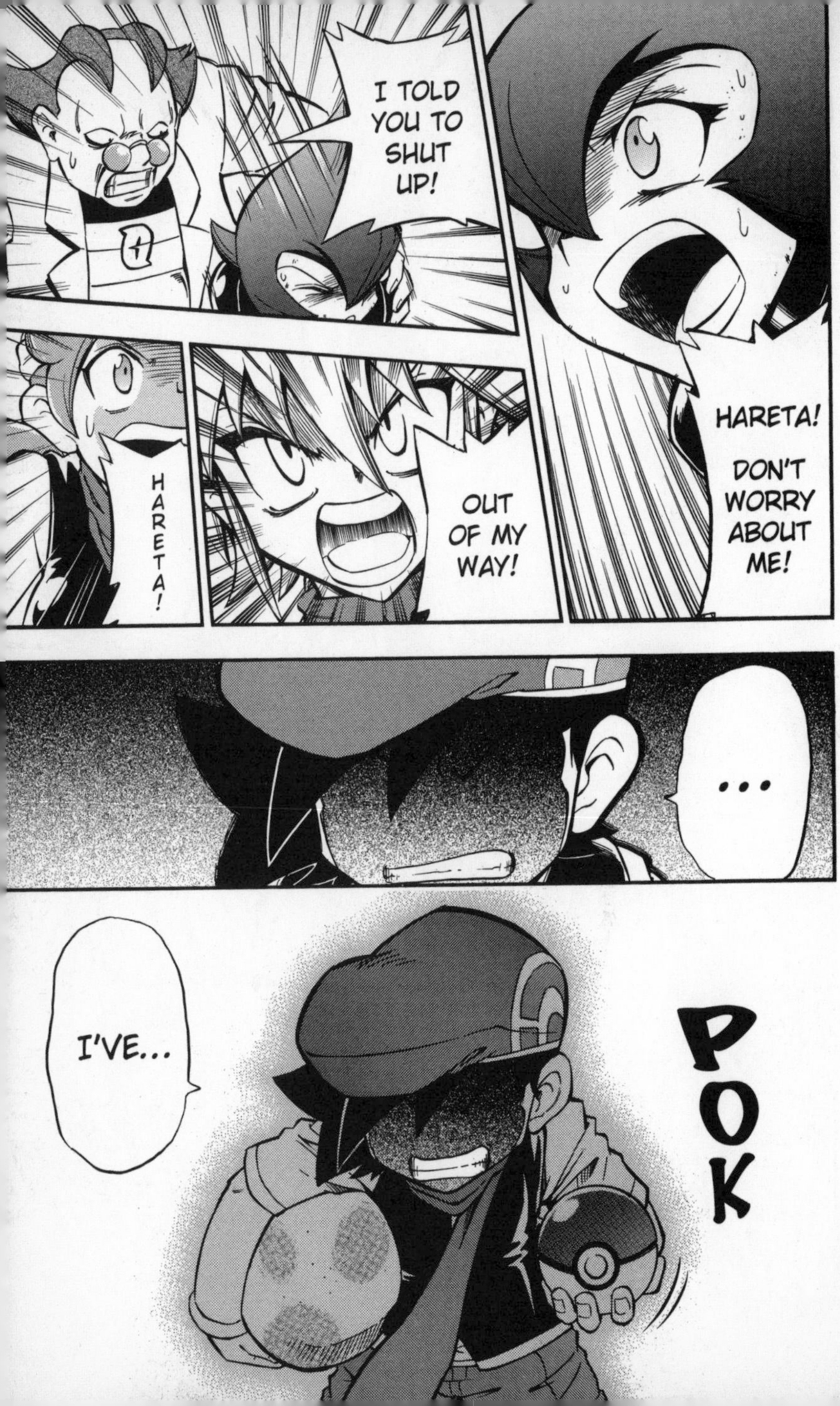
HARETA!
DON'T WORRY ABOUT ME!
I TOLD YOU TO SHUT UP!
OUT OF MY WAY!
HARETA!
...
POK
I'VE...

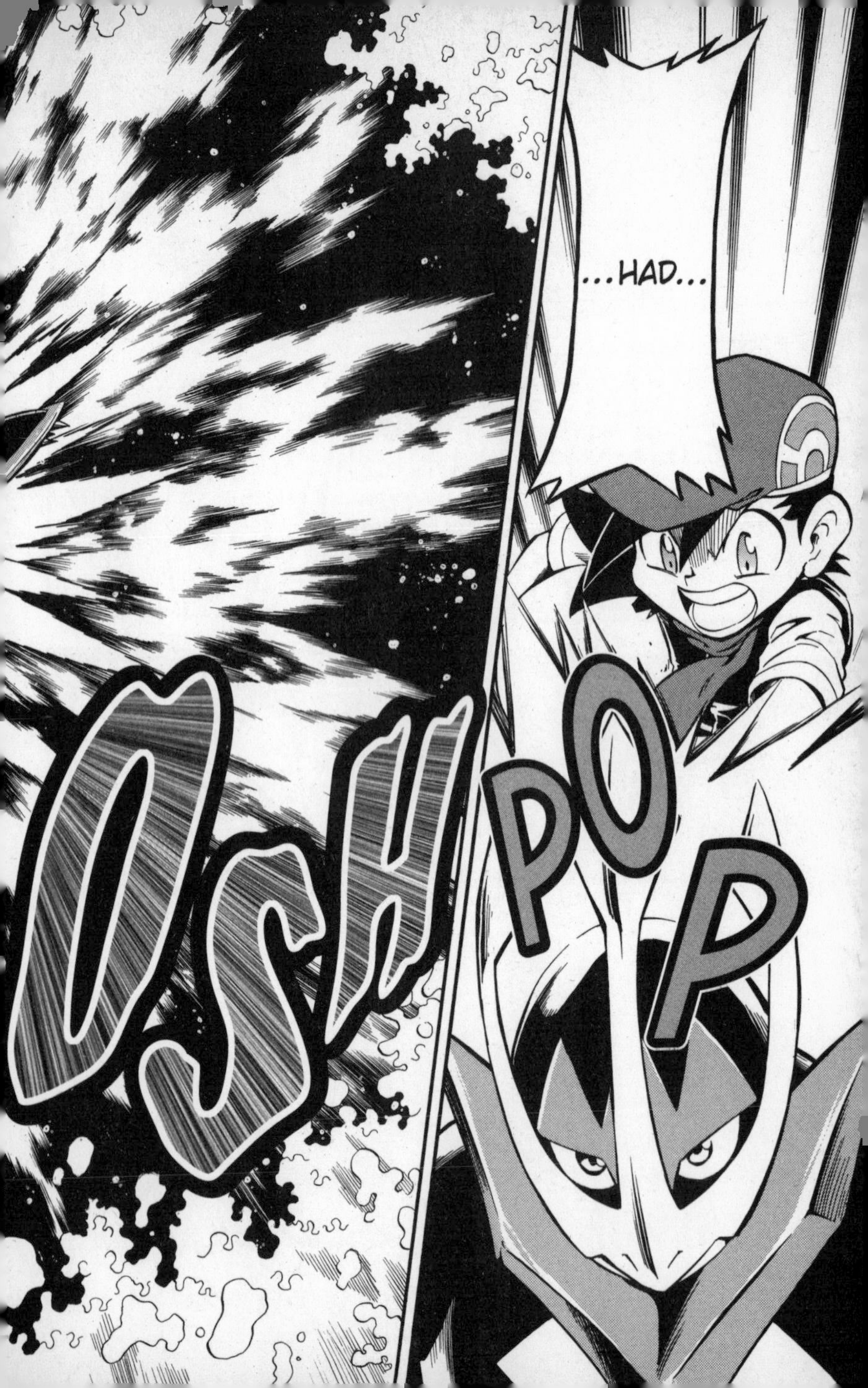
...HAD...
POP
OSH

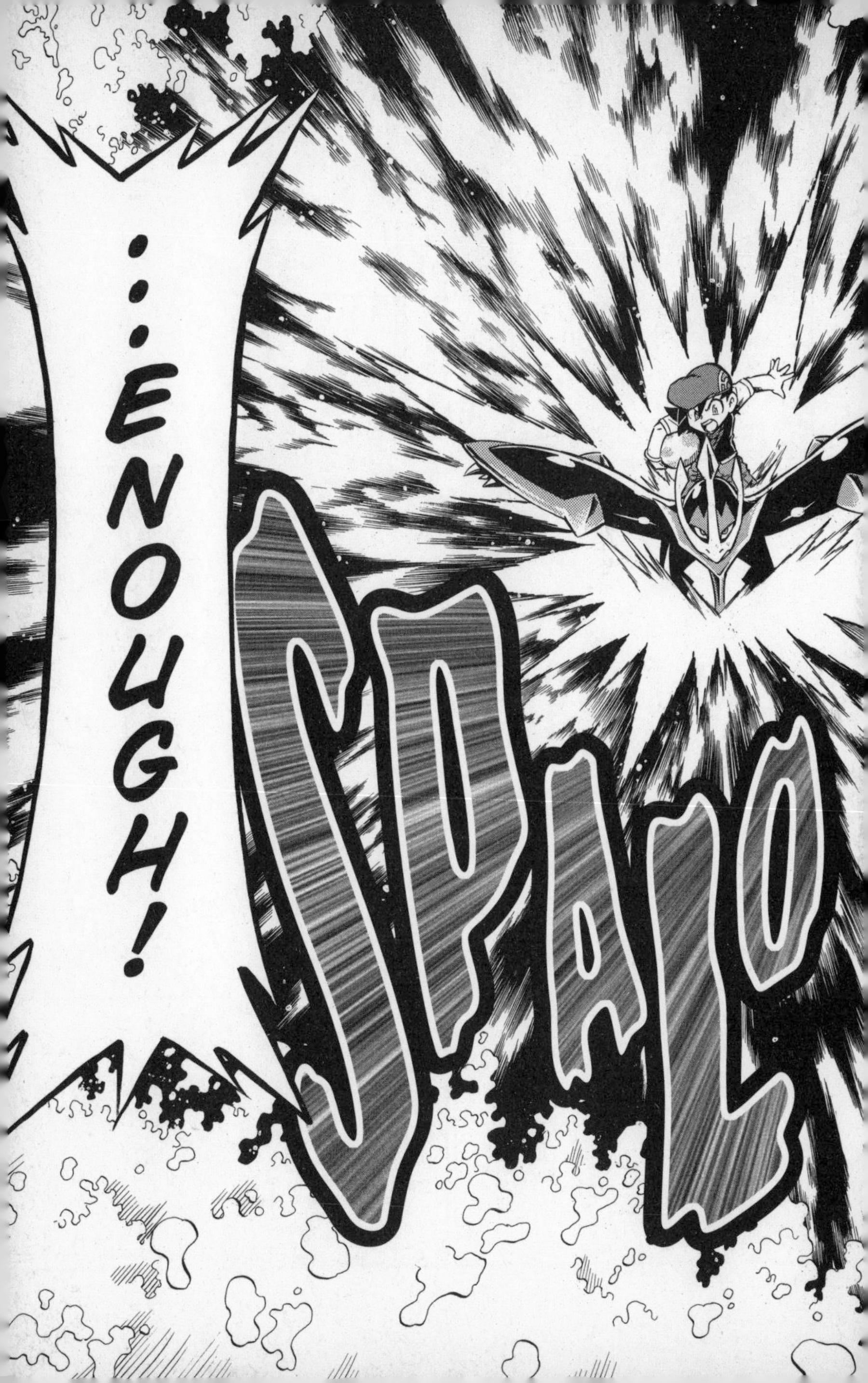
...ENOUGH!

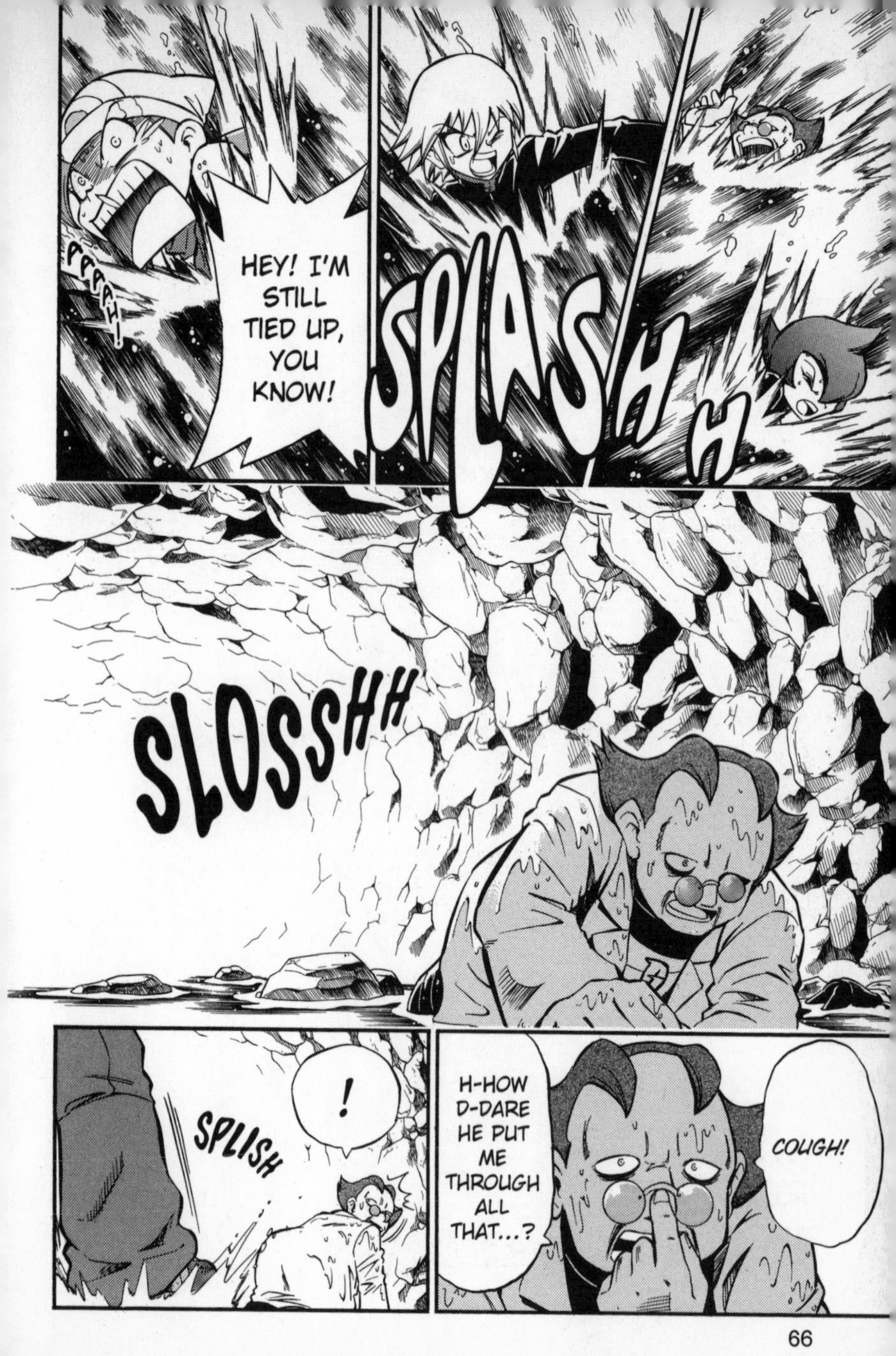
SPLASHH
HEY! I'M STILL TIED UP, YOU KNOW!
AAAAH!
SLOSSHH
COUGH!
H-HOW D-DARE HE PUT ME THROUGH ALL THAT...?
!
SPLISH

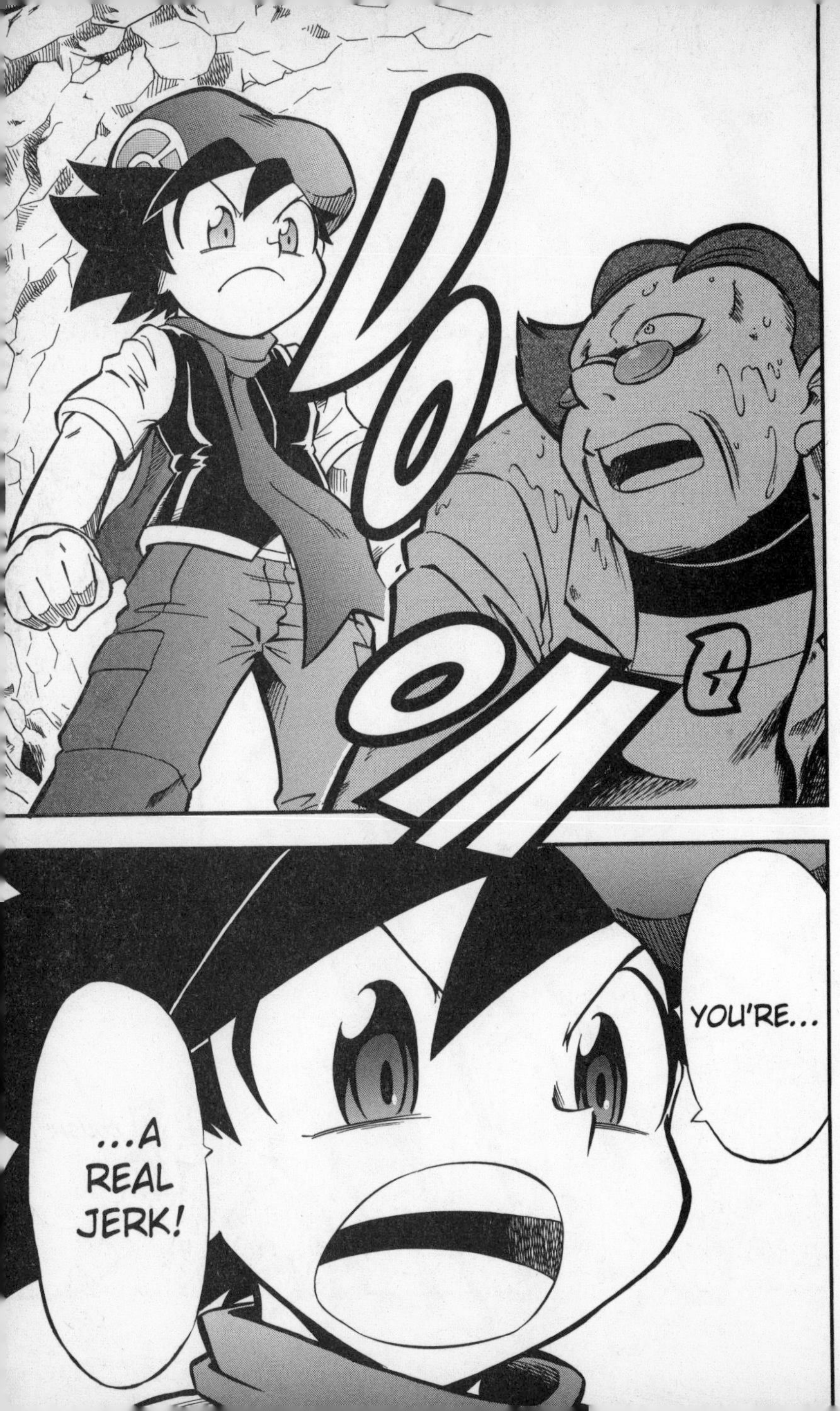
YOU'RE...
...A REAL JERK!

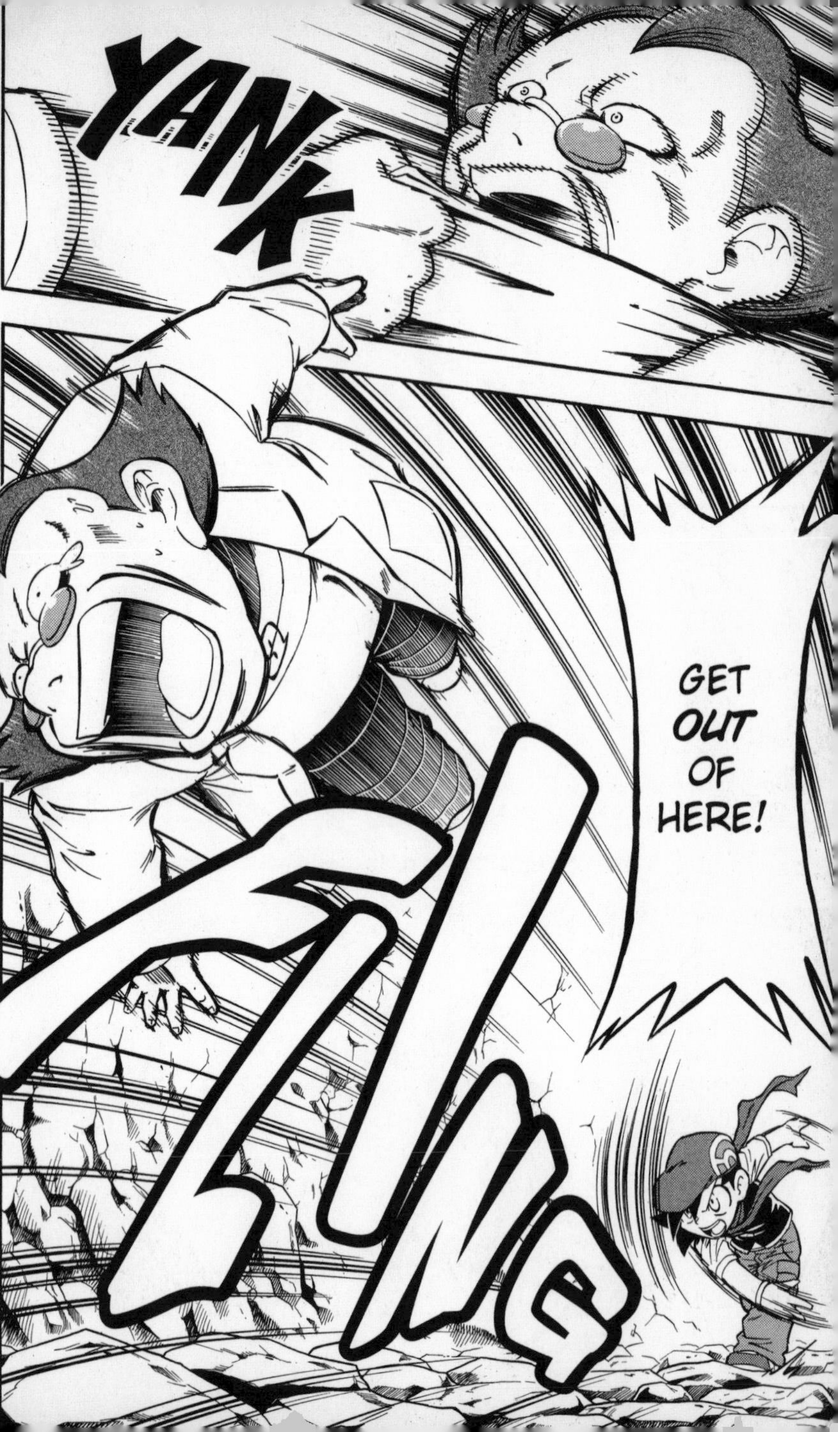
YANK
GET OUT OF HERE!
ZING

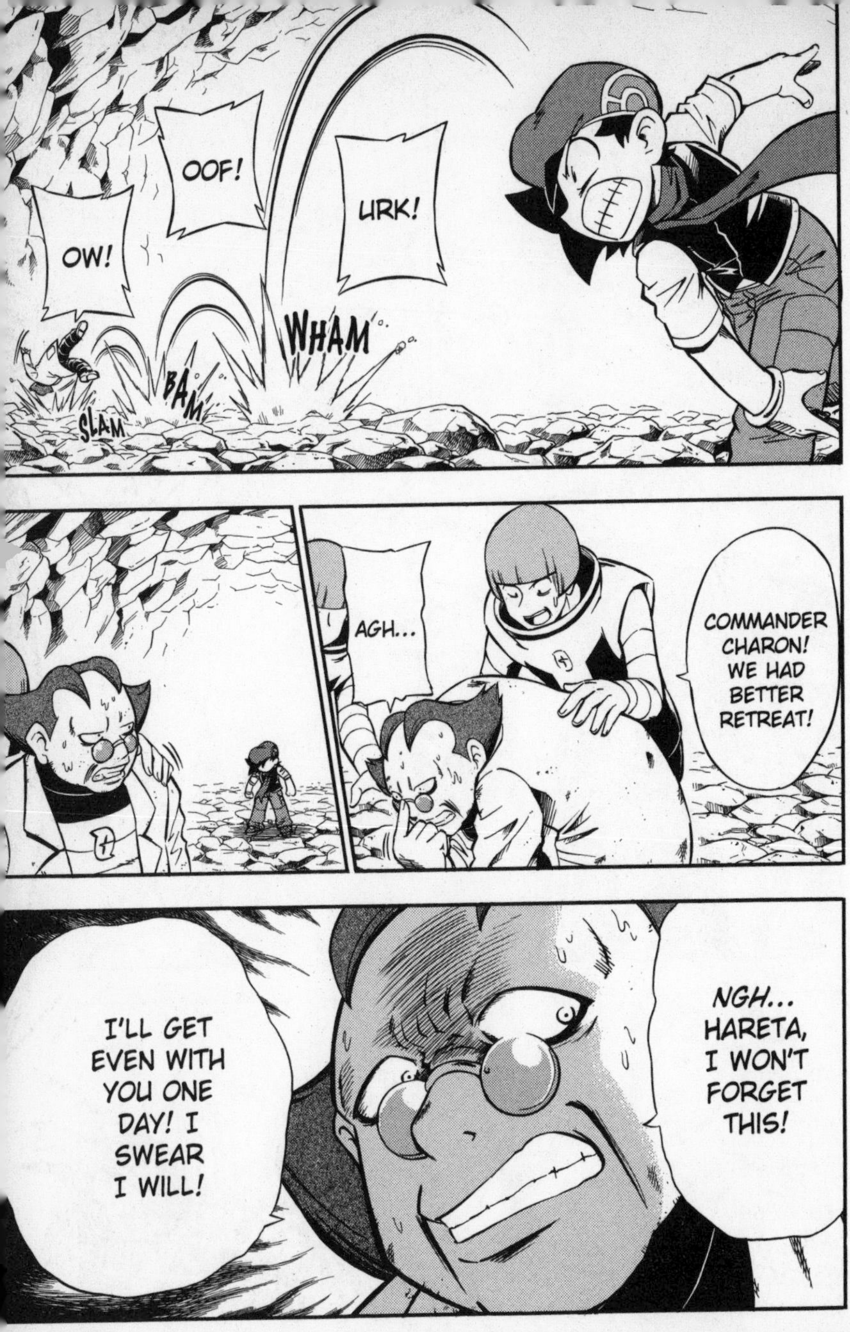
URK!
OOF!
OW!
WHAM
BAM
SLAM
COMMANDER CHARON! WE HAD BETTER RETREAT!
AGH...
NGH... HARETA, I WON'T FORGET THIS!
I'LL GET EVEN WITH YOU ONE DAY! I SWEAR I WILL!

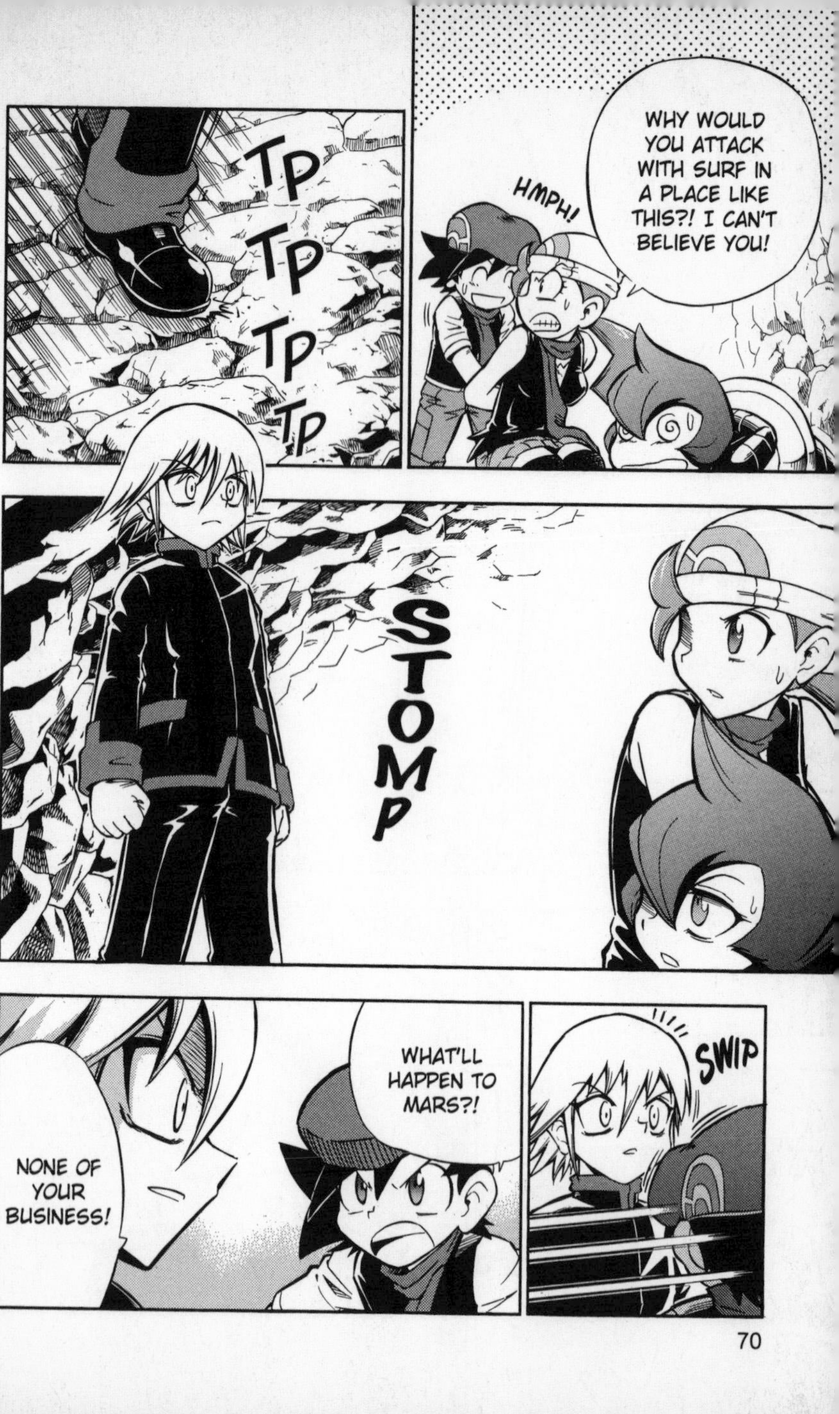
WHY WOULD YOU ATTACK WITH SURF IN A PLACE LIKE THIS?! I CAN'T BELIEVE YOU!
HMPH!
TP TP TP TP
STOMP
SWIP
WHAT'LL HAPPEN TO MARS?!
NONE OF YOUR BUSINESS!

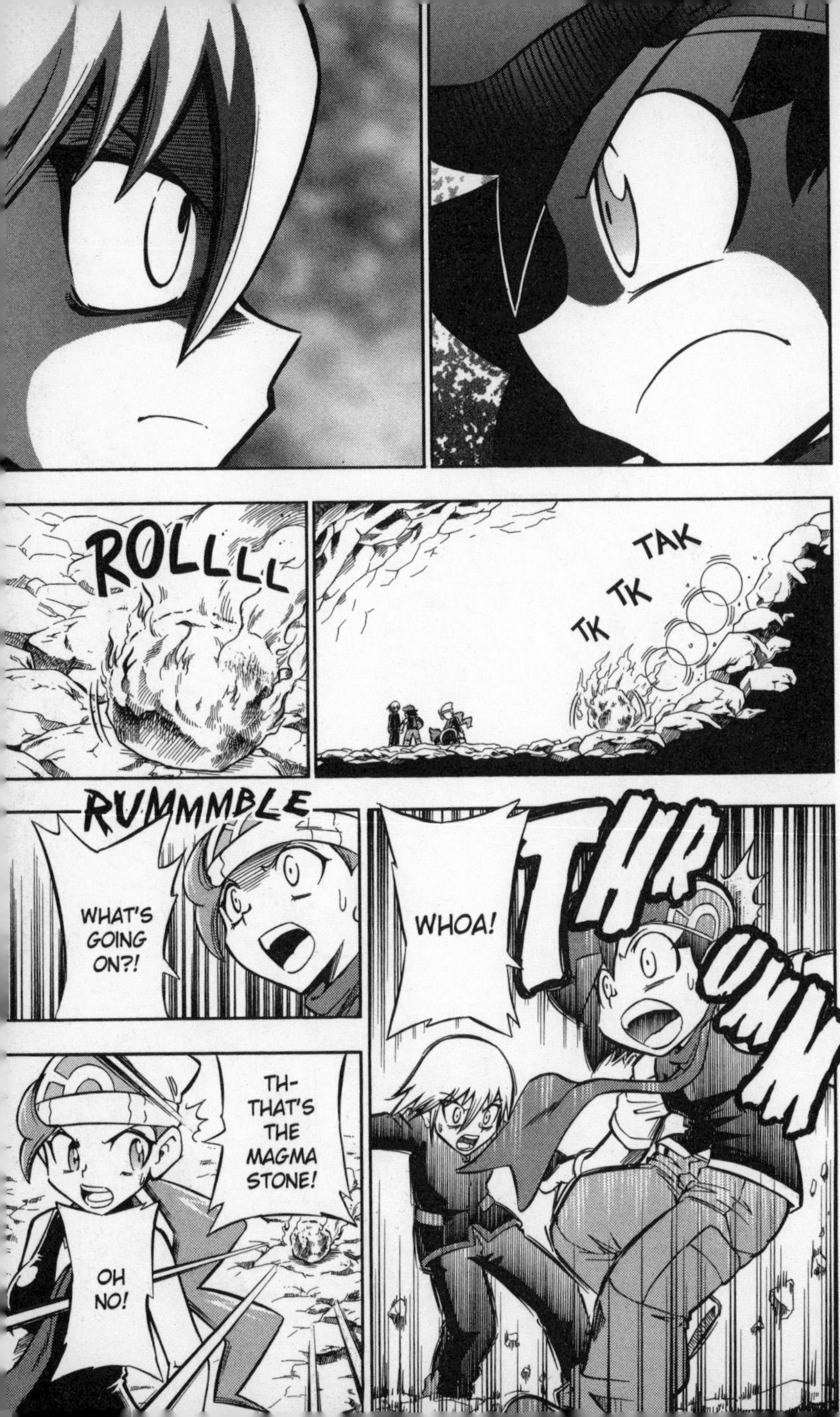
TAK
TK
TK
ROLLLLL
WHOA!
THROWN
RUMMMBLE
WHAT'S GOING ON?!
TH- THAT'S THE MAGMA STONE!
OH NO!

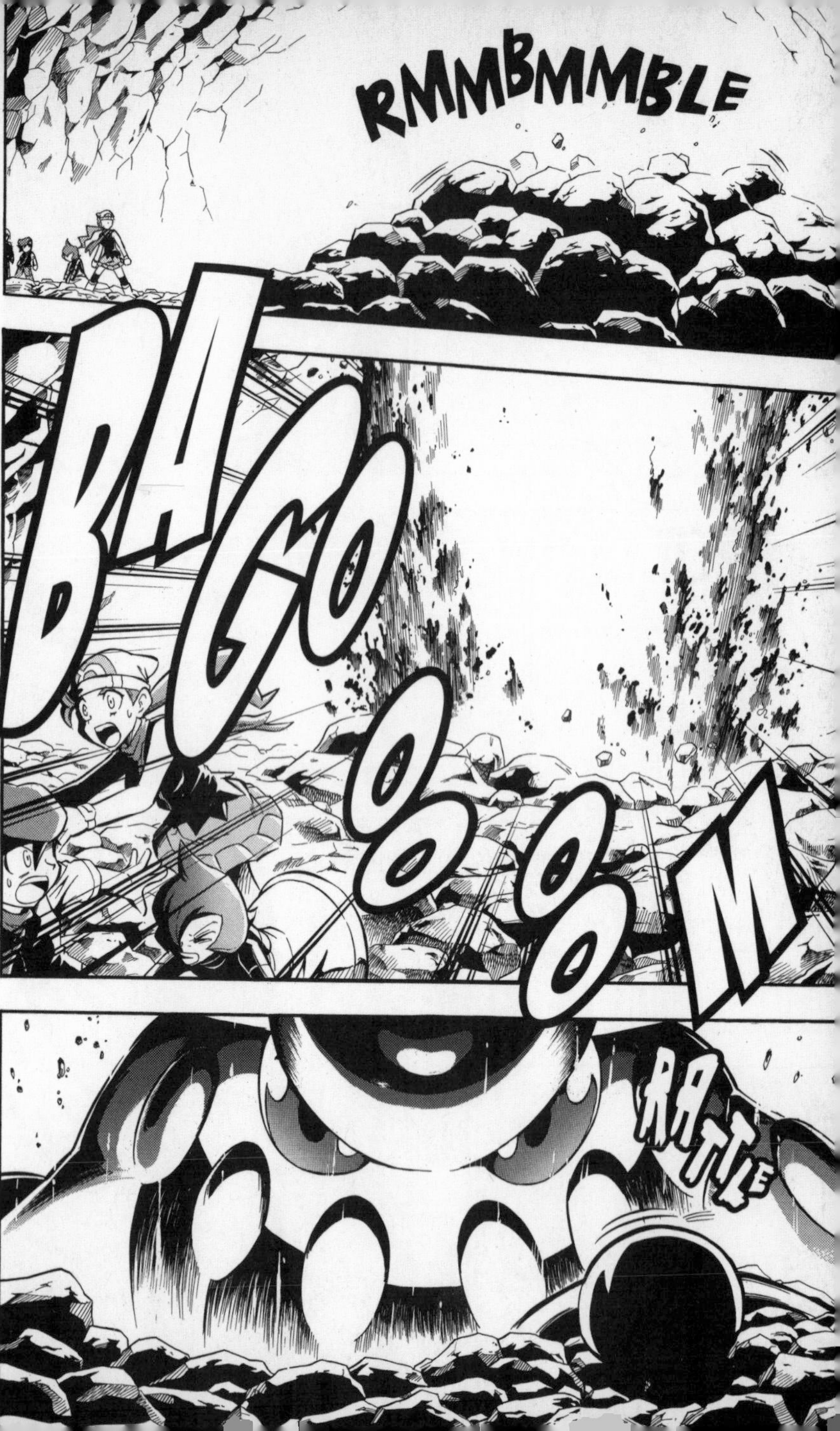
RMMBMMBLE
BAGOOOOOM
RATTLE

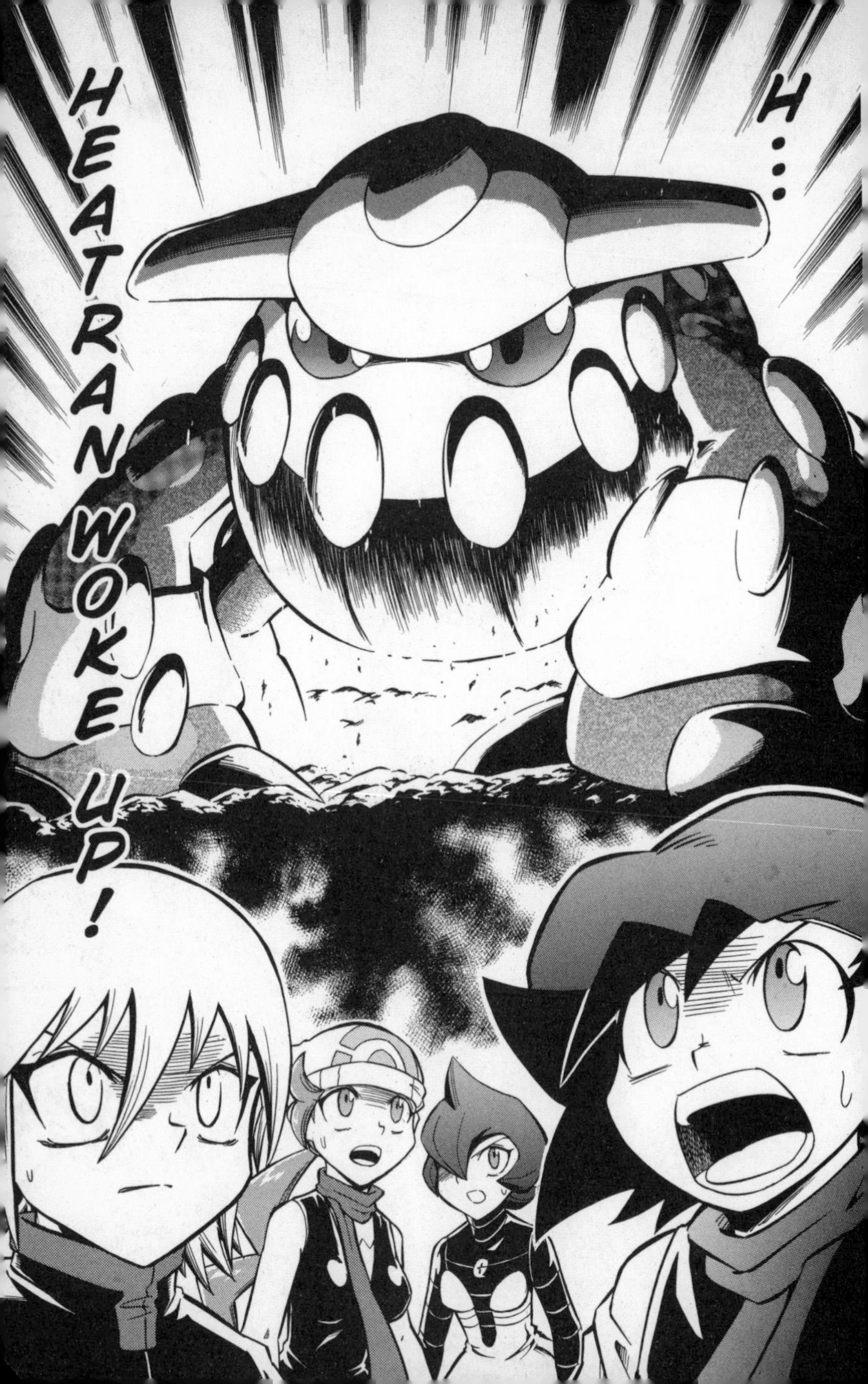
H...
HEATRAN WOKE UP!

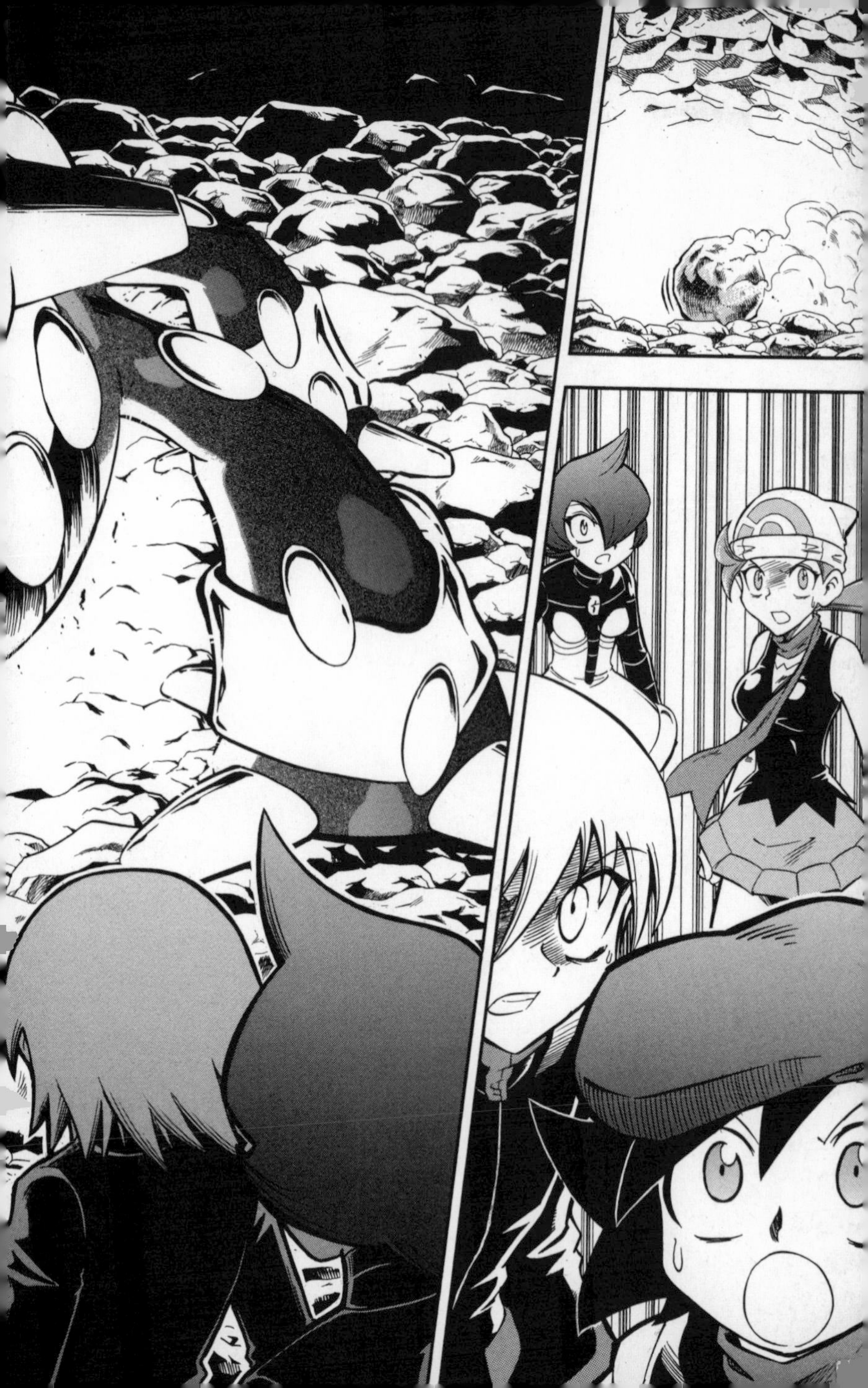

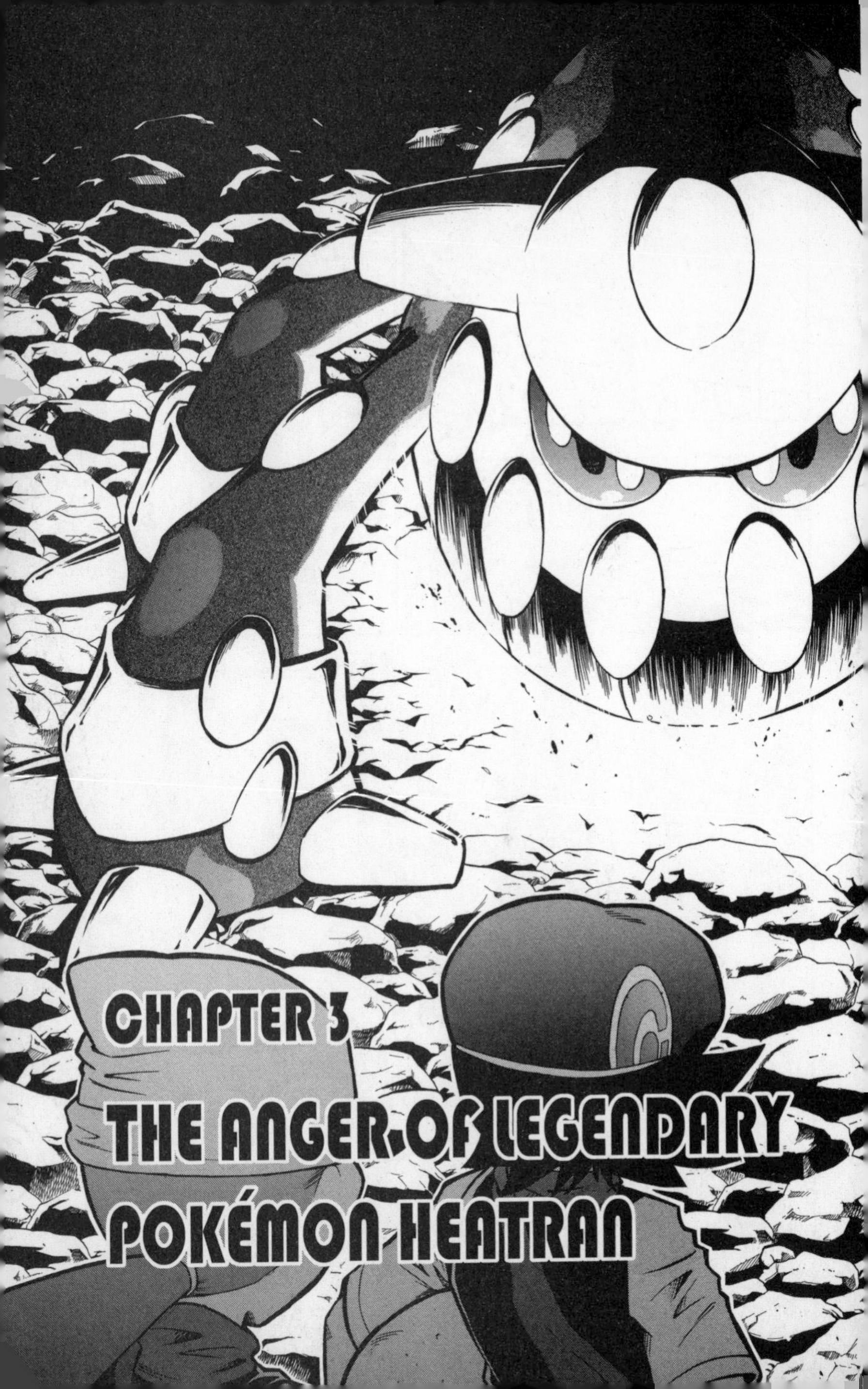
CHAPTER 3
THE ANGER OF LEGENDARY POKéMON HEATRAN

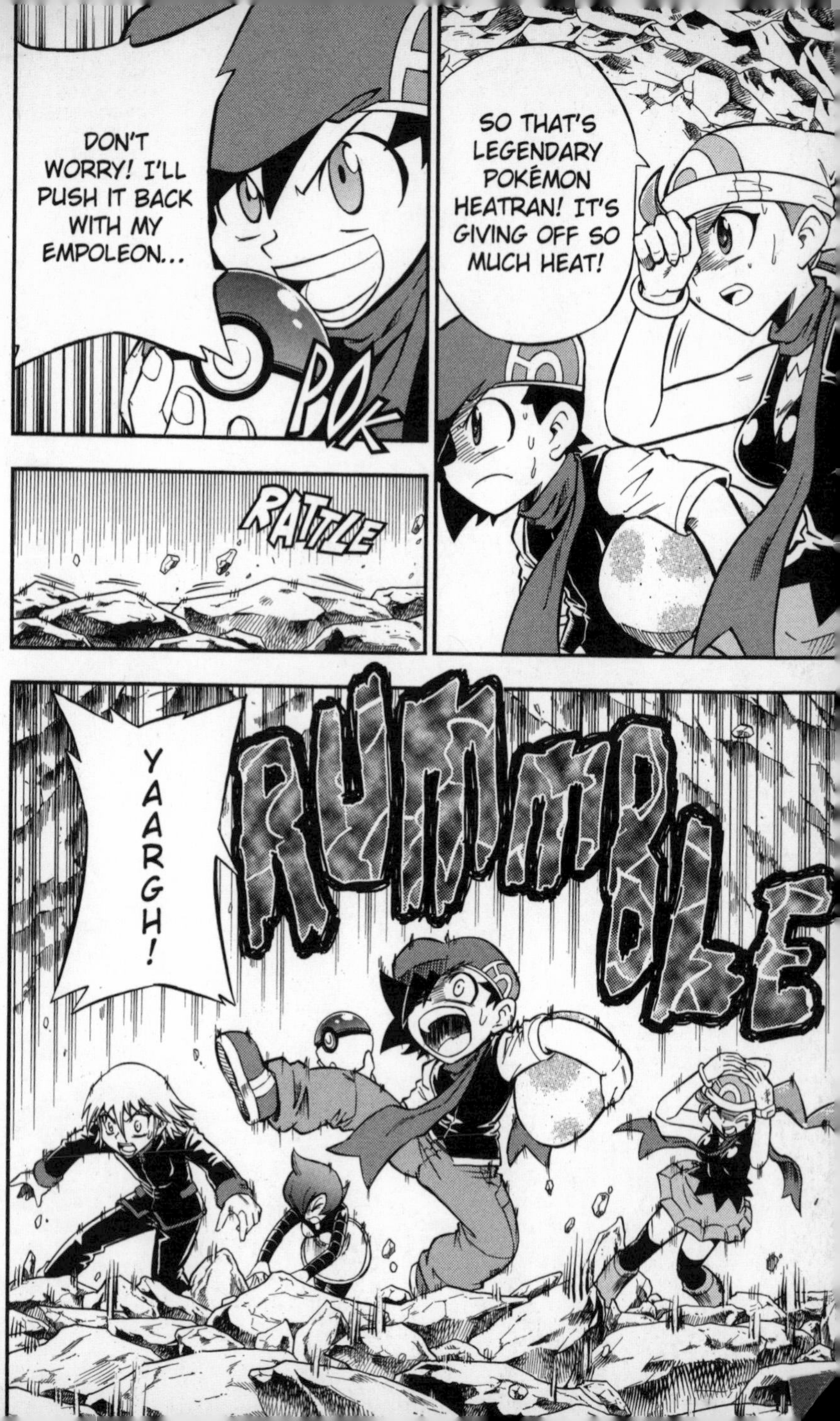
SO THAT'S LEGENDARY POKéMON HEATRAN! IT'S GIVING OFF SO MUCH HEAT!
DON'T WORRY! I'LL PUSH IT BACK WITH MY EMPOLEON...
POK
RATTLE
RUMBLE
YAARGH!

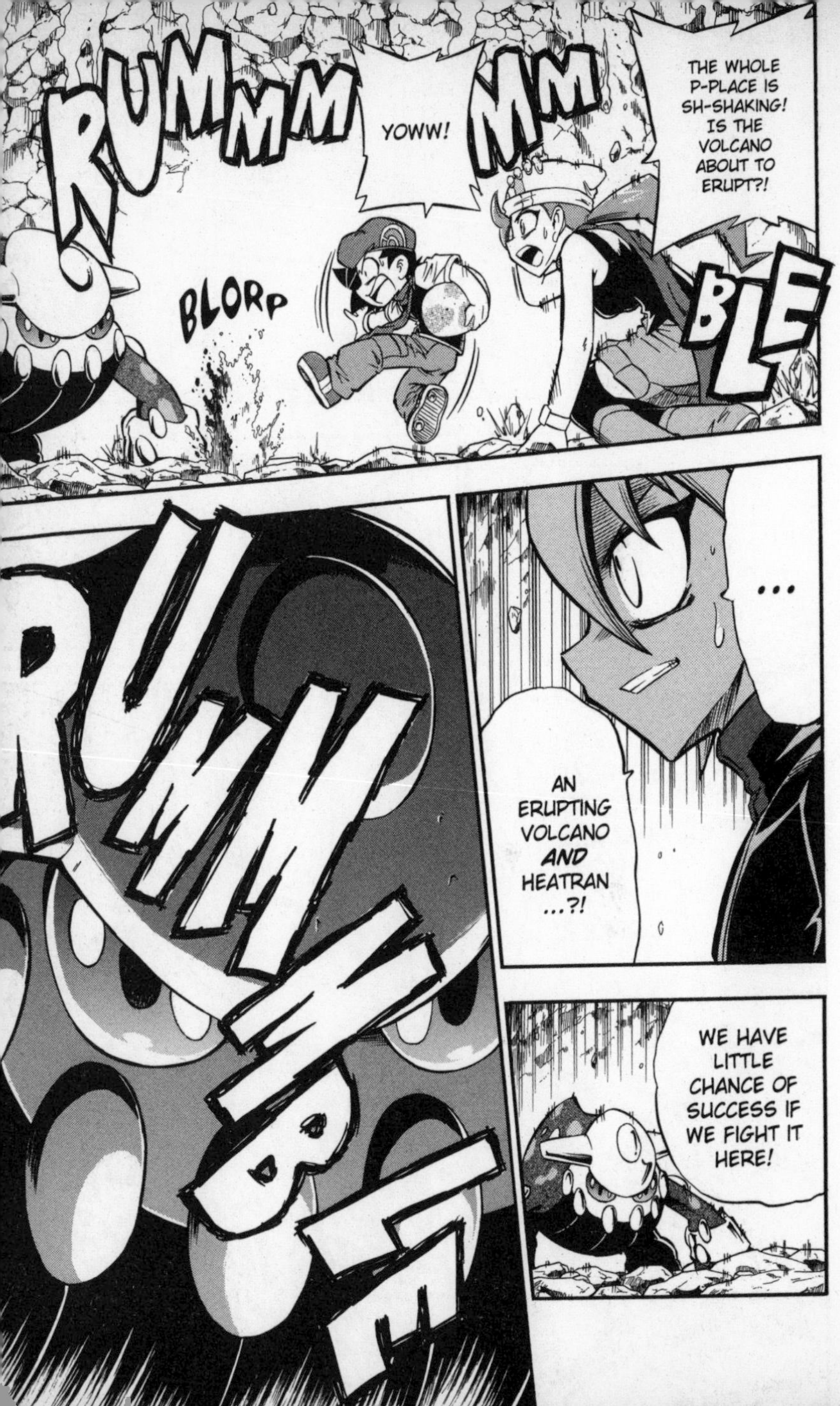
THE WHOLE P-PLACE IS SH-SHAKING! IS THE VOLCANO ABOUT TO ERUPT?!
YOWW!
RUMMMMMM
BLE
BLORP
...
AN ERUPTING VOLCANO *AND* HEATRAN ...?!
WE HAVE LITTLE CHANCE OF SUCCESS IF WE FIGHT IT HERE!
RUMMBLE

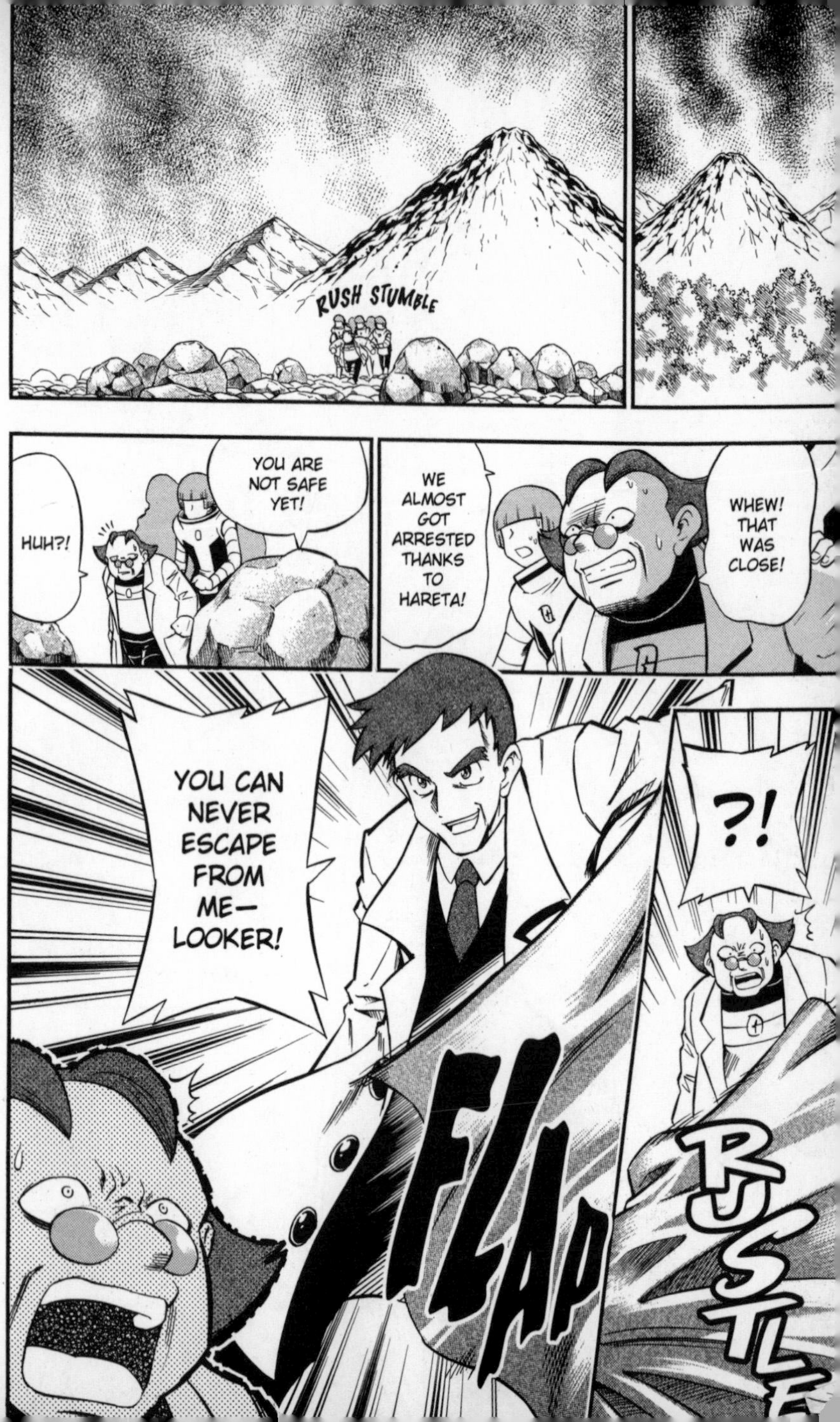
RUSH STUMBLE
WHEW! THAT WAS CLOSE!
WE ALMOST GOT ARRESTED THANKS TO HARETA!
YOU ARE NOT SAFE YET!
HUH?!
YOU CAN NEVER ESCAPE FROM ME—LOOKER!
?!
RUSTLE
FLAP

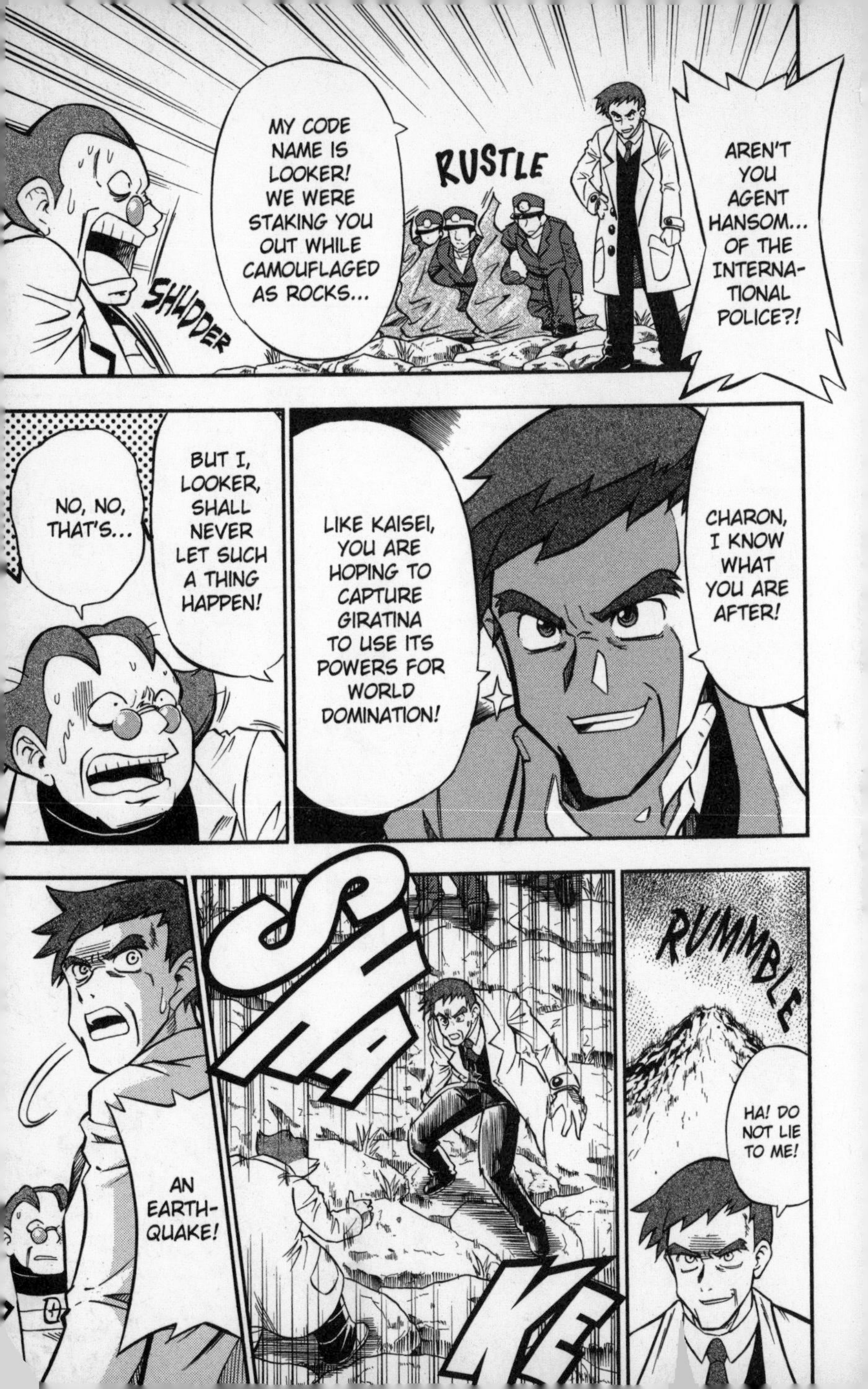
AREN'T YOU AGENT HANSOM... OF THE INTERNATIONAL POLICE?!
RUSTLE
MY CODE NAME IS LOOKER! WE WERE STAKING YOU OUT WHILE CAMOUFLAGED AS ROCKS...
SHUDDER
CHARON, I KNOW WHAT YOU ARE AFTER!
LIKE KAISEI, YOU ARE HOPING TO CAPTURE GIRATINA TO USE ITS POWERS FOR WORLD DOMINATION!
BUT I, LOOKER, SHALL NEVER LET SUCH A THING HAPPEN!
NO, NO, THAT'S...
RUMMBLE
HA! DO NOT LIE TO ME!
SHAKE
AN EARTHQUAKE!

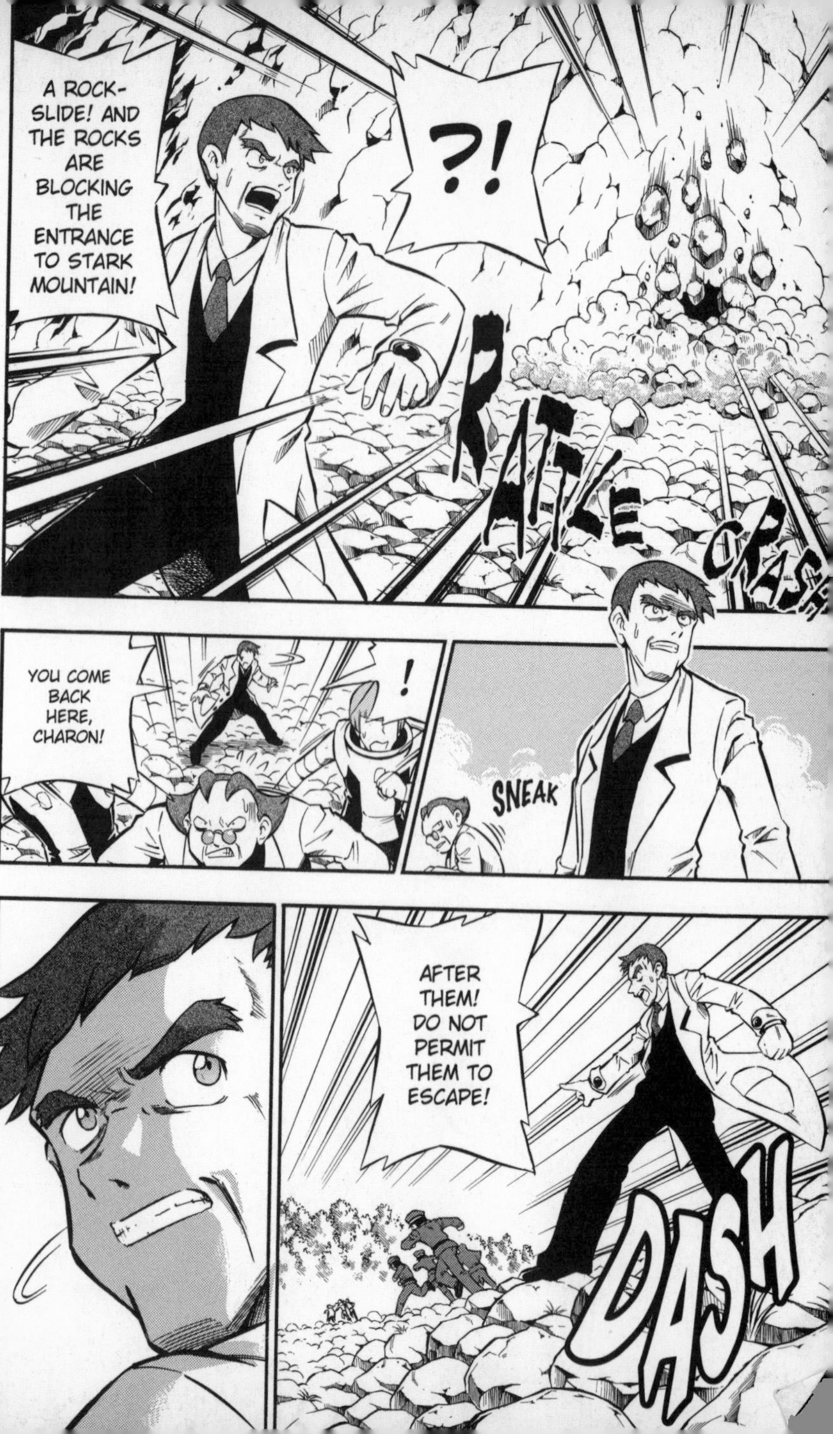
?!
A ROCK-SLIDE! AND THE ROCKS ARE BLOCKING THE ENTRANCE TO STARK MOUNTAIN!
RATTLE
CRASH
SNEAK
!
YOU COME BACK HERE, CHARON!
AFTER THEM! DO NOT PERMIT THEM TO ESCAPE!
DASH

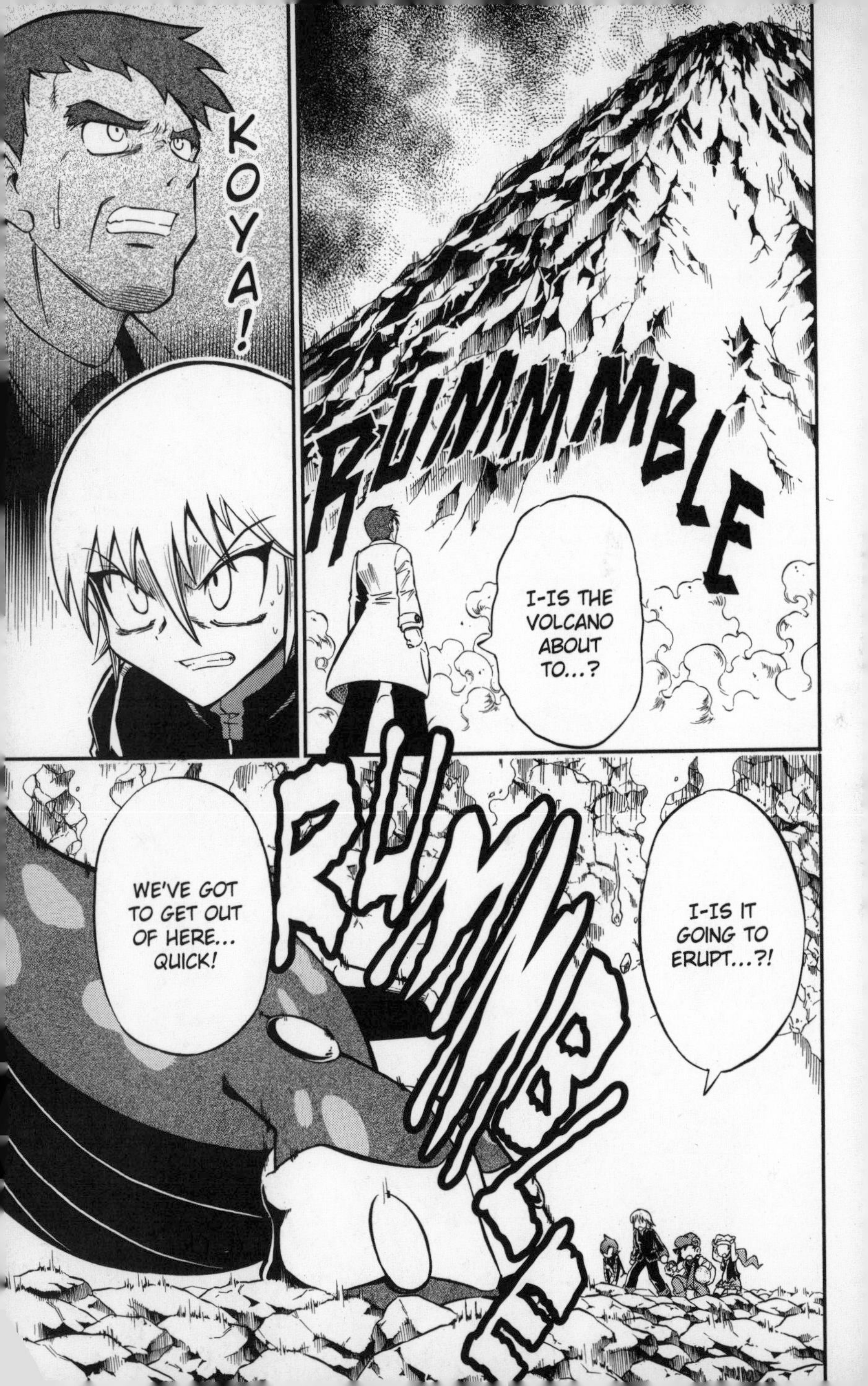
RUMMMBLE
I-IS THE VOLCANO ABOUT TO...?
KOYA!
I-IS IT GOING TO ERUPT...?!
WE'VE GOT TO GET OUT OF HERE... QUICK!

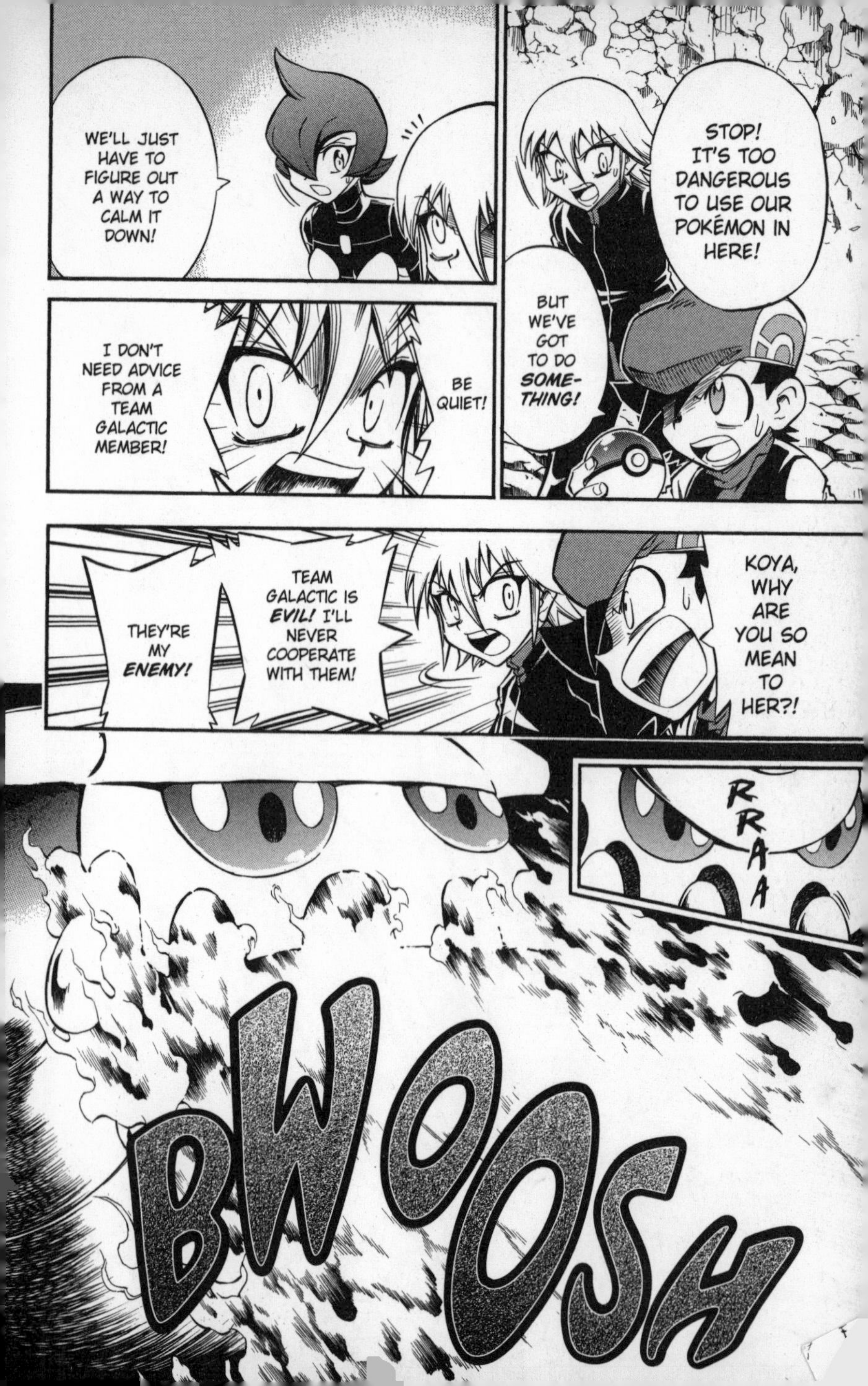
STOP! IT'S TOO DANGEROUS TO USE OUR POKÉMON IN HERE!
BUT WE'VE GOT TO DO *SOME-THING!*
WE'LL JUST HAVE TO FIGURE OUT A WAY TO CALM IT DOWN!
BE QUIET!
I DON'T NEED ADVICE FROM A TEAM GALACTIC MEMBER!
KOYA, WHY ARE YOU SO MEAN TO HER?!
TEAM GALACTIC IS *EVIL!* I'LL NEVER COOPERATE WITH THEM!
THEY'RE MY *ENEMY!*
RRAAA
BWOOSH

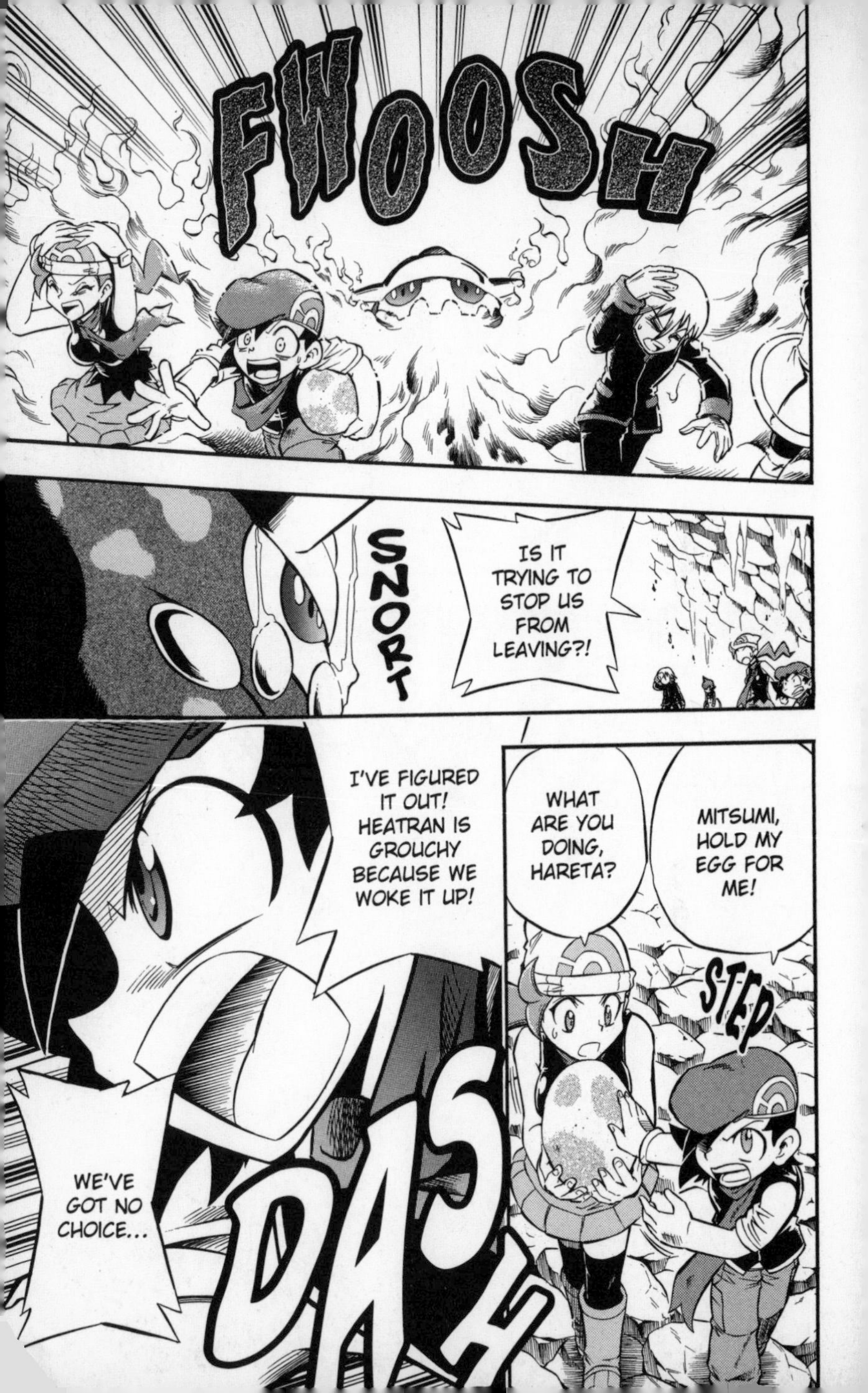
FWOOSH
IS IT TRYING TO STOP US FROM LEAVING?!
SNORT
MITSUMI, HOLD MY EGG FOR ME!
WHAT ARE YOU DOING, HARETA?
STEP
I'VE FIGURED IT OUT! HEATRAN IS GROUCHY BECAUSE WE WOKE IT UP!
WE'VE GOT NO CHOICE...
DASH

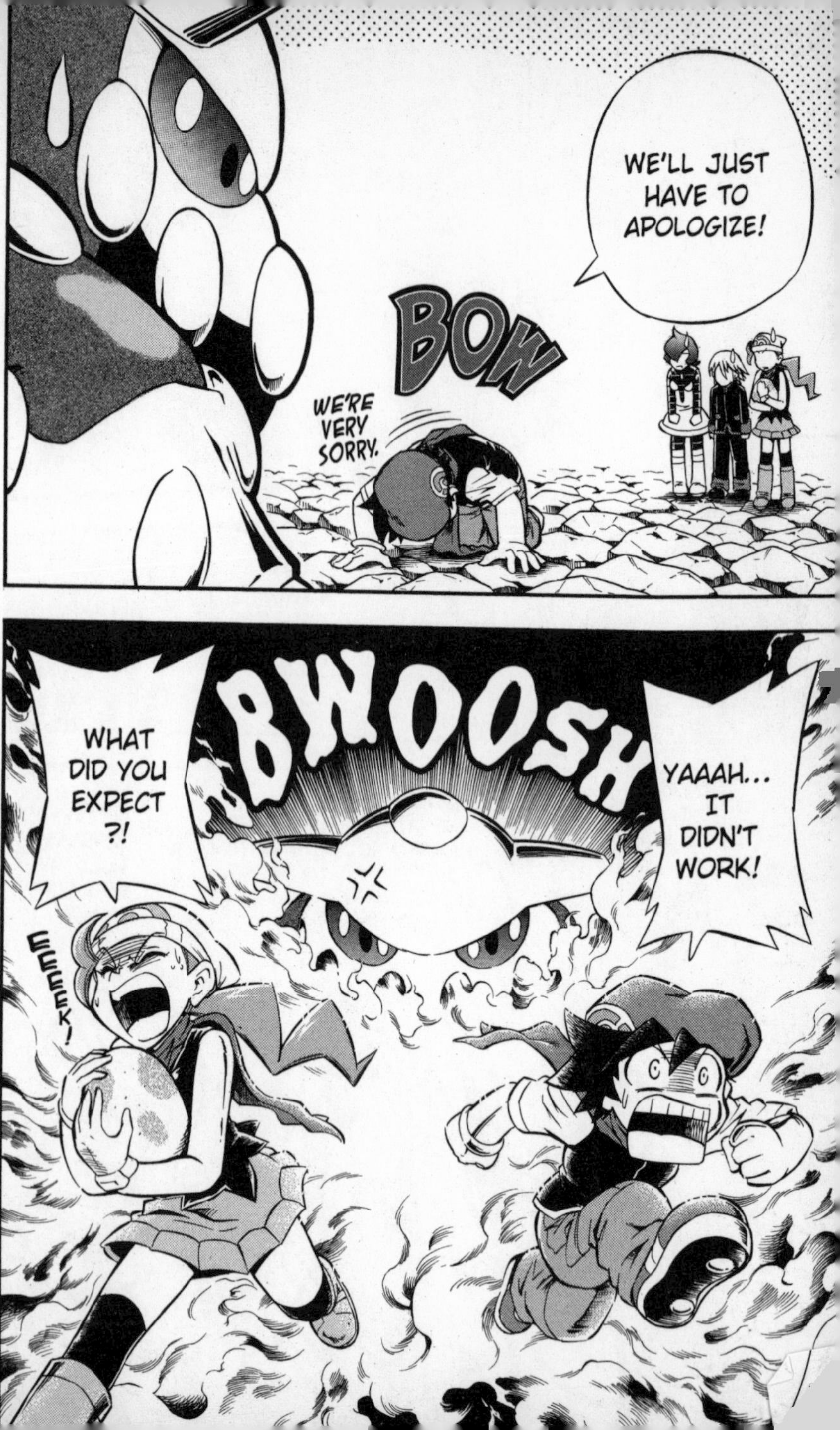
WE'LL JUST HAVE TO APOLOGIZE!
BOW
WE'RE VERY SORRY.
YAAAH... IT DIDN'T WORK!
BWOOSH
WHAT DID YOU EXPECT?!
EEEEK!

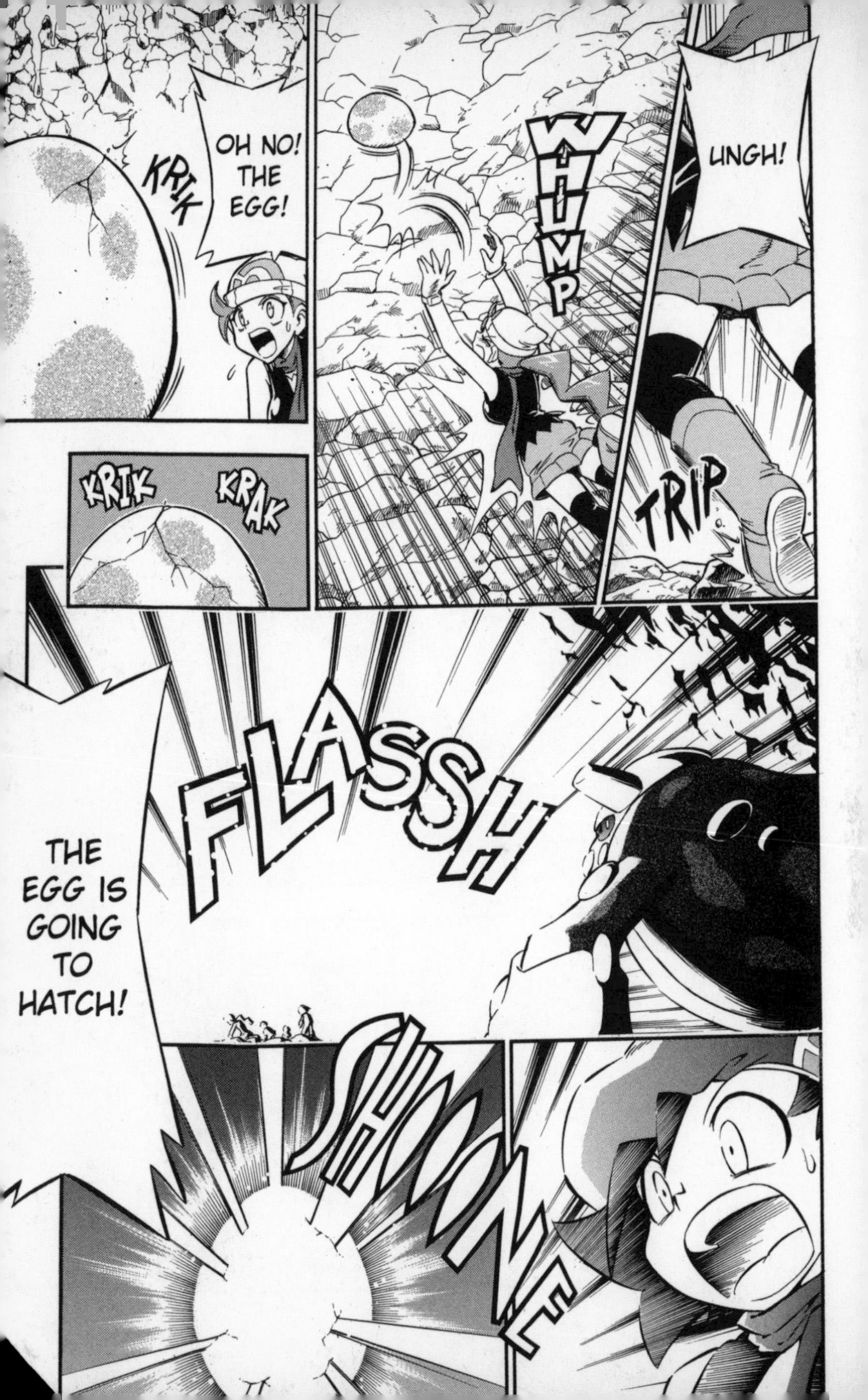
UNGH!
TRIP
WHUMP
OH NO! THE EGG!
KRIK
KRIK
KRAK
FLASSH
THE EGG IS GOING TO HATCH!

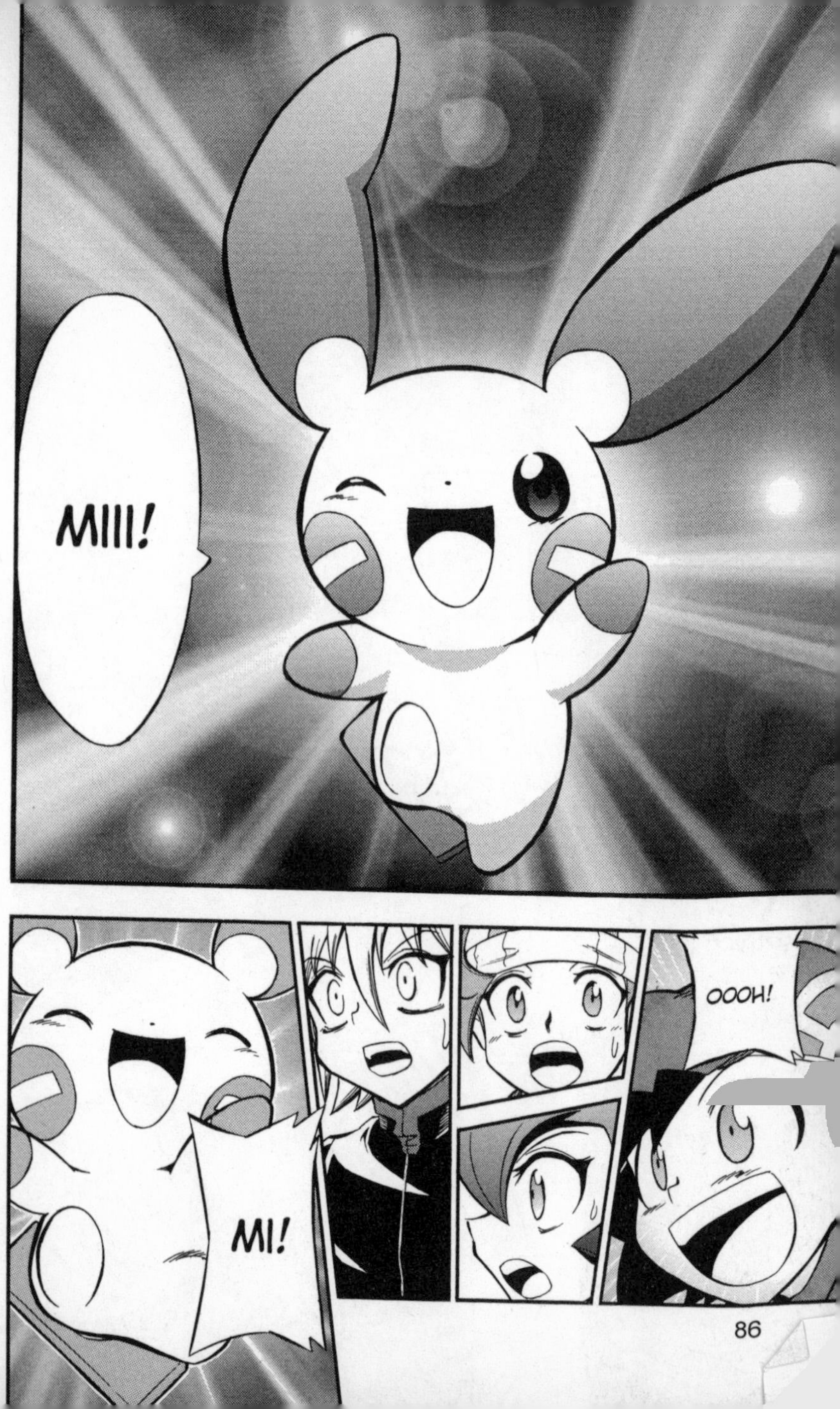
MIII!
OOOH!
MI!

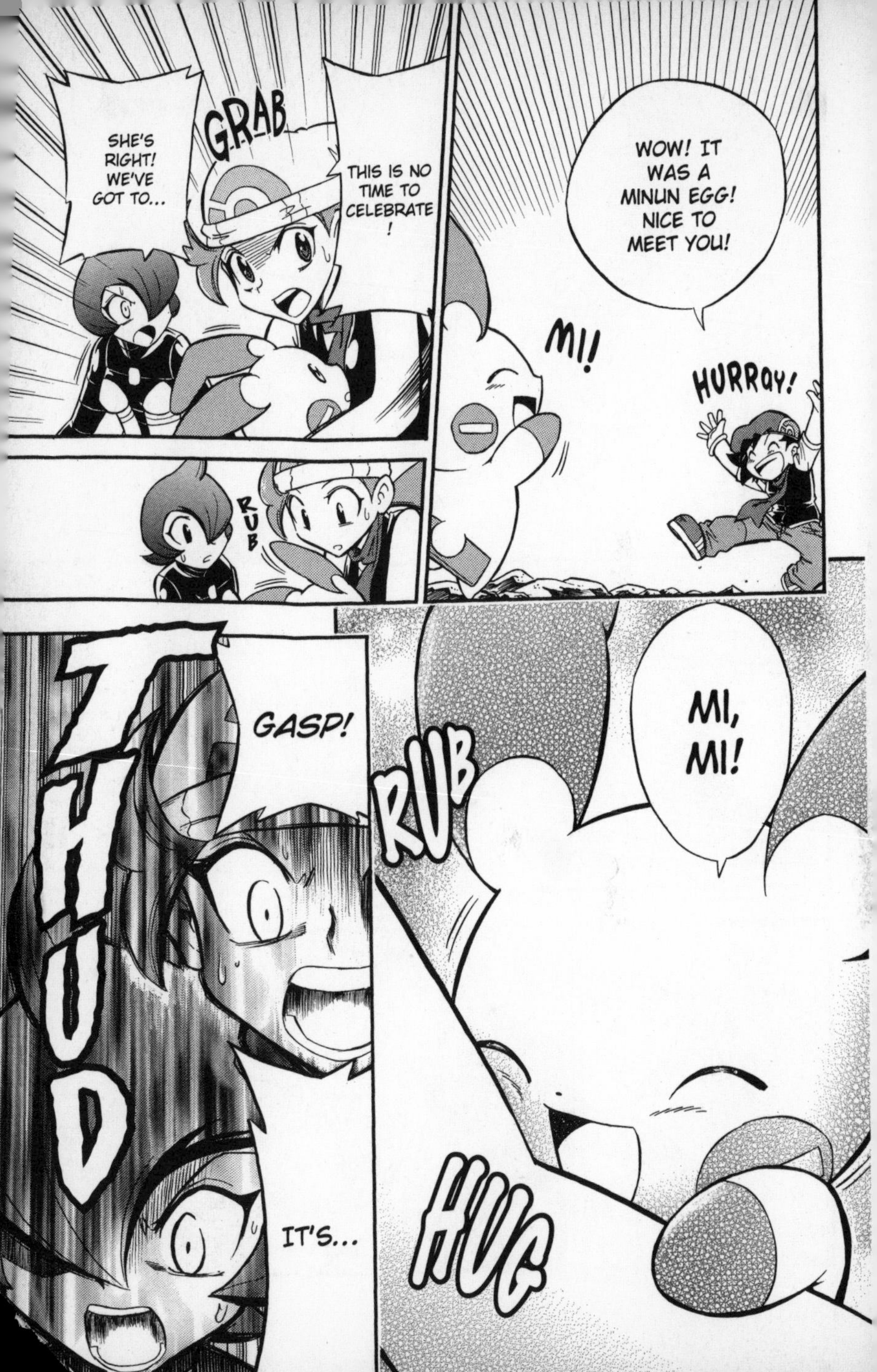
WOW! IT WAS A MINUN EGG! NICE TO MEET YOU!
HURRAY!
MI!
THIS IS NO TIME TO CELEBRATE !
GRAB
SHE'S RIGHT! WE'VE GOT TO...
RUB
MI, MI!
RUB
HUG
GASP!
THUD
IT'S...

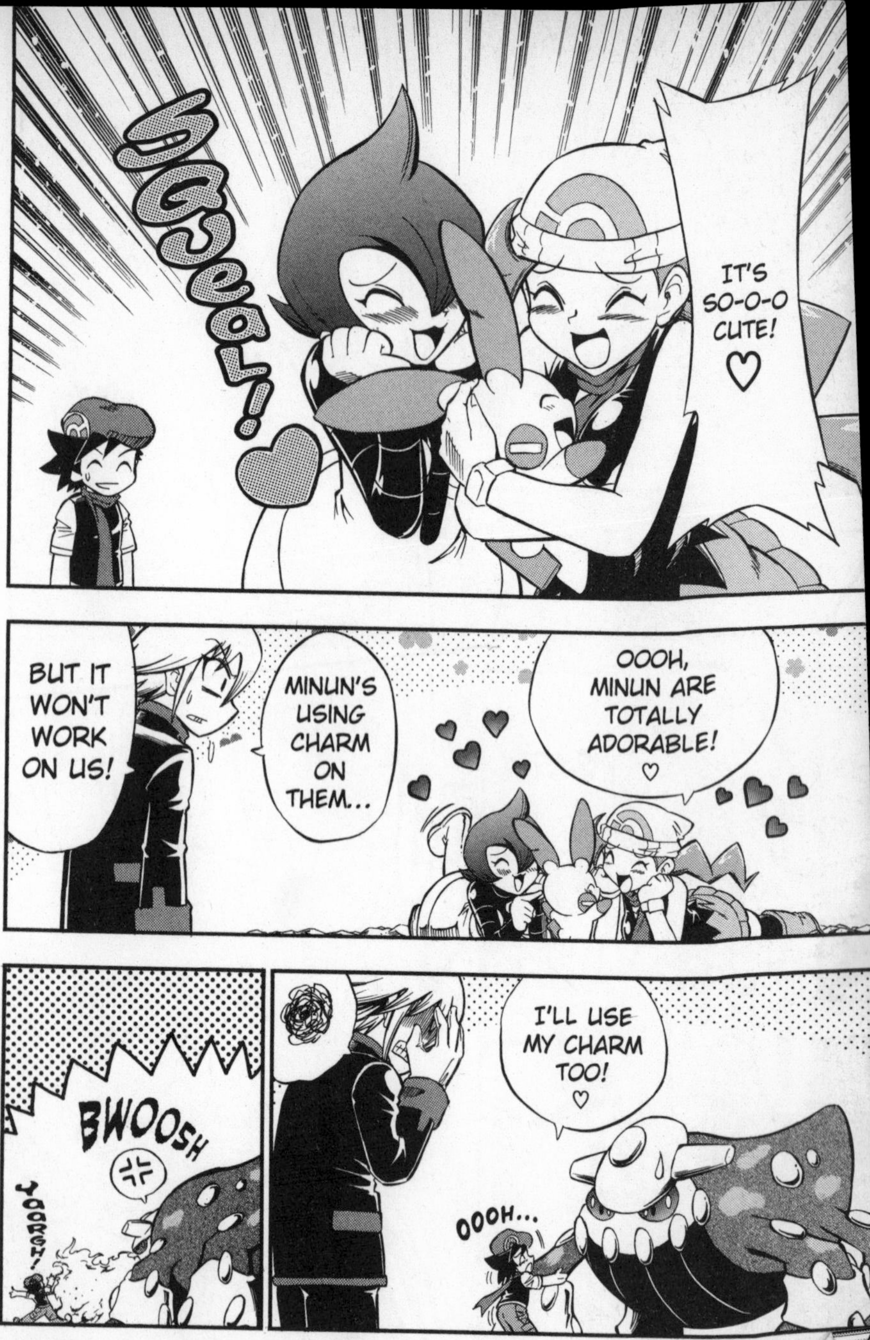
IT'S SO-O-O CUTE! ♡
SQUEAL!
OOOH, MINUN ARE TOTALLY ADORABLE! ♡
MINUN'S USING CHARM ON THEM...
BUT IT WON'T WORK ON US!
I'LL USE MY CHARM TOO! ♡
OOOH...
BWOOSH
YAARGH!

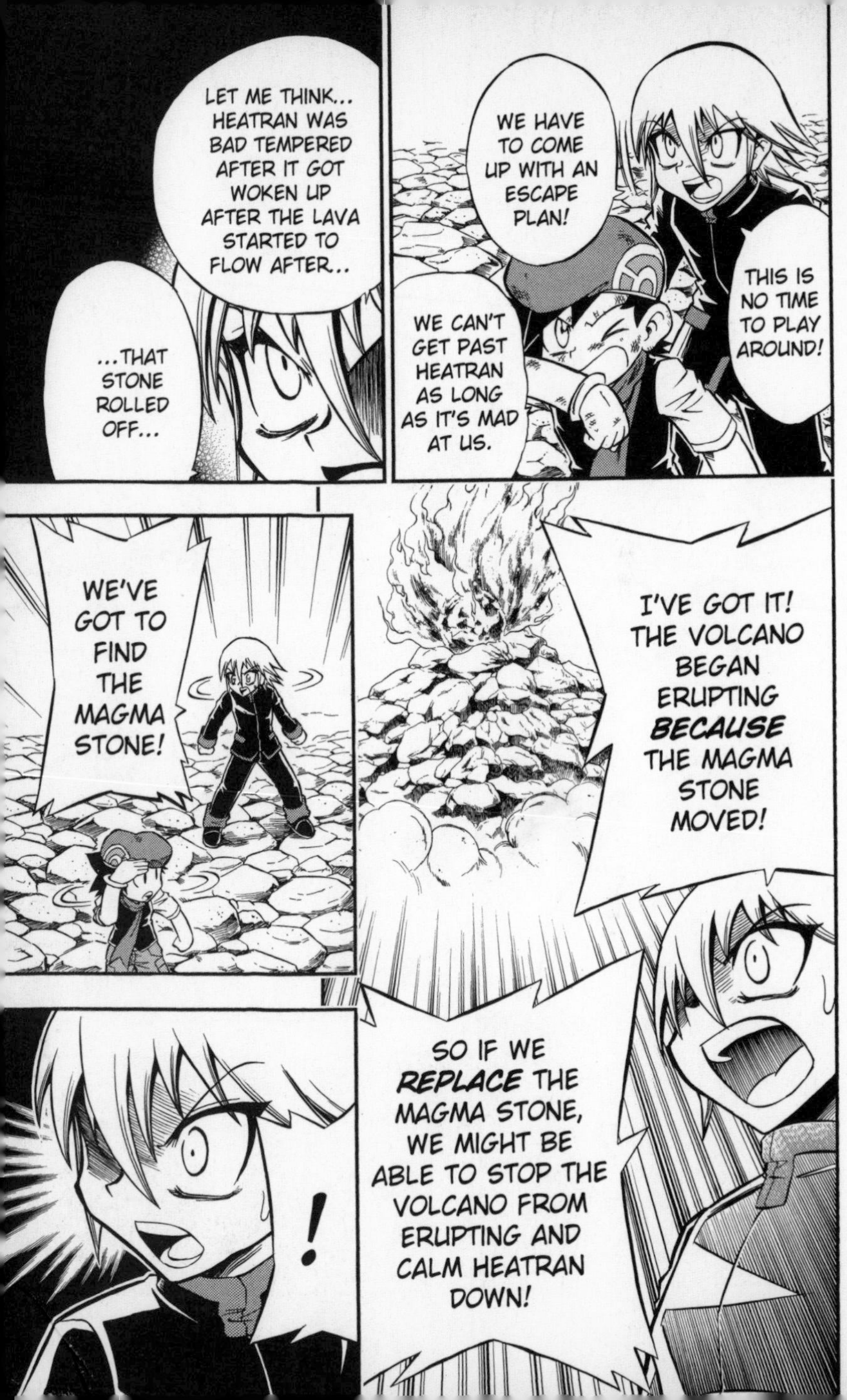

WE HAVE TO COME UP WITH AN ESCAPE PLAN!
THIS IS NO TIME TO PLAY AROUND!
WE CAN'T GET PAST HEATRAN AS LONG AS IT'S MAD AT US.
LET ME THINK... HEATRAN WAS BAD TEMPERED AFTER IT GOT WOKEN UP AFTER THE LAVA STARTED TO FLOW AFTER...
...THAT STONE ROLLED OFF...
I'VE GOT IT! THE VOLCANO BEGAN ERUPTING *BECAUSE* THE MAGMA STONE MOVED!
SO IF WE *REPLACE* THE MAGMA STONE, WE MIGHT BE ABLE TO STOP THE VOLCANO FROM ERUPTING AND CALM HEATRAN DOWN!
WE'VE GOT TO FIND THE MAGMA STONE!
!

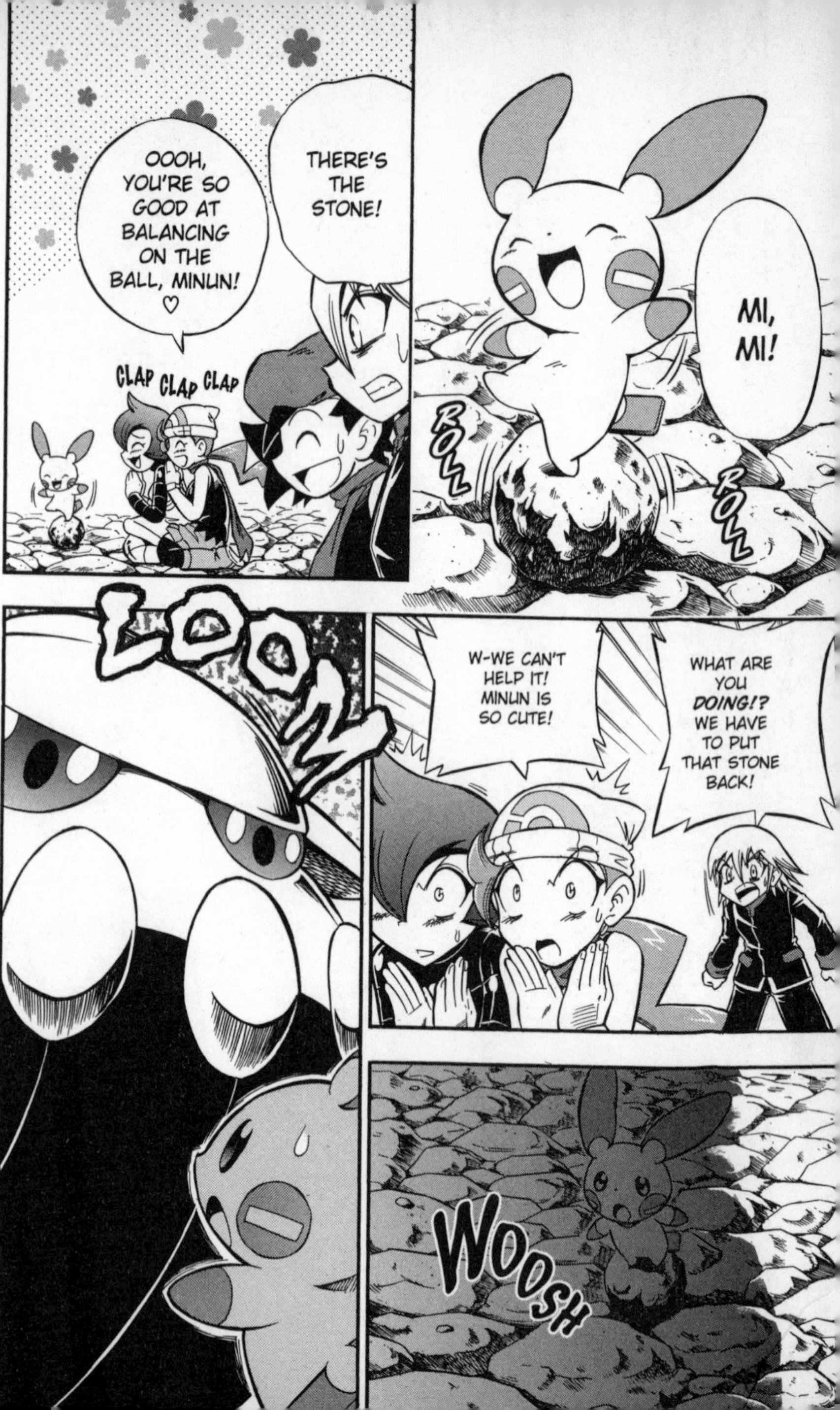
MI, MI!
ROLL
ROLL
THERE'S THE STONE!
OOOH, YOU'RE SO GOOD AT BALANCING ON THE BALL, MINUN! ♡
CLAP CLAP CLAP
WHAT ARE YOU *DOING!?* WE HAVE TO PUT THAT STONE BACK!
W-WE CAN'T HELP IT! MINUN IS SO CUTE!
WOOSH
LOOOM

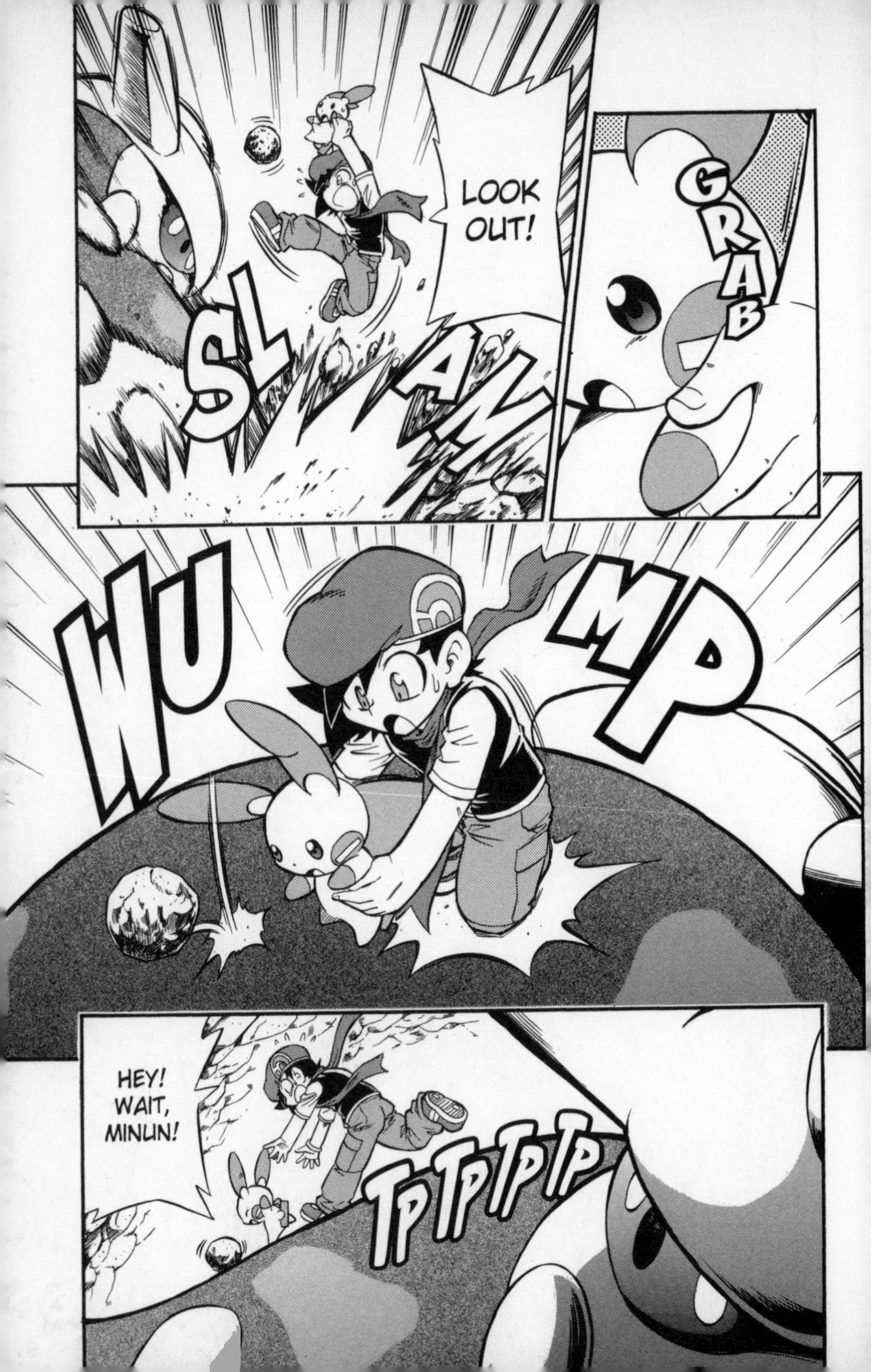
GRAB
LOOK OUT!
SLAM
WHUMP
HEY! WAIT, MINUN!
TpTpTpTp

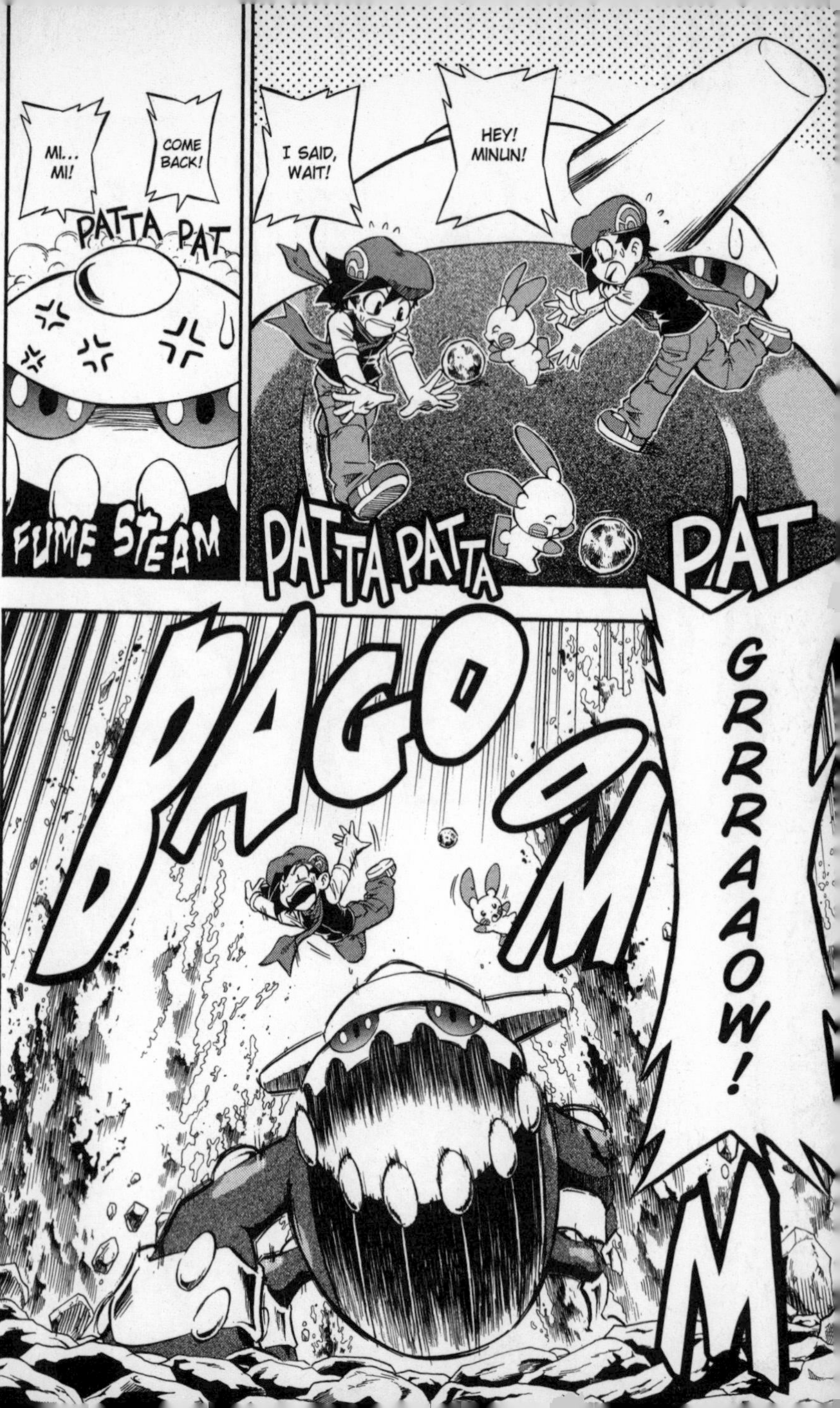
HEY! MINUN!
I SAID, WAIT!
PAT
PATTA PATTA
COME BACK!
MI... MI!
PATTA PAT
FUME STEAM
GRRRAAOW!
DAGOOMM

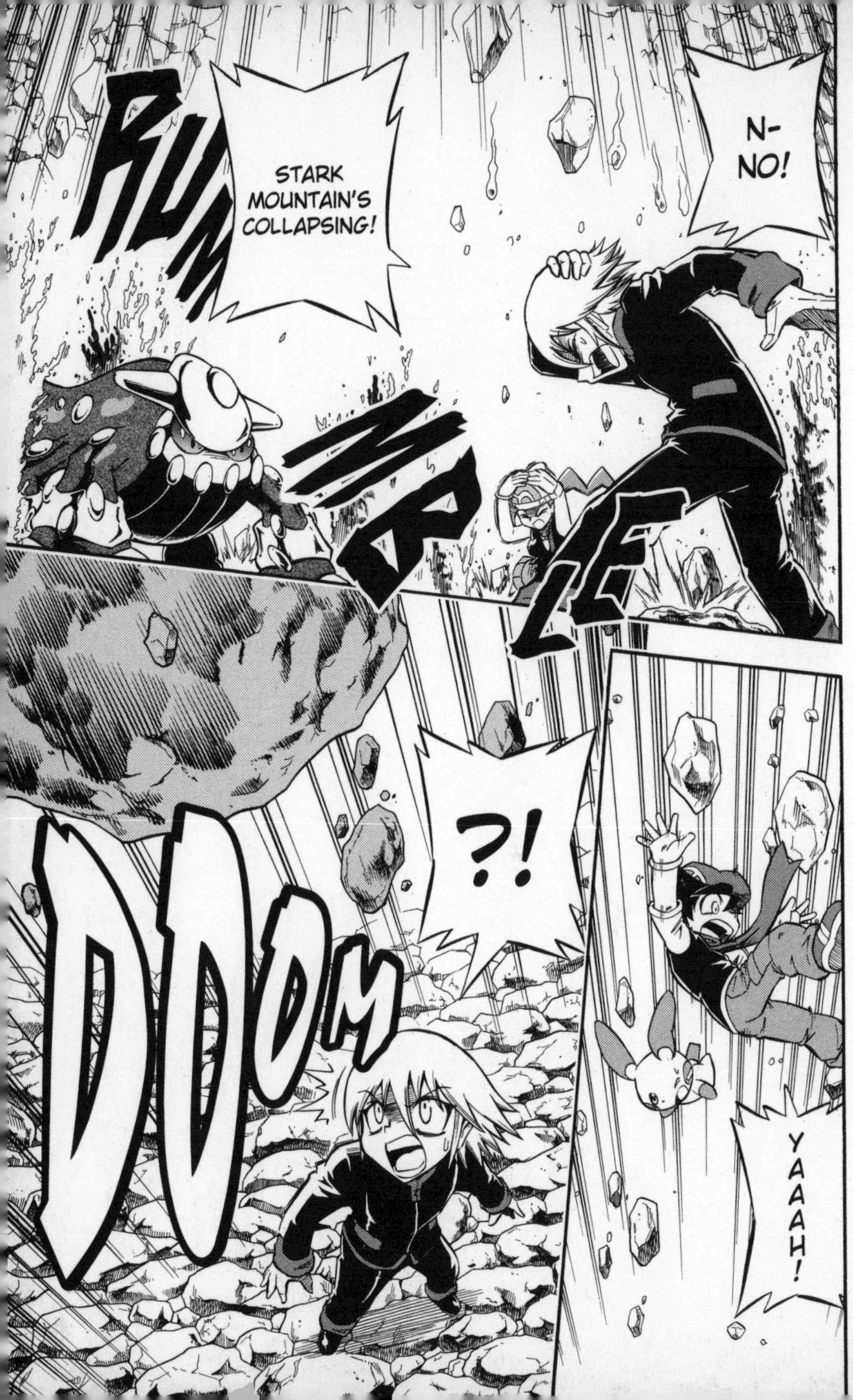
N-
NO!
STARK MOUNTAIN'S COLLAPSING!
RUMMBLE
YAAAH!
?!
DOOM

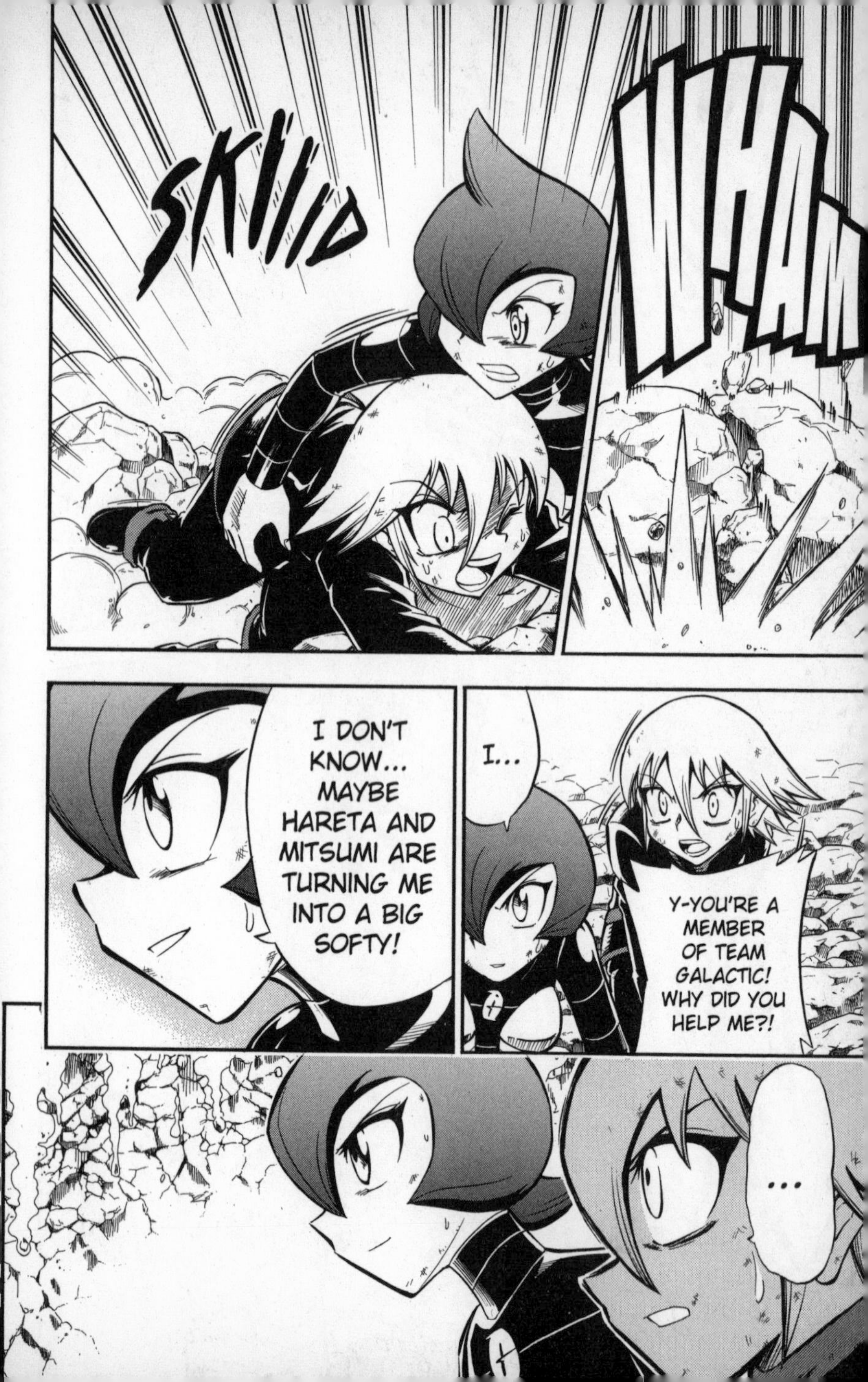
W-HAM
SKIIID
Y-YOU'RE A MEMBER OF TEAM GALACTIC! WHY DID YOU HELP ME?!
I...
I DON'T KNOW... MAYBE HARETA AND MITSUMI ARE TURNING ME INTO A BIG SOFTY!
...

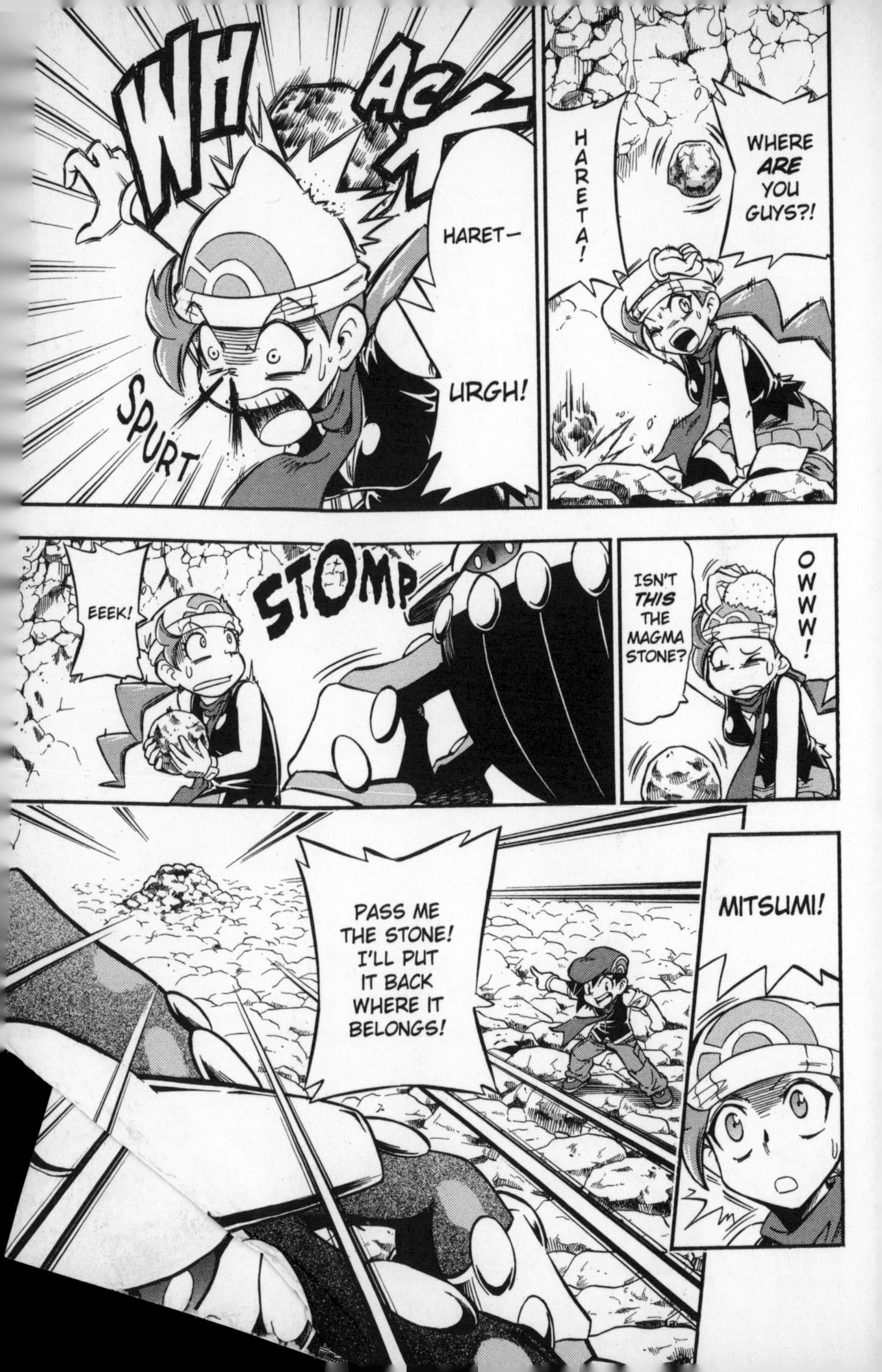
WHERE ARE YOU GUYS?!
HARETA!
WHAC
HARET—
URGH!
SPURT
OWWW!
ISN'T THIS THE MAGMA STONE?
STOMP
EEEK!
MITSUMI!
PASS ME THE STONE! I'LL PUT IT BACK WHERE IT BELONGS!

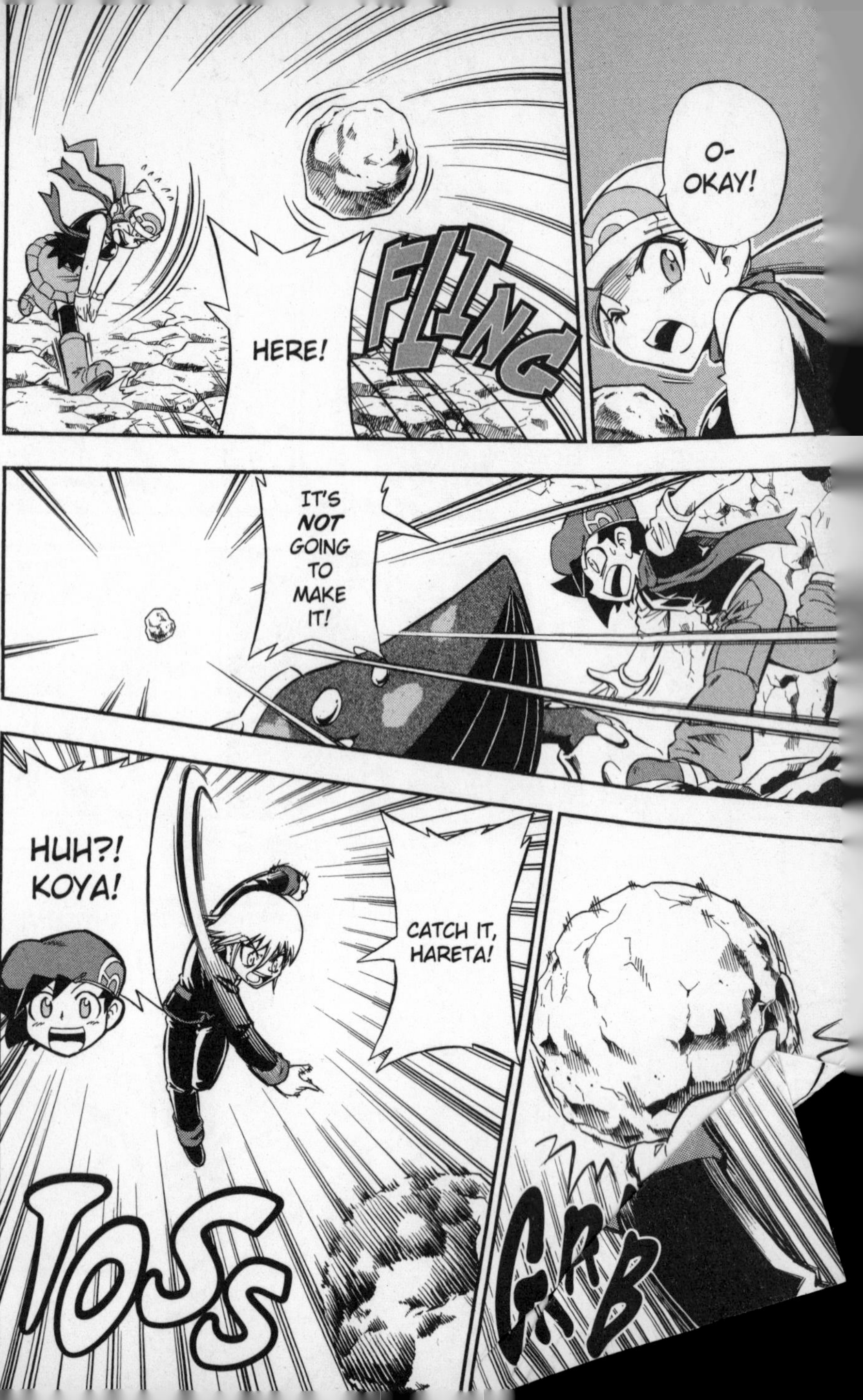
O-
OKAY!
FLING
HERE!
IT'S *NOT* GOING TO MAKE IT!
GRAB
CATCH IT, HARETA!
HUH?! KOYA!
TOSS

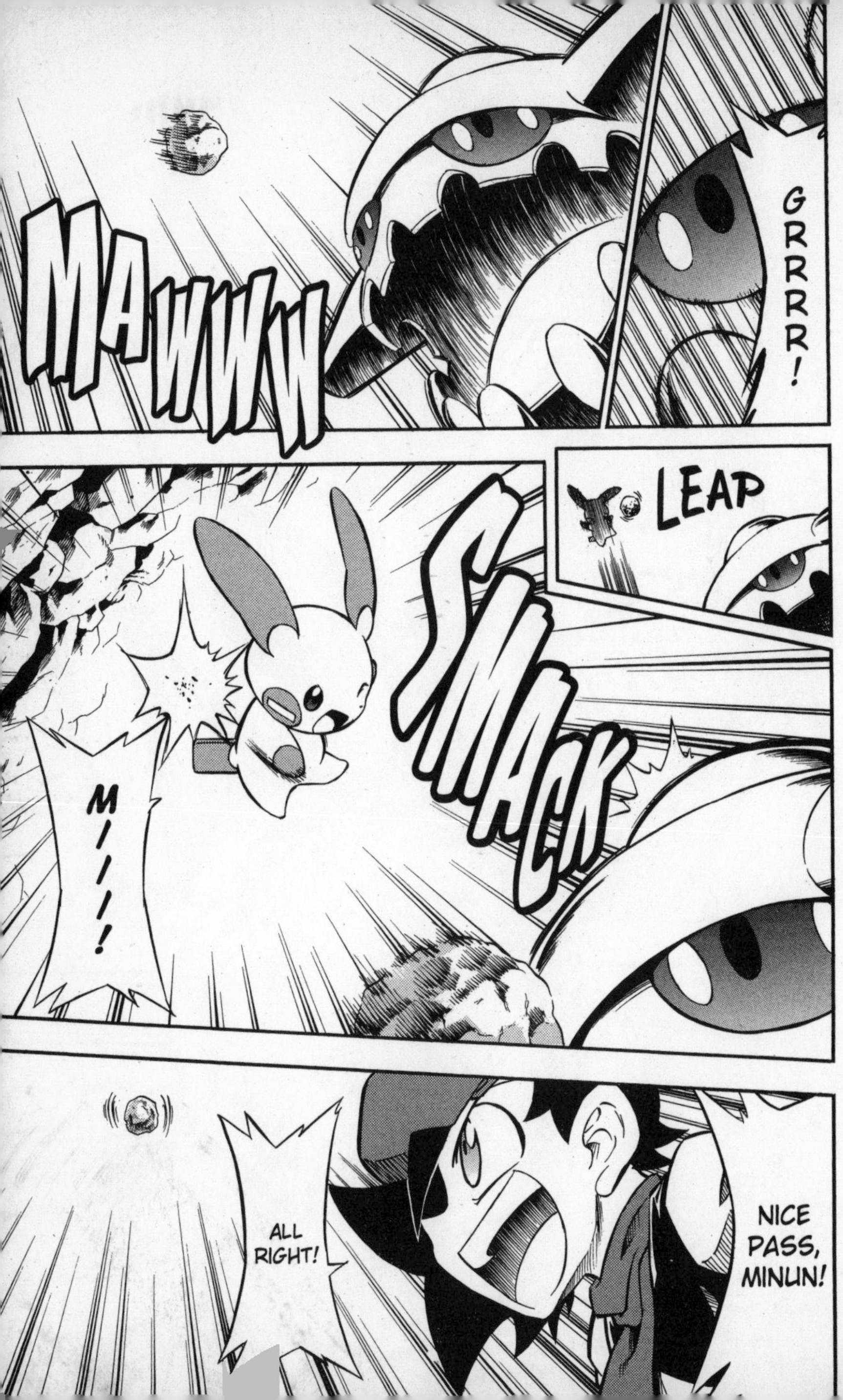
GRRRR!
MAWWWN
LEAP
SMACK
M...!
NICE PASS, MINUN!
ALL RIGHT!

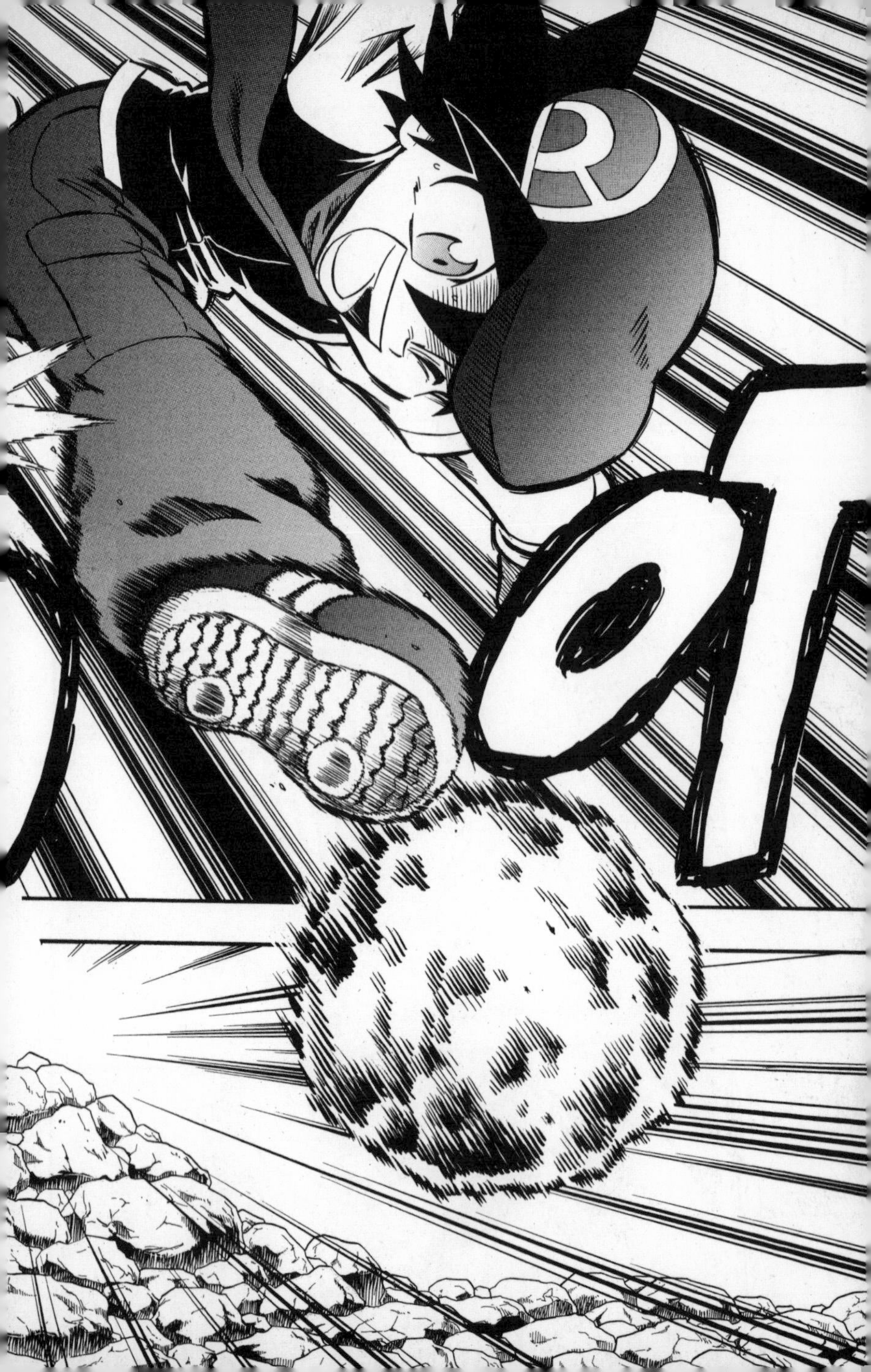

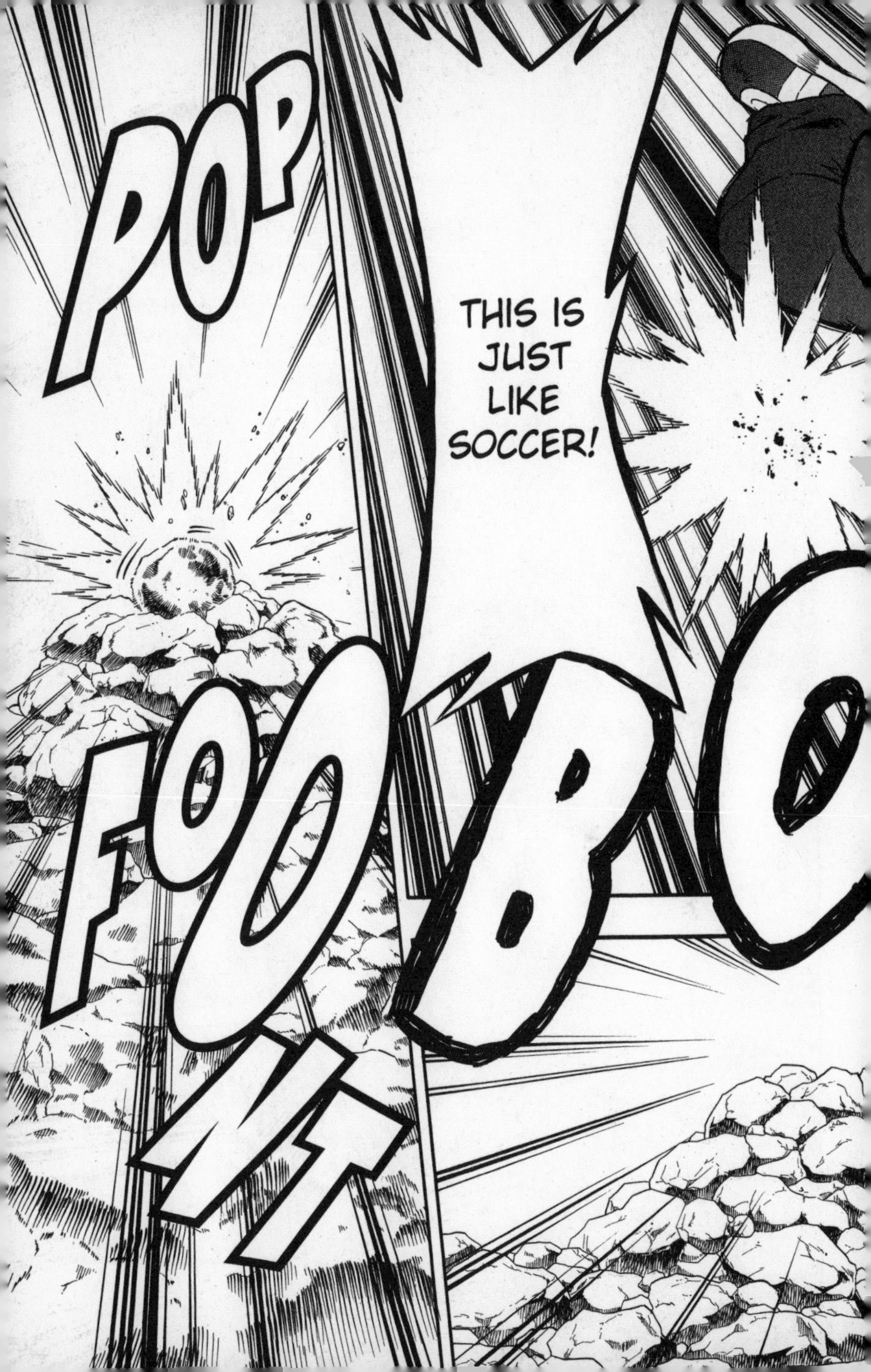
THIS IS JUST LIKE SOCCER!
POP

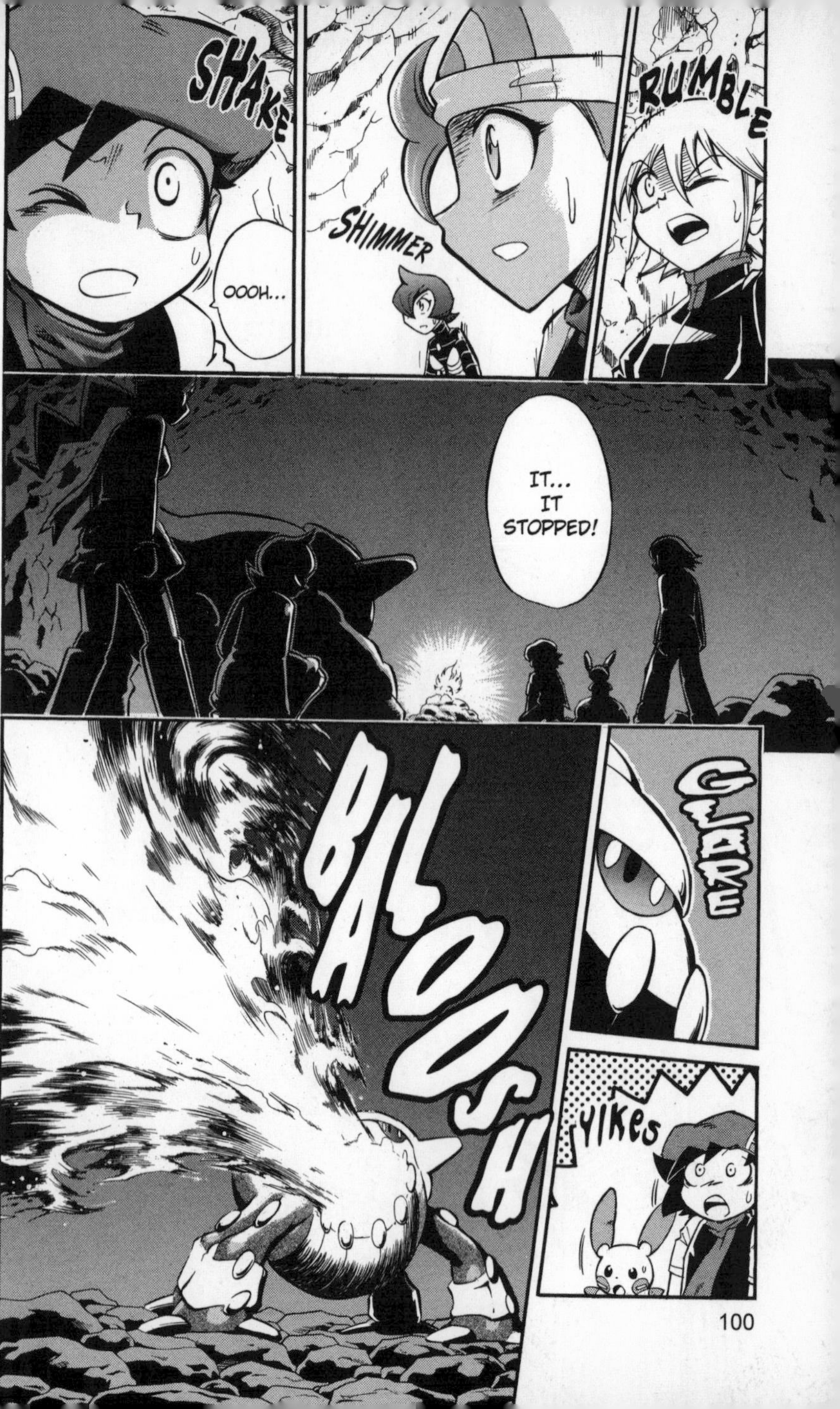
RUMBLE
SHIMMER
SHAKE
OOOH...
IT... IT STOPPED!
GLARE
YIKES
BLAOOSH

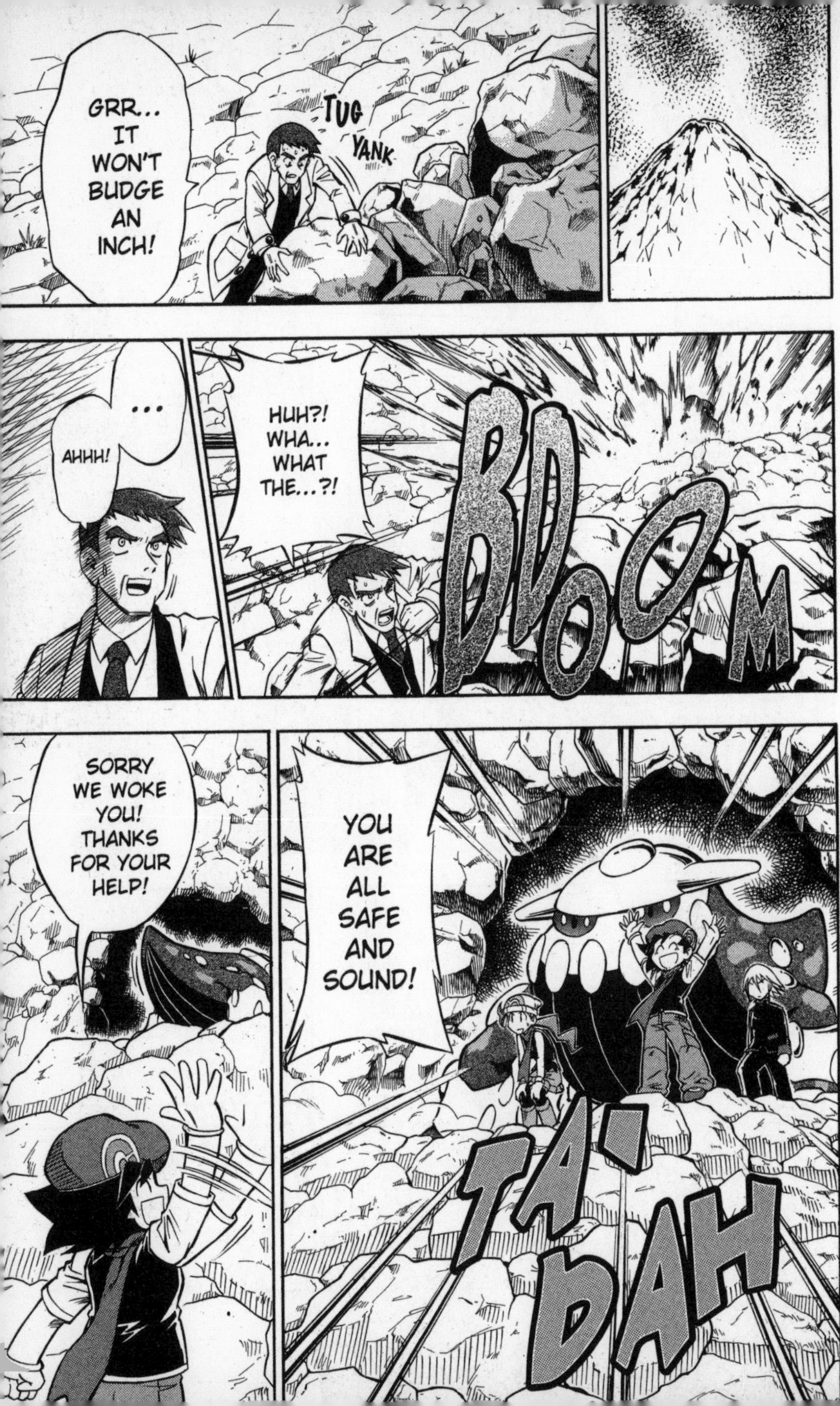
TUG
YANK
GRR... IT WON'T BUDGE AN INCH!
BOOOOM
HUH?! WHA... WHAT THE...?!
...
AHHH!
YOU ARE ALL SAFE AND SOUND!
TA-DAH
SORRY WE WOKE YOU! THANKS FOR YOUR HELP!

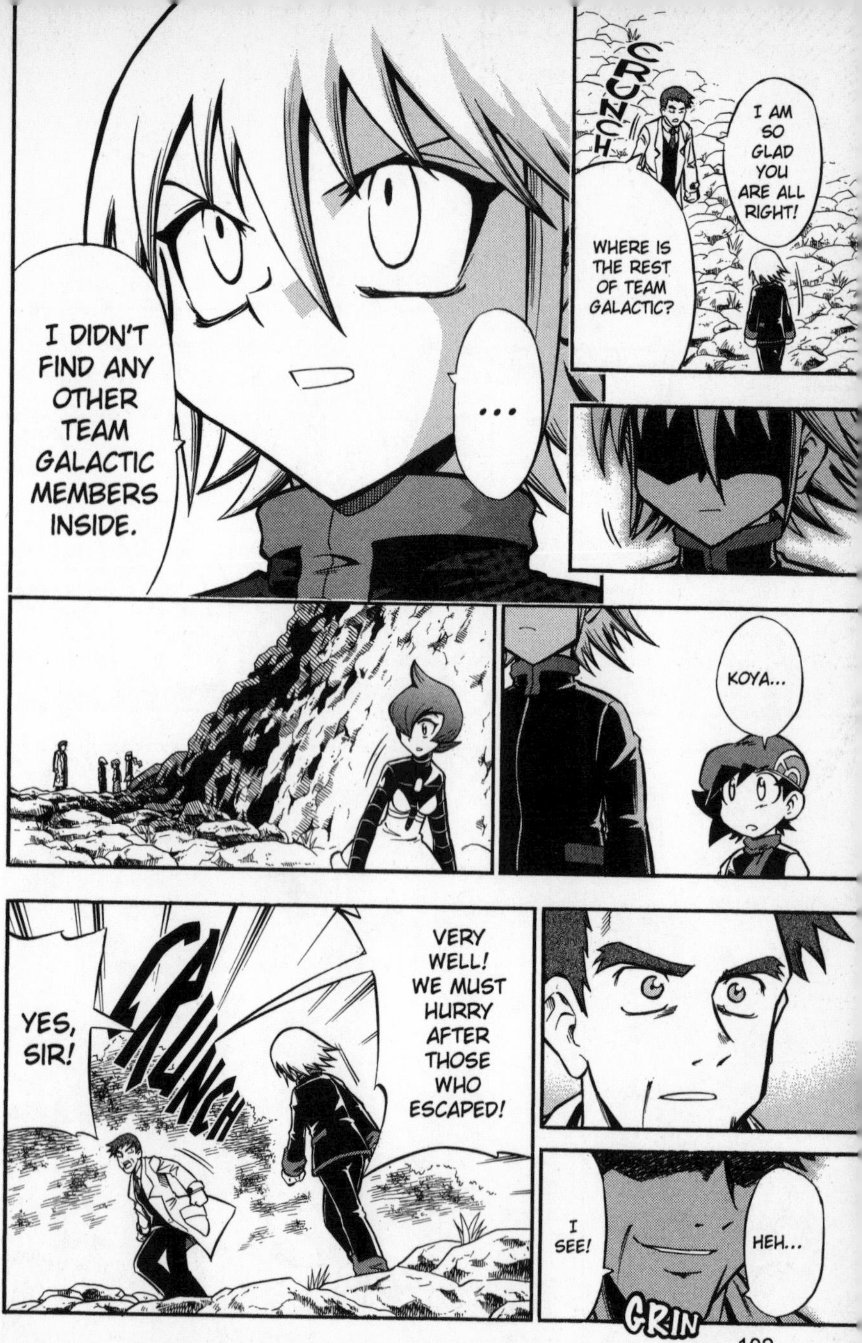
CRUNCH
I AM SO GLAD YOU ARE ALL RIGHT!
WHERE IS THE REST OF TEAM GALACTIC?
...
I DIDN'T FIND ANY OTHER TEAM GALACTIC MEMBERS INSIDE.
KOYA...
HEH...
I SEE!
GRIN
VERY WELL! WE MUST HURRY AFTER THOSE WHO ESCAPED!
CRUNCH
YES, SIR!

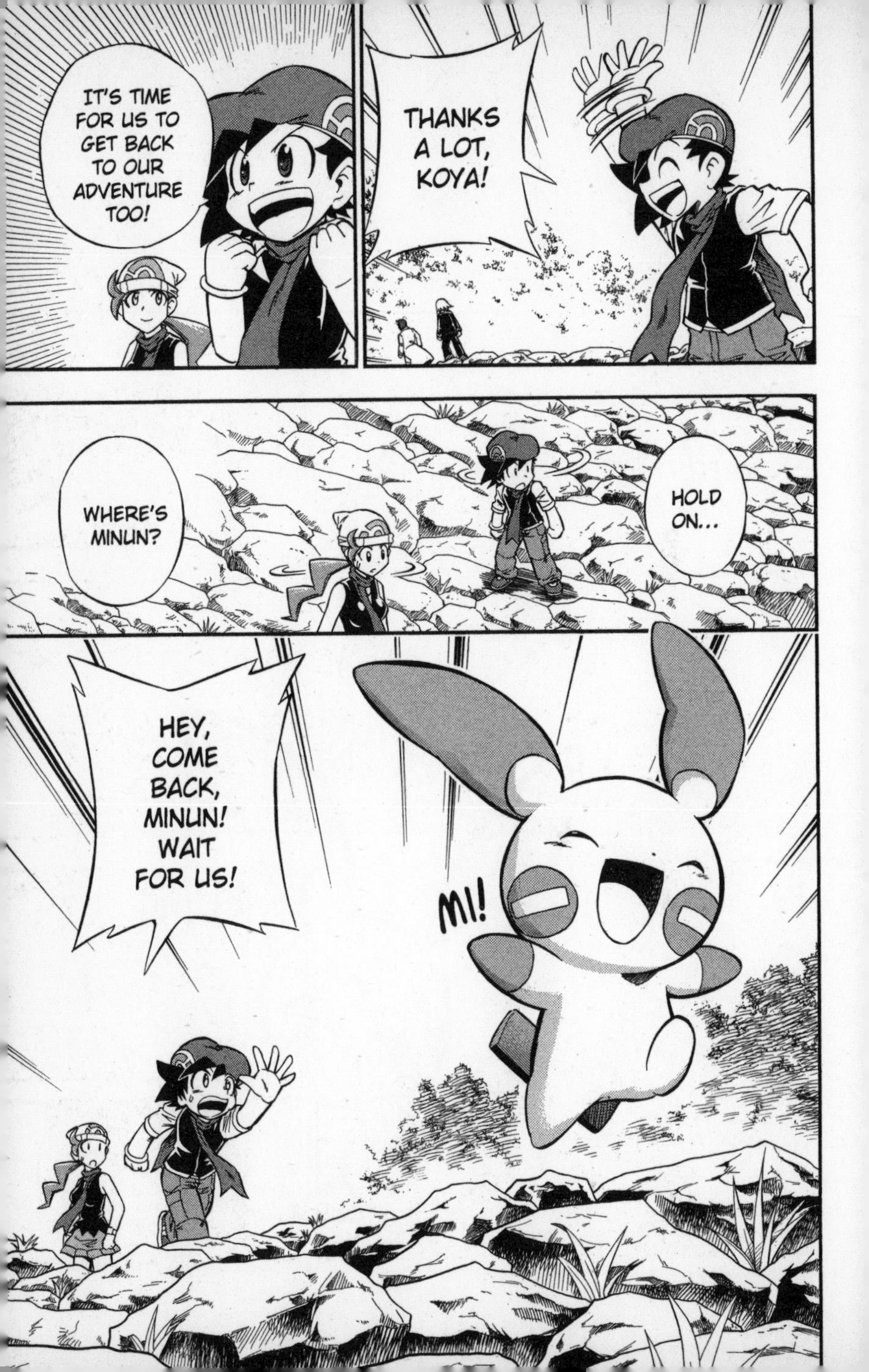
THANKS A LOT, KOYA!
IT'S TIME FOR US TO GET BACK TO OUR ADVENTURE TOO!
HOLD ON...
WHERE'S MINUN?
HEY, COME BACK, MINUN! WAIT FOR US!
MI!

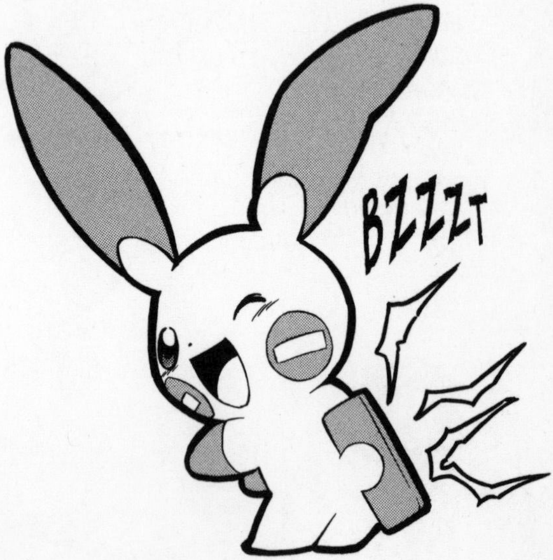
BZZZT

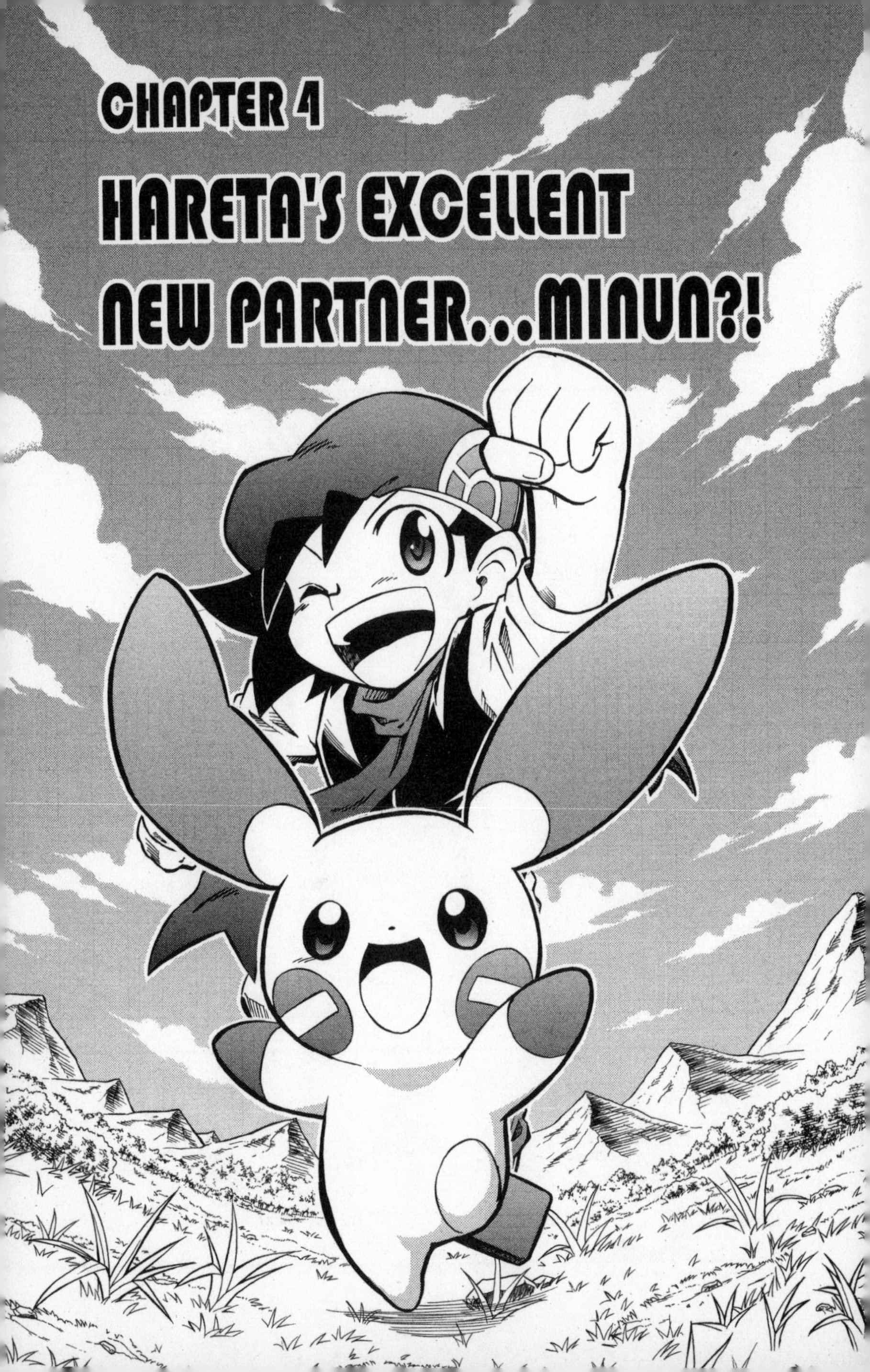
CHAPTER 4
HARETA'S EXCELLENT
NEW PARTNER...MINUN?!

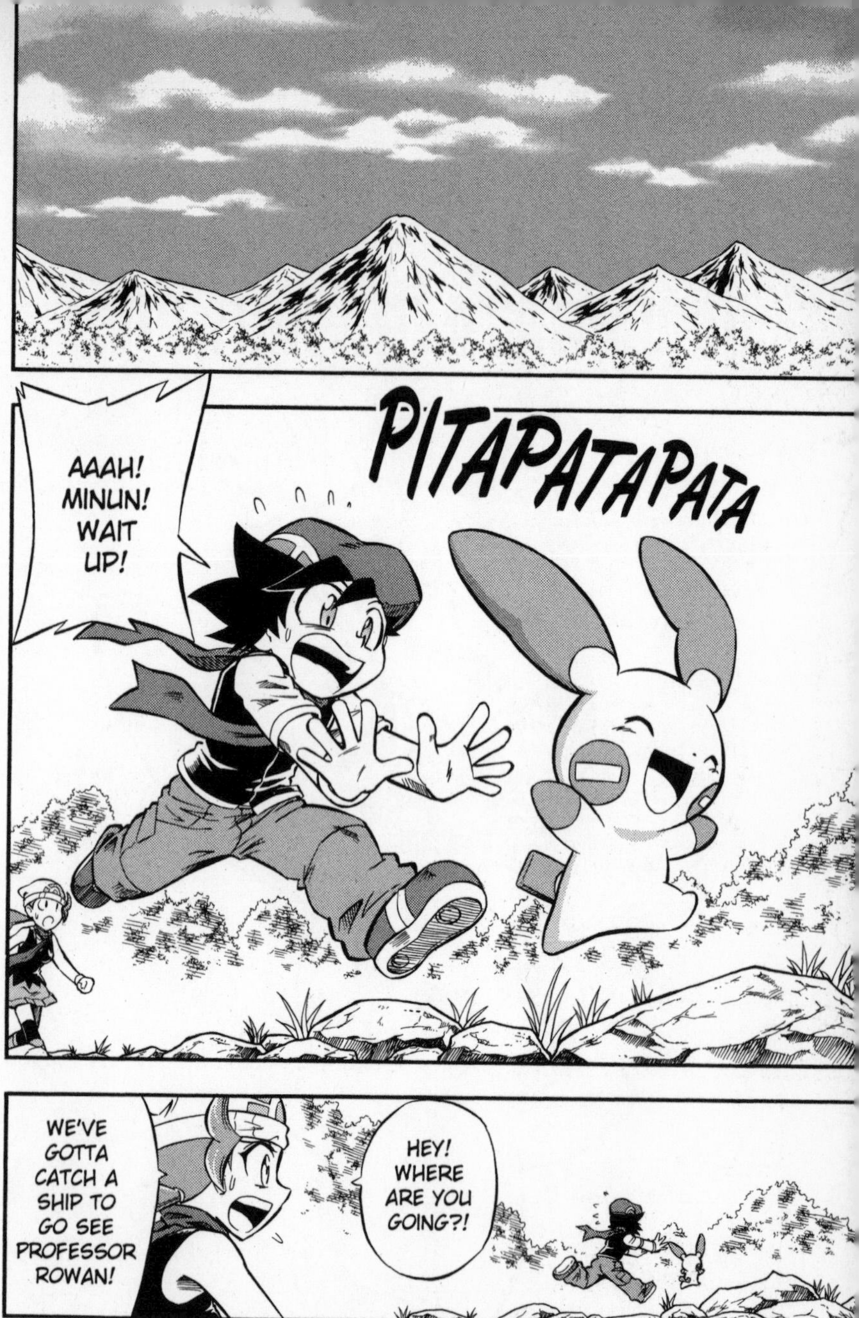
PITAPATAPATA
AAAH! MINUN! WAIT UP!
HEY! WHERE ARE YOU GOING?!
WE'VE GOTTA CATCH A SHIP TO GO SEE PROFESSOR ROWAN!

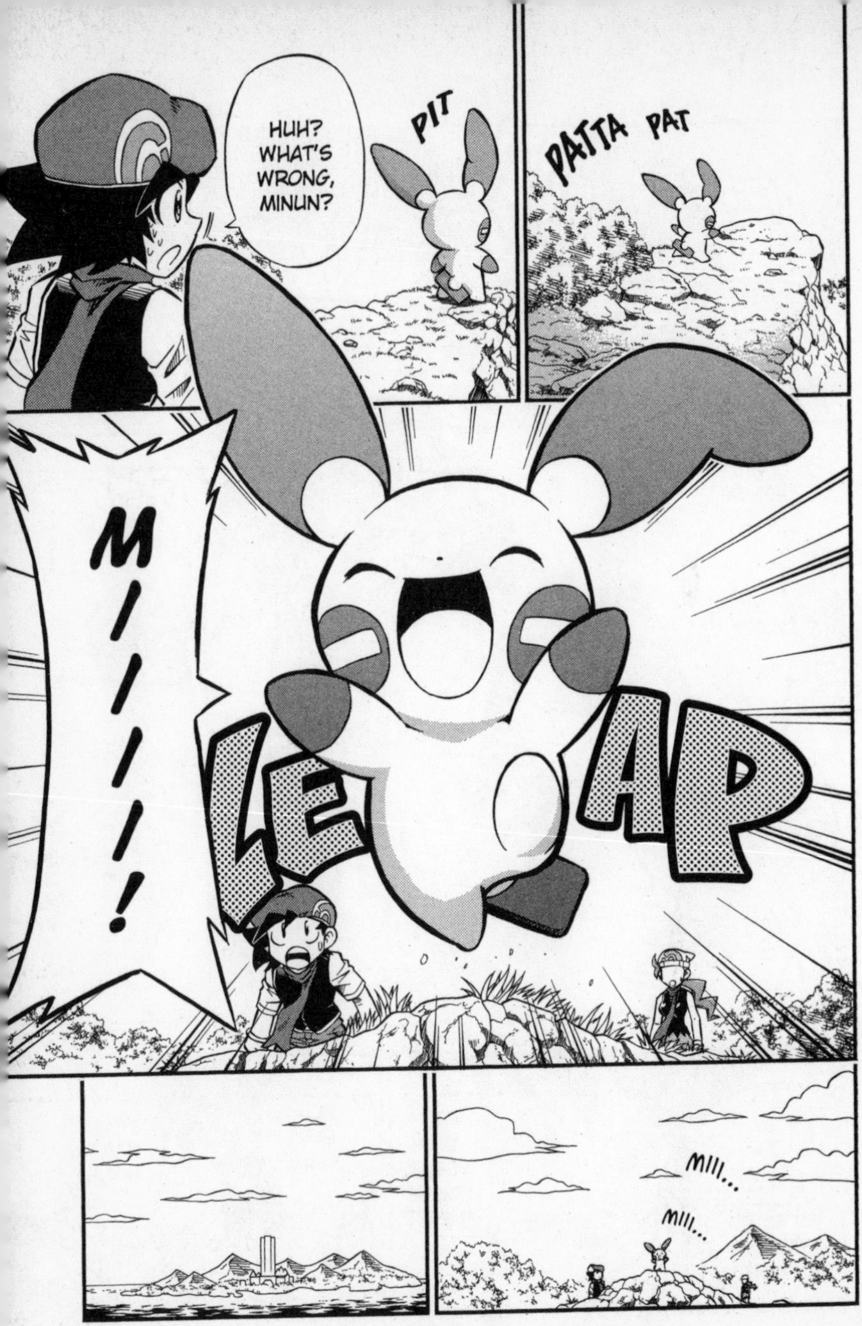
PATTA PAT
PIT
HUH? WHAT'S WRONG, MINUN?
M-I-I-I-I!
LEAP
MIII...
MIII...

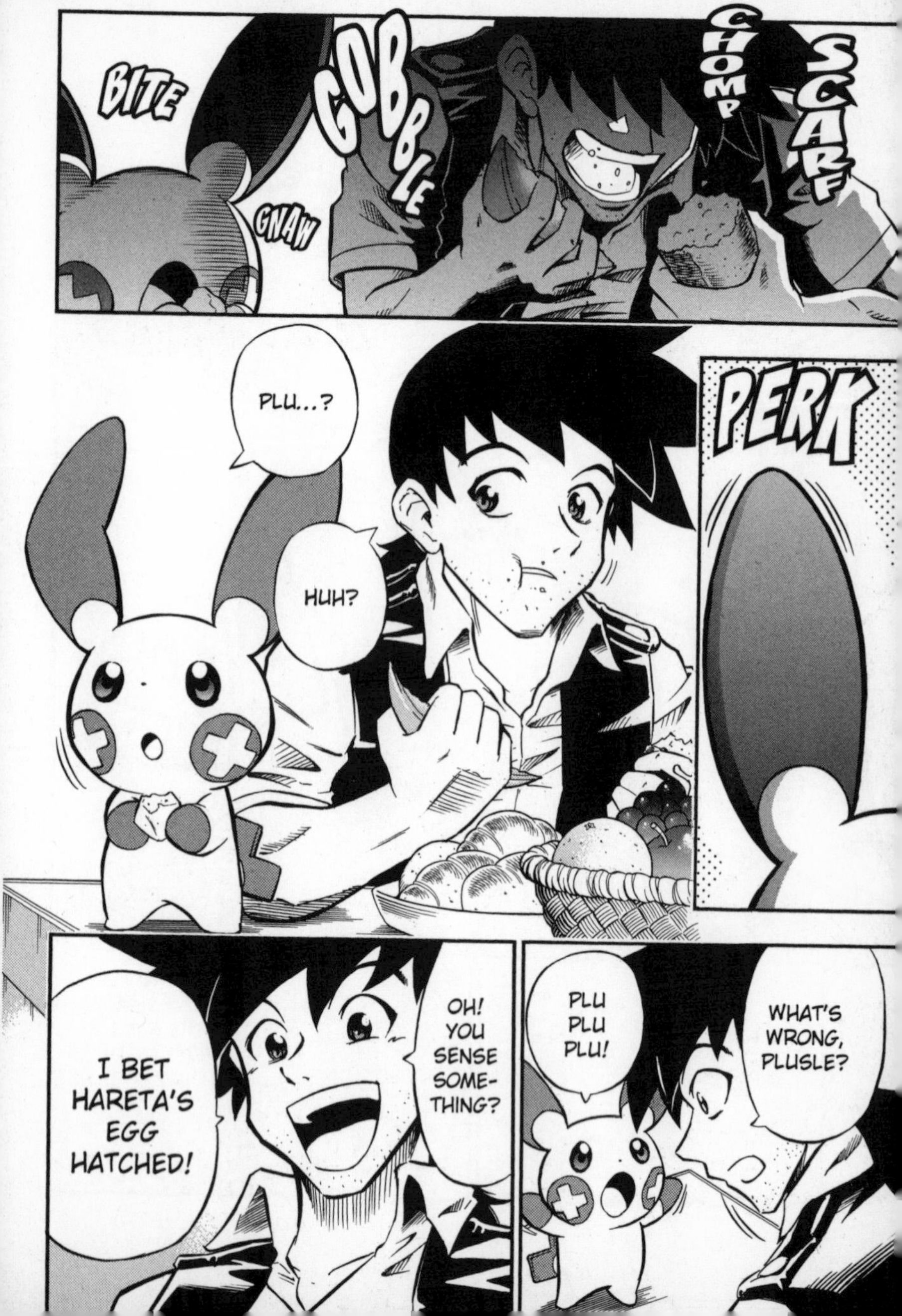
SCARF
CHOMP
GOBBLE
BITE
GNAW
PERK
PLU...?
HUH?
WHAT'S WRONG, PLUSLE?
PLU PLU PLU!
OH! YOU SENSE SOMETHING?
I BET HARETA'S EGG HATCHED!

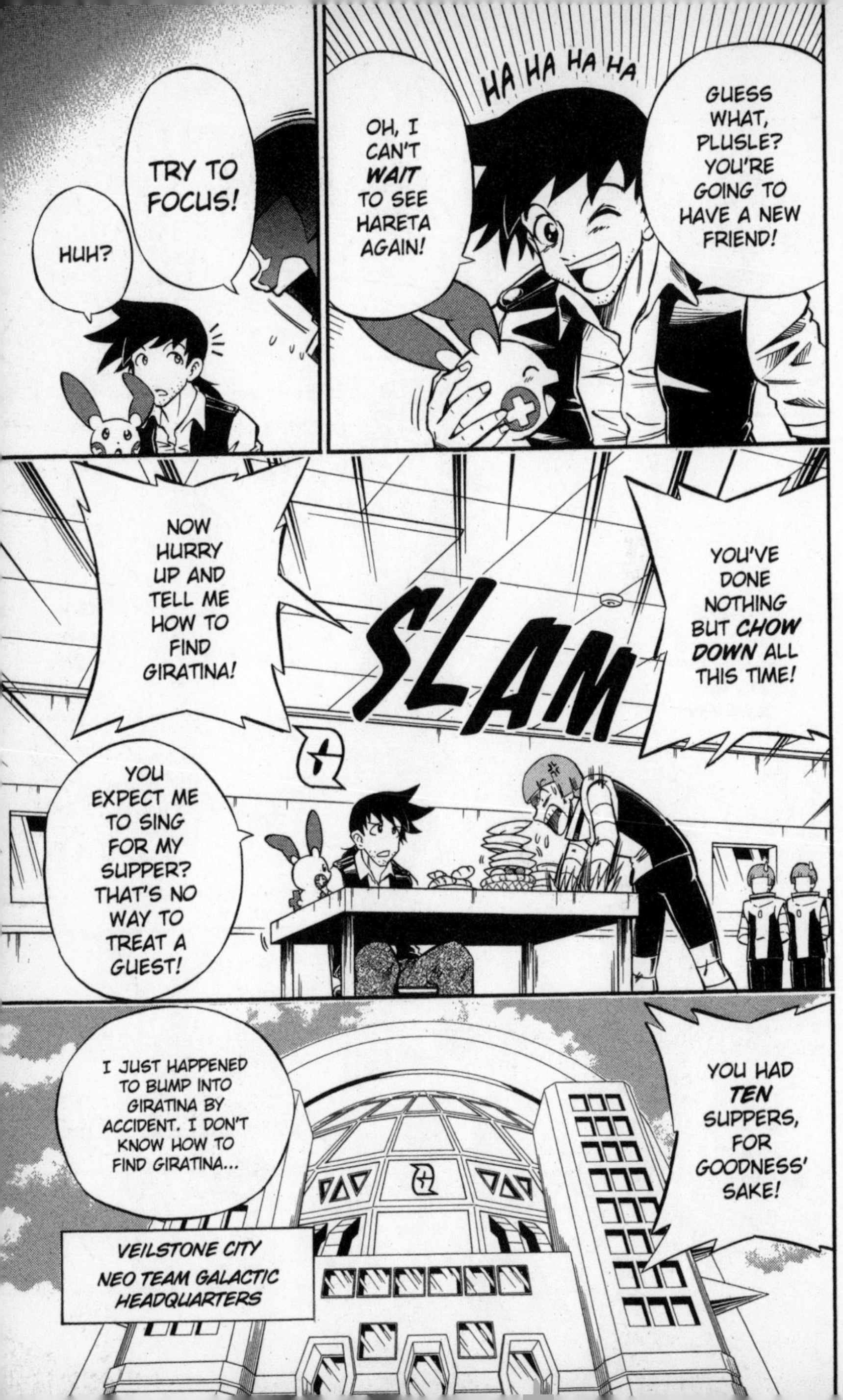
HA HA HA HA
GUESS WHAT, PLUSLE? YOU'RE GOING TO HAVE A NEW FRIEND!
OH, I CAN'T WAIT TO SEE HARETA AGAIN!
TRY TO FOCUS!
HUH?
YOU'VE DONE NOTHING BUT CHOW DOWN ALL THIS TIME!
SLAM
NOW HURRY UP AND TELL ME HOW TO FIND GIRATINA!
YOU EXPECT ME TO SING FOR MY SUPPER? THAT'S NO WAY TO TREAT A GUEST!
YOU HAD TEN SUPPERS, FOR GOODNESS' SAKE!
I JUST HAPPENED TO BUMP INTO GIRATINA BY ACCIDENT. I DON'T KNOW HOW TO FIND GIRATINA...
VEILSTONE CITY NEO TEAM GALACTIC HEADQUARTERS

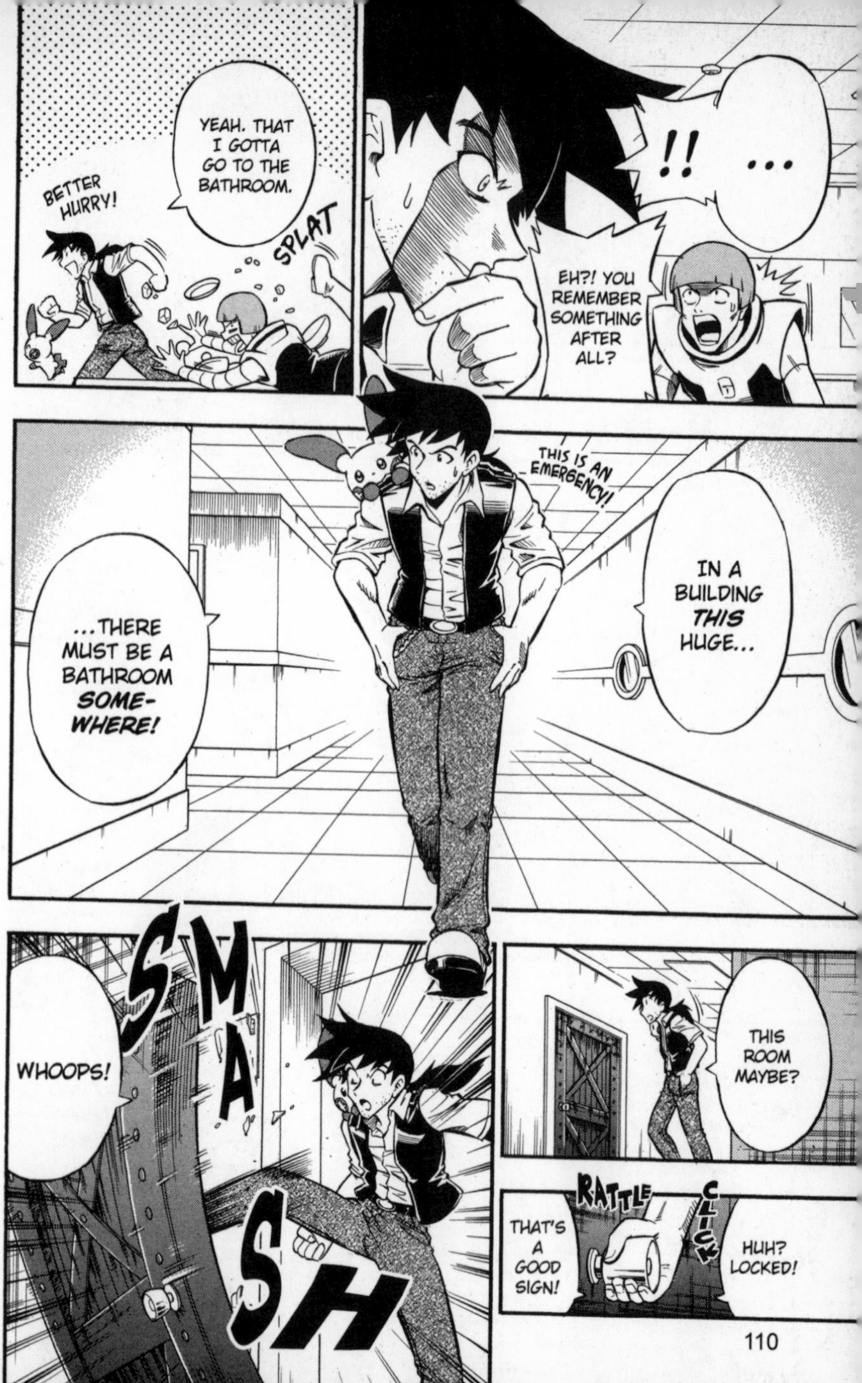
!! ...
EH?! YOU REMEMBER SOMETHING AFTER ALL?
YEAH. THAT I GOTTA GO TO THE BATHROOM.
SPLAT
BETTER HURRY!
THIS IS AN EMERGENCY!
IN A BUILDING THIS HUGE...
...THERE MUST BE A BATHROOM SOME-WHERE!
THIS ROOM MAYBE?
RATTLE
CLICK
HUH? LOCKED!
THAT'S A GOOD SIGN!
SMASH
WHOOPS!

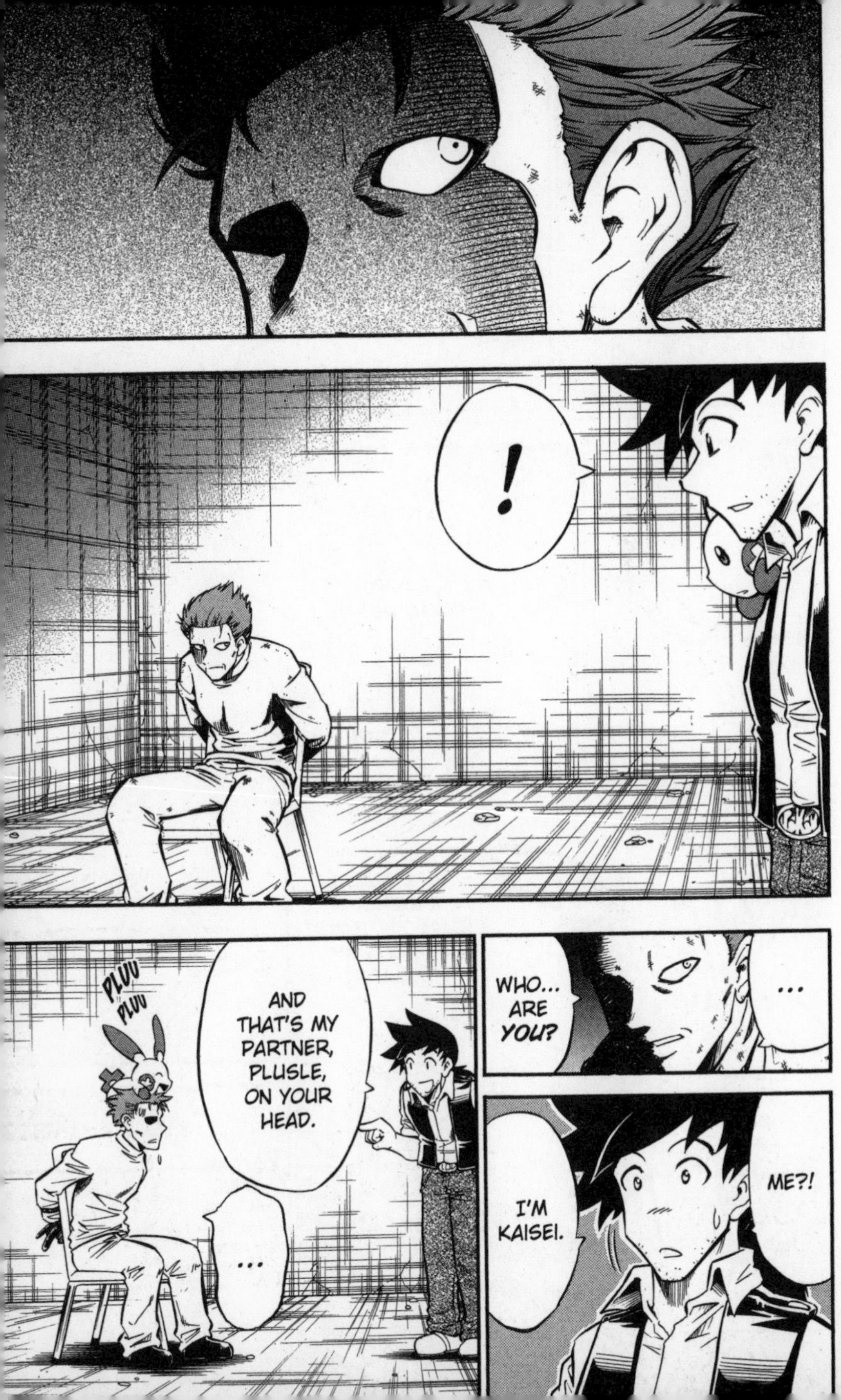
!
...
WHO... ARE YOU?
ME?!
I'M KAISEI.
AND THAT'S MY PARTNER, PLUSLE, ON YOUR HEAD.
PLUU PLUU
...

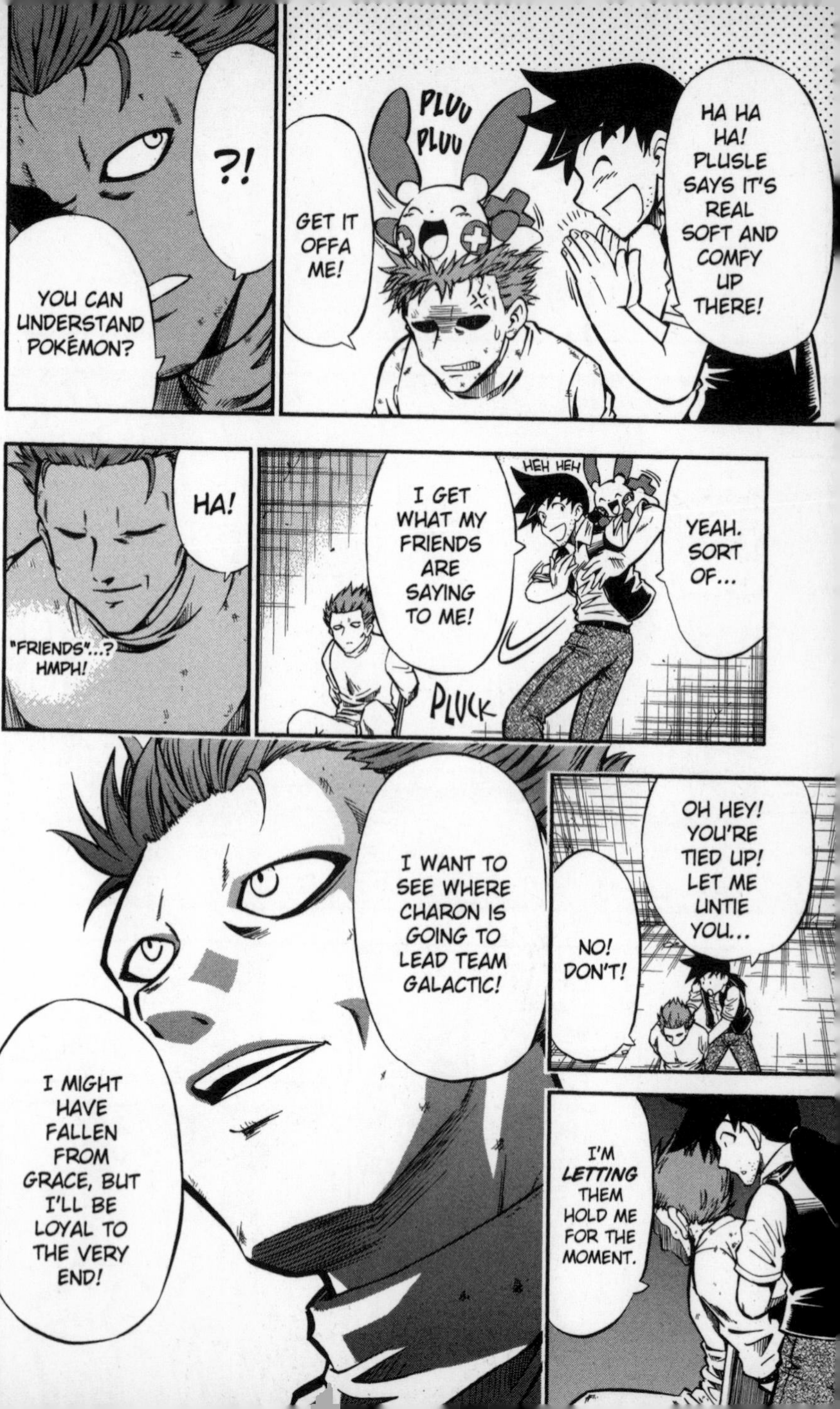
HA HA HA! PLUSLE SAYS IT'S REAL SOFT AND COMFY UP THERE!
PLUU PLUU
GET IT OFFA ME!
?!
YOU CAN UNDERSTAND POKÉMON?
YEAH. SORT OF...
HEH HEH
I GET WHAT MY FRIENDS ARE SAYING TO ME!
PLUCK
HA!
"FRIENDS"...? HMPH!
OH HEY! YOU'RE TIED UP! LET ME UNTIE YOU...
NO! DON'T!
I'M *LETTING* THEM HOLD ME FOR THE MOMENT.
I WANT TO SEE WHERE CHARON IS GOING TO LEAD TEAM GALACTIC!
I MIGHT HAVE FALLEN FROM GRACE, BUT I'LL BE LOYAL TO THE VERY END!

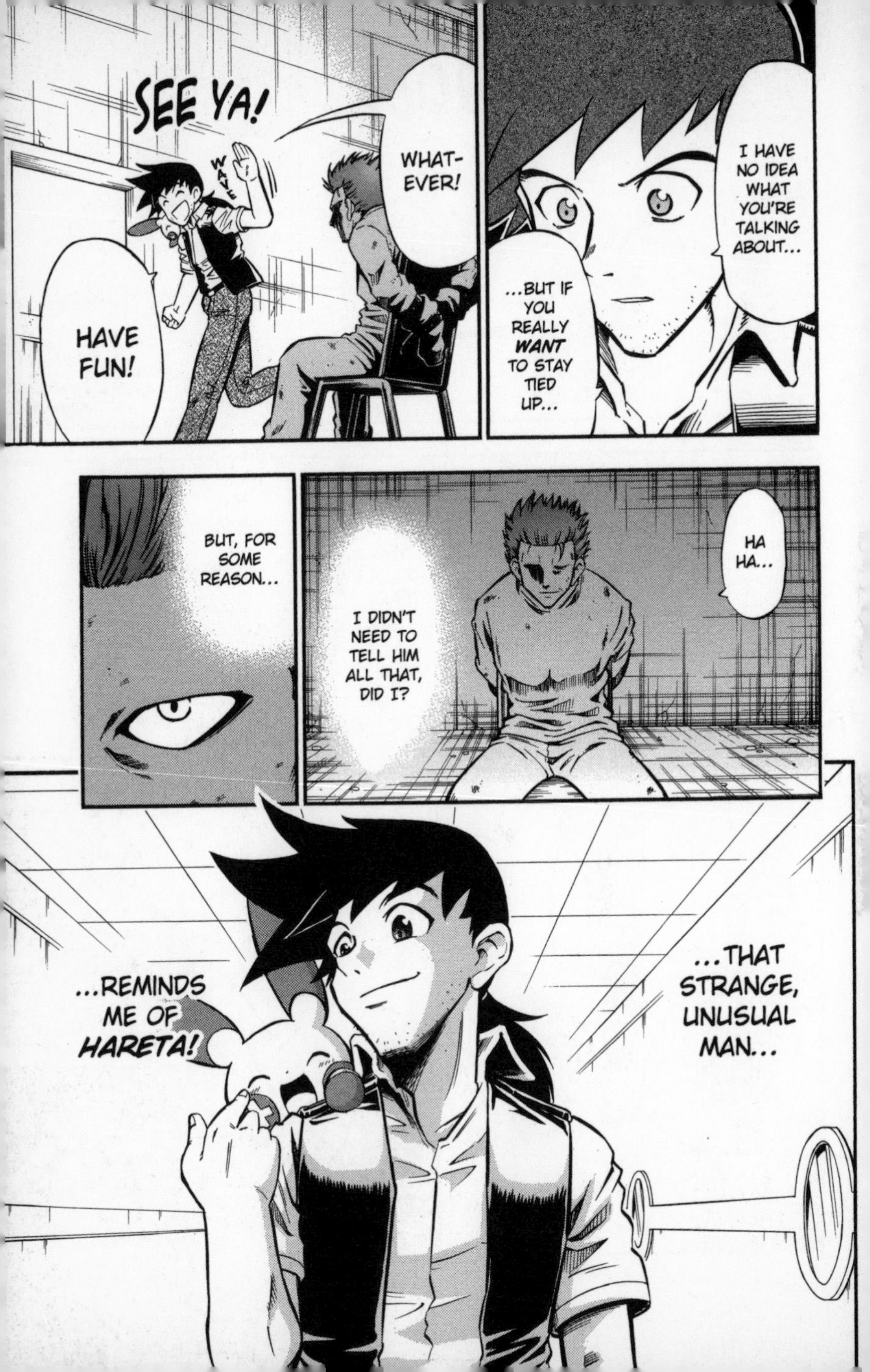
I HAVE NO IDEA WHAT YOU'RE TALKING ABOUT...
...BUT IF YOU REALLY *WANT* TO STAY TIED UP...
WHAT-EVER!
SEE YA!
WAVE
HAVE FUN!
HA HA...
I DIDN'T NEED TO TELL HIM ALL THAT, DID I?
BUT, FOR SOME REASON...
...THAT STRANGE, UNUSUAL MAN...
...REMINDS ME OF *HARETA!*

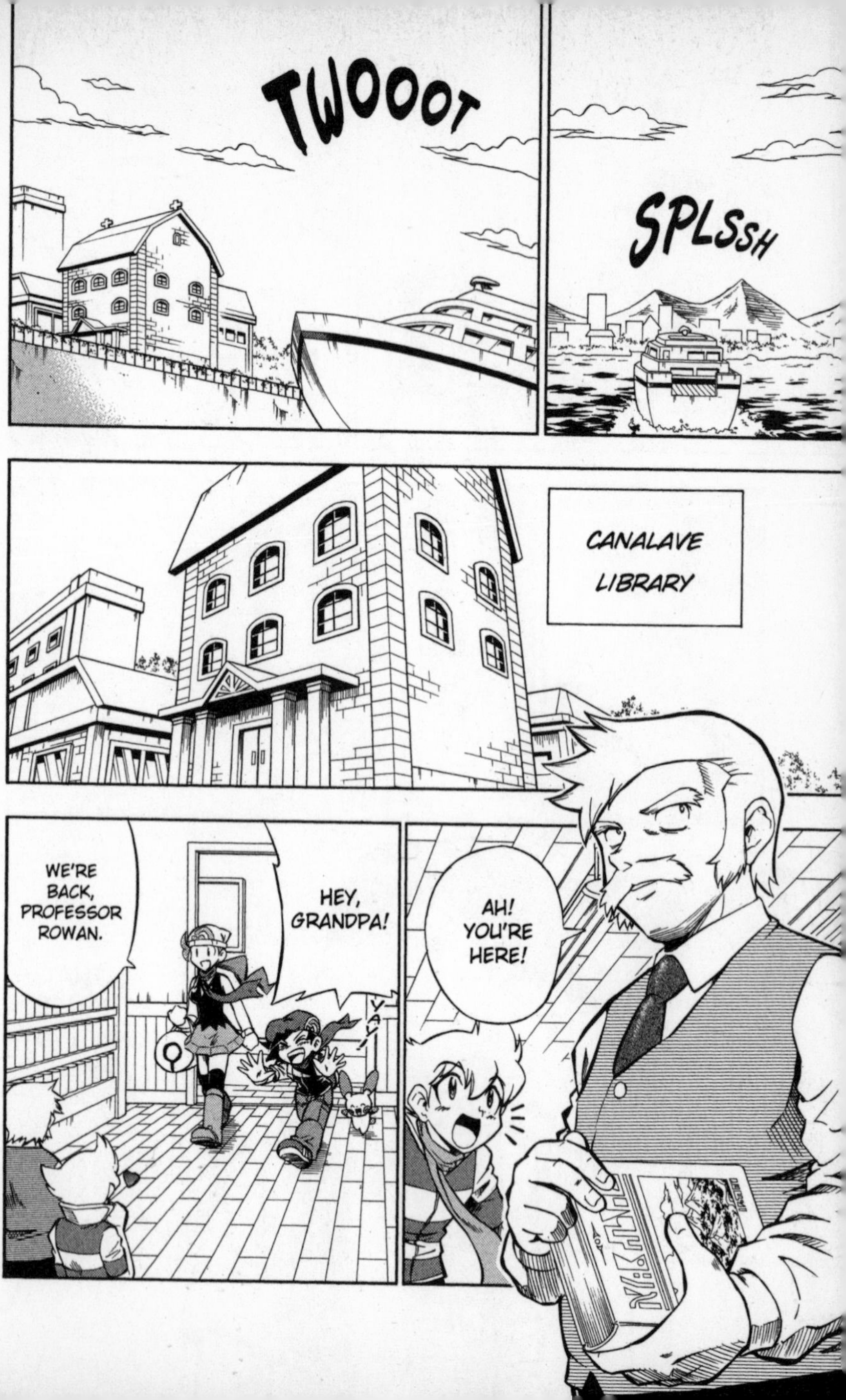
SPLSSH
TWOOOT
CANALAVE LIBRARY
AH! YOU'RE HERE!
HEY, GRANDPA!
YAY!
WE'RE BACK, PROFESSOR ROWAN.

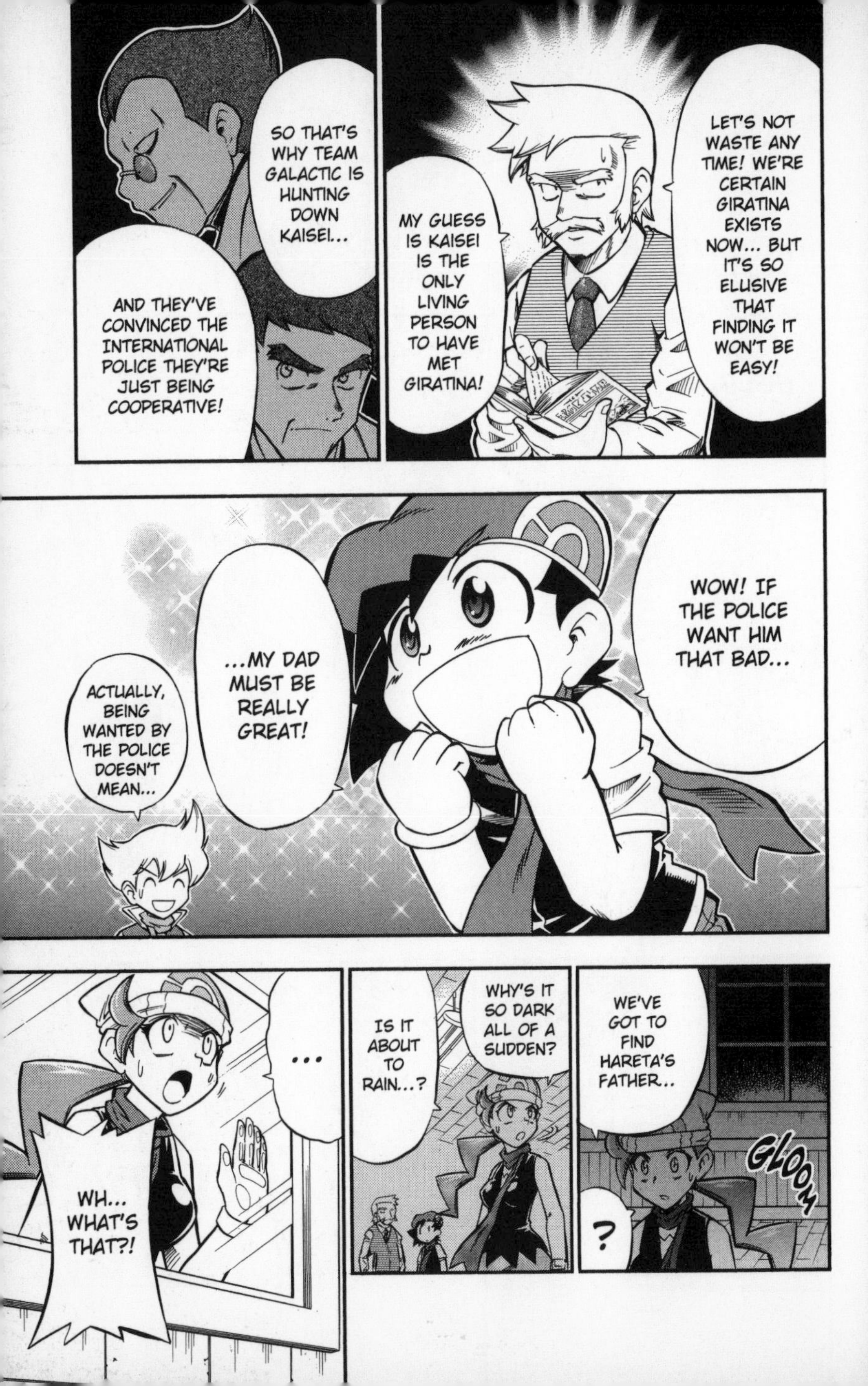
LET'S NOT WASTE ANY TIME! WE'RE CERTAIN GIRATINA EXISTS NOW... BUT IT'S SO ELUSIVE THAT FINDING IT WON'T BE EASY!
MY GUESS IS KAISEI IS THE ONLY LIVING PERSON TO HAVE MET GIRATINA!
SO THAT'S WHY TEAM GALACTIC IS HUNTING DOWN KAISEI...
AND THEY'VE CONVINCED THE INTERNATIONAL POLICE THEY'RE JUST BEING COOPERATIVE!
WOW! IF THE POLICE WANT HIM THAT BAD...
...MY DAD MUST BE REALLY GREAT!
ACTUALLY, BEING WANTED BY THE POLICE DOESN'T MEAN...
WE'VE GOT TO FIND HARETA'S FATHER...
GLOOM
?
WHY'S IT SO DARK ALL OF A SUDDEN?
IS IT ABOUT TO RAIN...?
...
WH... WHAT'S THAT?!

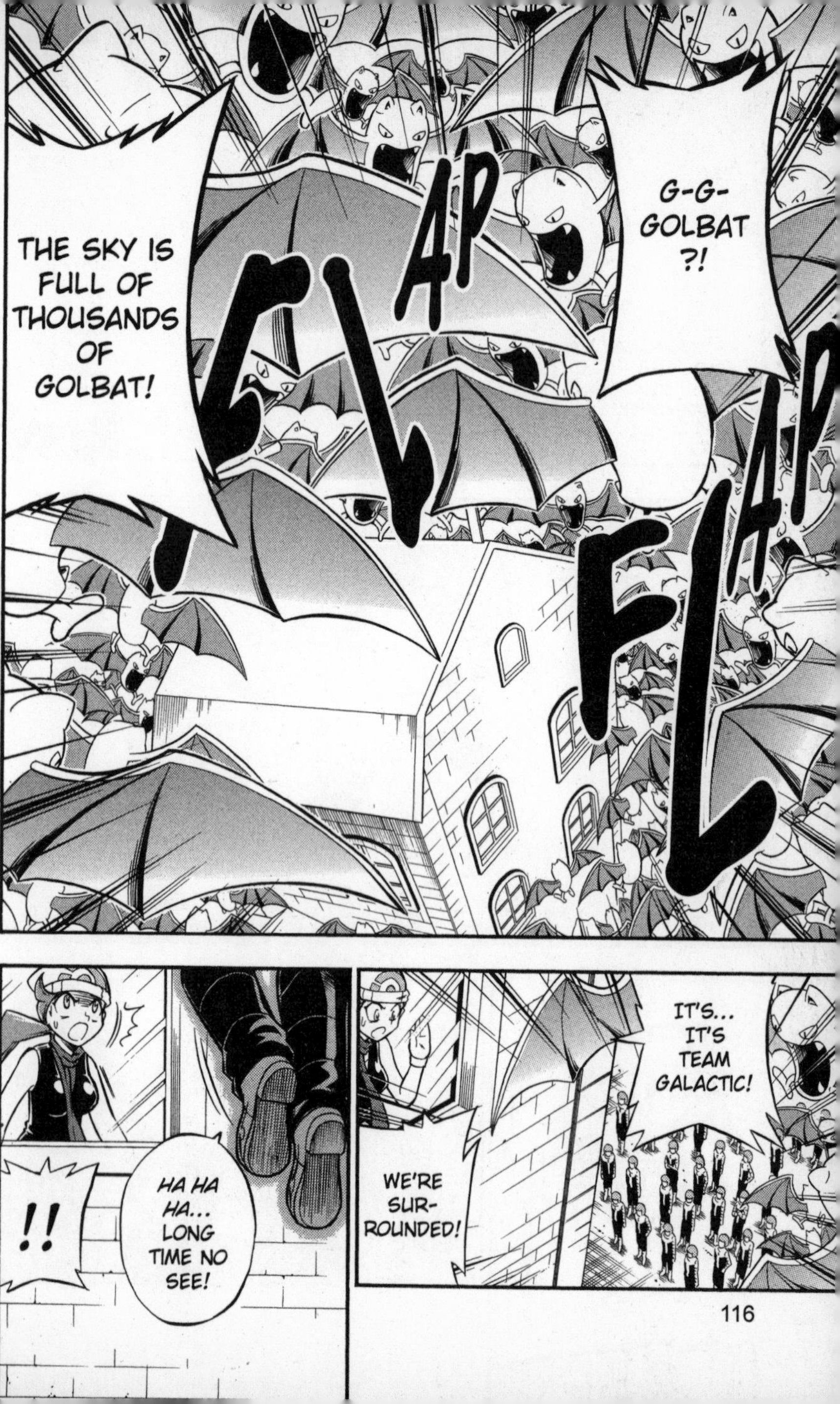
G-G-GOLBAT?!
FLAP
FLAP
THE SKY IS FULL OF THOUSANDS OF GOLBAT!
IT'S... IT'S TEAM GALACTIC!
WE'RE SUR-ROUNDED!
HA HA HA... LONG TIME NO SEE!
!!

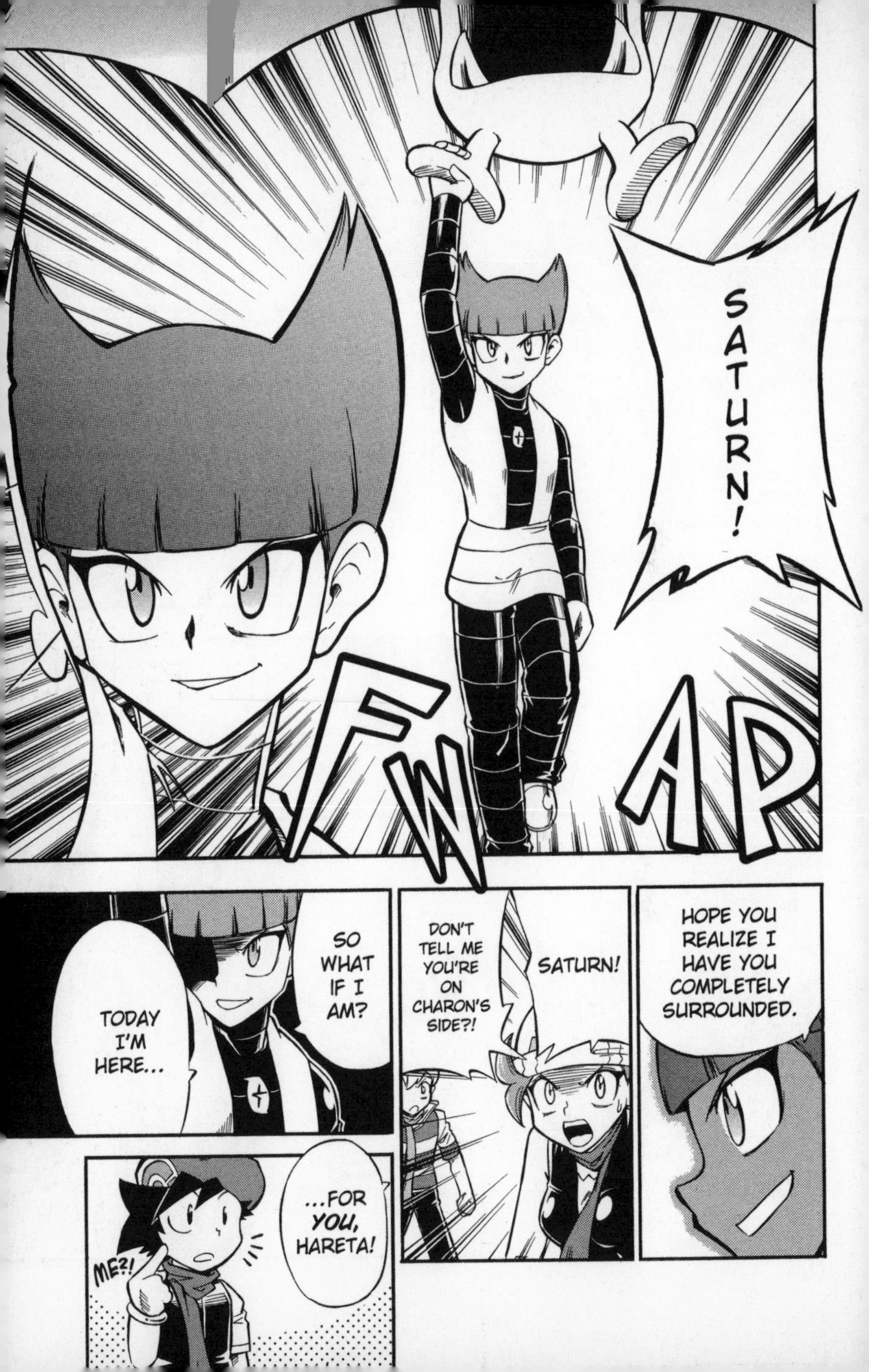
SATURN!
FWAP
HOPE YOU REALIZE I HAVE YOU COMPLETELY SURROUNDED.
SATURN!
DON'T TELL ME YOU'RE ON CHARON'S SIDE?!
SO WHAT IF I AM?
TODAY I'M HERE...
...FOR *YOU*, HARETA!
ME?!

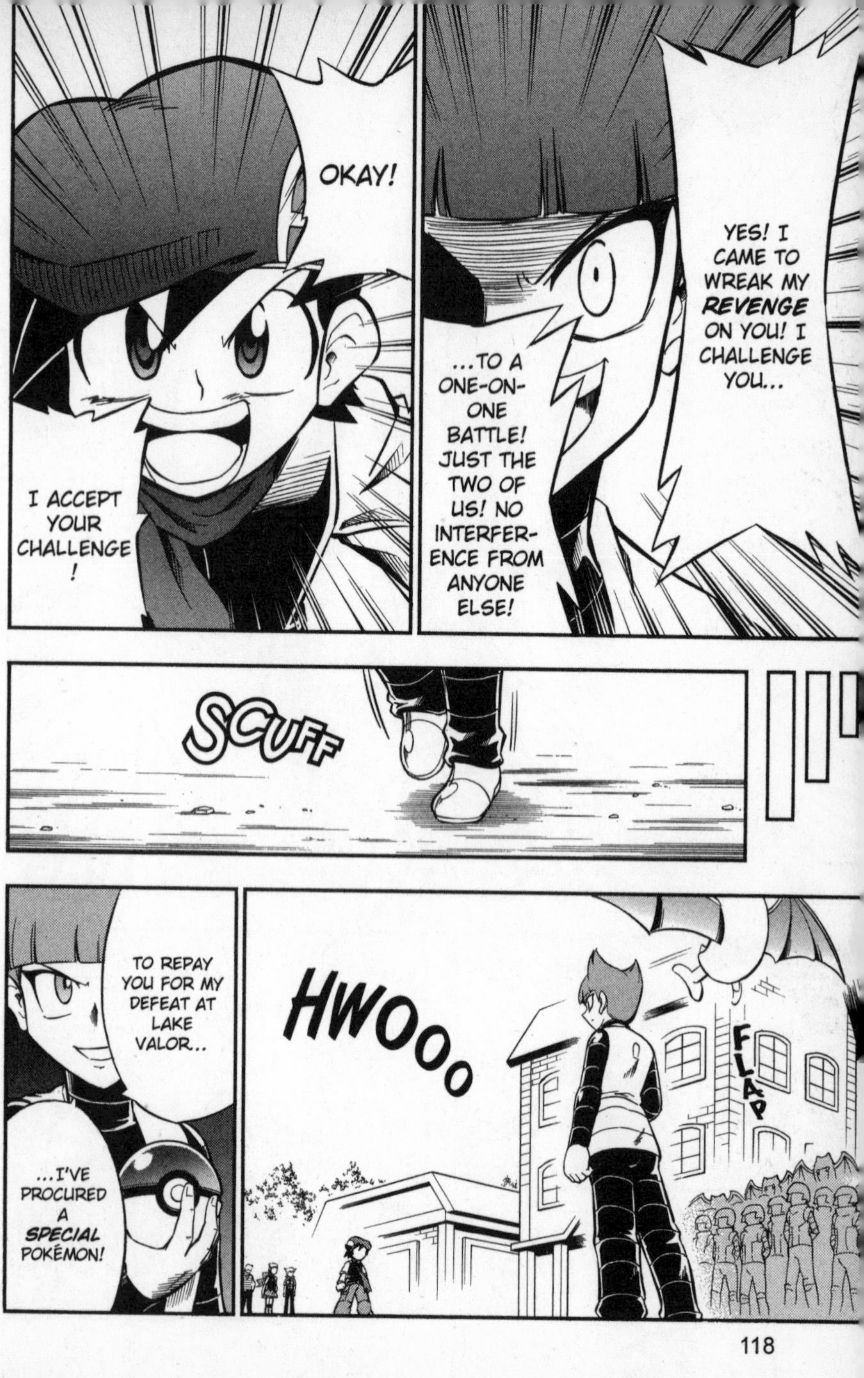
YES! I CAME TO WREAK MY ***REVENGE*** ON YOU! I CHALLENGE YOU...
...TO A ONE-ON-ONE BATTLE! JUST THE TWO OF US! NO INTERFERENCE FROM ANYONE ELSE!
OKAY!
I ACCEPT YOUR CHALLENGE!
SCUFF
HWOOOO
FLAP
TO REPAY YOU FOR MY DEFEAT AT LAKE VALOR...
...I'VE PROCURED A ***SPECIAL*** POKéMON!

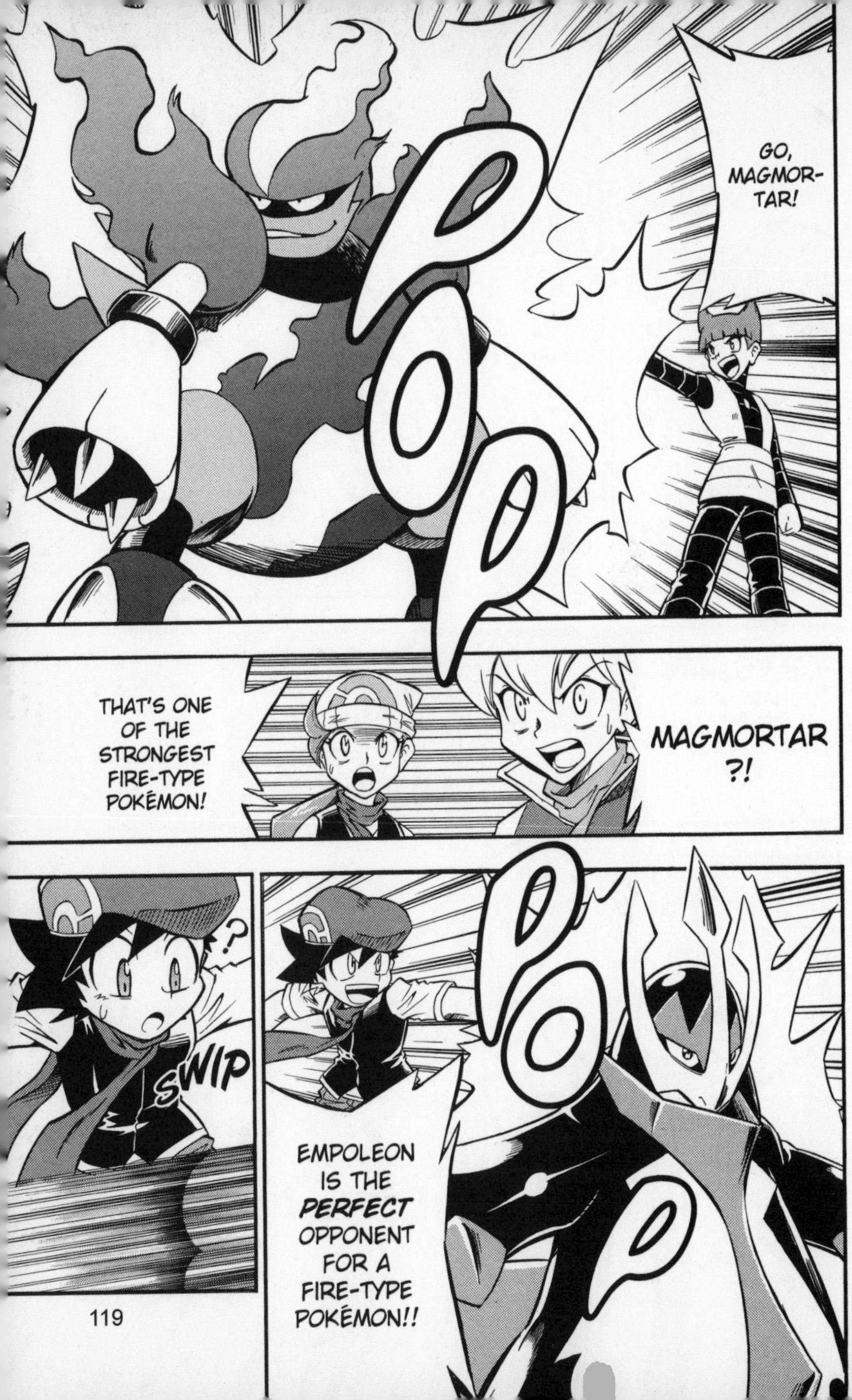

POP
GO, MAGMORTAR!
MAGMORTAR ?!
THAT'S ONE OF THE STRONGEST FIRE-TYPE POKÉMON!
POP
EMPOLEON IS THE PERFECT OPPONENT FOR A FIRE-TYPE POKÉMON!!
?
SWIP

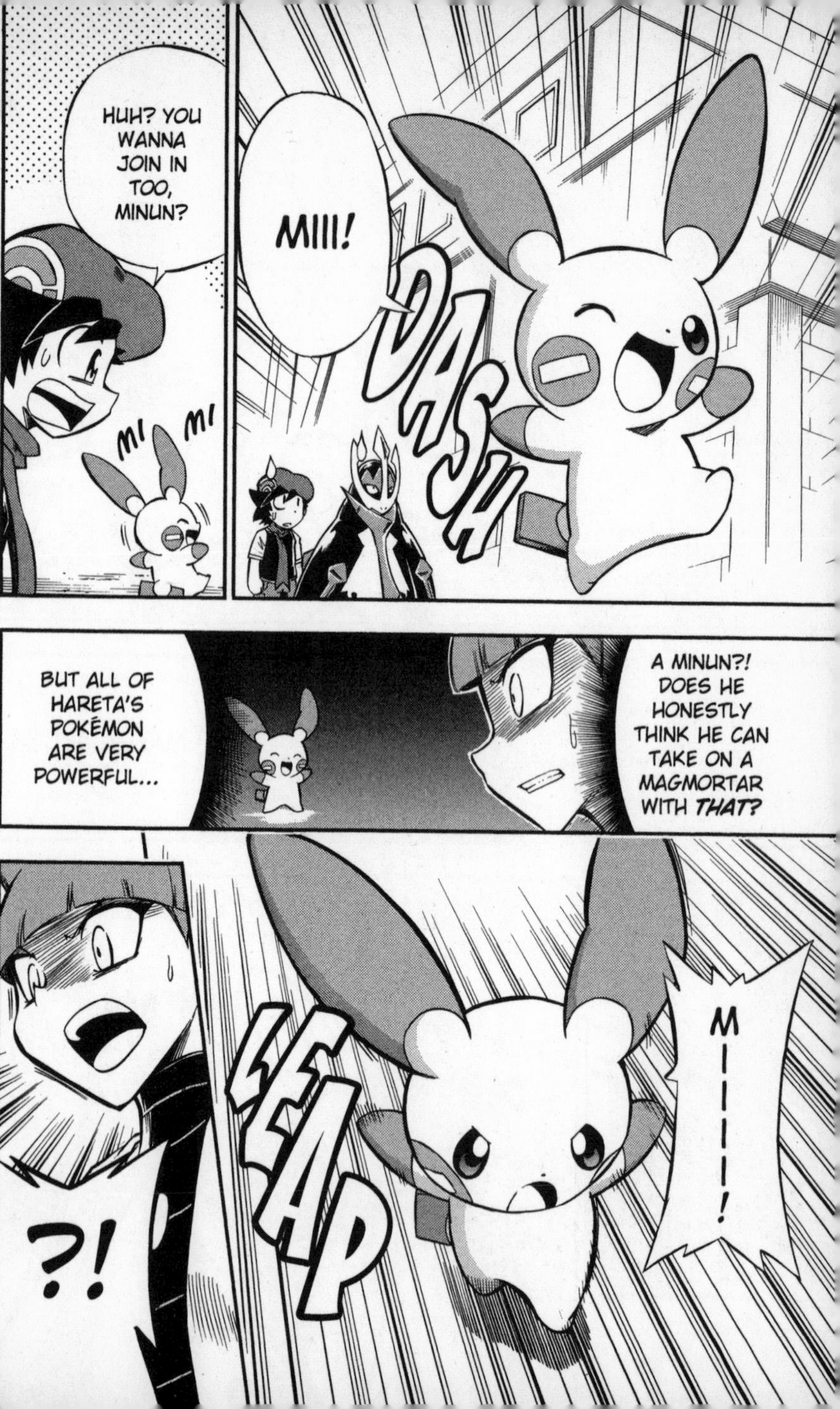
MIII!
DASH
HUH? YOU WANNA JOIN IN TOO, MINUN?
MI MI
A MINUN?! DOES HE HONESTLY THINK HE CAN TAKE ON A MAGMORTAR WITH *THAT?*
BUT ALL OF HARETA'S POKÉMON ARE VERY POWERFUL...
M——!
LEAP
?!

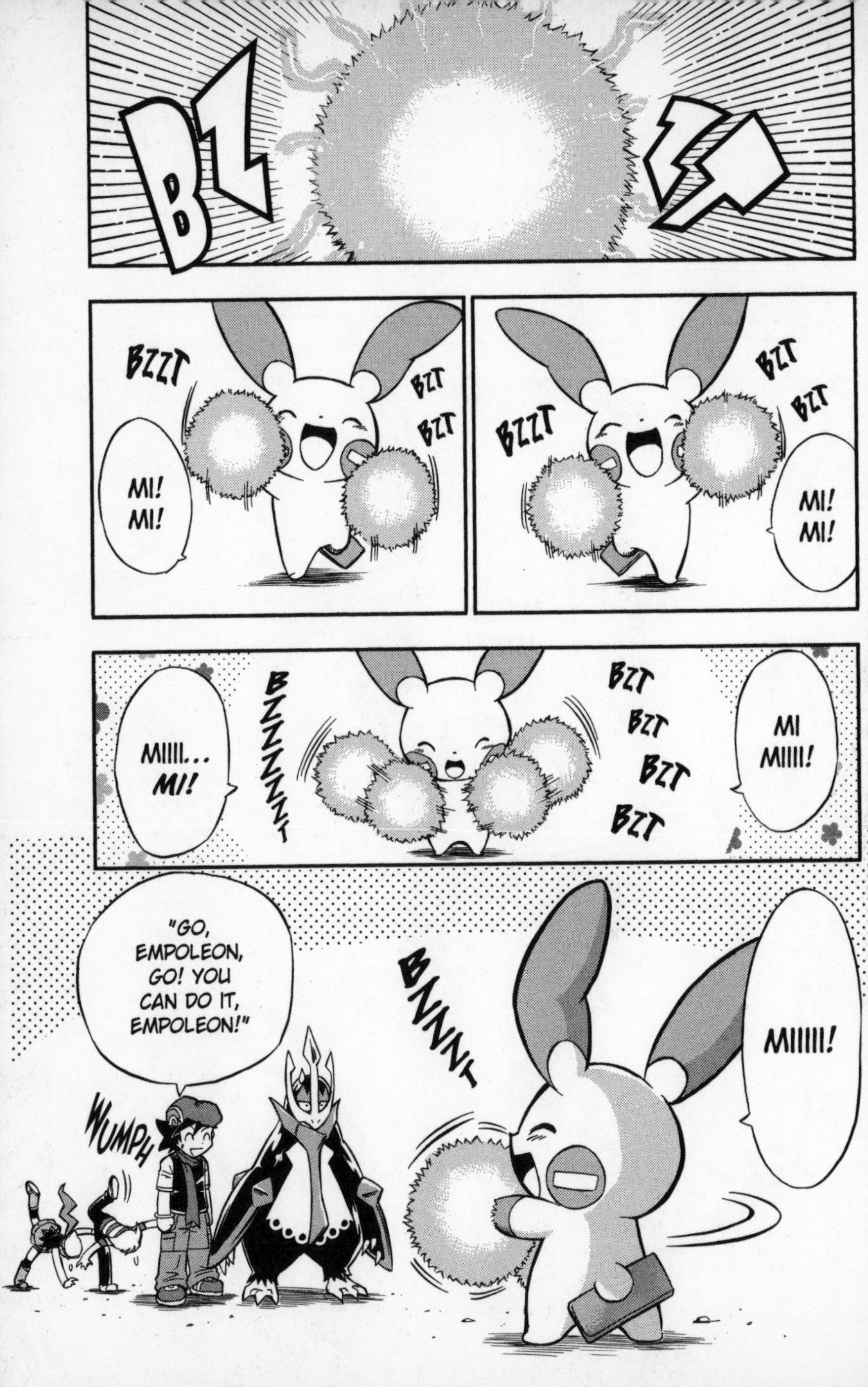
BZZT
BZT
BZT
BZZT
MI! MI!
BZZT
BZT
BZT
MI! MI!
MI MIIII!
BZT
BZT
BZT
BZT
BZZZZZZT
MIIII... MI!
MIIIII!
BZZZZT
"GO, EMPOLEON, GO! YOU CAN DO IT, EMPOLEON!"
WUMPH

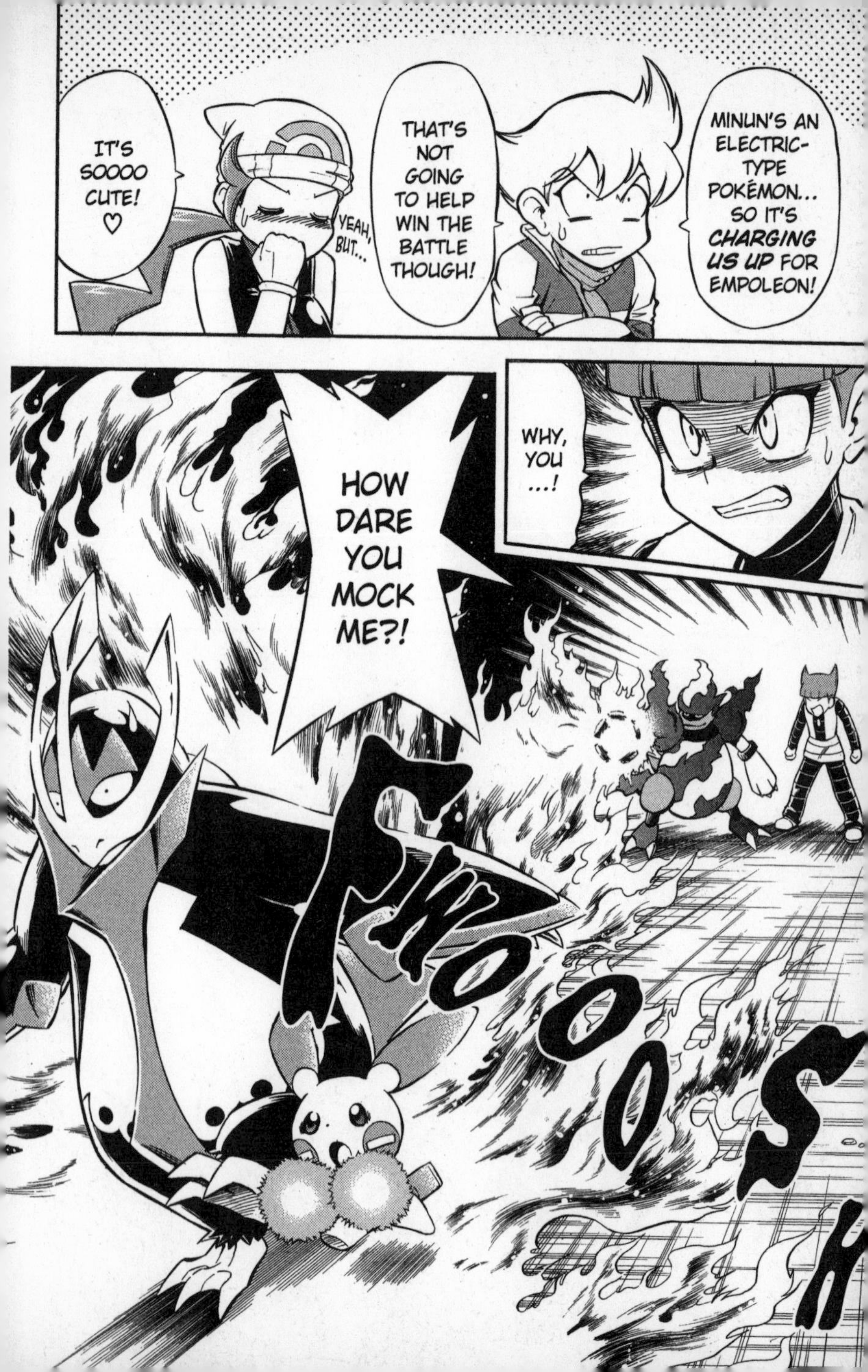
MINUN'S AN ELECTRIC-TYPE POKÉMON... SO IT'S **CHARGING US UP** FOR EMPOLEON!
THAT'S NOT GOING TO HELP WIN THE BATTLE THOUGH!
YEAH, BUT...
IT'S SOOOO CUTE! ♡
WHY, YOU ...!
HOW DARE YOU MOCK ME?!
FWOOOOSH

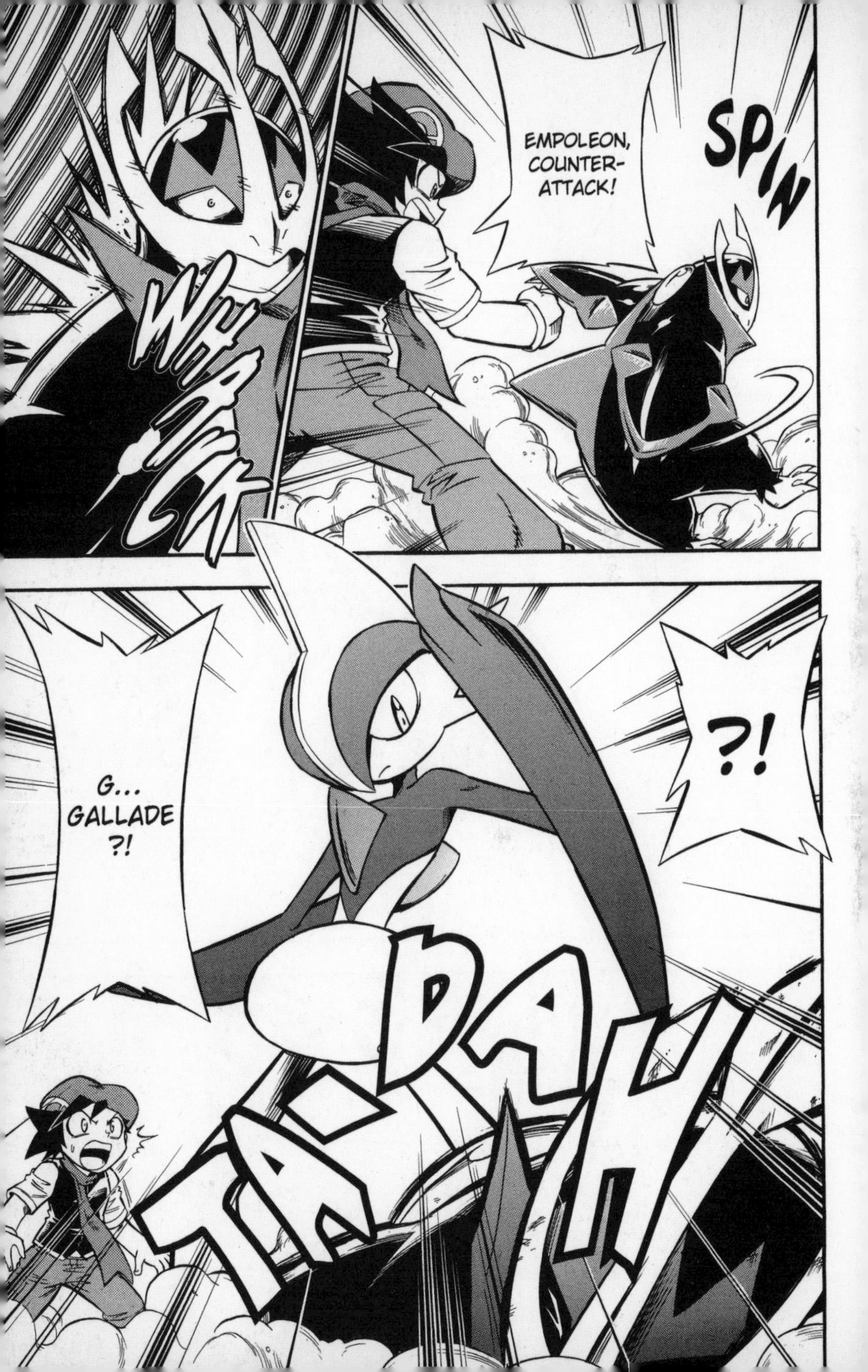
SPIN
EMPOLEON, COUNTER-ATTACK!
WHACK
?!
G... GALLADE ?!
TA-DAH!

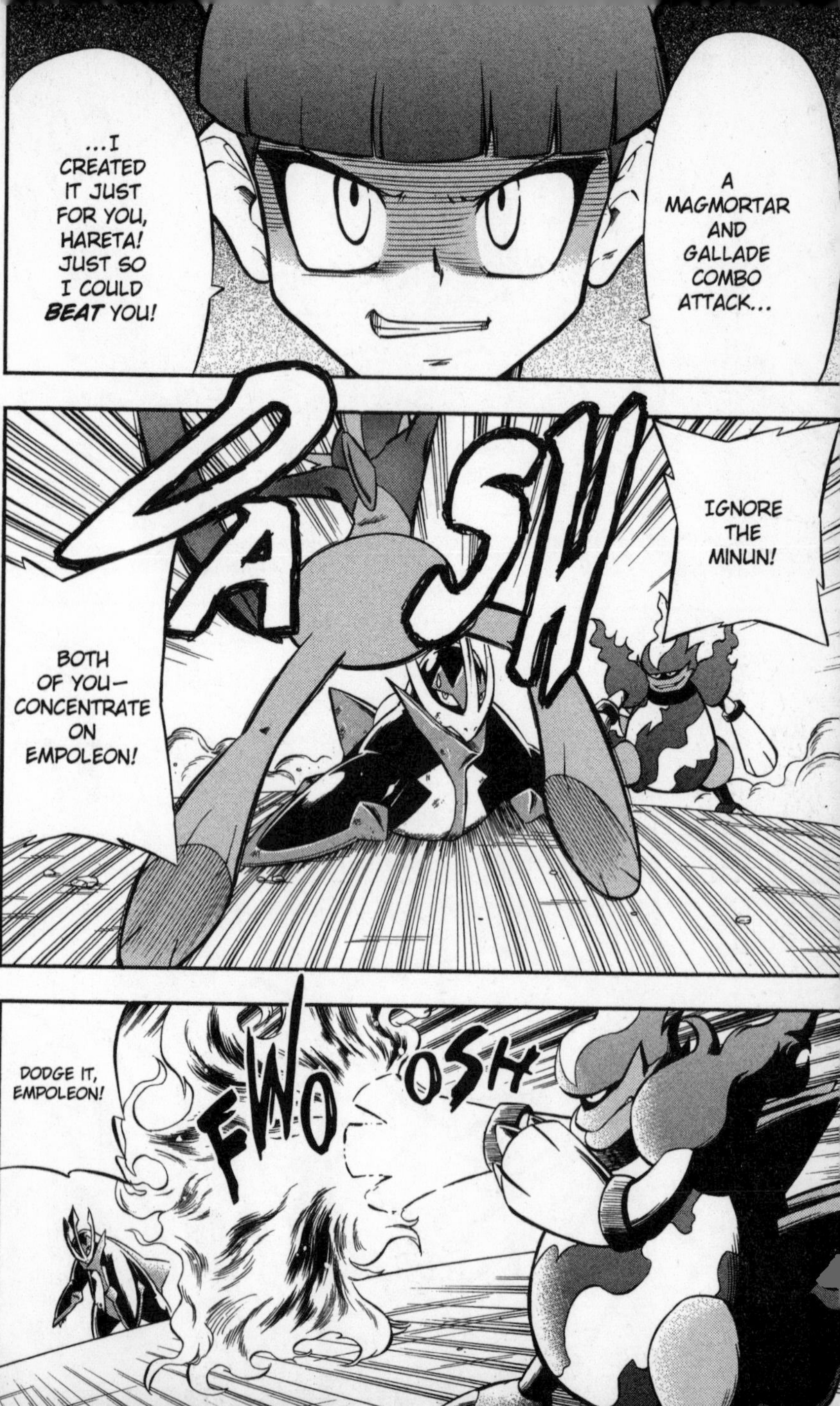
A MAGMORTAR AND GALLADE COMBO ATTACK...
...I CREATED IT JUST FOR YOU, HARETA! JUST SO I COULD BEAT YOU!
DASH
IGNORE THE MINUN!
BOTH OF YOU— CONCENTRATE ON EMPOLEON!
FWOOSH
DODGE IT, EMPOLEON!

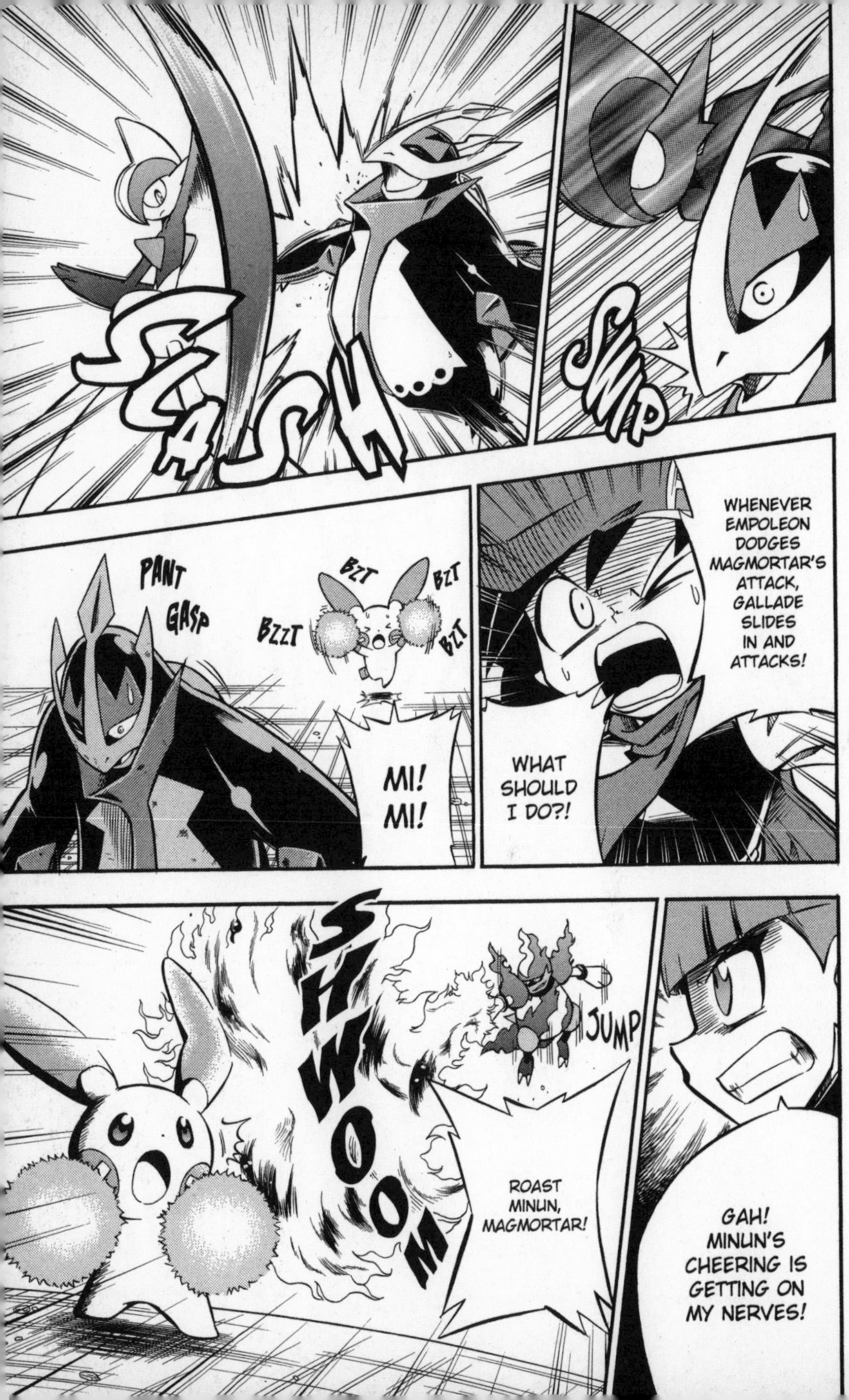
SWIP
SLASH
WHENEVER EMPOLEON DODGES MAGMORTAR'S ATTACK, GALLADE SLIDES IN AND ATTACKS!
WHAT SHOULD I DO?!
PANT
GASP
BZT
BZT
BZZT
BZT
MI! MI!
GAH! MINUN'S CHEERING IS GETTING ON MY NERVES!
JUMP
ROAST MINUN, MAGMORTAR!
SHWOOOM

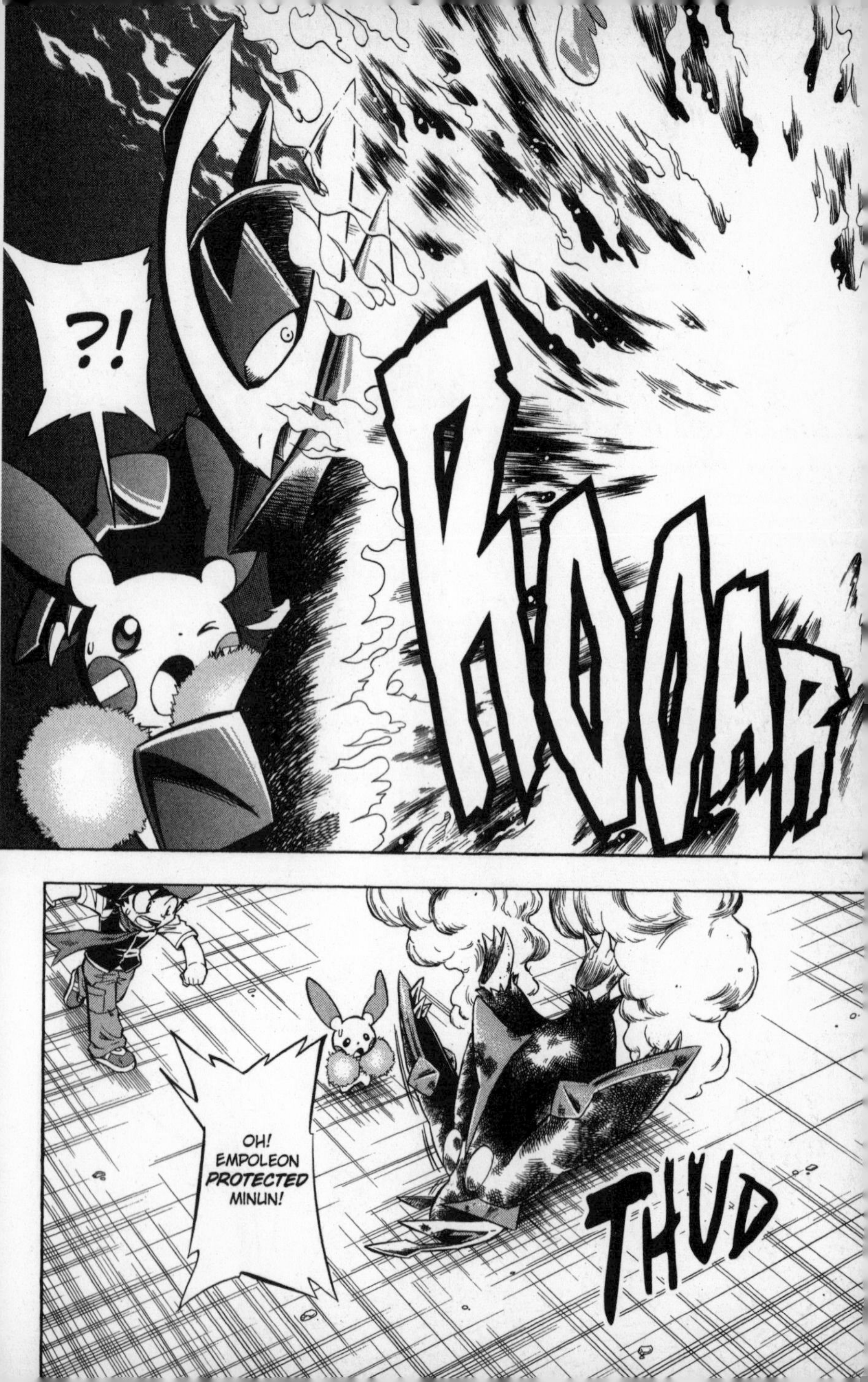
KOOAB
?!
THUD
OH! EMPOLEON PROTECTED MINUN!

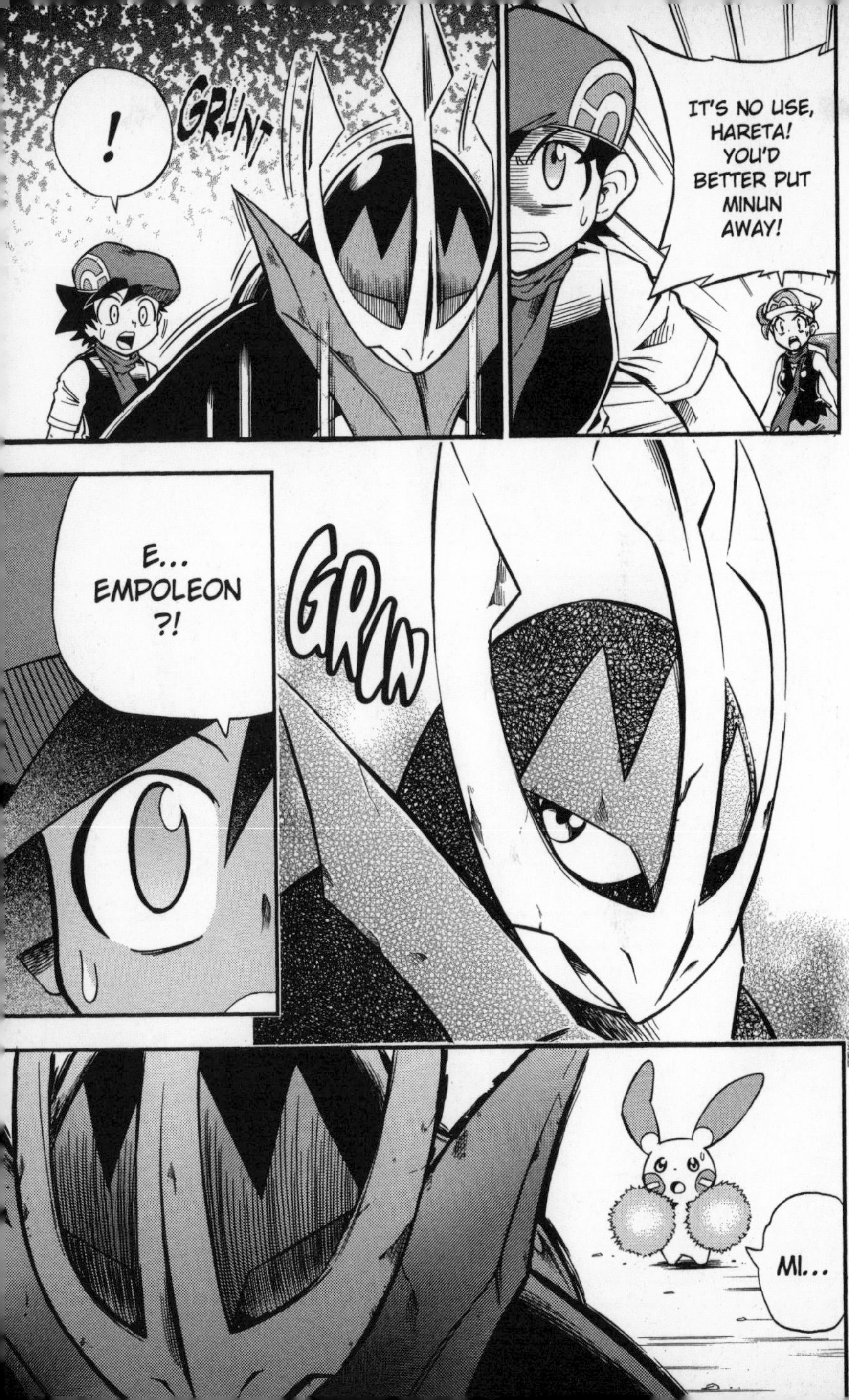
IT'S NO USE, HARETA! YOU'D BETTER PUT MINUN AWAY!
!
GRUNT
GRIN
E... EMPOLEON ?!
MI...

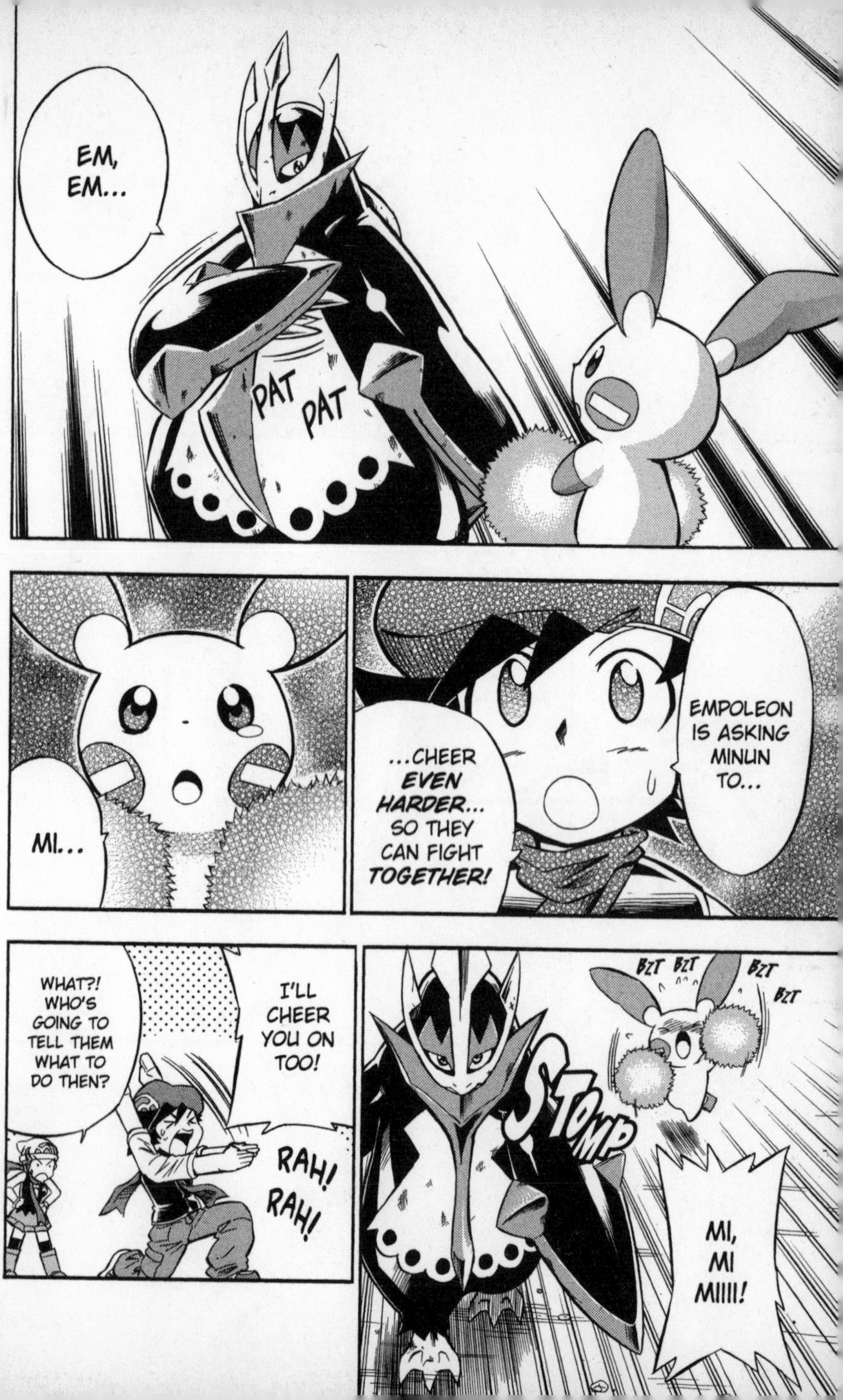
EM, EM...
PAT PAT
EMPOLEON IS ASKING MINUN TO...
...CHEER *EVEN HARDER*... SO THEY CAN FIGHT *TOGETHER!*
MI...
BZT BZT BZT BZT
STOMP
MI, MI MIIII!
I'LL CHEER YOU ON TOO!
WHAT?! WHO'S GOING TO TELL THEM WHAT TO DO THEN?
RAH! RAH!

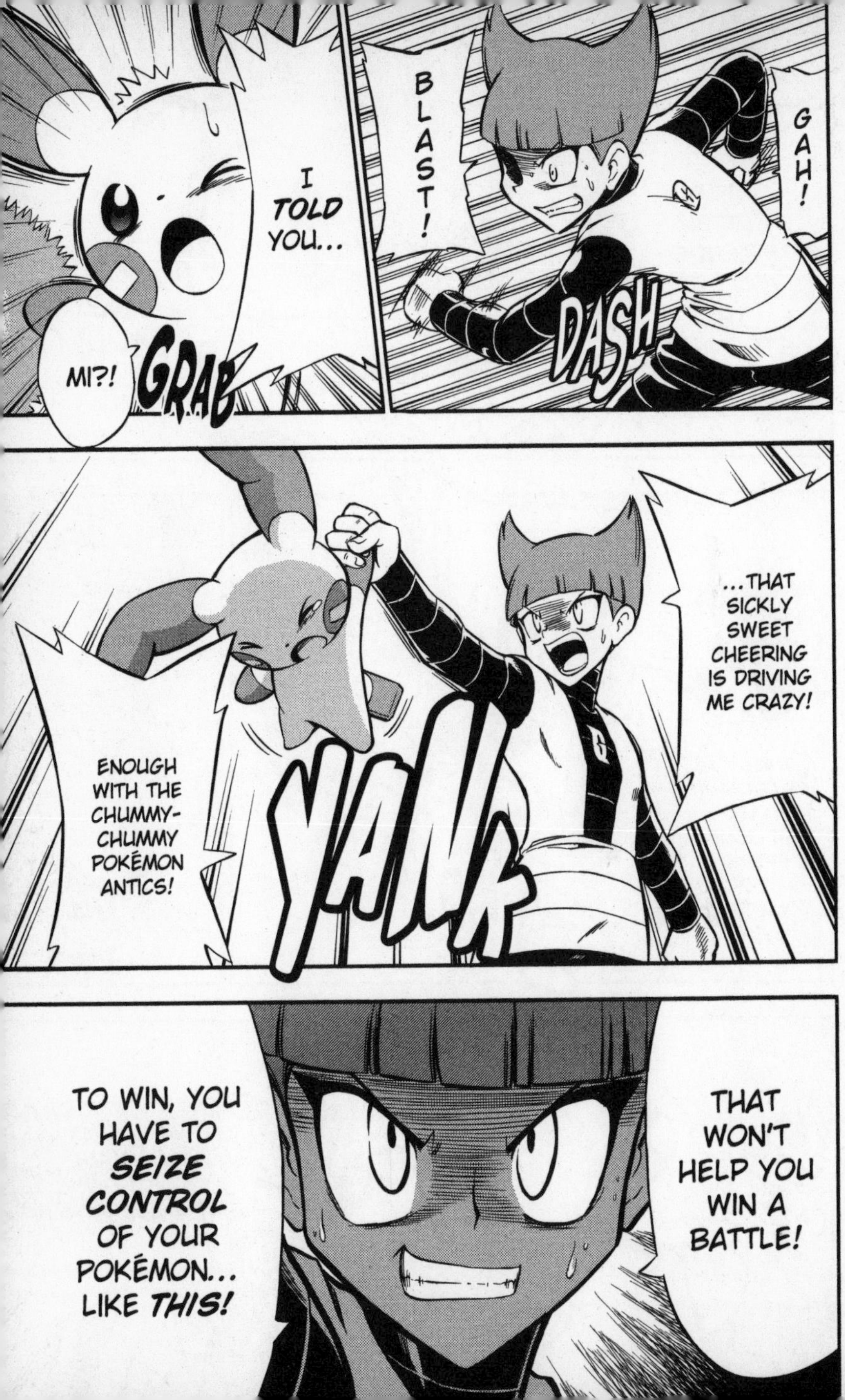
GAH!
BLAST!
DASH
I TOLD YOU...
MI?!
GRAB
...THAT SICKLY SWEET CHEERING IS DRIVING ME CRAZY!
ENOUGH WITH THE CHUMMY-CHUMMY POKÉMON ANTICS!
YANK
THAT WON'T HELP YOU WIN A BATTLE!
TO WIN, YOU HAVE TO *SEIZE CONTROL* OF YOUR POKÉMON... LIKE *THIS!*

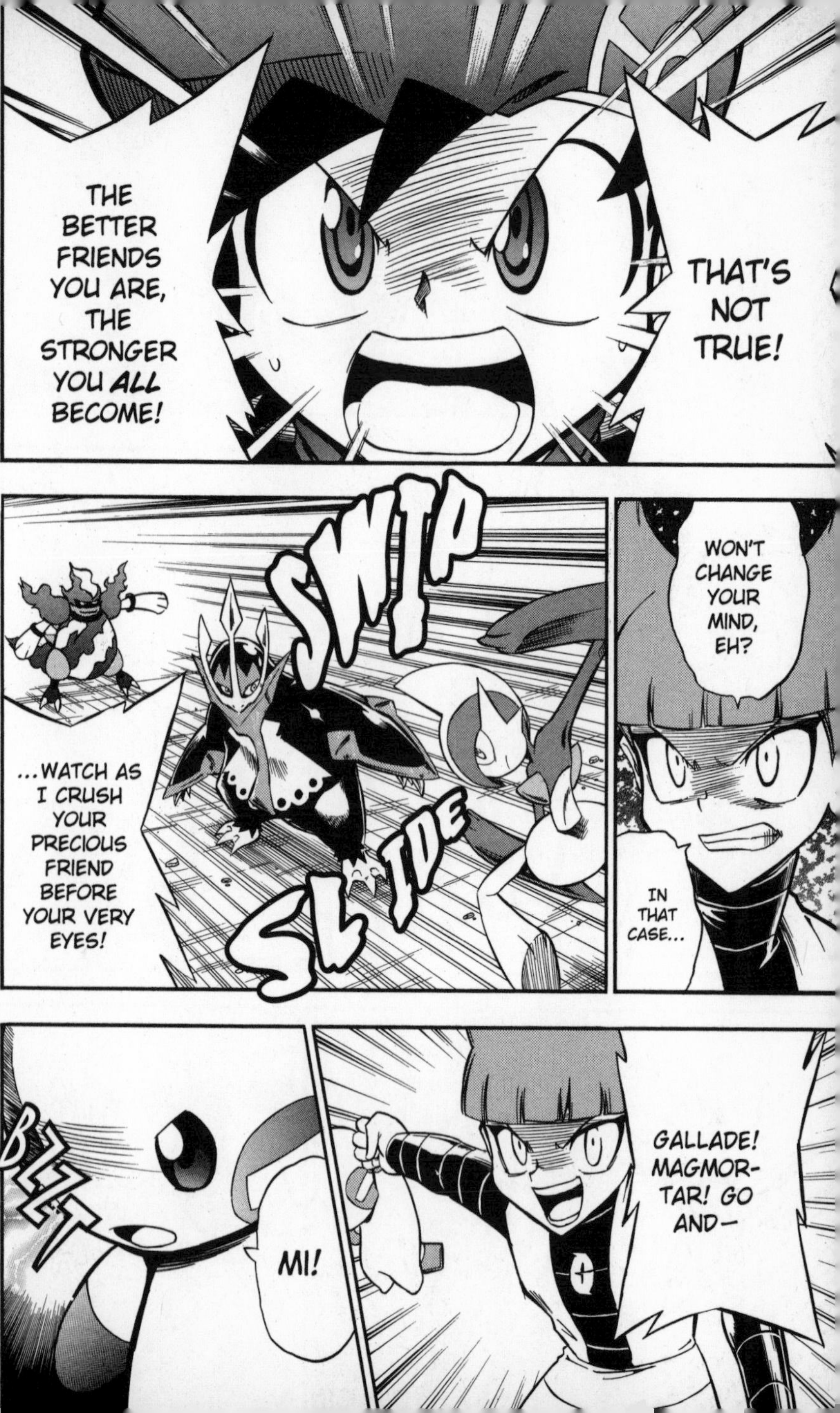
THAT'S NOT TRUE!
THE BETTER FRIENDS YOU ARE, THE STRONGER YOU ALL BECOME!
WON'T CHANGE YOUR MIND, EH?
IN THAT CASE...
SWIP
...WATCH AS I CRUSH YOUR PRECIOUS FRIEND BEFORE YOUR VERY EYES!
SLIDE
GALLADE! MAGMORTAR! GO AND—
MI!
BZZT

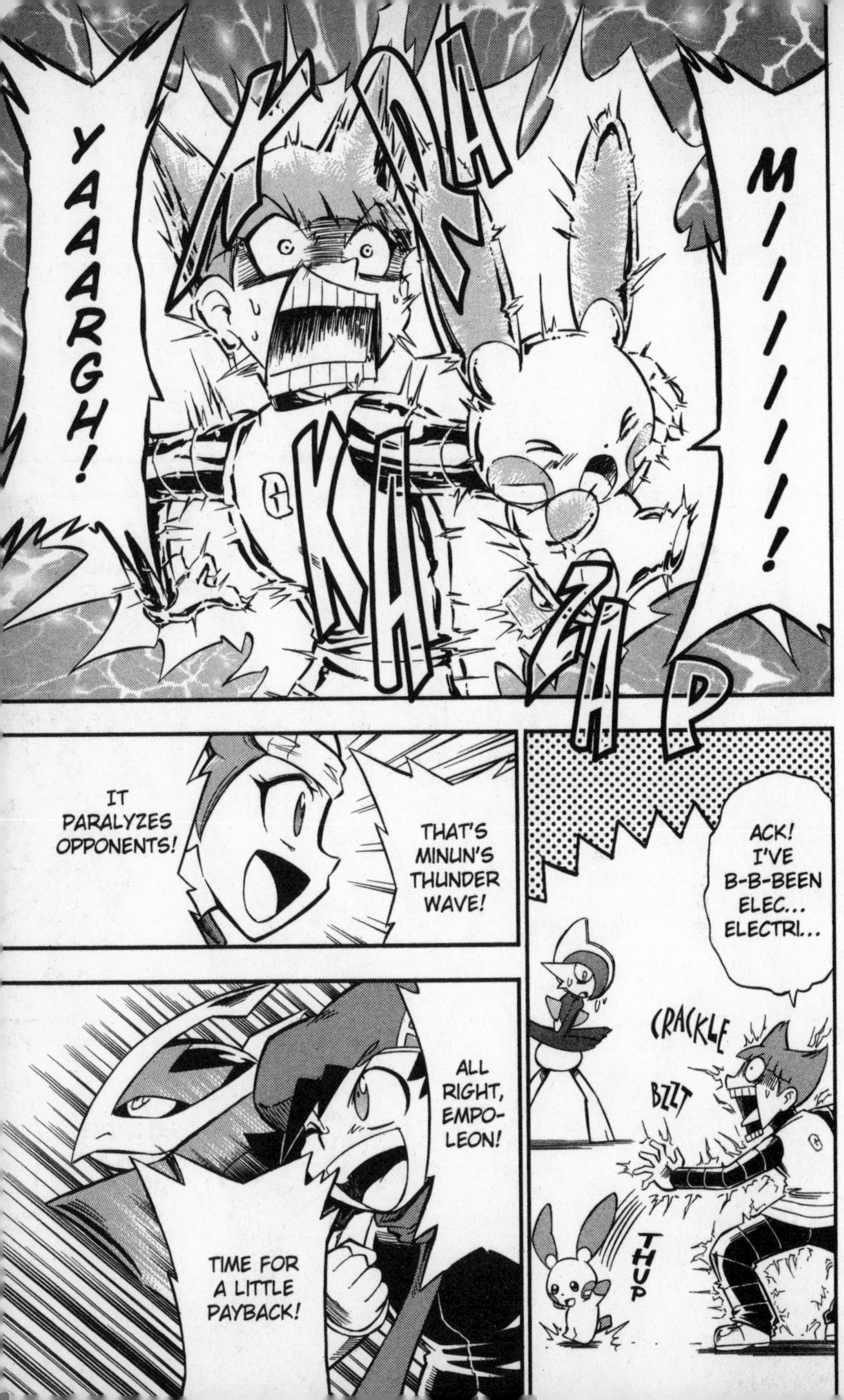
MI!!!!!!!
YAAAARGH!
KA
ZAAP
ACK! I'VE B-B-BEEN ELEC... ELECTRI...
CRACKLE
BZZT
THUP
THAT'S MINUN'S THUNDER WAVE!
IT PARALYZES OPPONENTS!
ALL RIGHT, EMPOLEON!
TIME FOR A LITTLE PAYBACK!

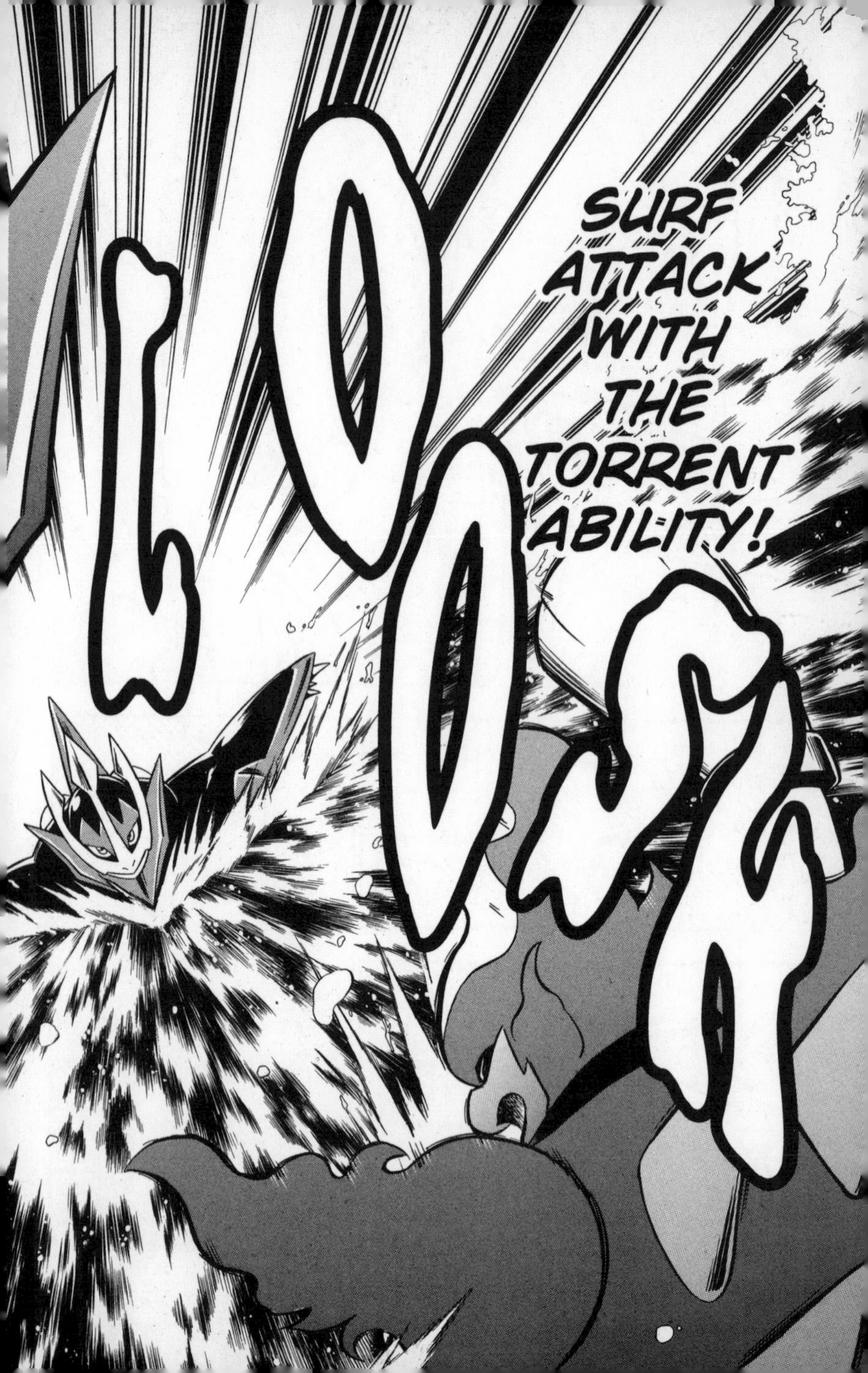
SURF ATTACK WITH THE TORRENT ABILITY!
LOOSH

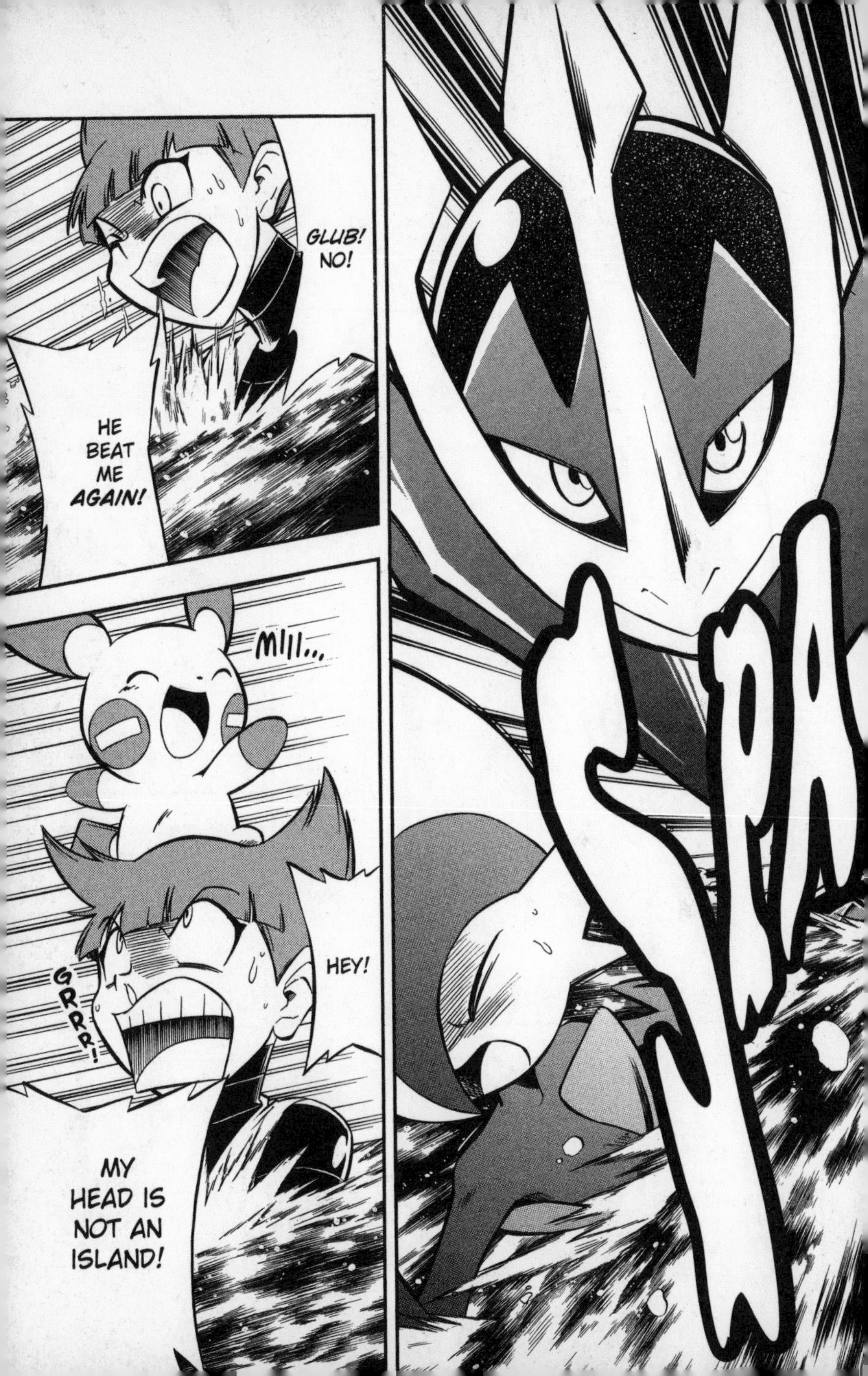
GLUB! NO!
HE BEAT ME AGAIN!
MIII...
HEY!
GRRR!
MY HEAD IS NOT AN ISLAND!

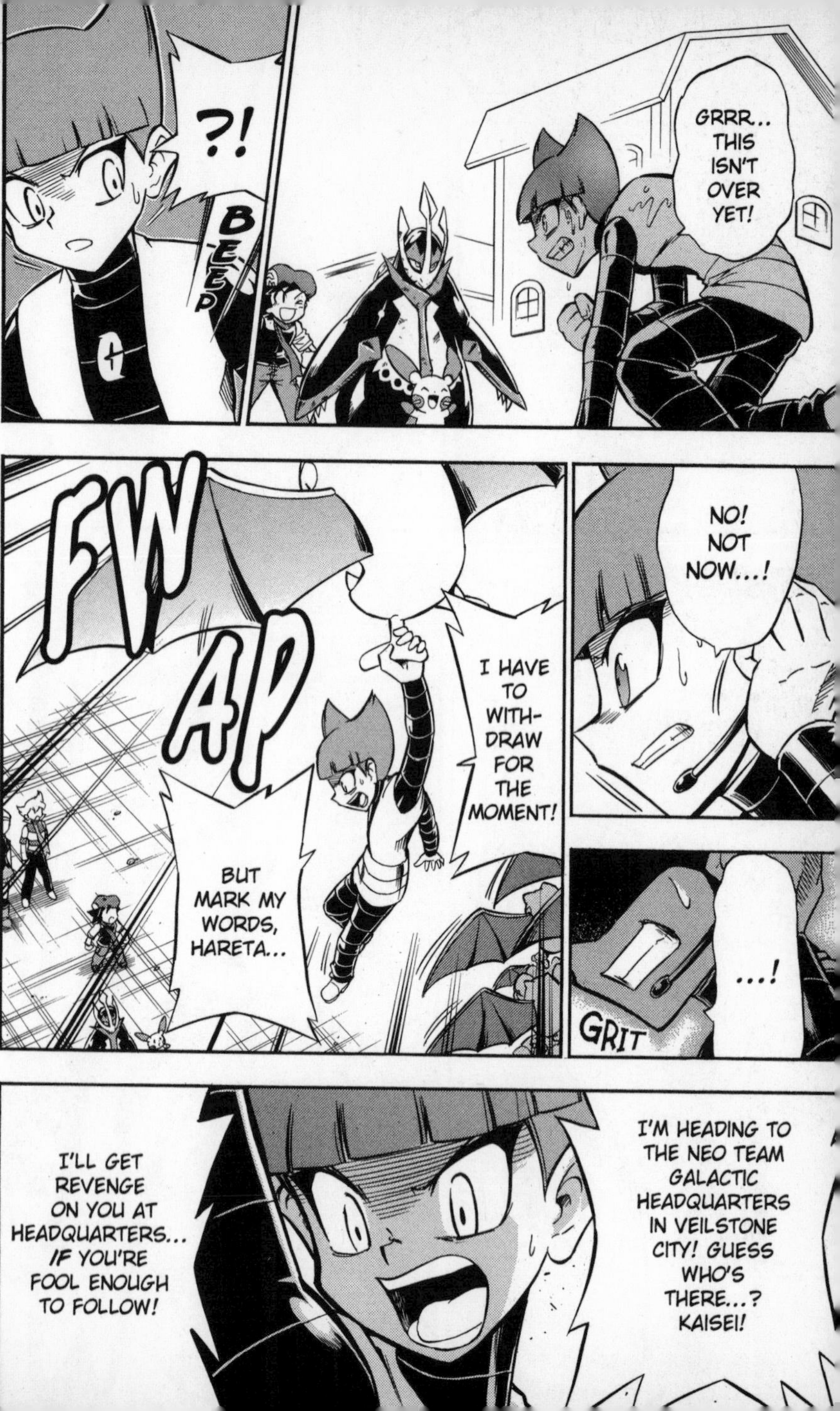
GRRR... THIS ISN'T OVER YET!
?!
BEEP
NO! NOT NOW...!
...!
GRIT
FWAP
I HAVE TO WITH-DRAW FOR THE MOMENT!
BUT MARK MY WORDS, HARETA...
I'M HEADING TO THE NEO TEAM GALACTIC HEADQUARTERS IN VEILSTONE CITY! GUESS WHO'S THERE...? KAISEI!
I'LL GET REVENGE ON YOU AT HEADQUARTERS... *IF* YOU'RE FOOL ENOUGH TO FOLLOW!

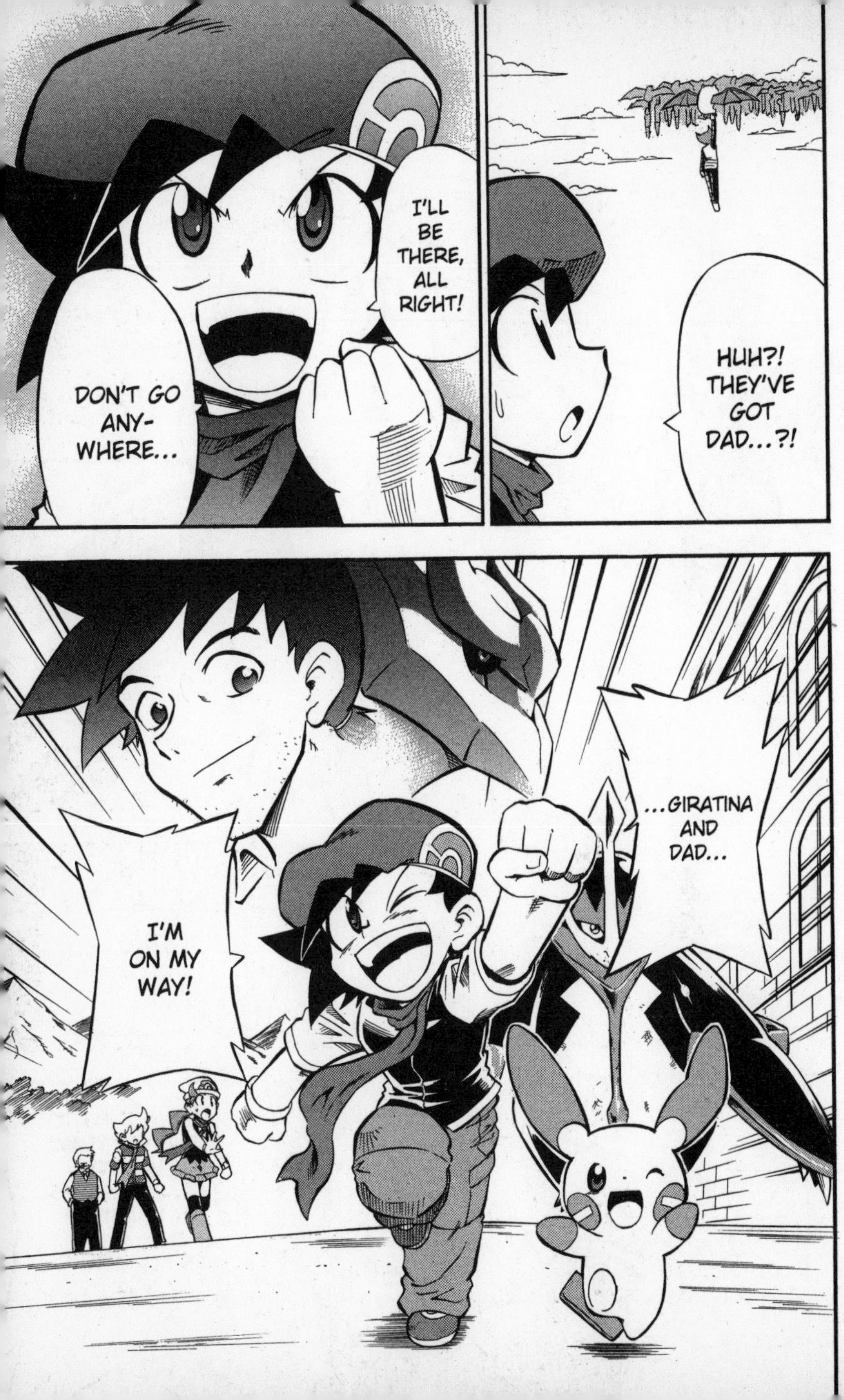
HUH?! THEY'VE GOT DAD...?!
I'LL BE THERE, ALL RIGHT!
DON'T GO ANY-WHERE...
...GIRATINA AND DAD...
I'M ON MY WAY!

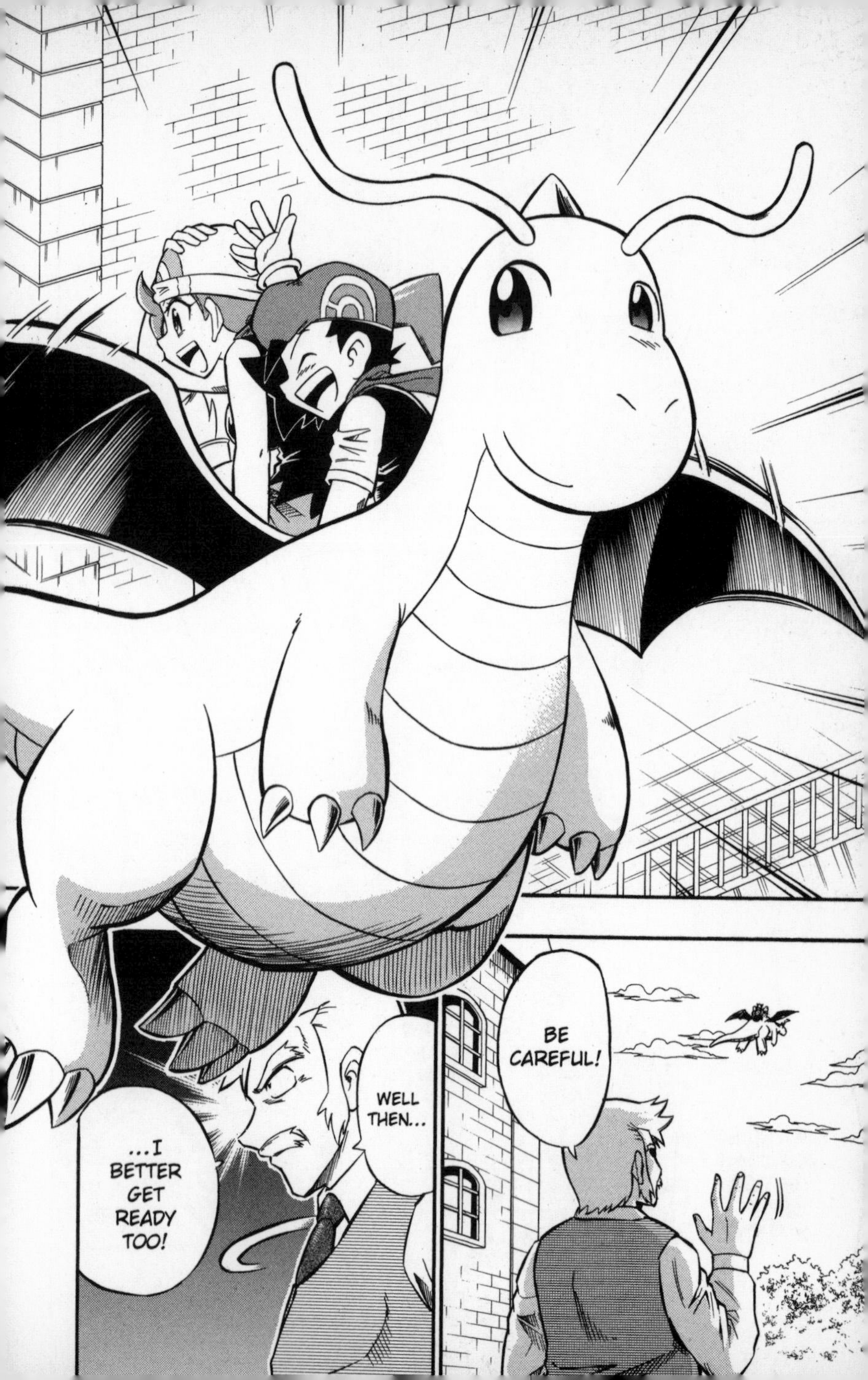
BE CAREFUL!
WELL THEN...
...I BETTER GET READY TOO!

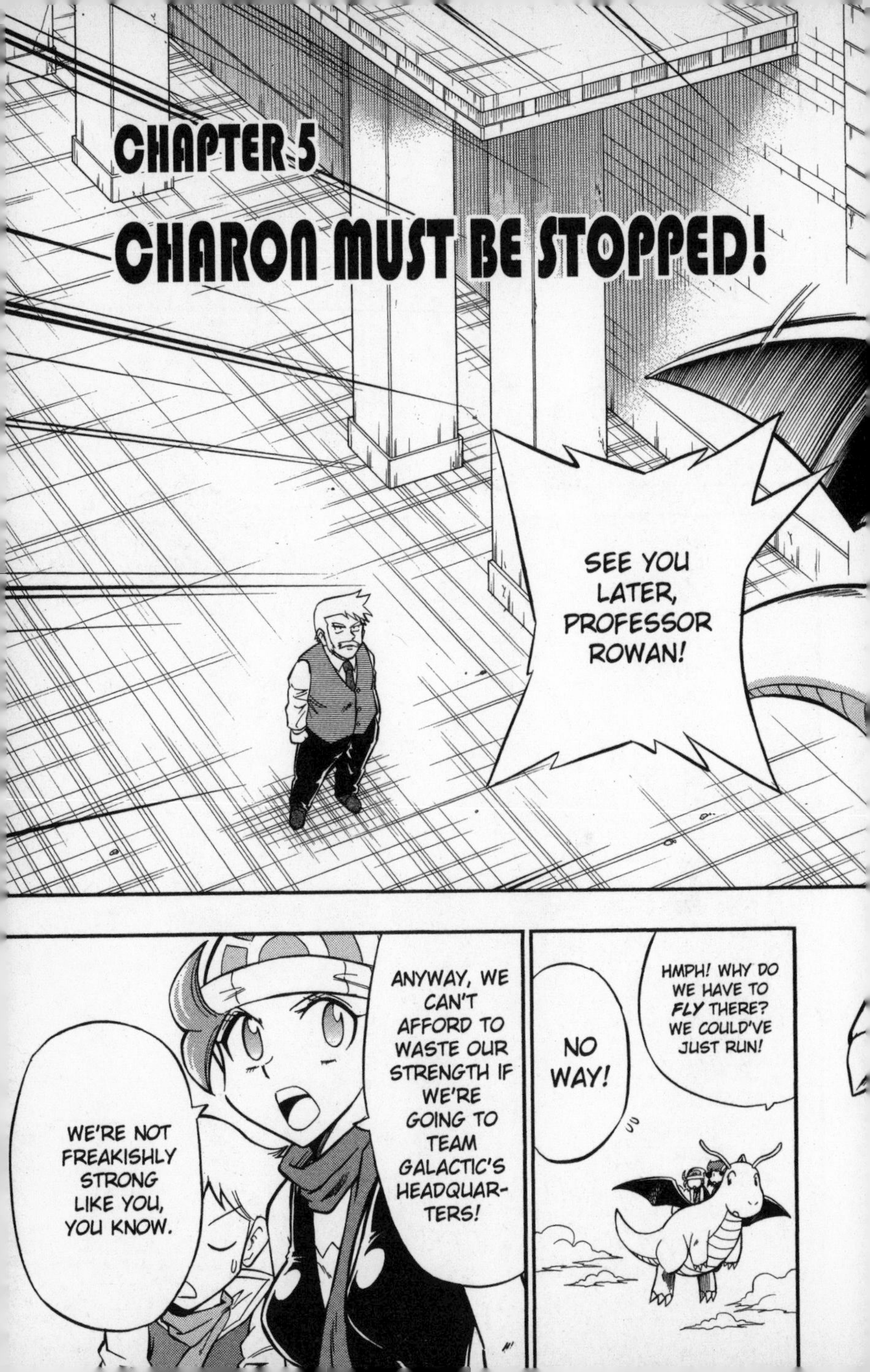
CHAPTER 5
CHARON MUST BE STOPPED!
SEE YOU LATER, PROFESSOR ROWAN!
HMPH! WHY DO WE HAVE TO *FLY* THERE? WE COULD'VE JUST RUN!
NO WAY!
ANYWAY, WE CAN'T AFFORD TO WASTE OUR STRENGTH IF WE'RE GOING TO TEAM GALACTIC'S HEADQUAR-TERS!
WE'RE NOT FREAKISHLY STRONG LIKE YOU, YOU KNOW.

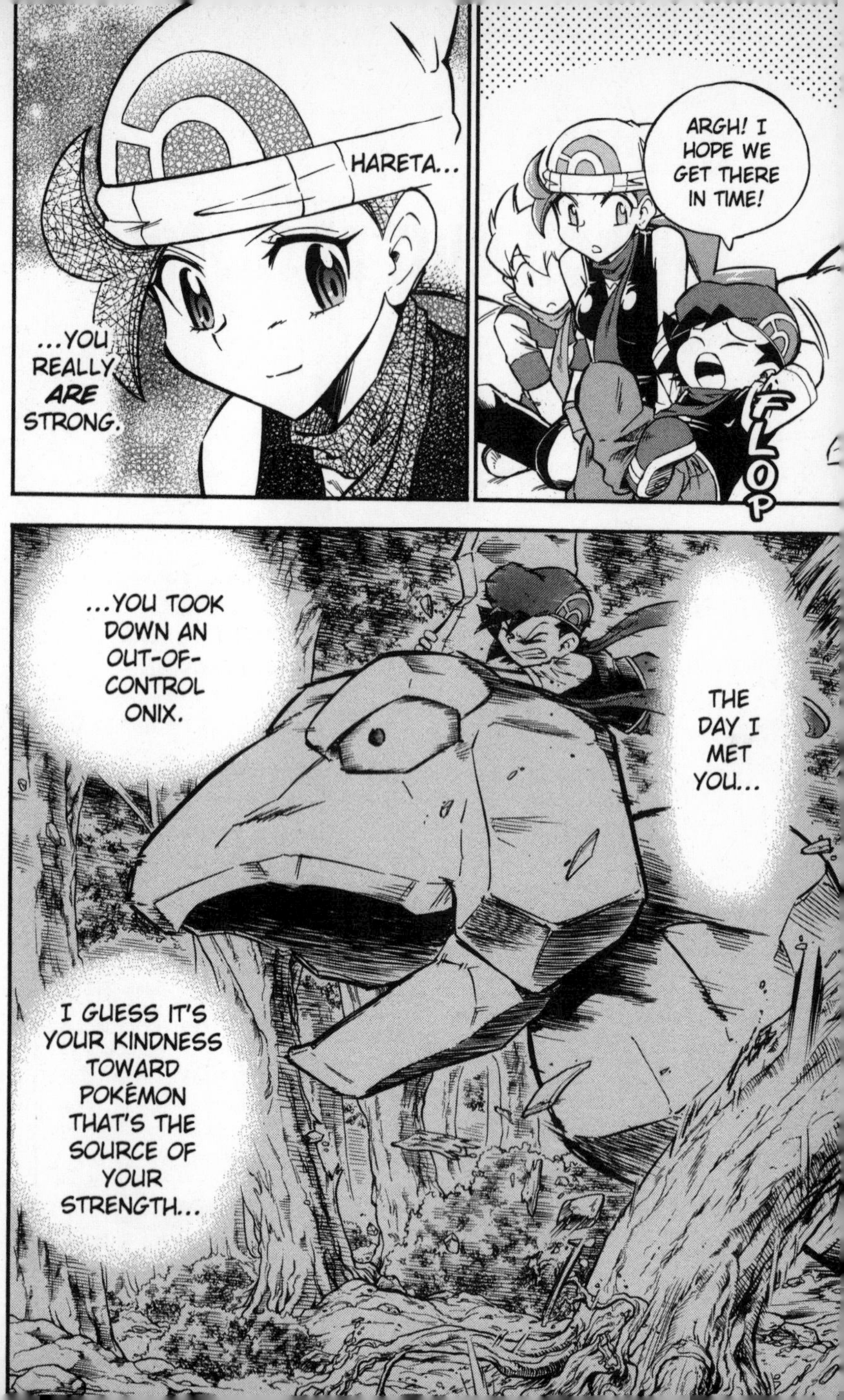
ARGH! I HOPE WE GET THERE IN TIME!
FLOP
HARETA...
...YOU REALLY ARE STRONG.
THE DAY I MET YOU...
...YOU TOOK DOWN AN OUT-OF-CONTROL ONIX.
I GUESS IT'S YOUR KINDNESS TOWARD POKÉMON THAT'S THE SOURCE OF YOUR STRENGTH...

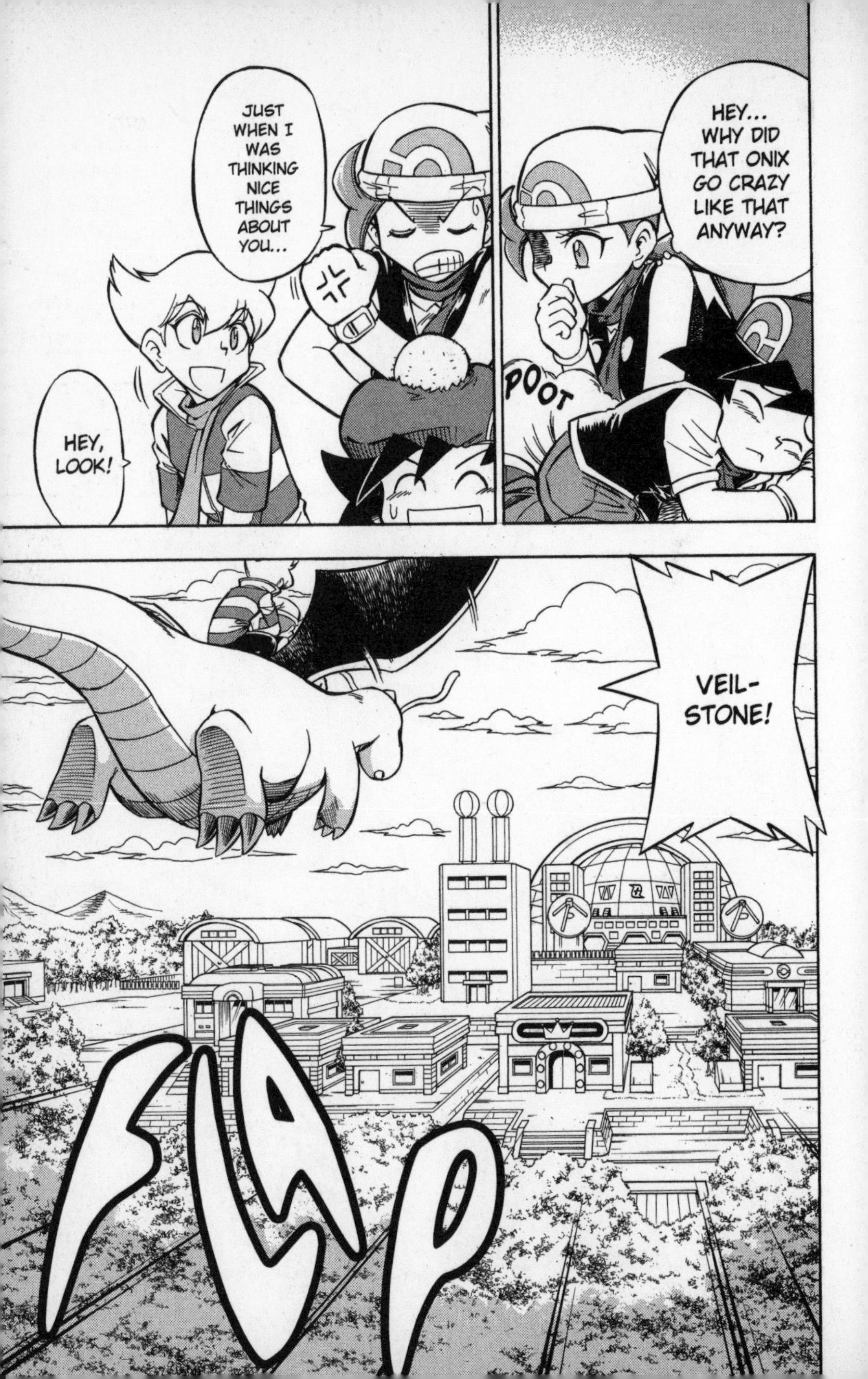
HEY... WHY DID THAT ONIX GO CRAZY LIKE THAT ANYWAY?
POOT
JUST WHEN I WAS THINKING NICE THINGS ABOUT YOU...
HEY, LOOK!
VEIL-STONE!
FLAP

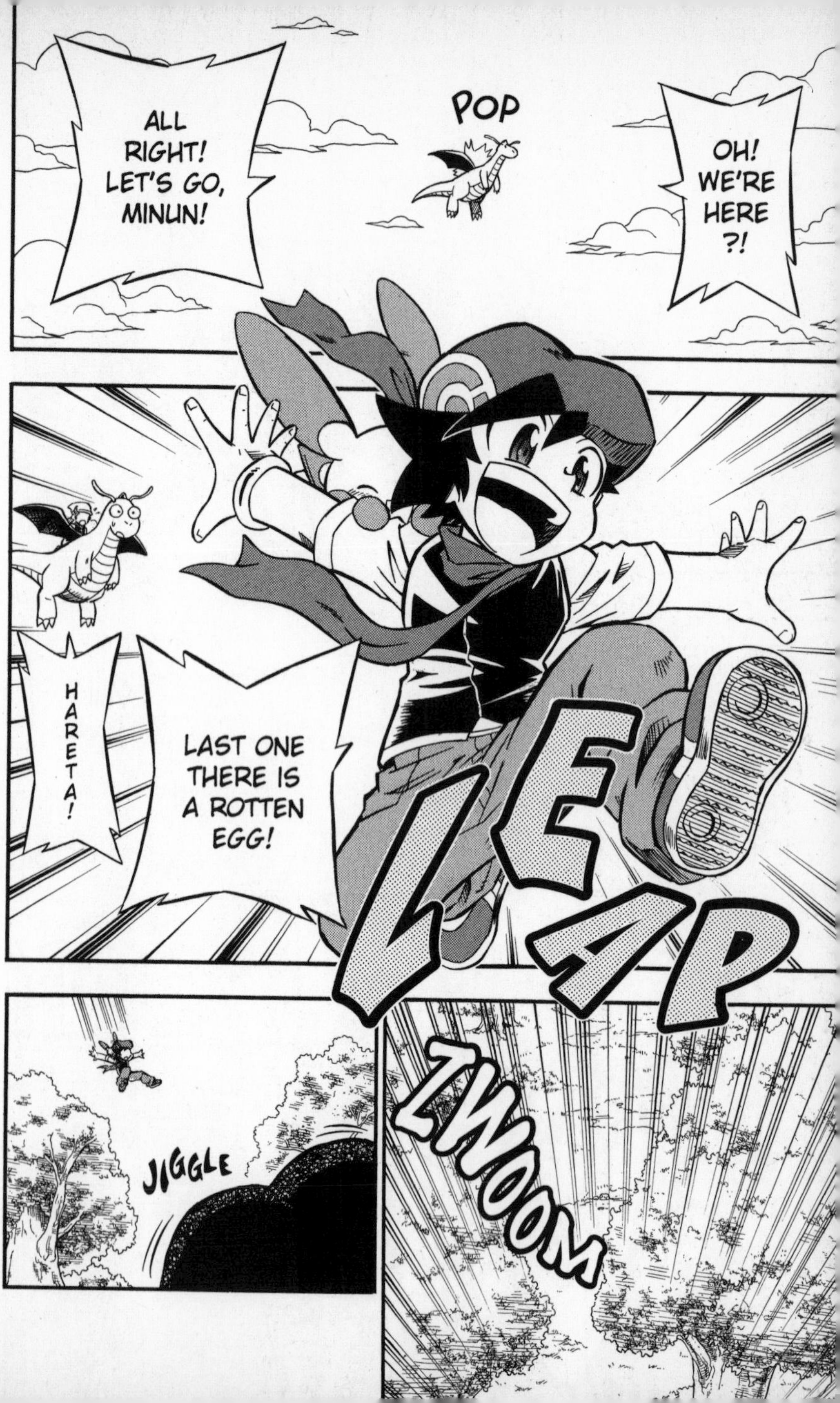
OH! WE'RE HERE ?!
POP
ALL RIGHT! LET'S GO, MINUN!
LEAP
LAST ONE THERE IS A ROTTEN EGG!
HARETA!
ZWOOM
JIGGLE

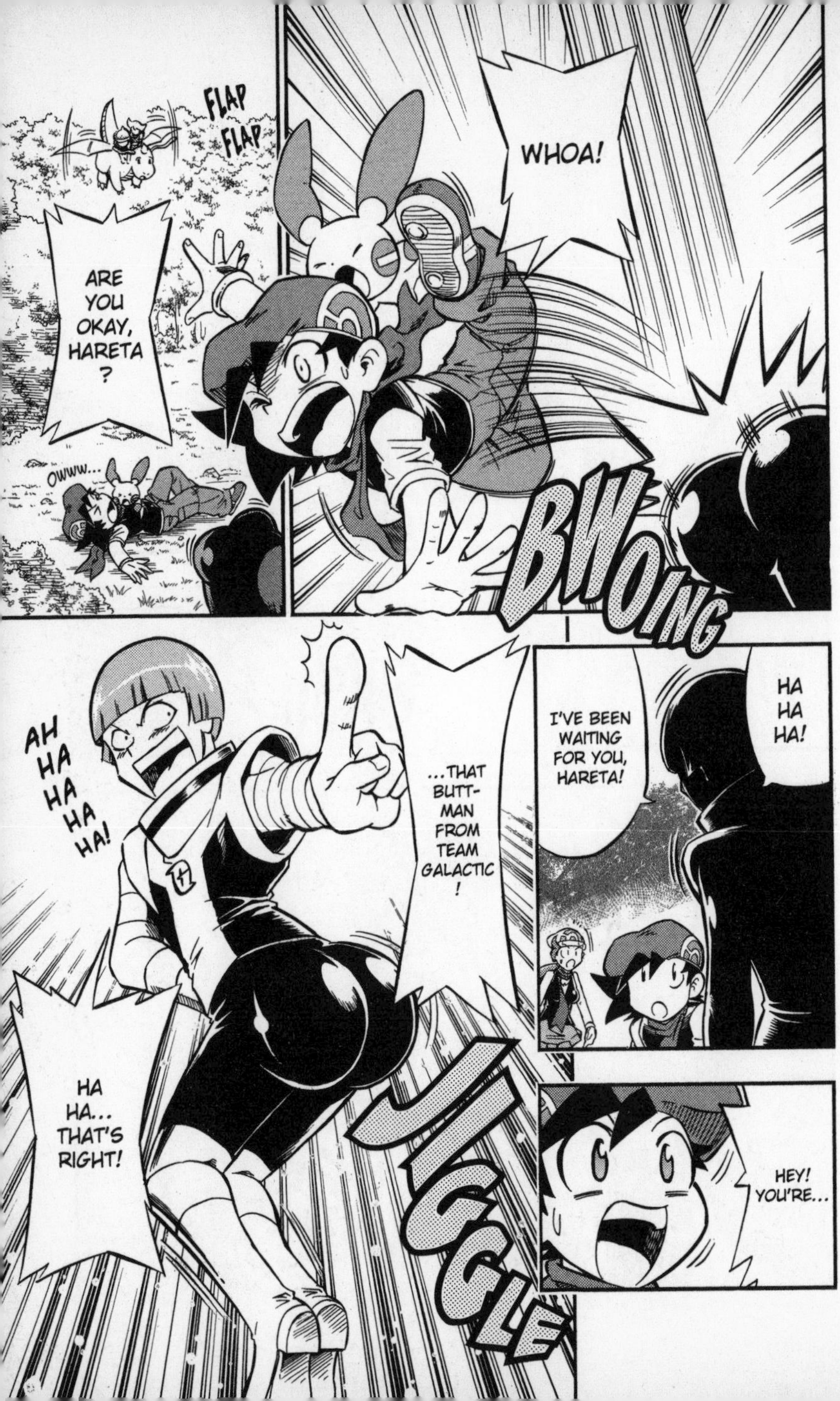
WHOA!
BWOING
FLAP FLAP
ARE YOU OKAY, HARETA?
OWWW...
HA HA HA!
I'VE BEEN WAITING FOR YOU, HARETA!
HEY! YOU'RE...
...THAT BUTT-MAN FROM TEAM GALACTIC!
AH HA HA HA HA!
HA HA... THAT'S RIGHT!
JIGGLE

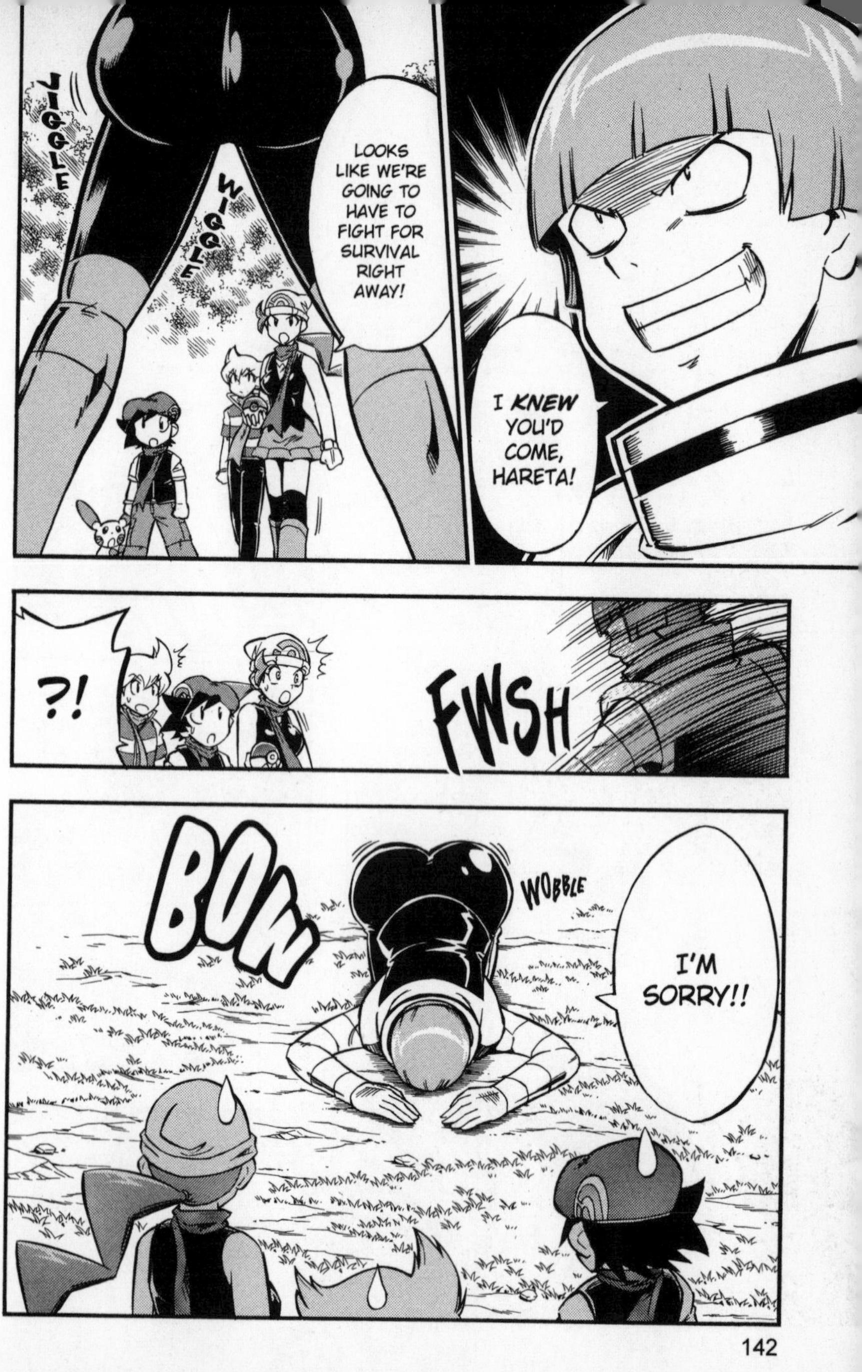
I KNEW YOU'D COME, HARETA!
JIGGLE
WIGGLE
LOOKS LIKE WE'RE GOING TO HAVE TO FIGHT FOR SURVIVAL RIGHT AWAY!
FWSH
?!
I'M SORRY!!
WOBBLE
BOW

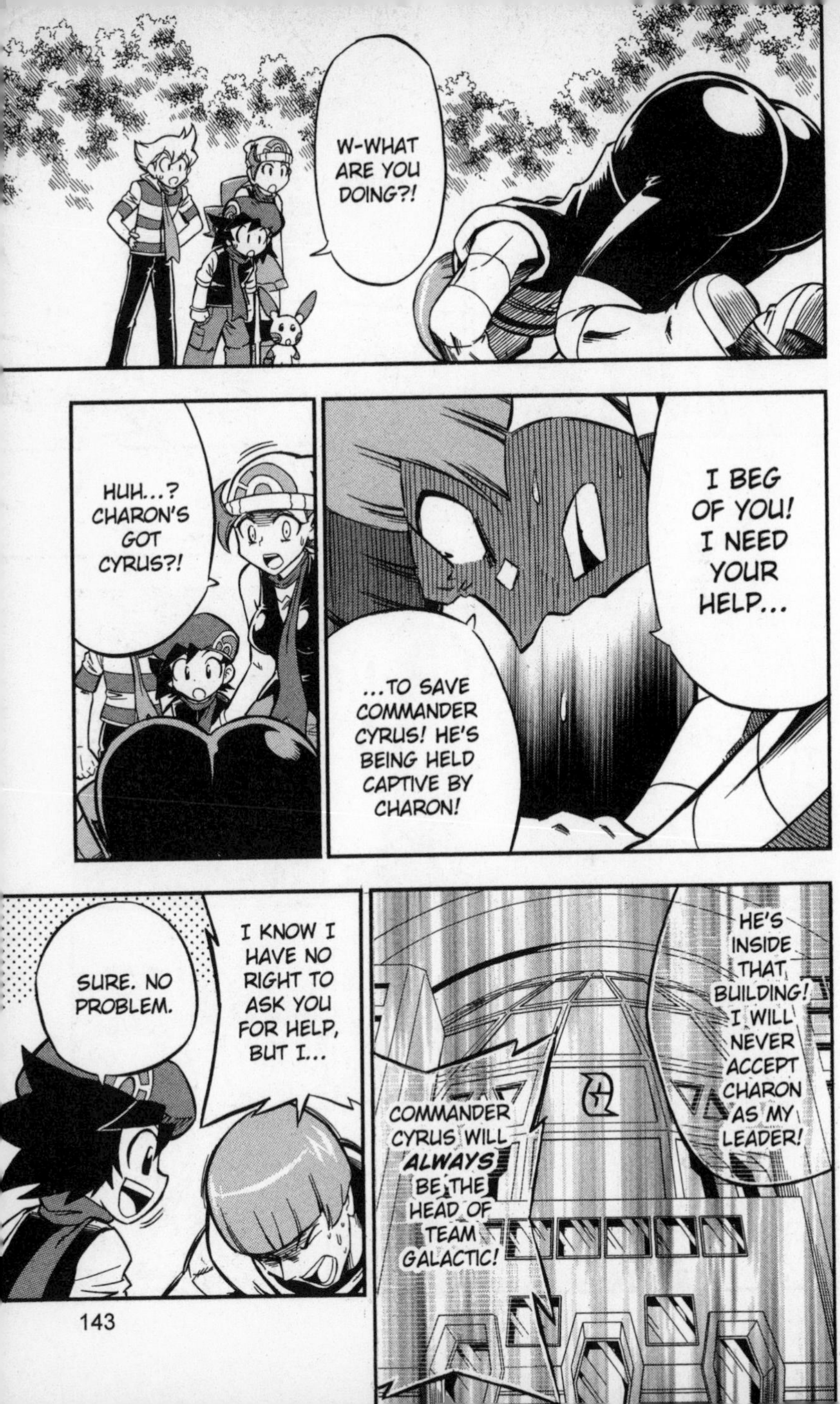
W-WHAT ARE YOU DOING?!
I BEG OF YOU! I NEED YOUR HELP...
...TO SAVE COMMANDER CYRUS! HE'S BEING HELD CAPTIVE BY CHARON!
HUH...? CHARON'S GOT CYRUS?!
HE'S INSIDE THAT BUILDING! I WILL NEVER ACCEPT CHARON AS MY LEADER!
COMMANDER CYRUS WILL ***ALWAYS*** BE THE HEAD OF TEAM GALACTIC!
I KNOW I HAVE NO RIGHT TO ASK YOU FOR HELP, BUT I...
SURE. NO PROBLEM.

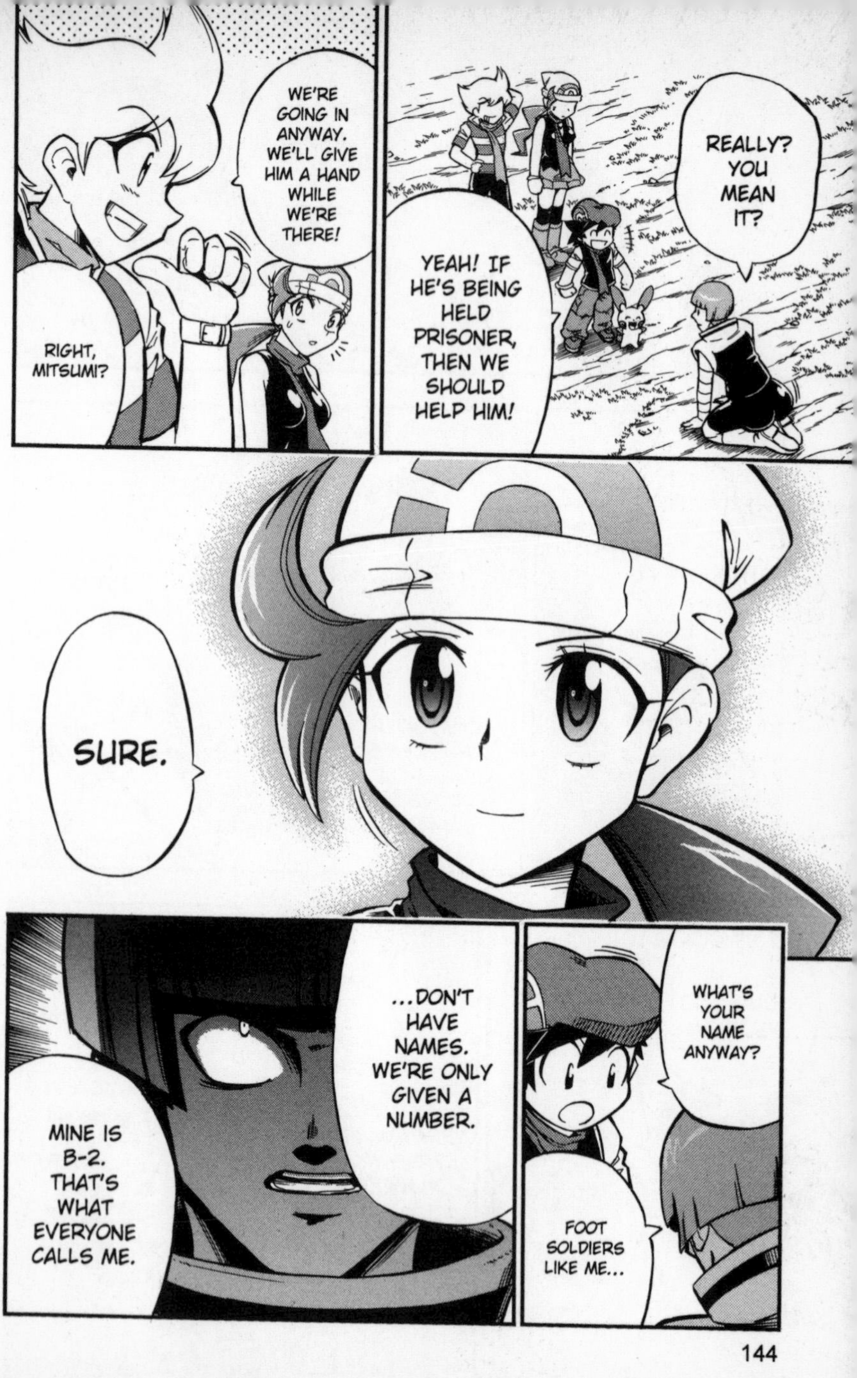
REALLY? YOU MEAN IT?
YEAH! IF HE'S BEING HELD PRISONER, THEN WE SHOULD HELP HIM!
WE'RE GOING IN ANYWAY. WE'LL GIVE HIM A HAND WHILE WE'RE THERE!
RIGHT, MITSUMI?
SURE.
WHAT'S YOUR NAME ANYWAY?
FOOT SOLDIERS LIKE ME...
...DON'T HAVE NAMES. WE'RE ONLY GIVEN A NUMBER.
MINE IS B-2. THAT'S WHAT EVERYONE CALLS ME.

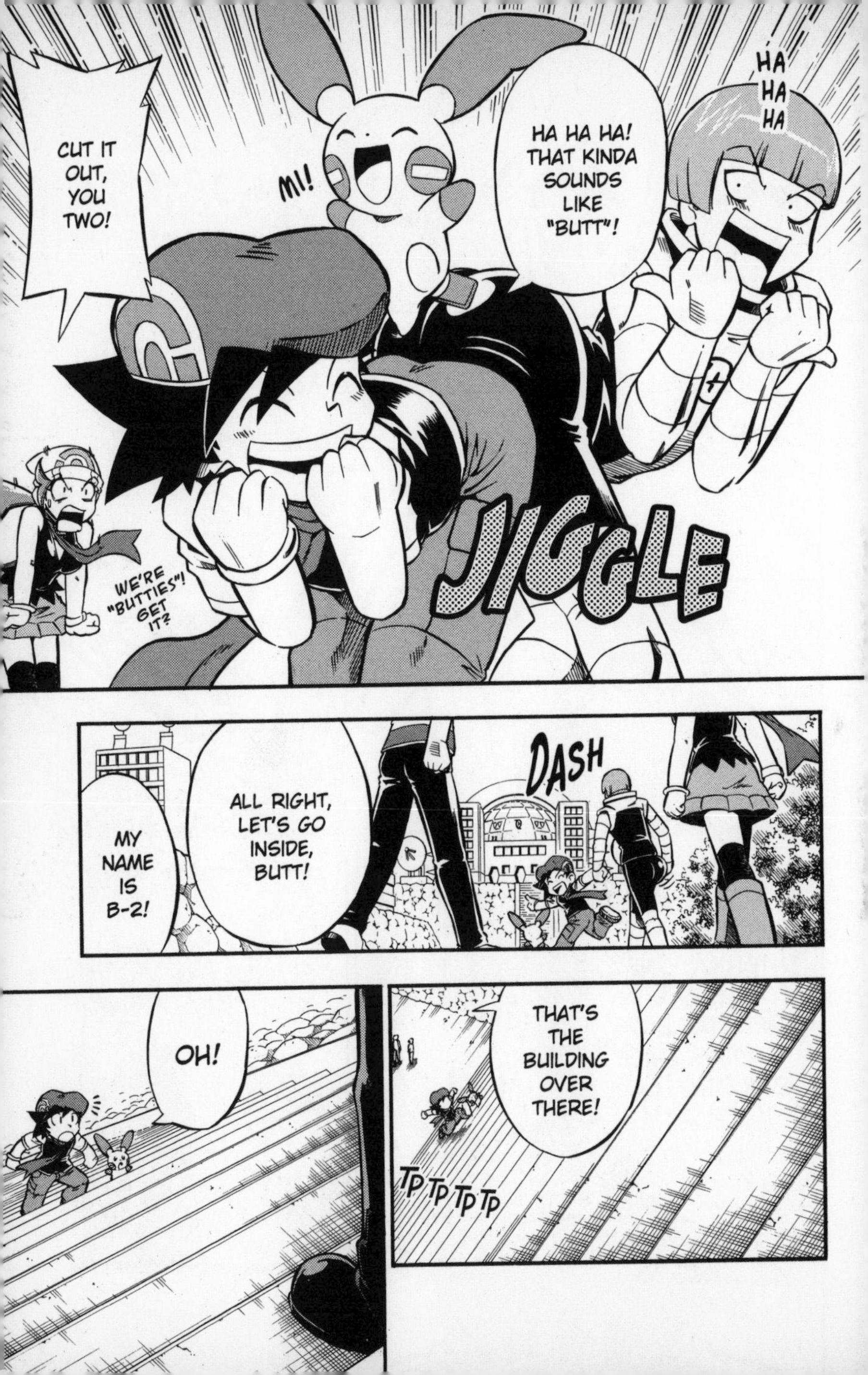
HA HA HA
HA HA HA! THAT KINDA SOUNDS LIKE "BUTT"!
MI!
CUT IT OUT, YOU TWO!
JIGGLE
WE'RE "BUTTIES"! GET IT?
DASH
ALL RIGHT, LET'S GO INSIDE, BUTT!
MY NAME IS B-2!
THAT'S THE BUILDING OVER THERE!
TP TP TP TP
OH!

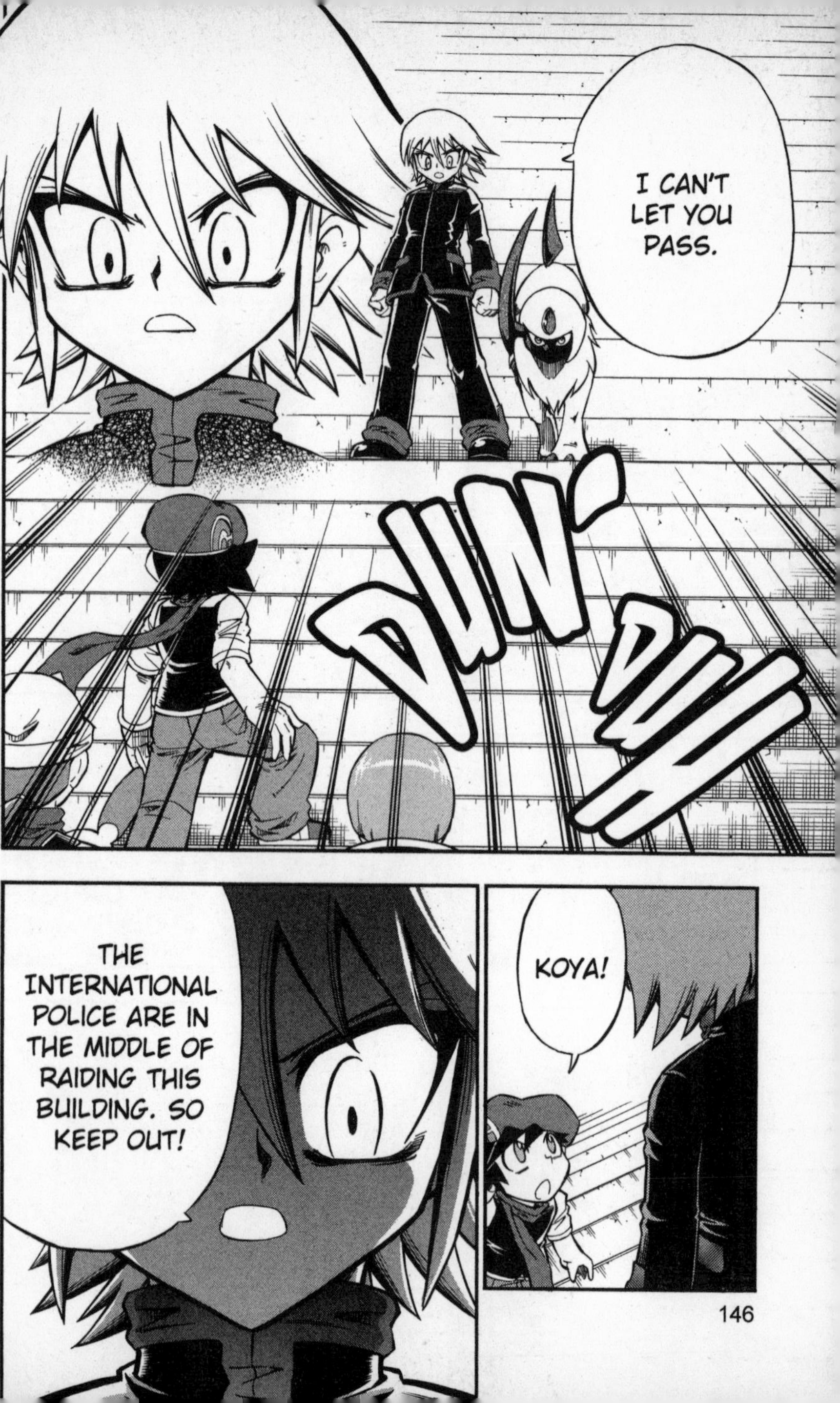
I CAN'T LET YOU PASS.
DUN DUH
KOYA!
THE INTERNATIONAL POLICE ARE IN THE MIDDLE OF RAIDING THIS BUILDING. SO KEEP OUT!

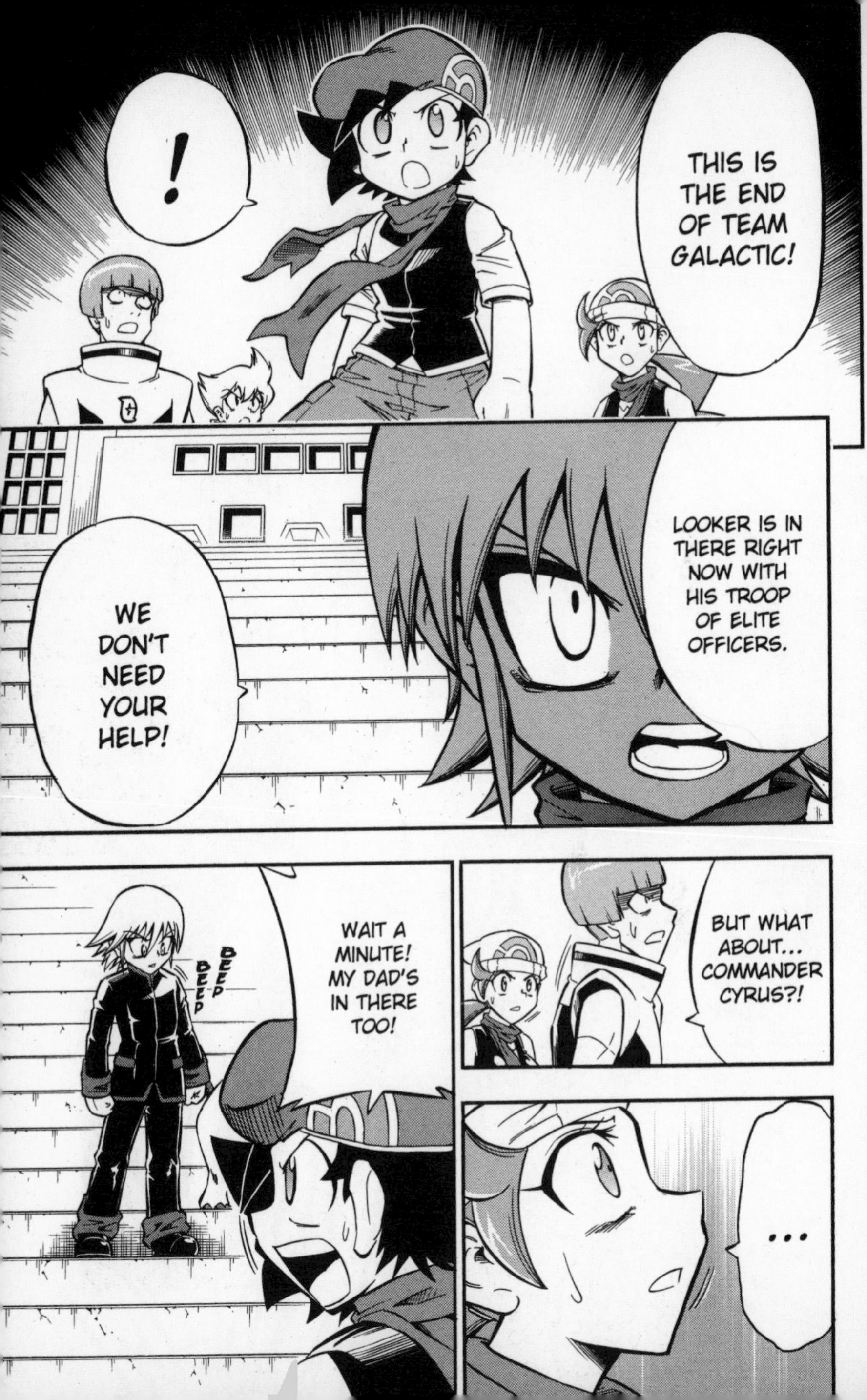
THIS IS THE END OF TEAM GALACTIC!
!
LOOKER IS IN THERE RIGHT NOW WITH HIS TROOP OF ELITE OFFICERS.
WE DON'T NEED YOUR HELP!
BUT WHAT ABOUT... COMMANDER CYRUS?!
...
WAIT A MINUTE! MY DAD'S IN THERE TOO!
BEEP BEEP

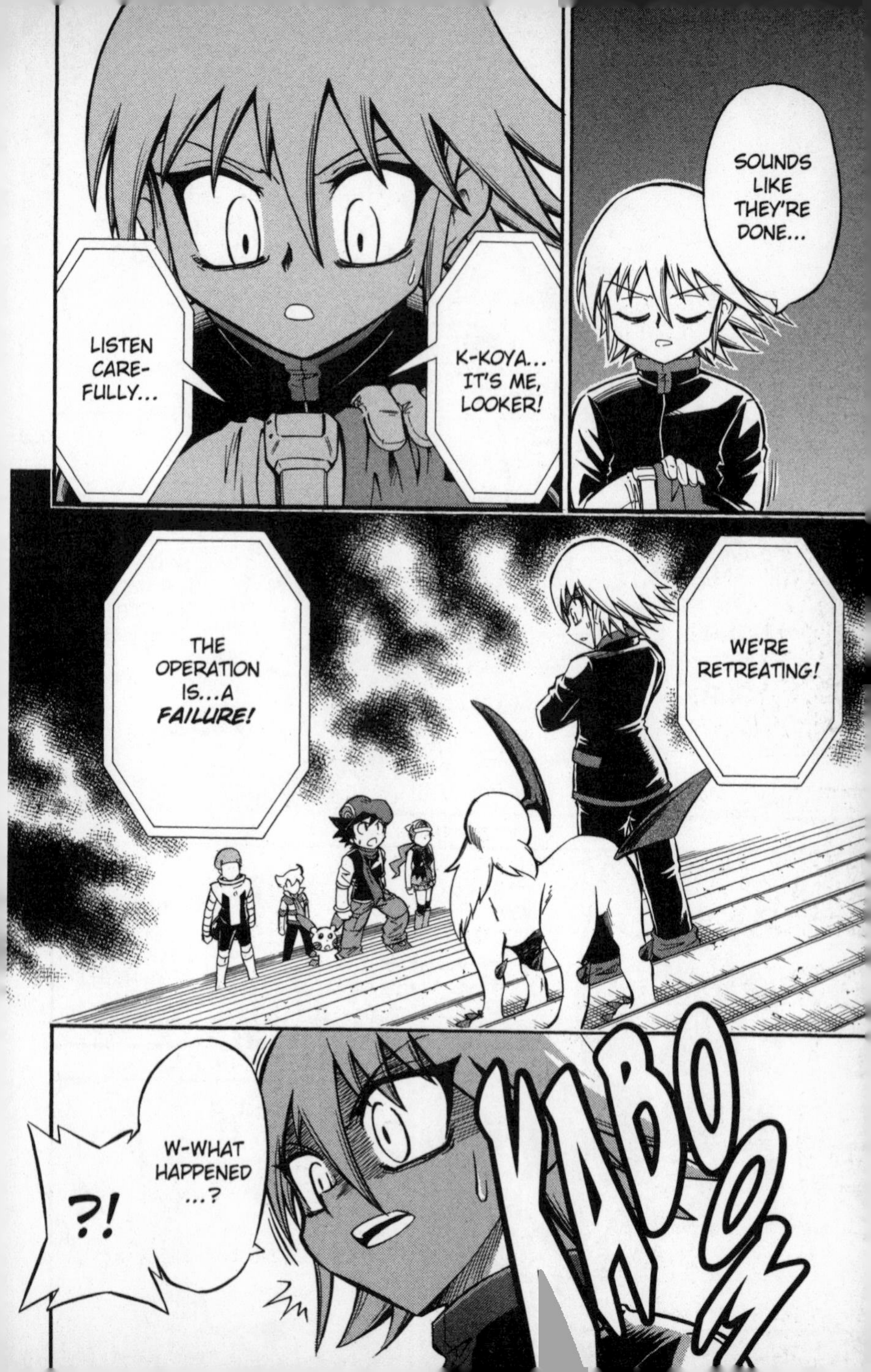
SOUNDS LIKE THEY'RE DONE...
K-KOYA... IT'S ME, LOOKER!
LISTEN CARE-FULLY...
WE'RE RETREATING!
THE OPERATION IS...A *FAILURE!*
KABOOM
W-WHAT HAPPENED ...?
?!

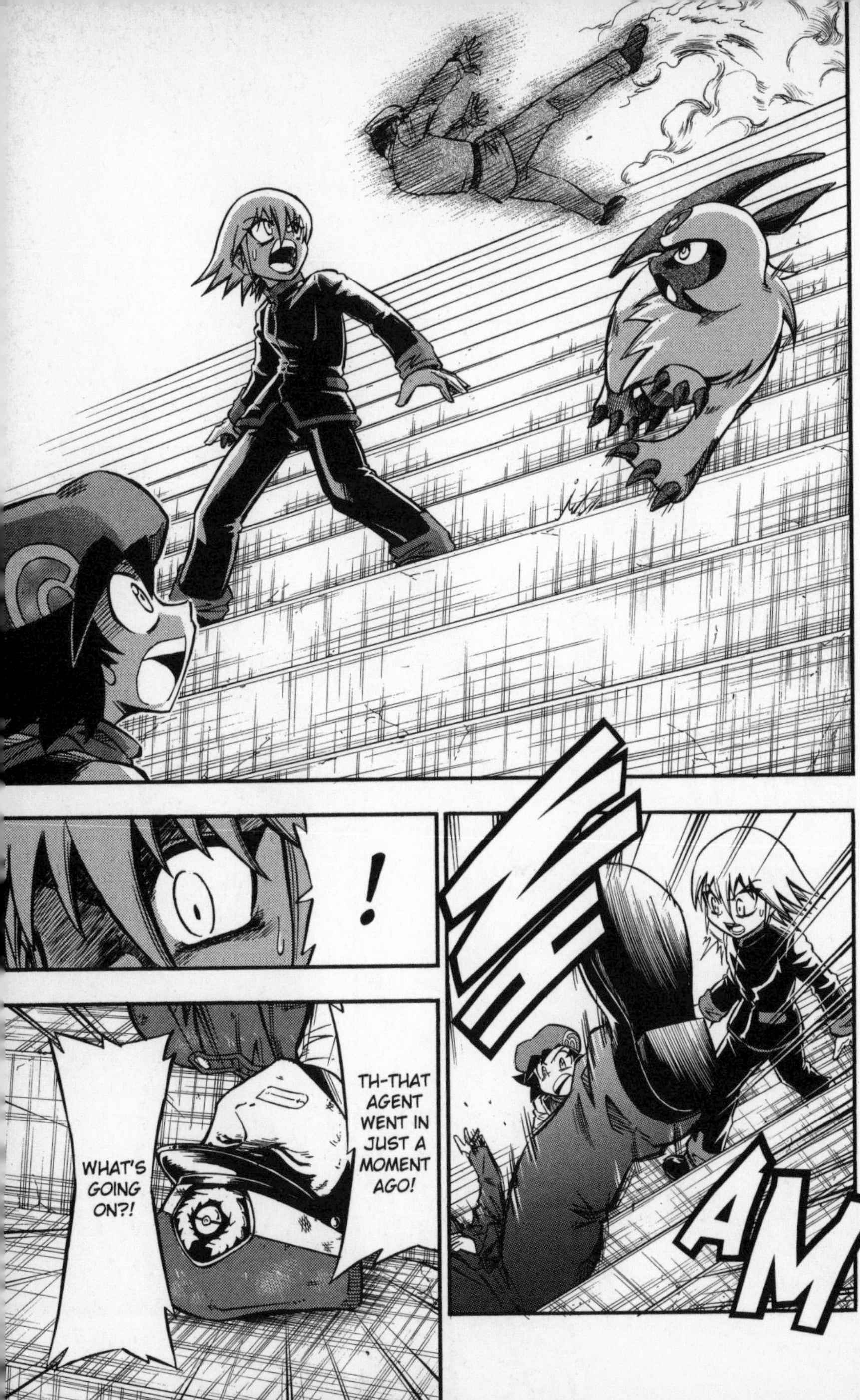
WHAM
!
TH-THAT AGENT WENT IN JUST A MOMENT AGO!
WHAT'S GOING ON?!

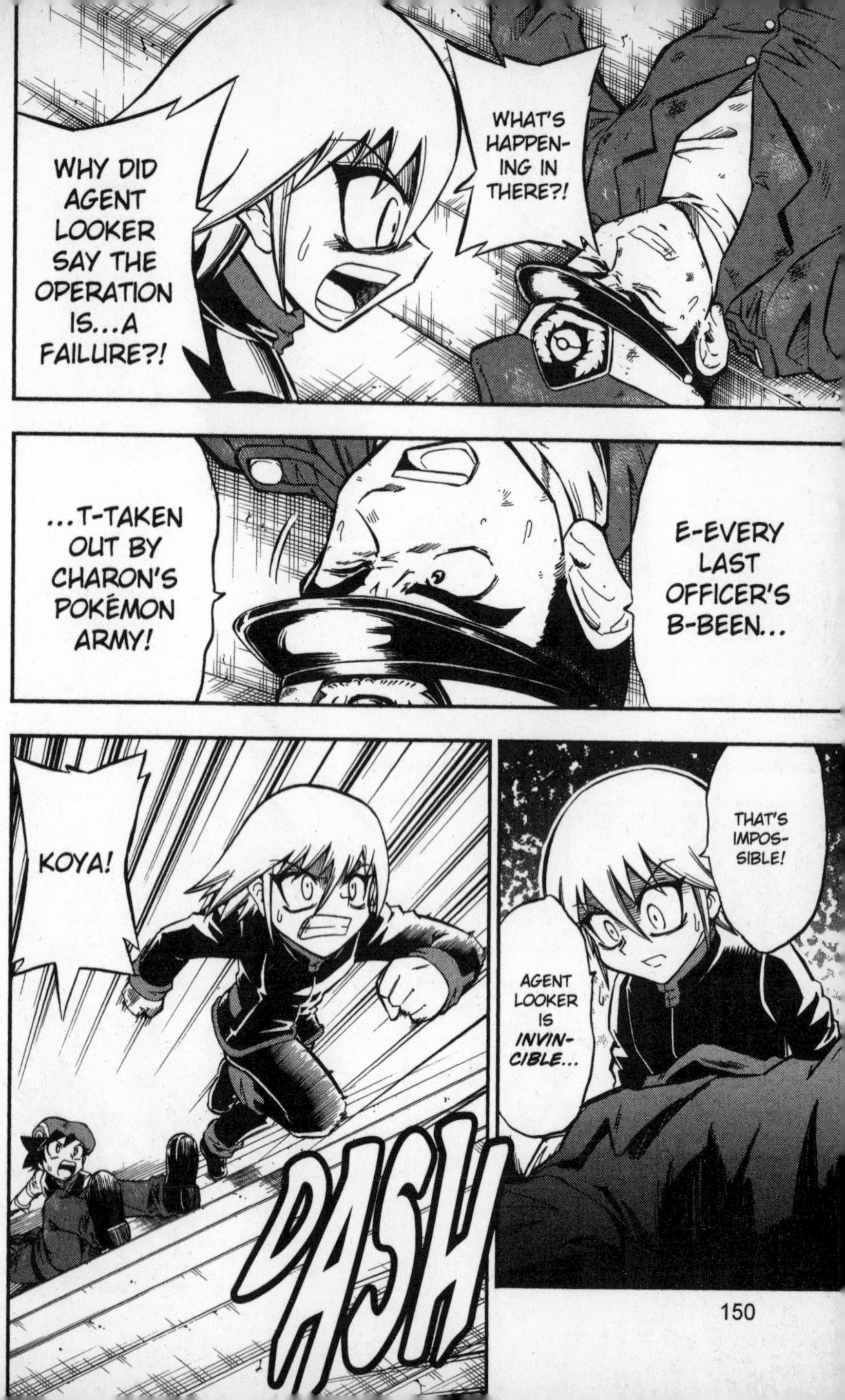
WHAT'S HAPPENING IN THERE?!
WHY DID AGENT LOOKER SAY THE OPERATION IS...A FAILURE?!
E-EVERY LAST OFFICER'S B-BEEN...
...T-TAKEN OUT BY CHARON'S POKÉMON ARMY!
THAT'S IMPOSSIBLE!
AGENT LOOKER IS *INVINCIBLE*...
KOYA!
DASH

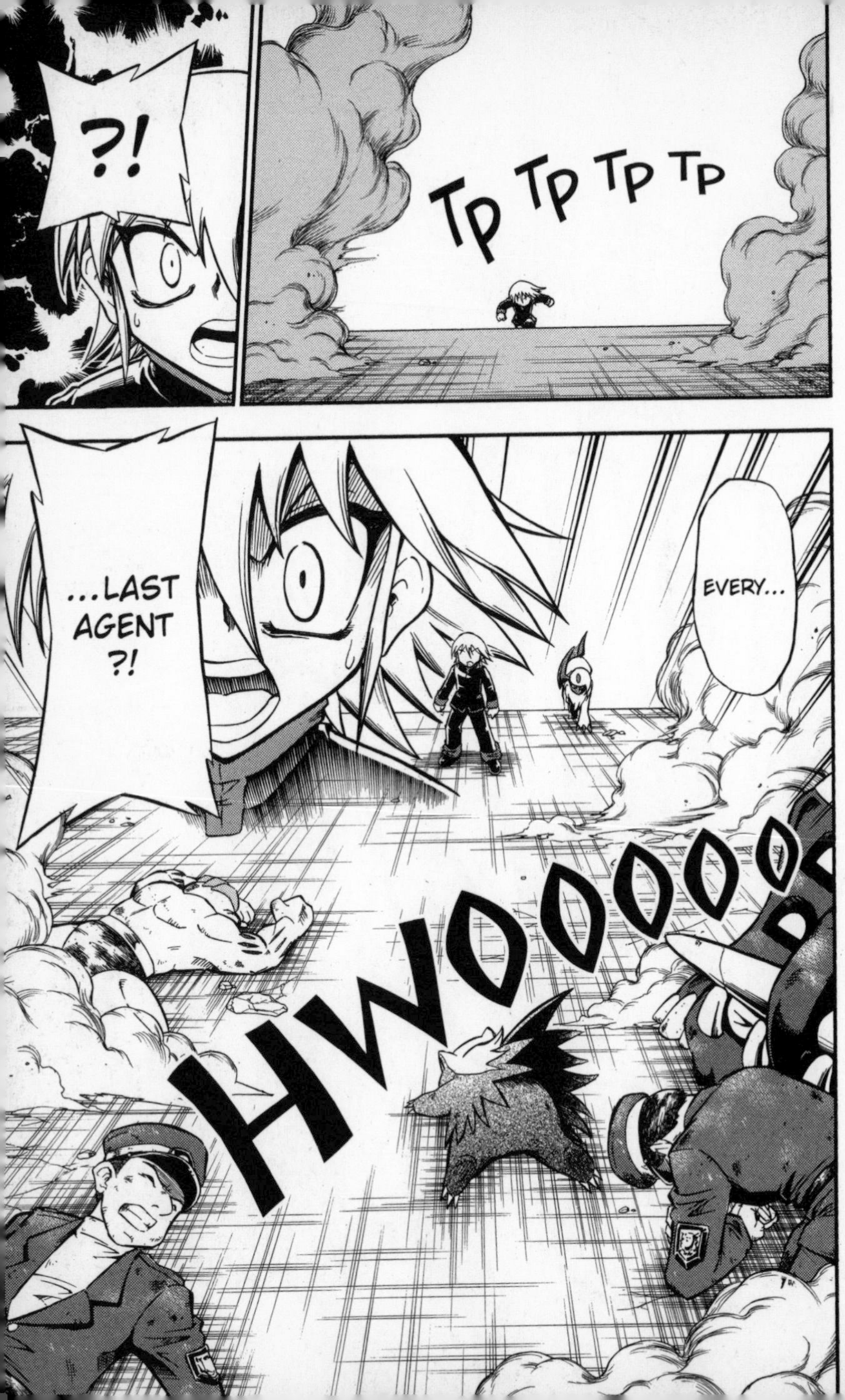
TP TP TP TP
?!
EVERY...
...LAST AGENT ?!
HWOOOOOO

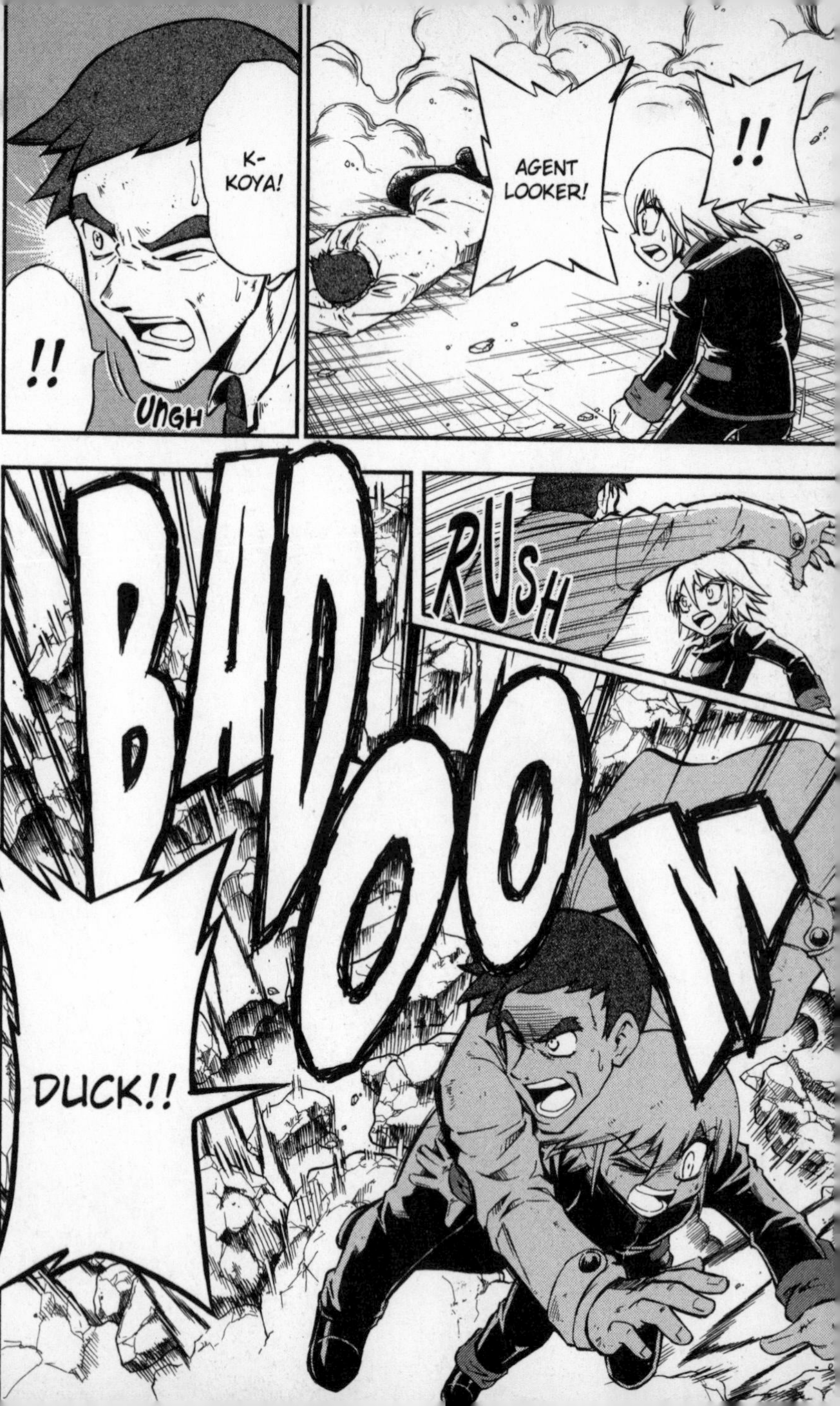
!!
AGENT LOOKER!
K-KOYA!
!!
UNGH
RUSH
BADOOM
DUCK!!

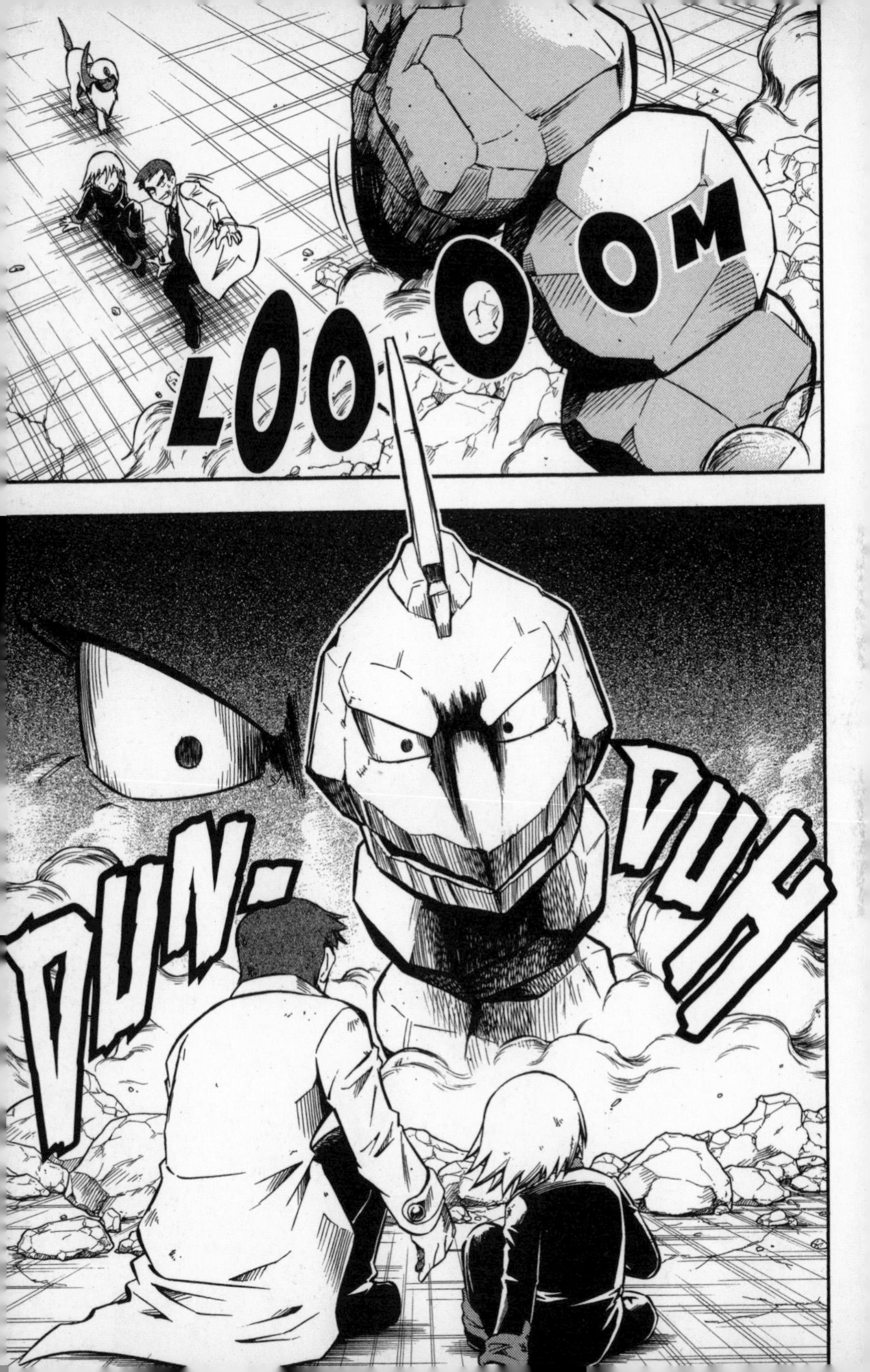
LOO-O-OOM
DUN-DUH

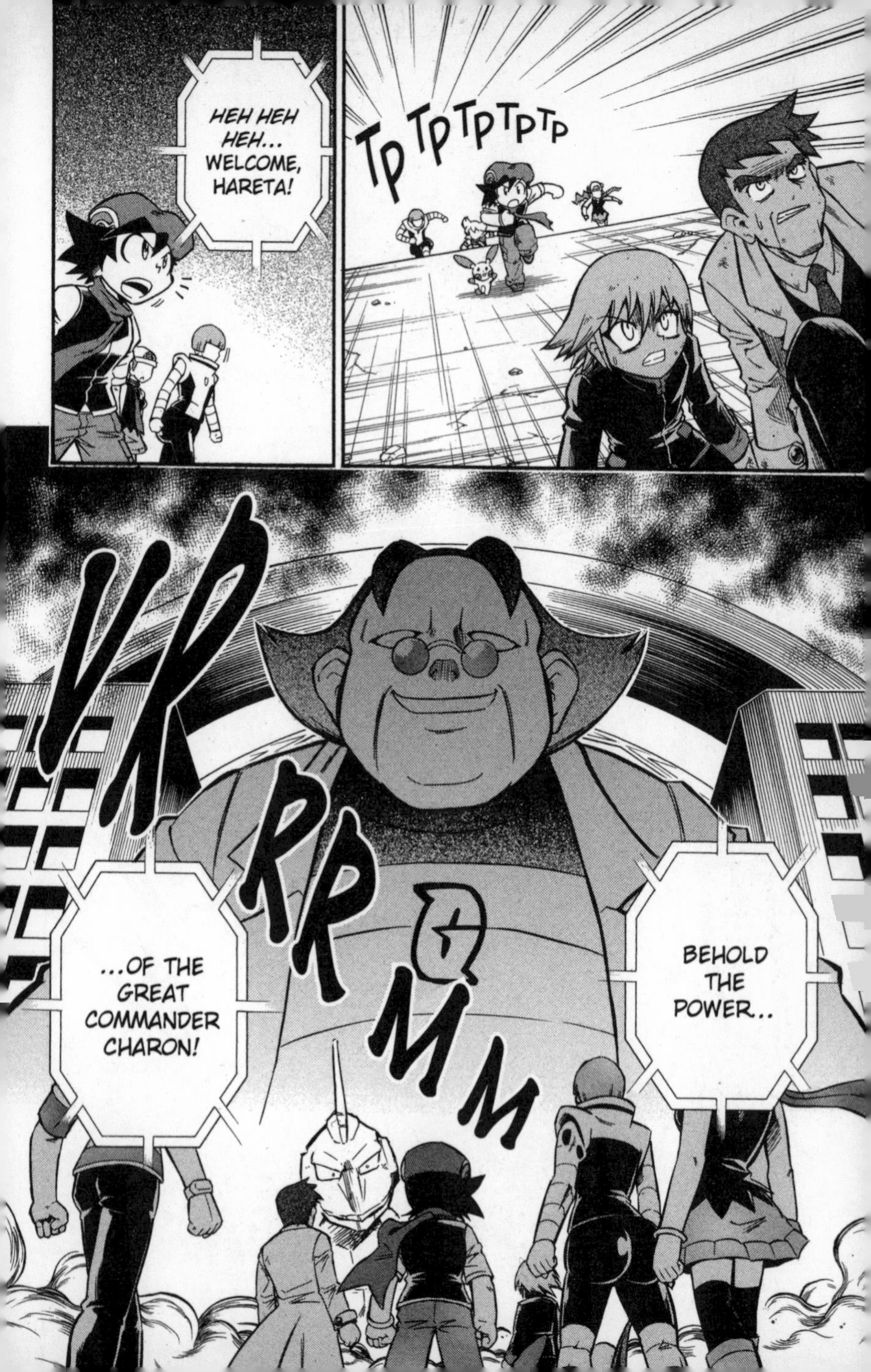
TPTPTPTPTP
HEH HEH HEH... WELCOME, HARETA!
BEHOLD THE POWER...
VRRRRMMM
...OF THE GREAT COMMANDER CHARON!

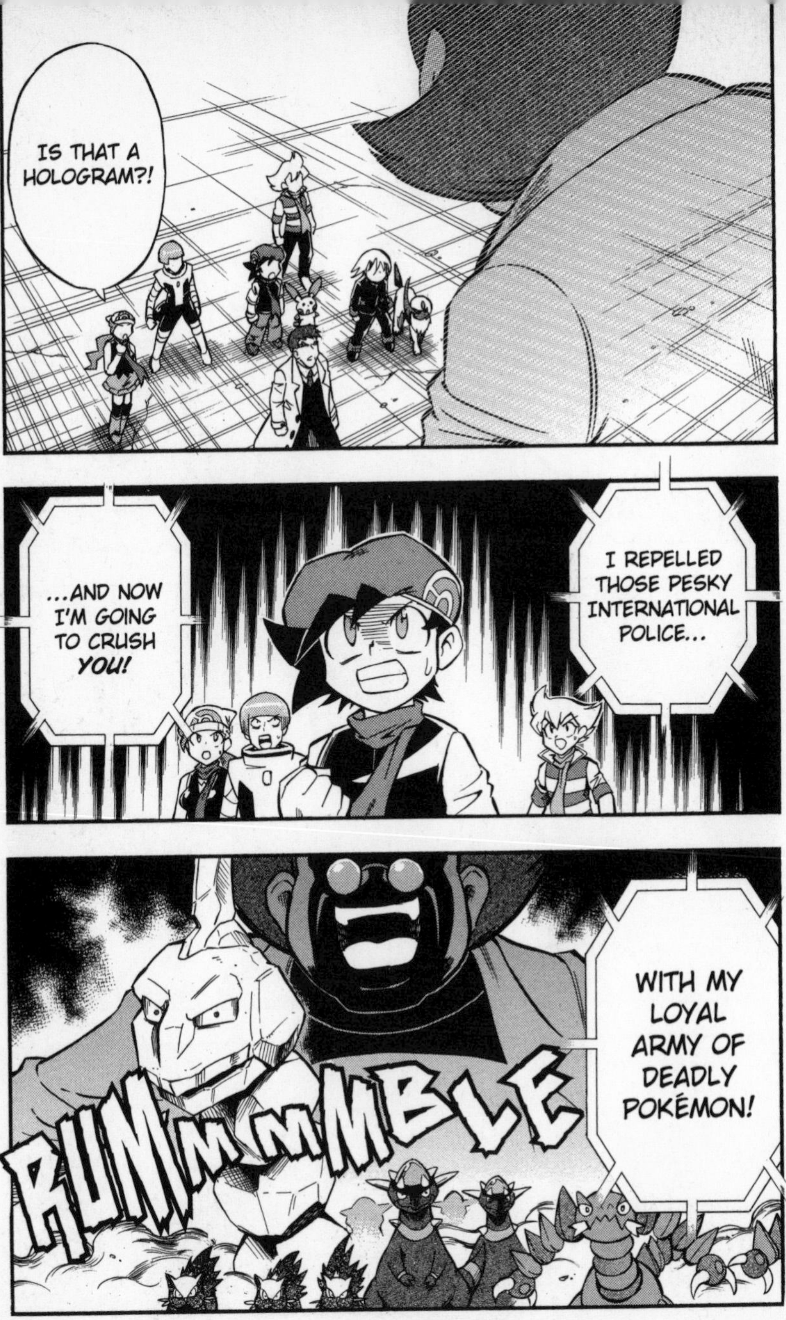
IS THAT A HOLOGRAM?!
I REPELLED THOSE PESKY INTERNATIONAL POLICE...
...AND NOW I'M GOING TO CRUSH *YOU!*
WITH MY LOYAL ARMY OF DEADLY POKÉMON!
RUMMMMMBLE

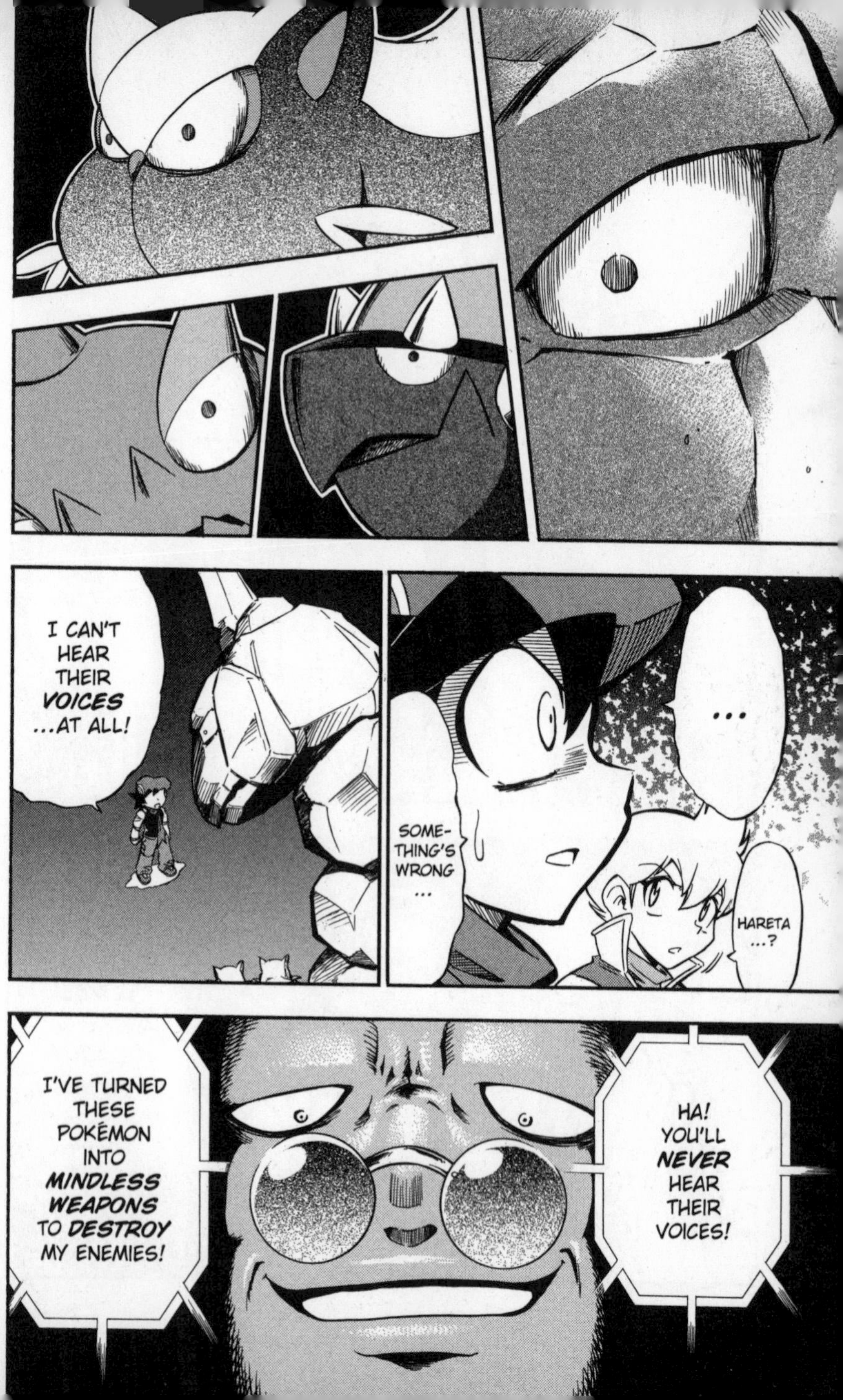

...
HARETA ...?
SOME-THING'S WRONG ...
I CAN'T HEAR THEIR **VOICES** ...AT ALL!
HA! YOU'LL **NEVER** HEAR THEIR VOICES!
I'VE TURNED THESE POKéMON INTO **MINDLESS WEAPONS** TO **DESTROY** MY ENEMIES!

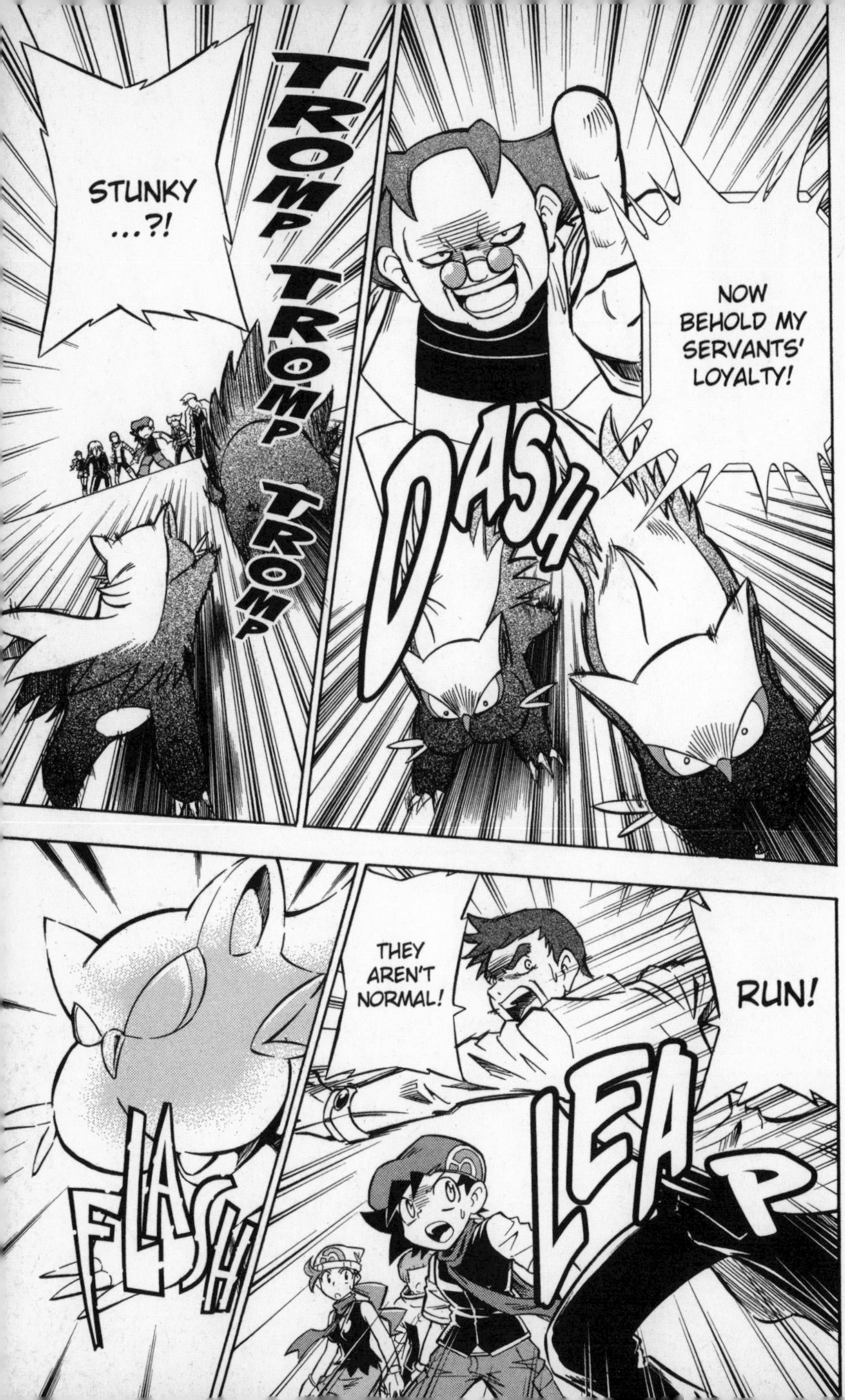
NOW BEHOLD MY SERVANTS' LOYALTY!
DASH
STUNKY ...?!
TROMP TROMP TROMP TROMP
RUN!
THEY AREN'T NORMAL!
LEAP
FLASH

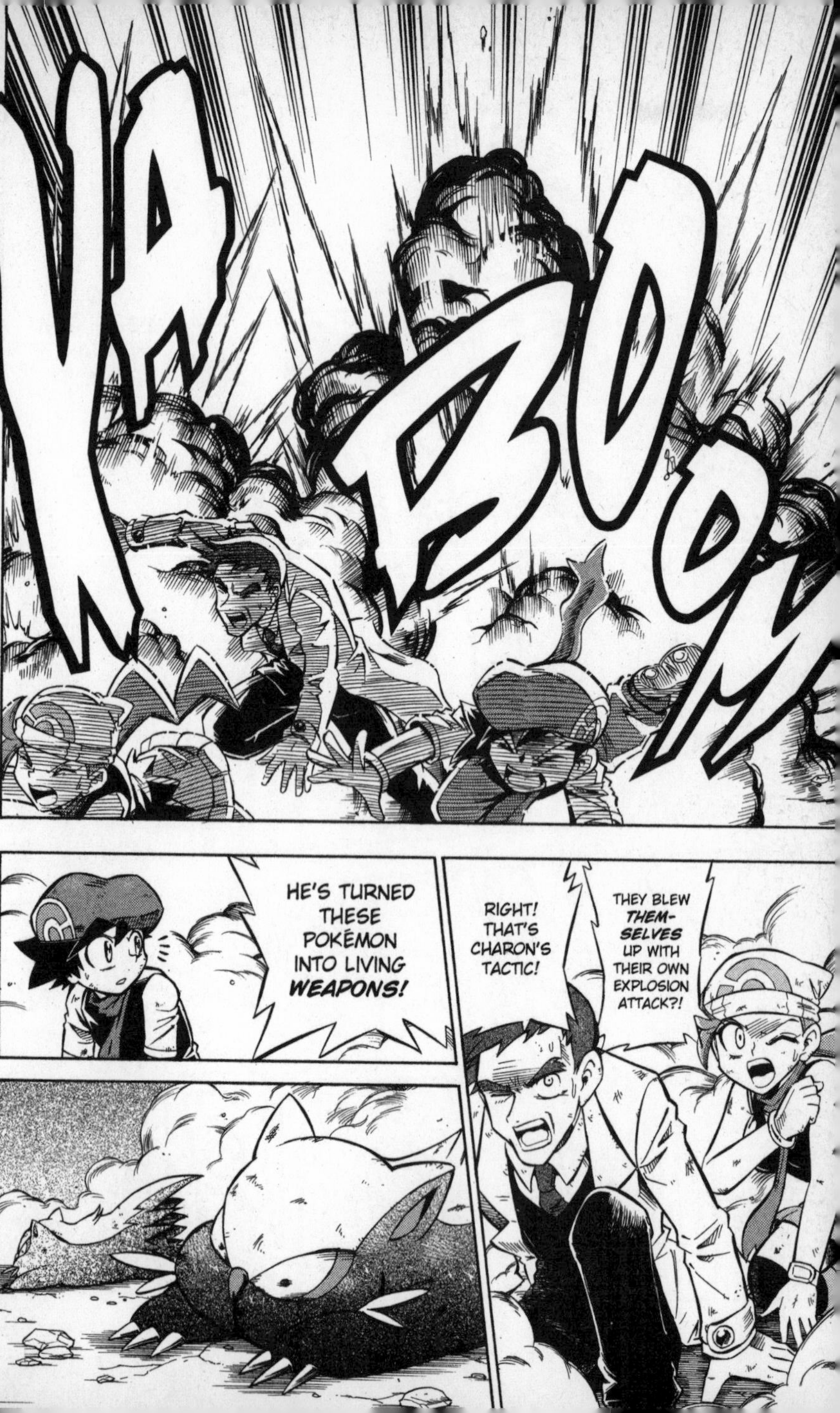
KABOOM
THEY BLEW THEMSELVES UP WITH THEIR OWN EXPLOSION ATTACK?!
RIGHT! THAT'S CHARON'S TACTIC!
HE'S TURNED THESE POKÉMON INTO LIVING WEAPONS!

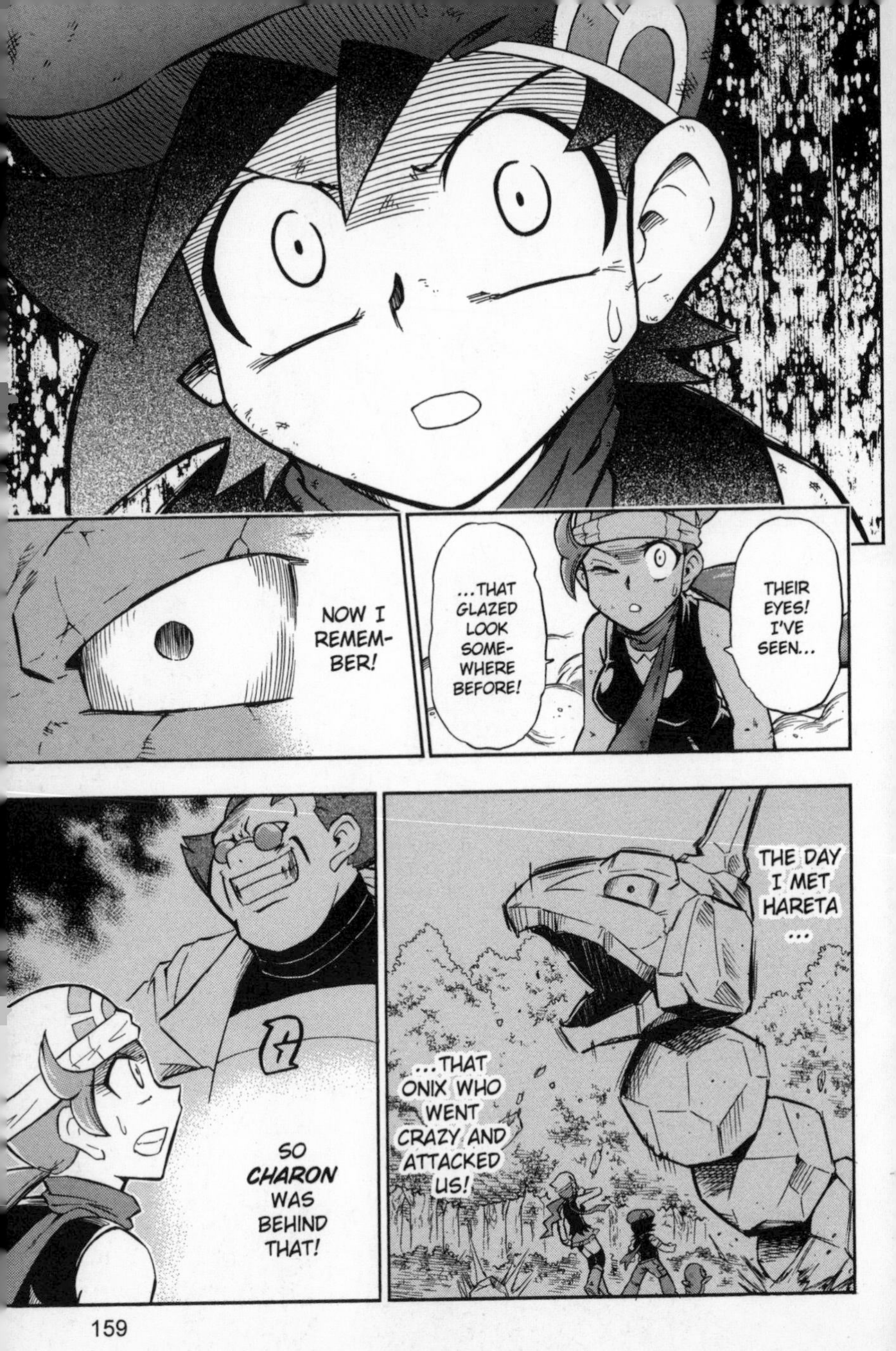
THEIR EYES! I'VE SEEN...
...THAT GLAZED LOOK SOMEWHERE BEFORE!
NOW I REMEMBER!
THE DAY I MET HARETA ...
...THAT ONIX WHO WENT CRAZY AND ATTACKED US!
SO CHARON WAS BEHIND THAT!

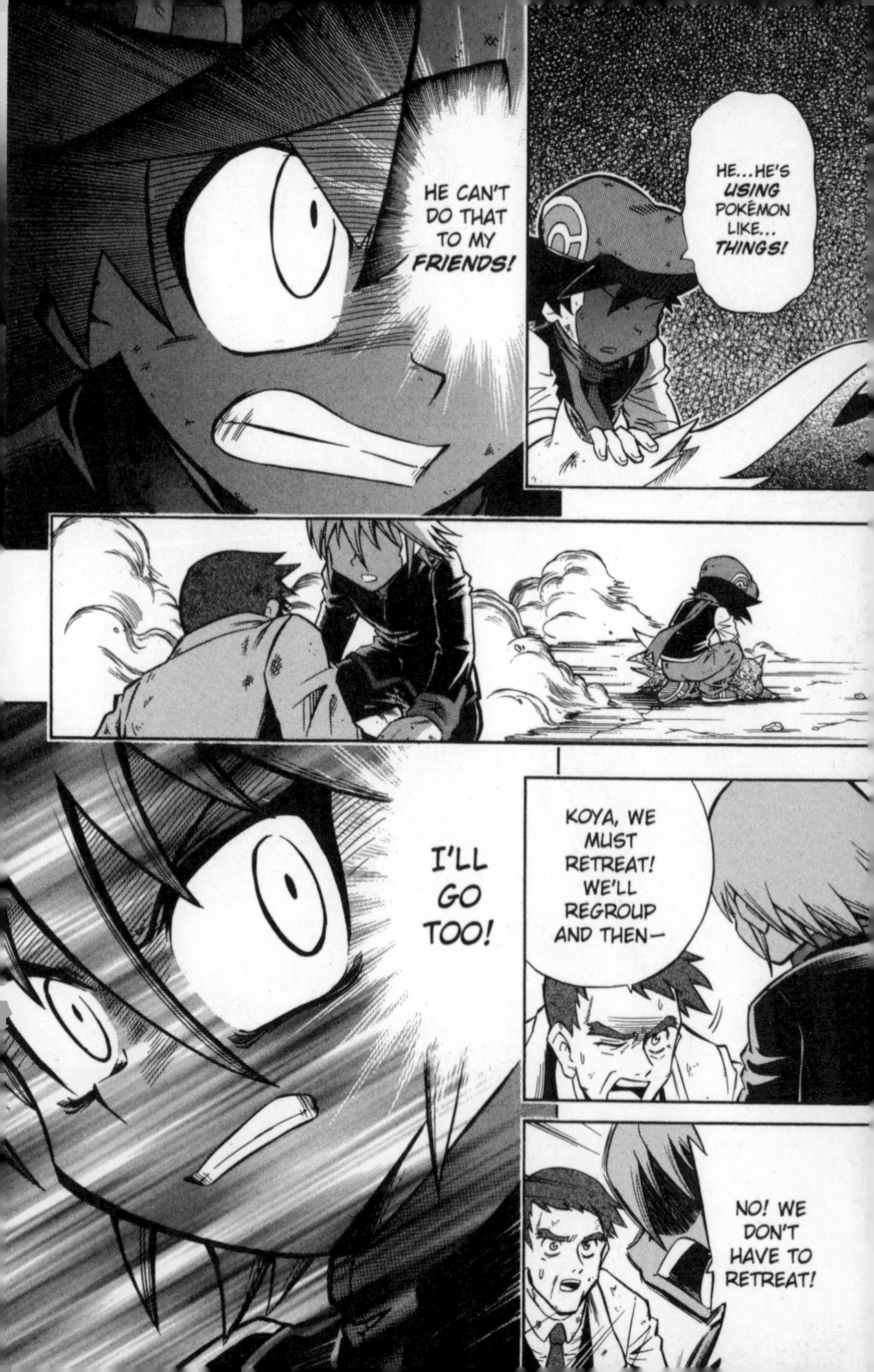
HE...HE'S USING POKÉMON LIKE... THINGS!
HE CAN'T DO THAT TO MY FRIENDS!
KOYA, WE MUST RETREAT! WE'LL REGROUP AND THEN—
NO! WE DON'T HAVE TO RETREAT!
I'LL GO TOO!

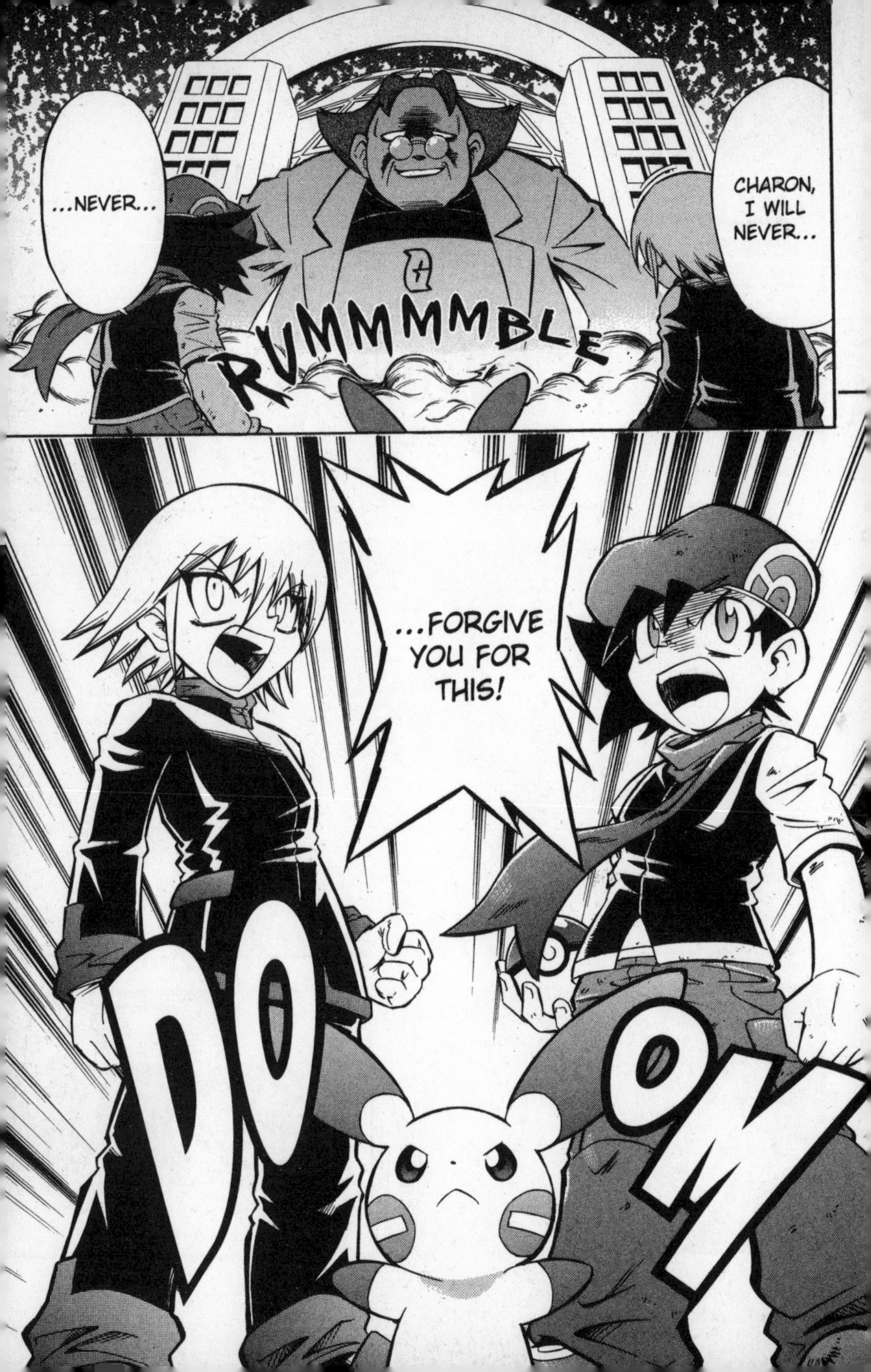
CHARON, I WILL NEVER...
...NEVER...
RUMMMMBLE
...FORGIVE YOU FOR THIS!
DOOM

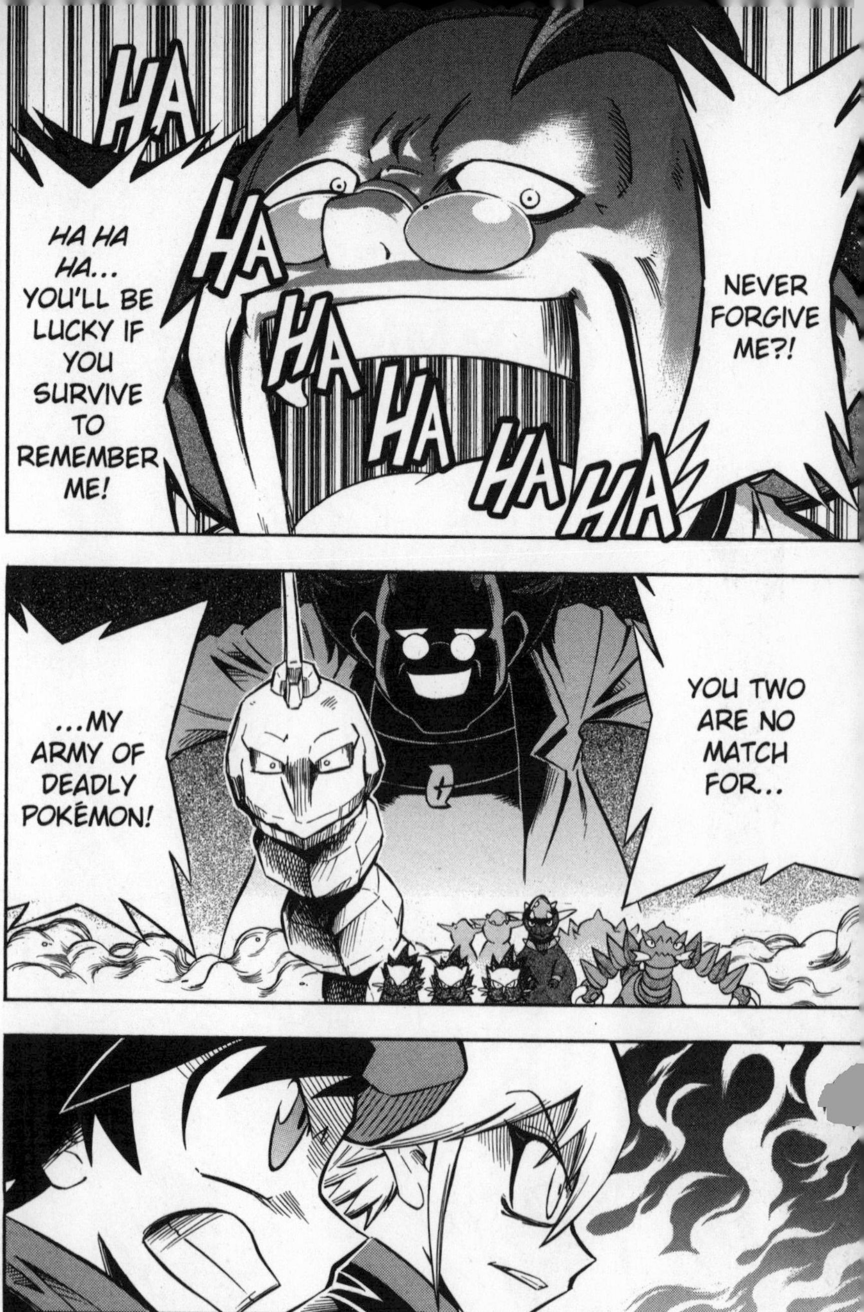
NEVER FORGIVE ME?!
HA HA HA HA HA HA HA
HA HA HA... YOU'LL BE LUCKY IF YOU SURVIVE TO REMEMBER ME!
YOU TWO ARE NO MATCH FOR...
...MY ARMY OF DEADLY POKÉMON!

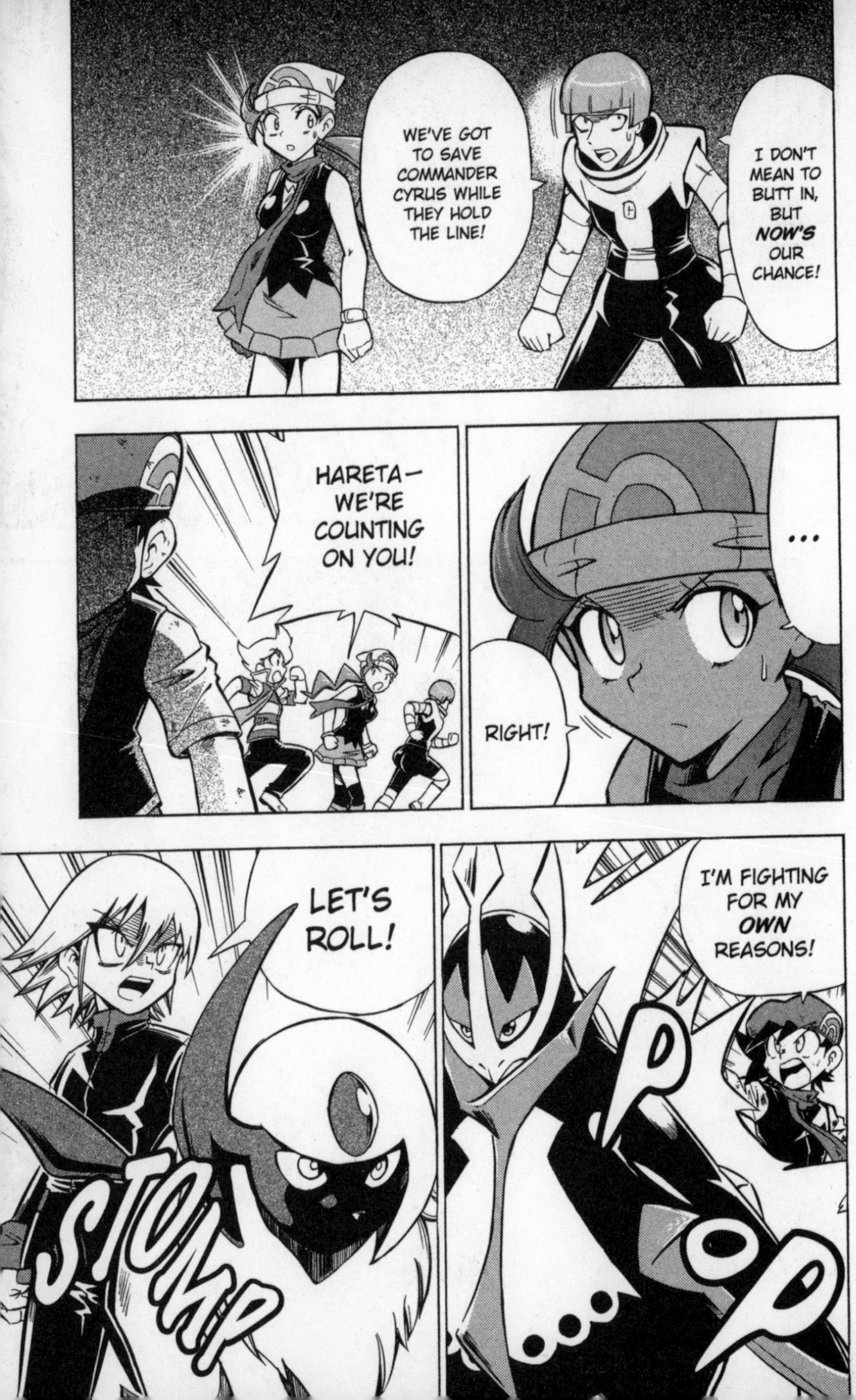
I DON'T MEAN TO BUTT IN, BUT **NOW'S** OUR CHANCE!
WE'VE GOT TO SAVE COMMANDER CYRUS WHILE THEY HOLD THE LINE!
...
RIGHT!
HARETA— WE'RE COUNTING ON YOU!
I'M FIGHTING FOR MY **OWN** REASONS!
POP...POP
LET'S ROLL!
STOMP

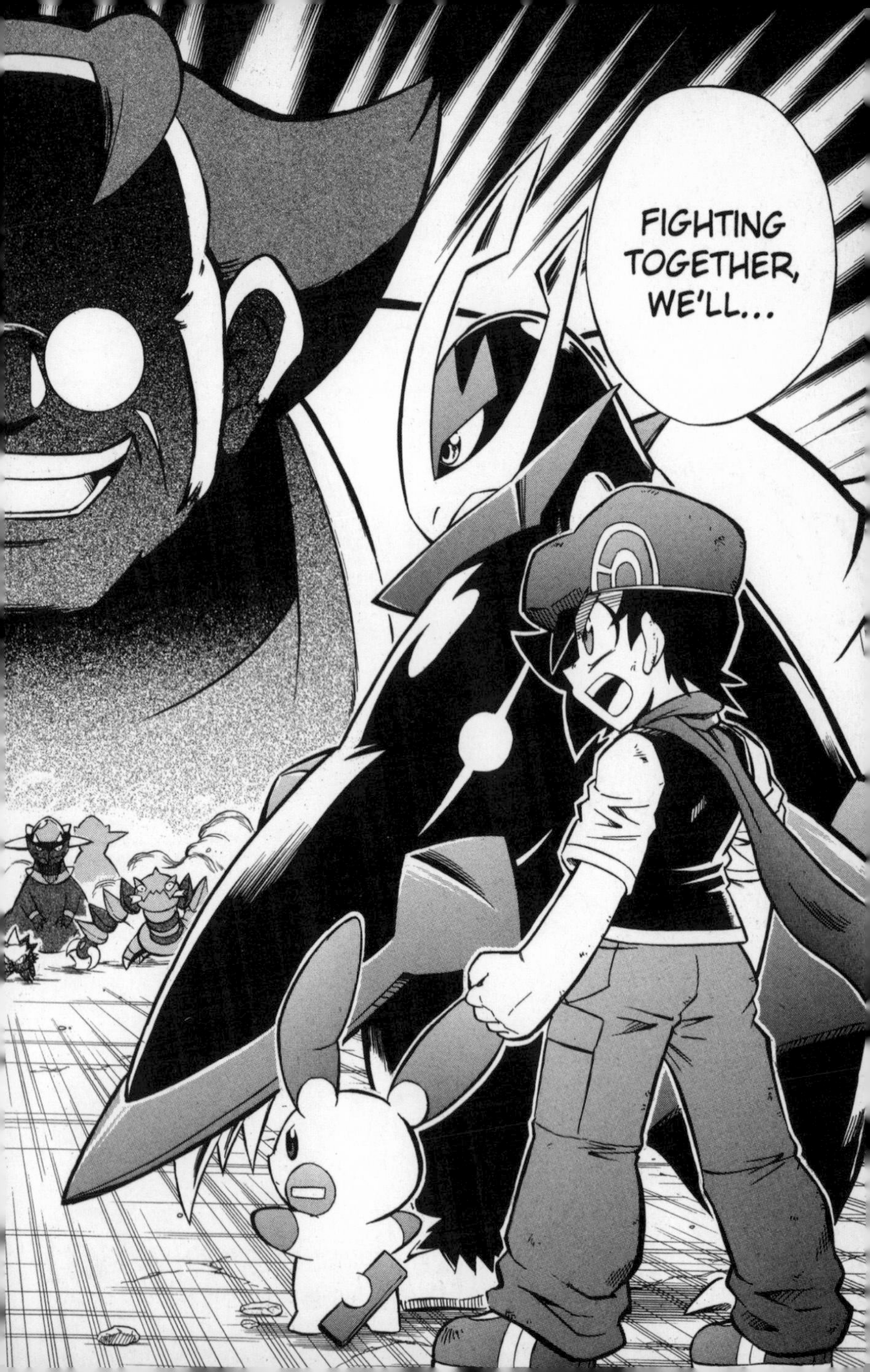
FIGHTING TOGETHER, WE'LL...

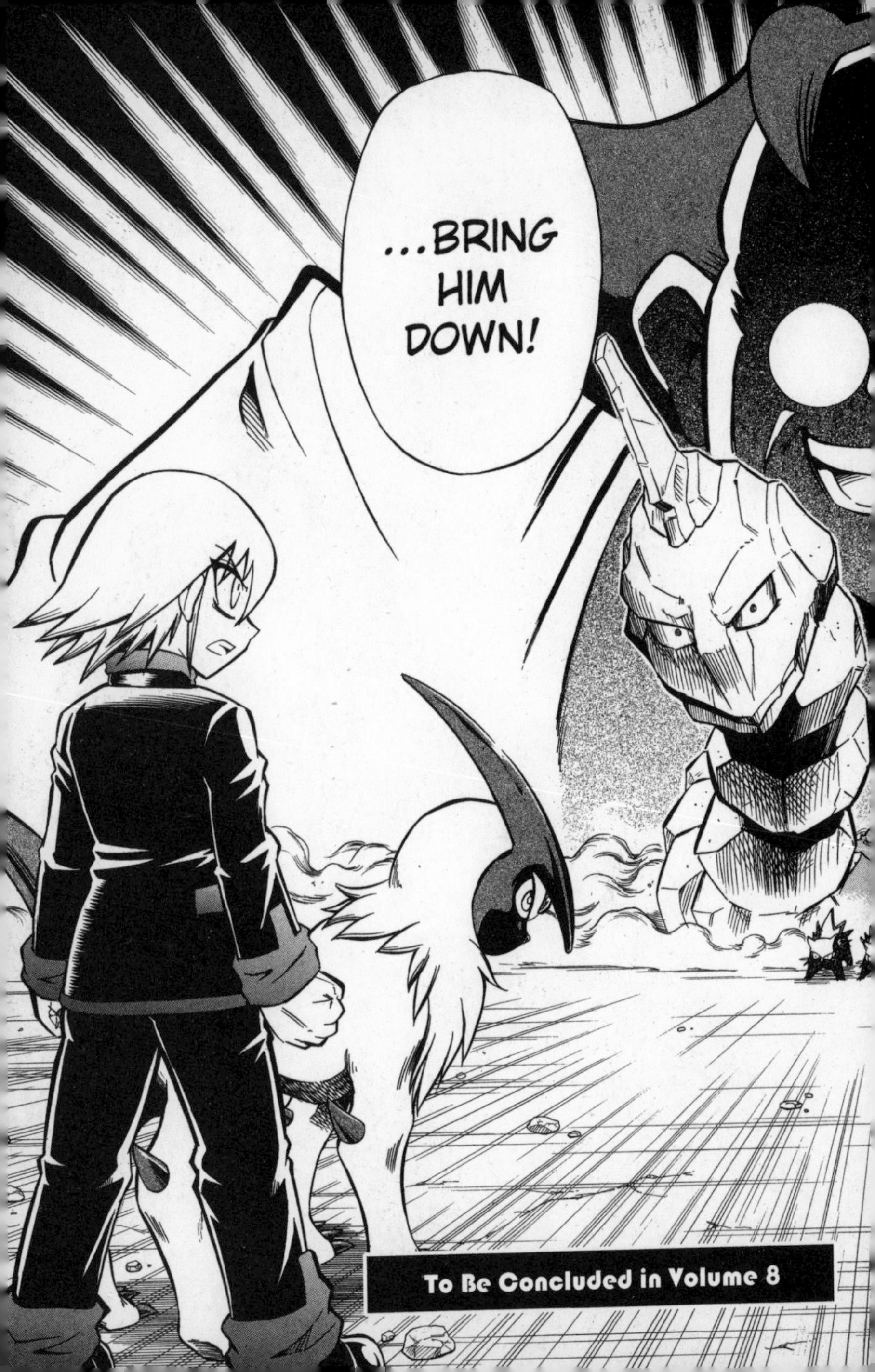
...BRING HIM DOWN!
To Be Concluded in Volume 8

POKEMON DIAMOND AND PEARL BONUS STORY

RETURN TO HARETA'S HOME FOREST!

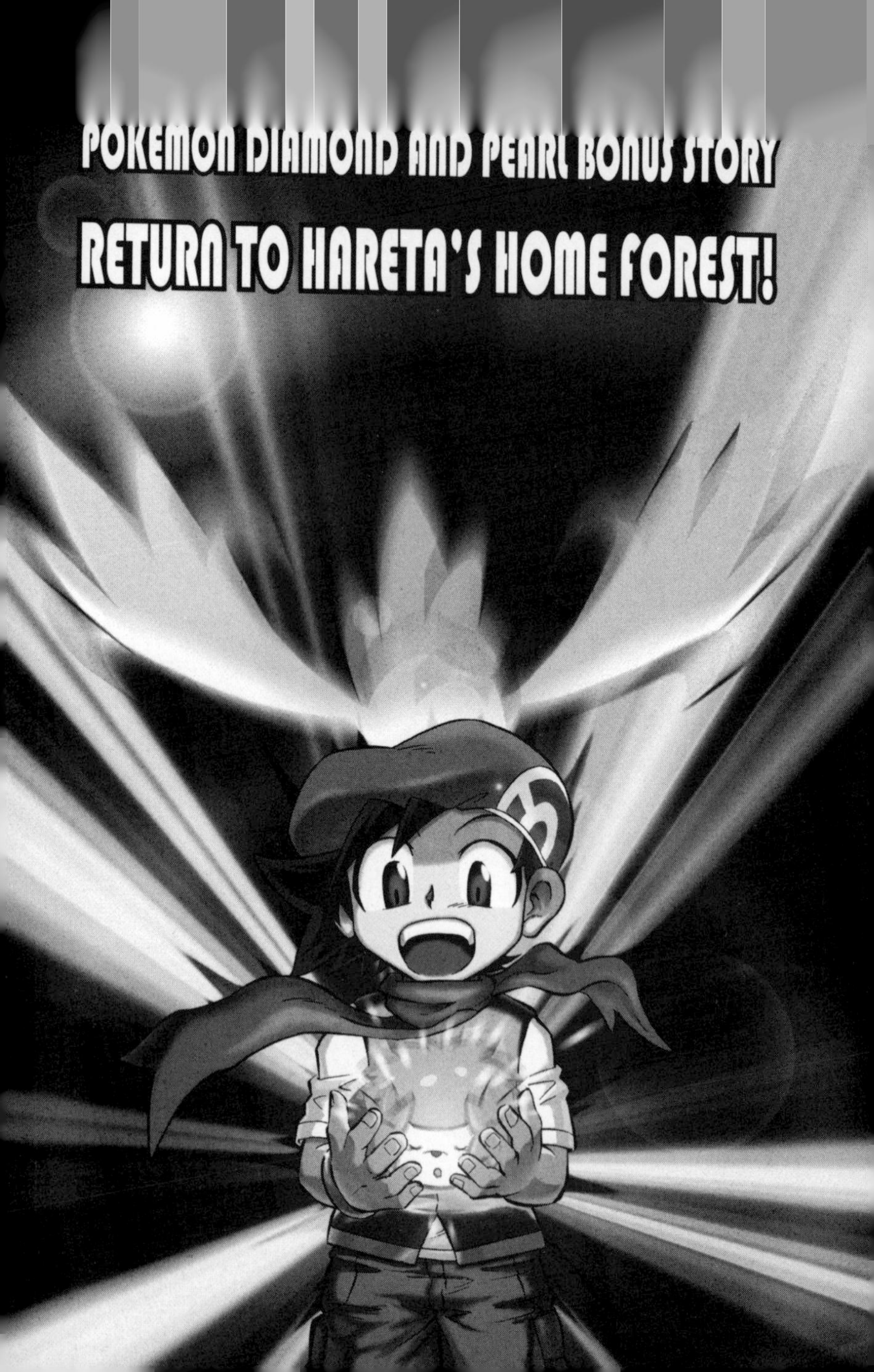

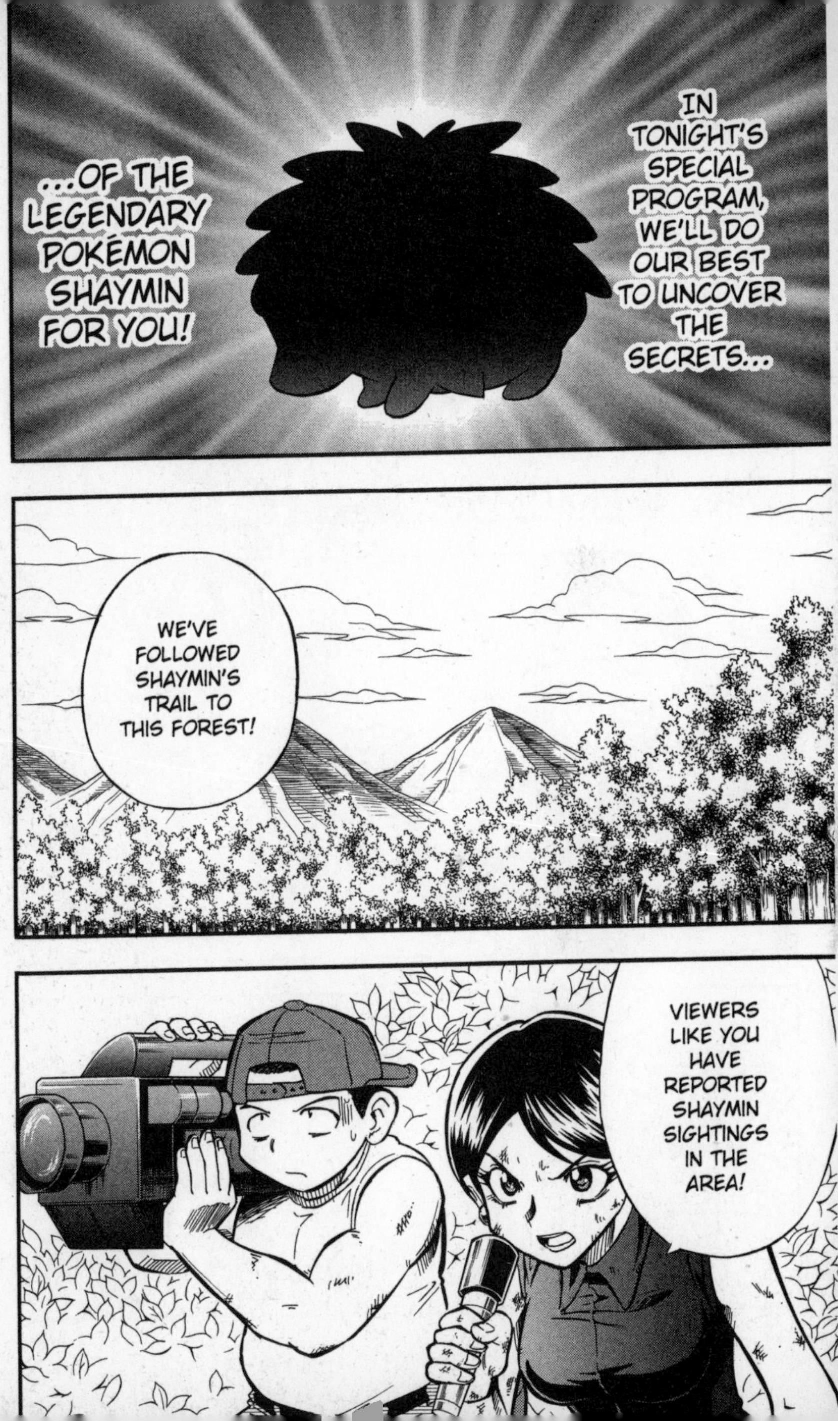
IN TONIGHT'S SPECIAL PROGRAM, WE'LL DO OUR BEST TO UNCOVER THE SECRETS...
...OF THE LEGENDARY POKÉMON SHAYMIN FOR YOU!
WE'VE FOLLOWED SHAYMIN'S TRAIL TO THIS FOREST!
VIEWERS LIKE YOU HAVE REPORTED SHAYMIN SIGHTINGS IN THE AREA!

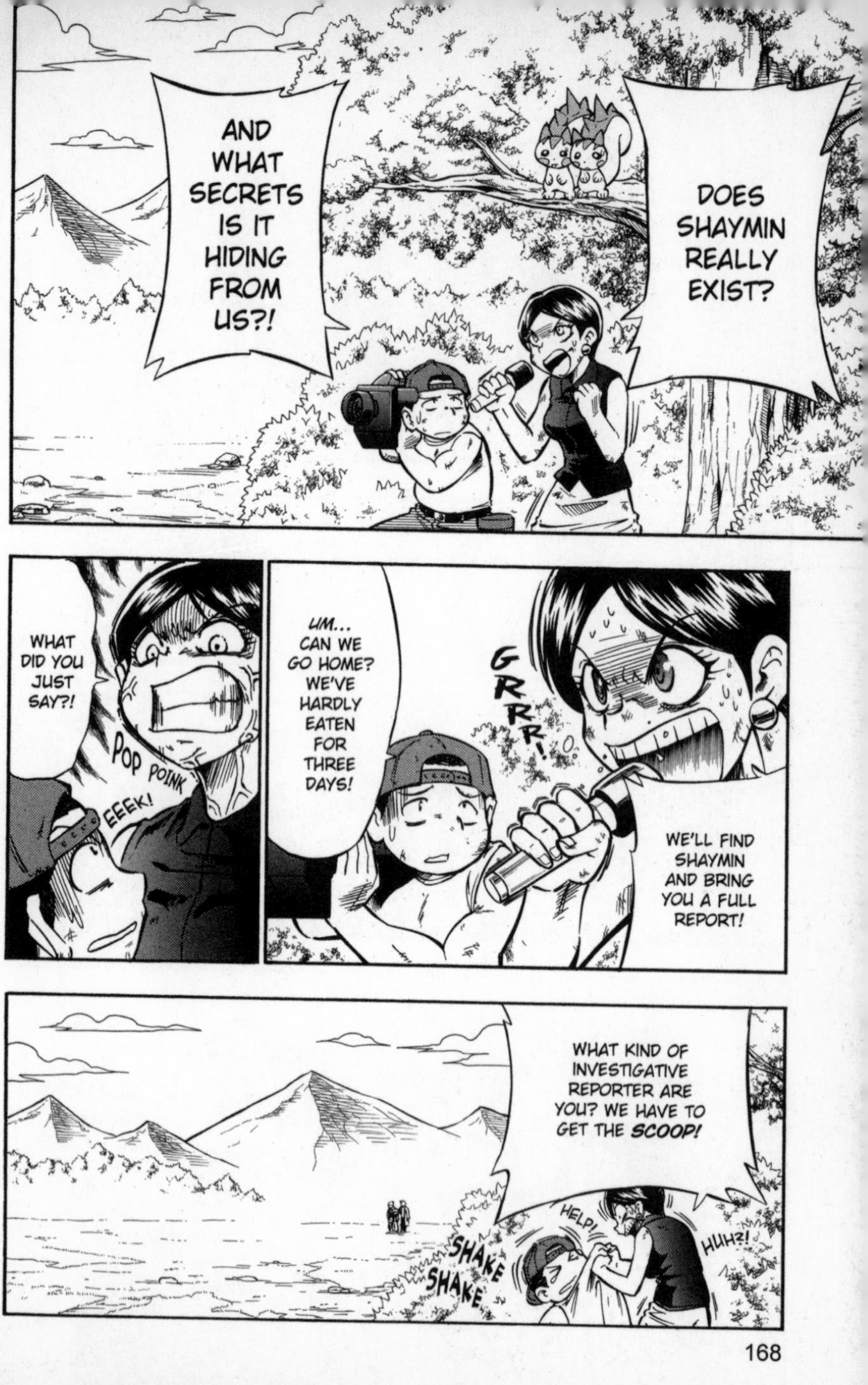
DOES SHAYMIN REALLY EXIST?
AND WHAT SECRETS IS IT HIDING FROM US?!
WE'LL FIND SHAYMIN AND BRING YOU A FULL REPORT!
UM... CAN WE GO HOME? WE'VE HARDLY EATEN FOR THREE DAYS!
GRRR!
WHAT DID YOU JUST SAY?!
POP POINK
EEEK!
WHAT KIND OF INVESTIGATIVE REPORTER ARE YOU? WE HAVE TO GET THE *SCOOP!*
HUH?!
HELP!
SHAKE SHAKE

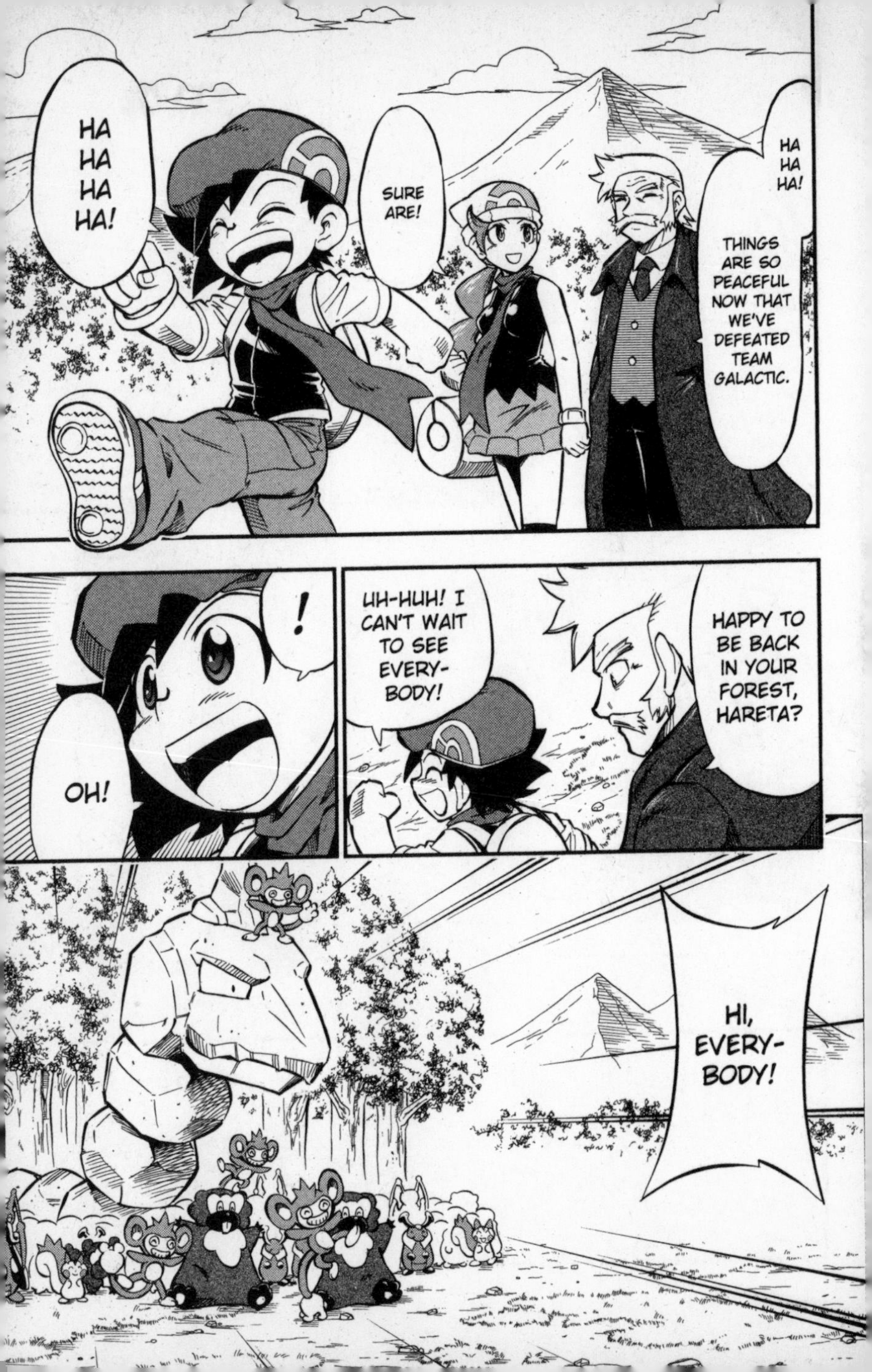
HA HA HA!
THINGS ARE SO PEACEFUL NOW THAT WE'VE DEFEATED TEAM GALACTIC.
SURE ARE!
HA HA HA HA!
HAPPY TO BE BACK IN YOUR FOREST, HARETA?
UH-HUH! I CAN'T WAIT TO SEE EVERY-BODY!
!
OH!
HI, EVERY-BODY!

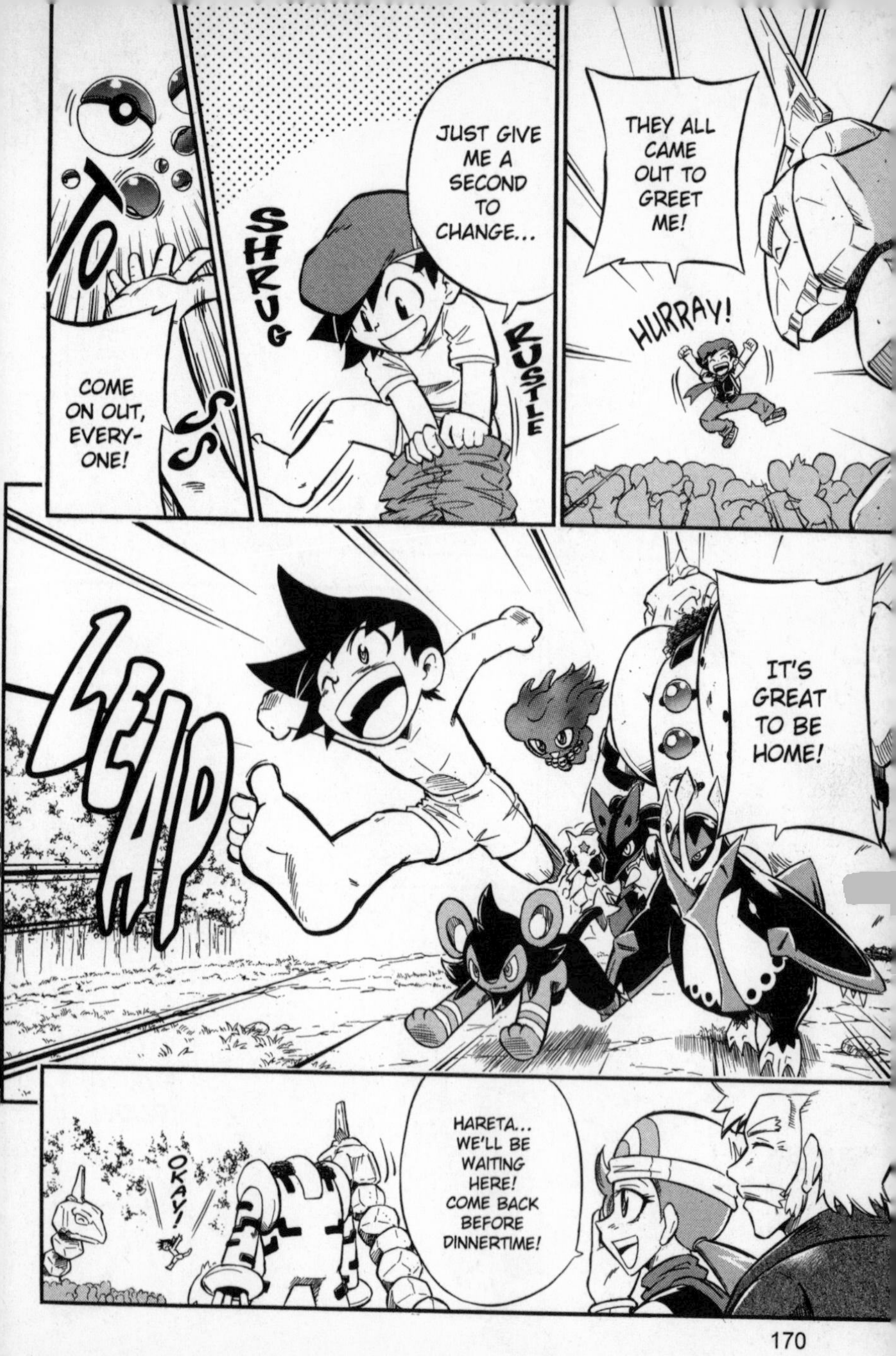
THEY ALL CAME OUT TO GREET ME!
HURRAY!
JUST GIVE ME A SECOND TO CHANGE...
SHRUG
RUSTLE
TO
SS
COME ON OUT, EVERY-ONE!
IT'S GREAT TO BE HOME!
LEAP
HARETA... WE'LL BE WAITING HERE! COME BACK BEFORE DINNERTIME!
OKAY!

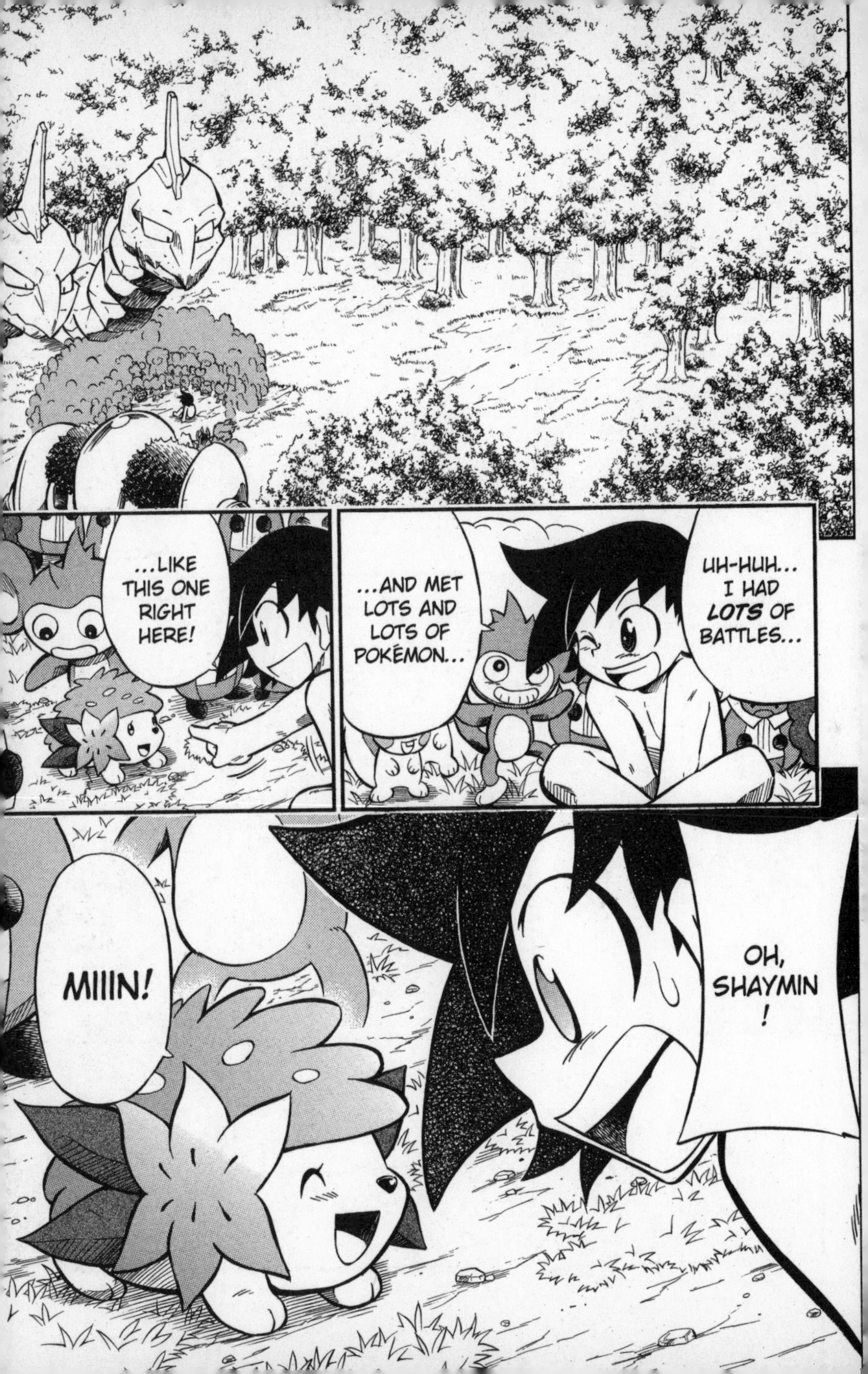
UH-HUH... I HAD ***LOTS*** OF BATTLES...
...AND MET LOTS AND LOTS OF POKÉMON...
...LIKE THIS ONE RIGHT HERE!
OH, SHAYMIN!
MIIIN!

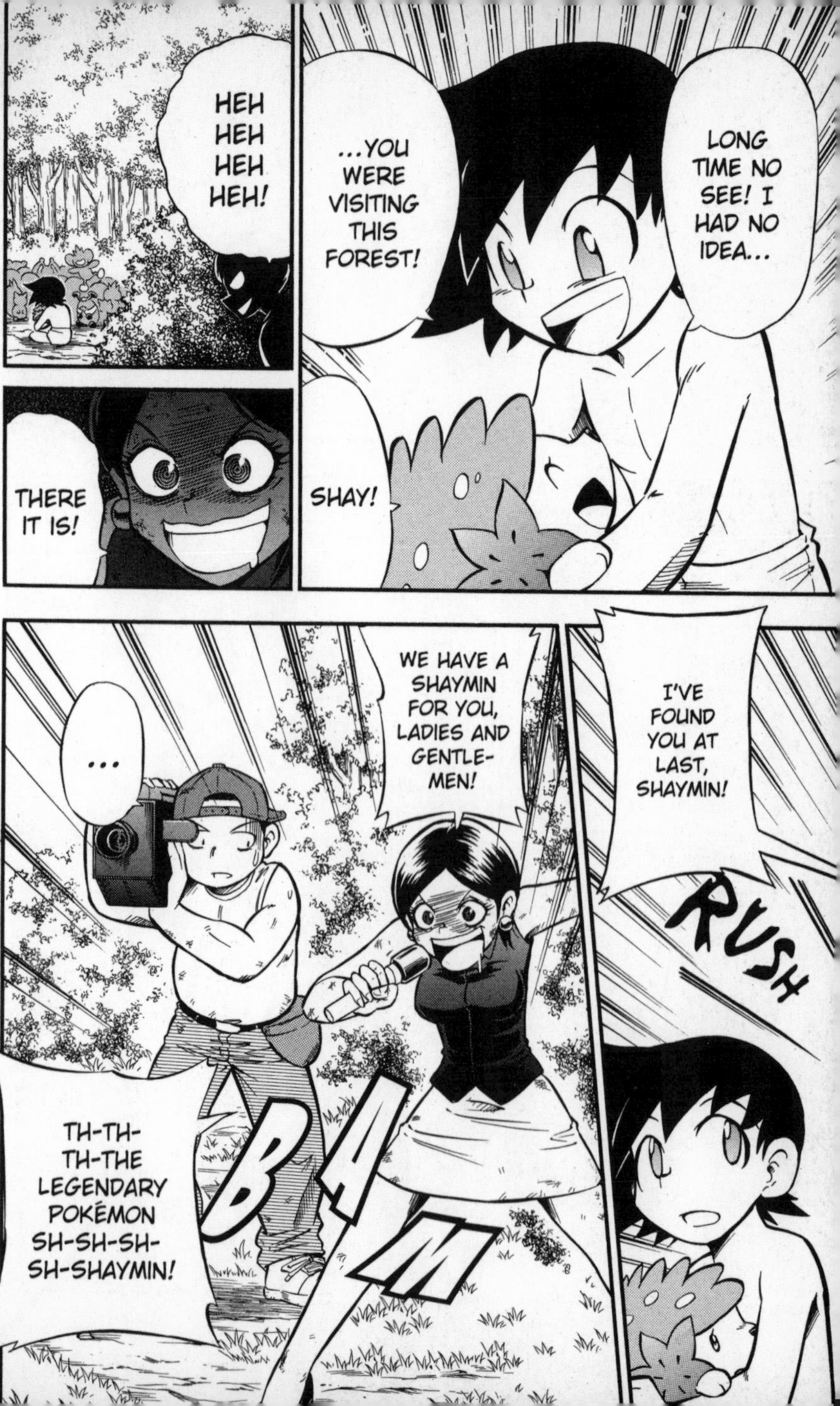
LONG TIME NO SEE! I HAD NO IDEA...
...YOU WERE VISITING THIS FOREST!
SHAY!
HEH HEH HEH HEH!
THERE IT IS!
I'VE FOUND YOU AT LAST, SHAYMIN!
RUSH
WE HAVE A SHAYMIN FOR YOU, LADIES AND GENTLE-MEN!
...
TH-TH-TH-THE LEGENDARY POKÉMON SH-SH-SH-SH-SHAYMIN!
BAM

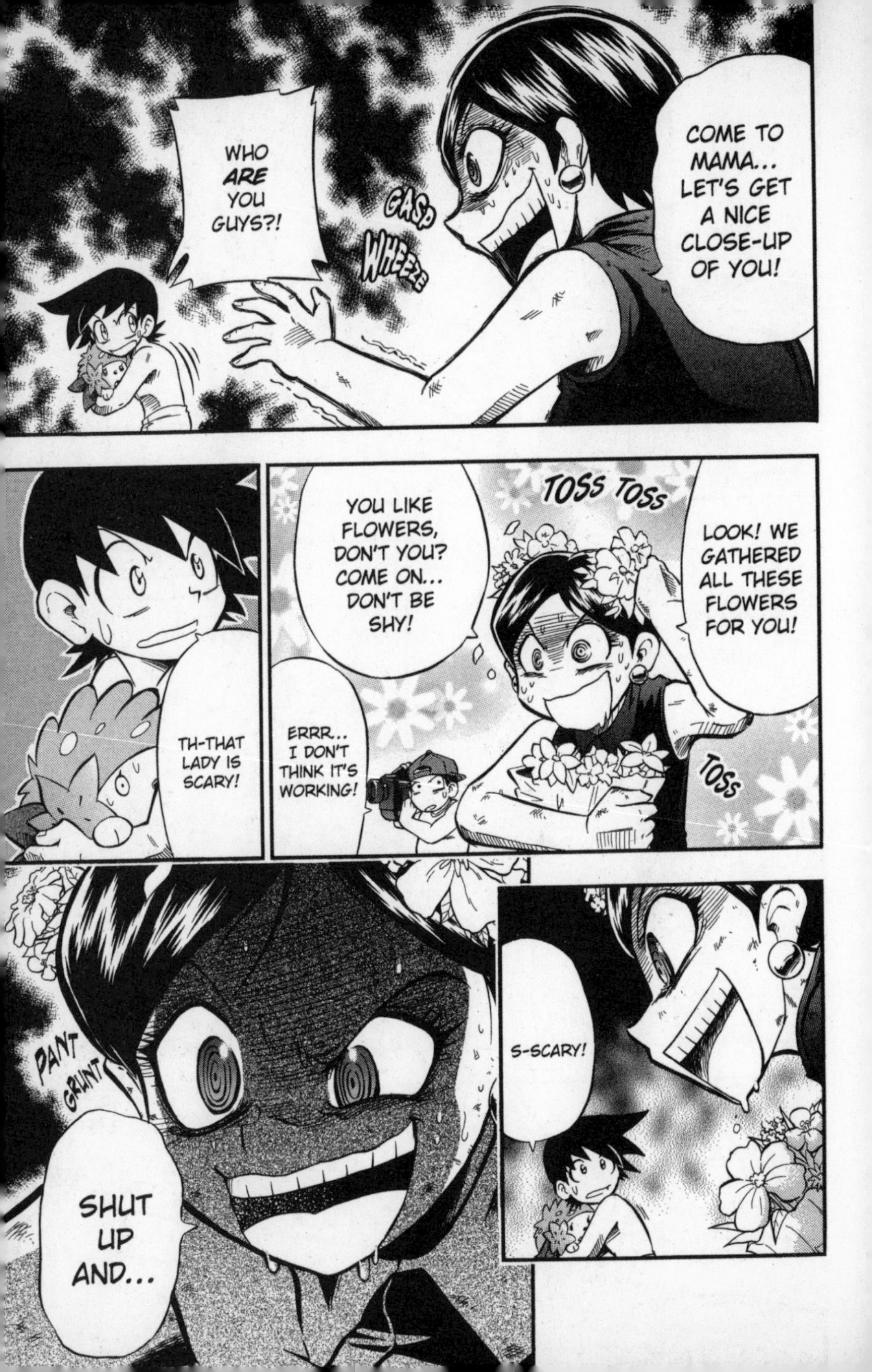
COME TO MAMA... LET'S GET A NICE CLOSE-UP OF YOU!
GASP
WHEEZE
WHO ARE YOU GUYS?!
TOSS TOSS
LOOK! WE GATHERED ALL THESE FLOWERS FOR YOU!
YOU LIKE FLOWERS, DON'T YOU? COME ON... DON'T BE SHY!
TOSS
ERRR.. I DON'T THINK IT'S WORKING!
TH-THAT LADY IS SCARY!
S-SCARY!
PANT
GRUNT
SHUT UP AND...

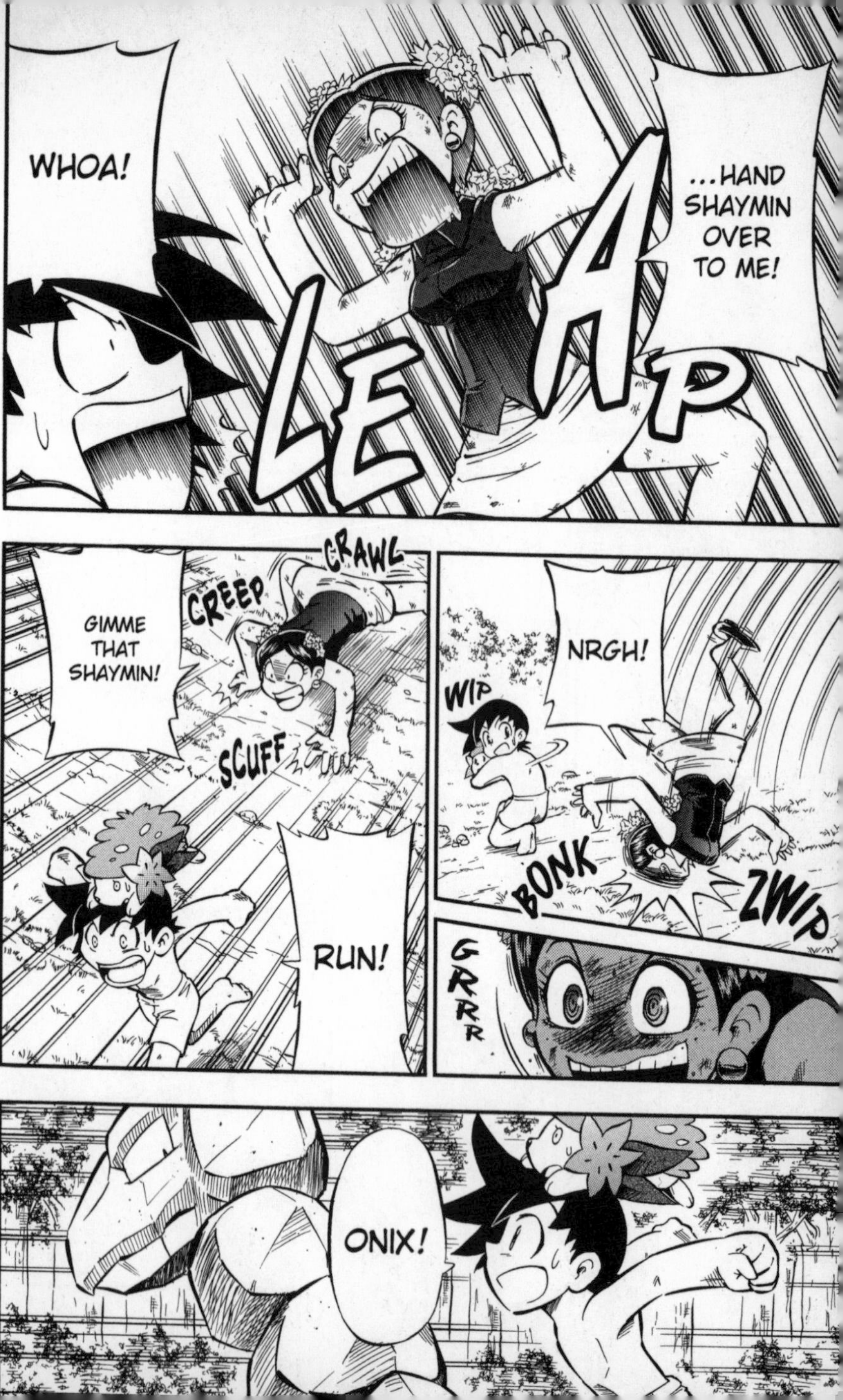
...HAND SHAYMIN OVER TO ME!
LEAP
WHOA!
NRGH!
WIP
BONK
ZWIP
GRRR
CRAWL
CREEP
GIMME THAT SHAYMIN!
SCUFF
RUN!
ONIX!

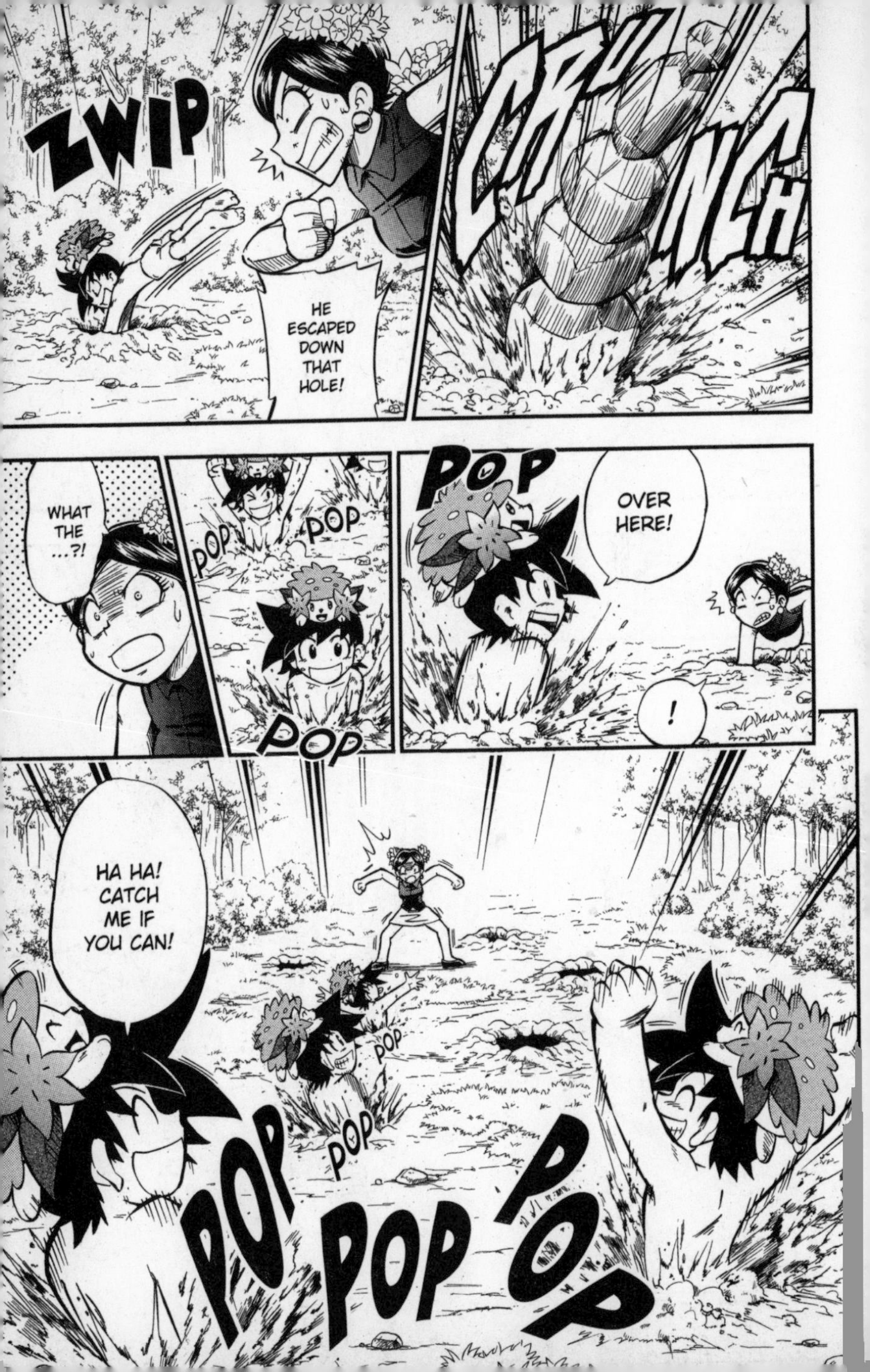
CRUNCH
ZWIP
HE ESCAPED DOWN THAT HOLE!
POP
OVER HERE!
!
POP
POP
POP
WHAT THE ...?!
HA HA! CATCH ME IF YOU CAN!
POP
POP
POP
POP
POP
POP

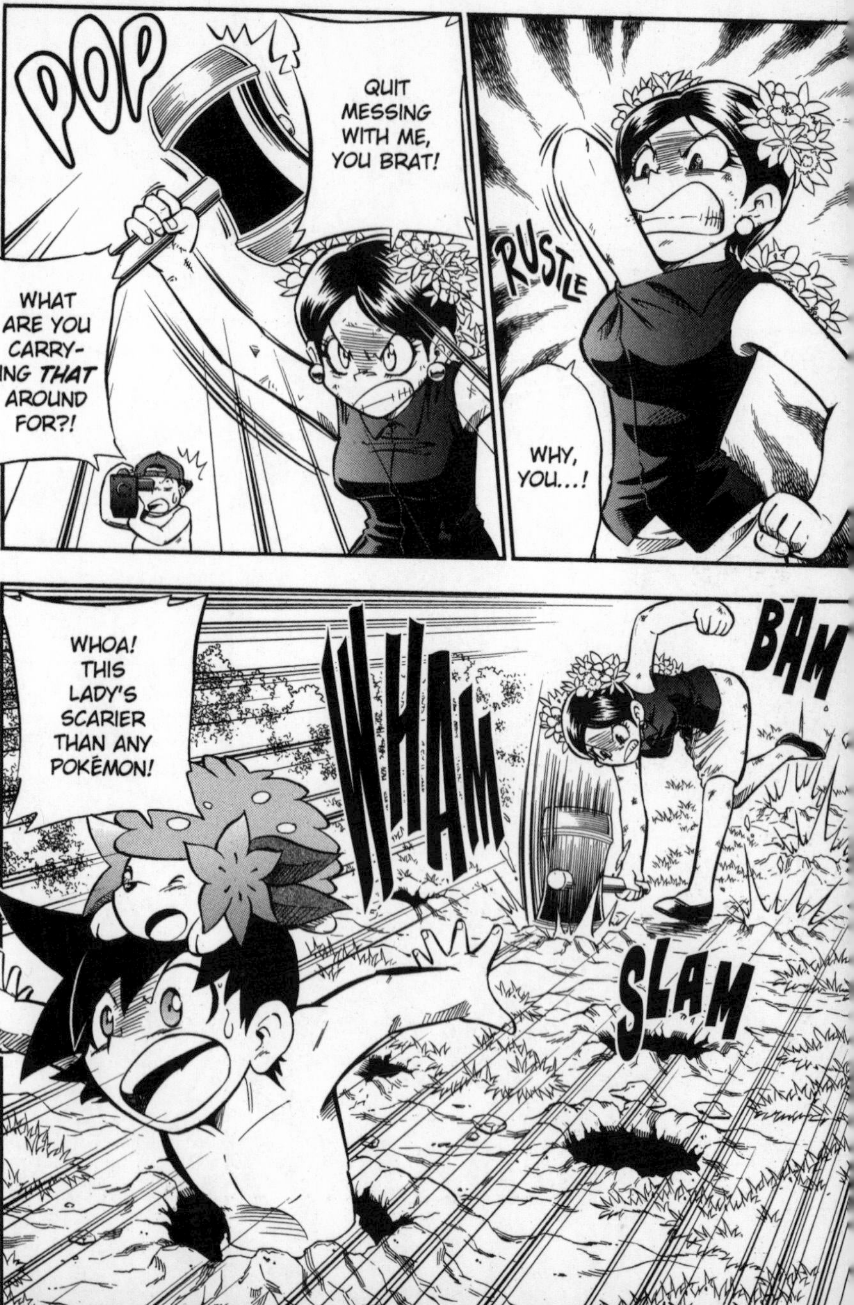
RUSTLE
WHY, YOU...!
QUIT MESSING WITH ME, YOU BRAT!
POP
WHAT ARE YOU CARRYING *THAT* AROUND FOR?!
BAM
WHAM
WHOA! THIS LADY'S SCARIER THAN ANY POKÉMON!
SLAM

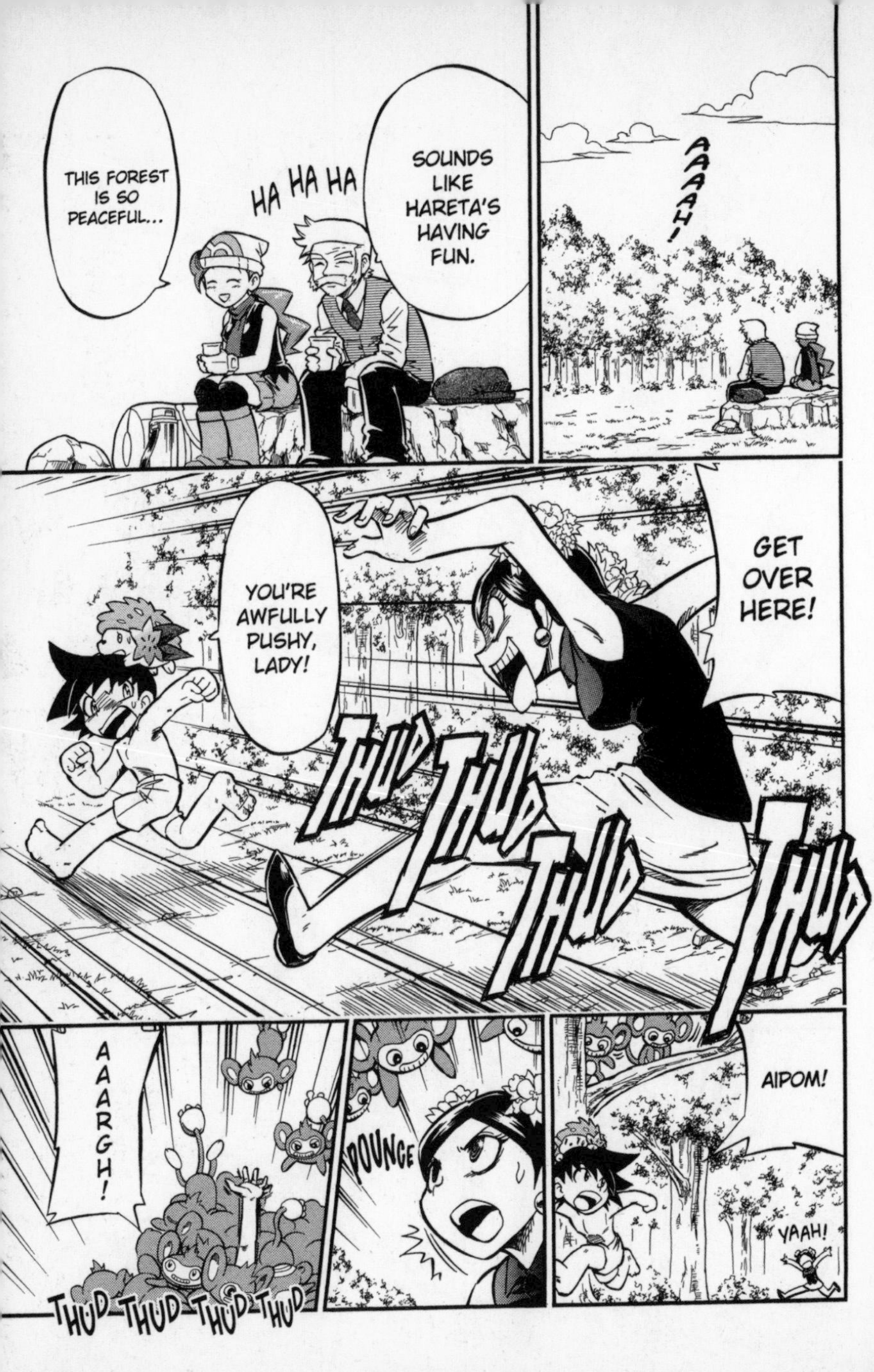
AAAAH!
SOUNDS LIKE HARETA'S HAVING FUN.
HA HA HA
THIS FOREST IS SO PEACEFUL...
GET OVER HERE!
YOU'RE AWFULLY PUSHY, LADY!
THUD THUD THUD THUD
AIPOM!
YAAH!
POUNCE
AAARGH!
THUD THUD THUD THUD

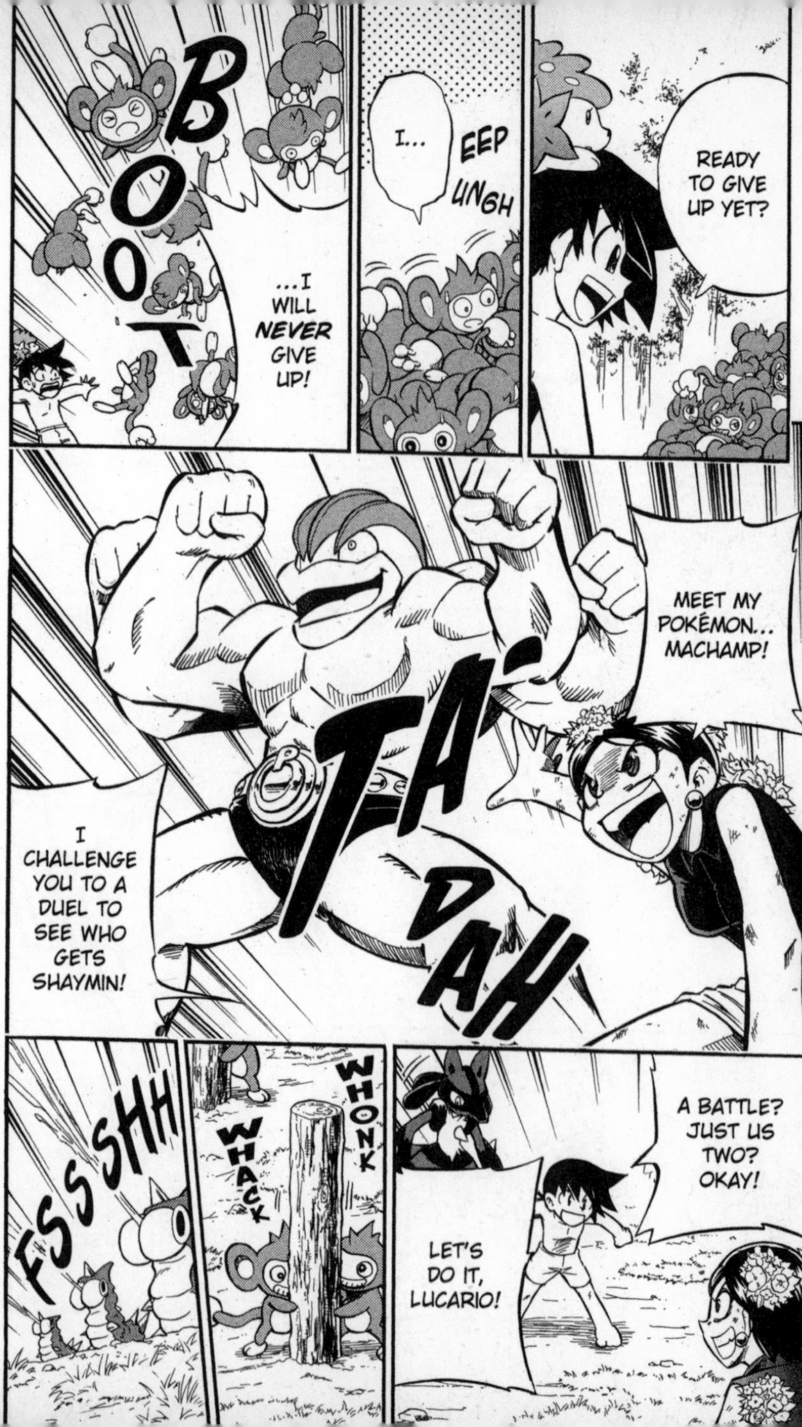
READY TO GIVE UP YET?
I...
EEP
UNGH
BOOT
...I WILL NEVER GIVE UP!
MEET MY POKÉMON... MACHAMP!
TA-DAH
I CHALLENGE YOU TO A DUEL TO SEE WHO GETS SHAYMIN!
A BATTLE? JUST US TWO? OKAY!
LET'S DO IT, LUCARIO!
WHONK
WHACK
FSSSHH

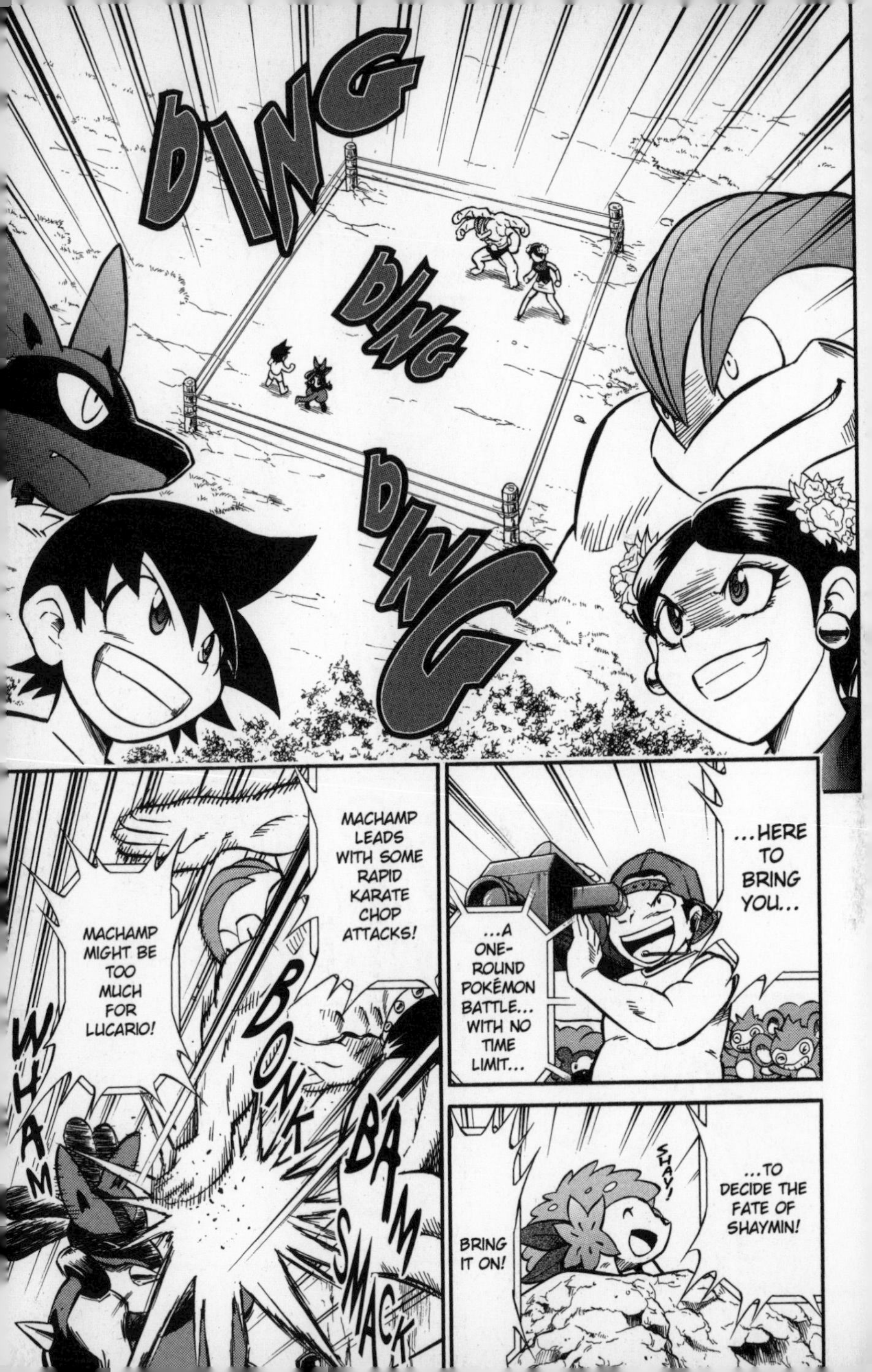
DING
DING
DING
...HERE TO BRING YOU...
...A ONE-ROUND POKÉMON BATTLE... WITH NO TIME LIMIT...
...TO DECIDE THE FATE OF SHAYMIN!
SHAY!
BRING IT ON!
MACHAMP LEADS WITH SOME RAPID KARATE CHOP ATTACKS!
MACHAMP MIGHT BE TOO MUCH FOR LUCARIO!
WHAM
BONK
BAM
SMACK

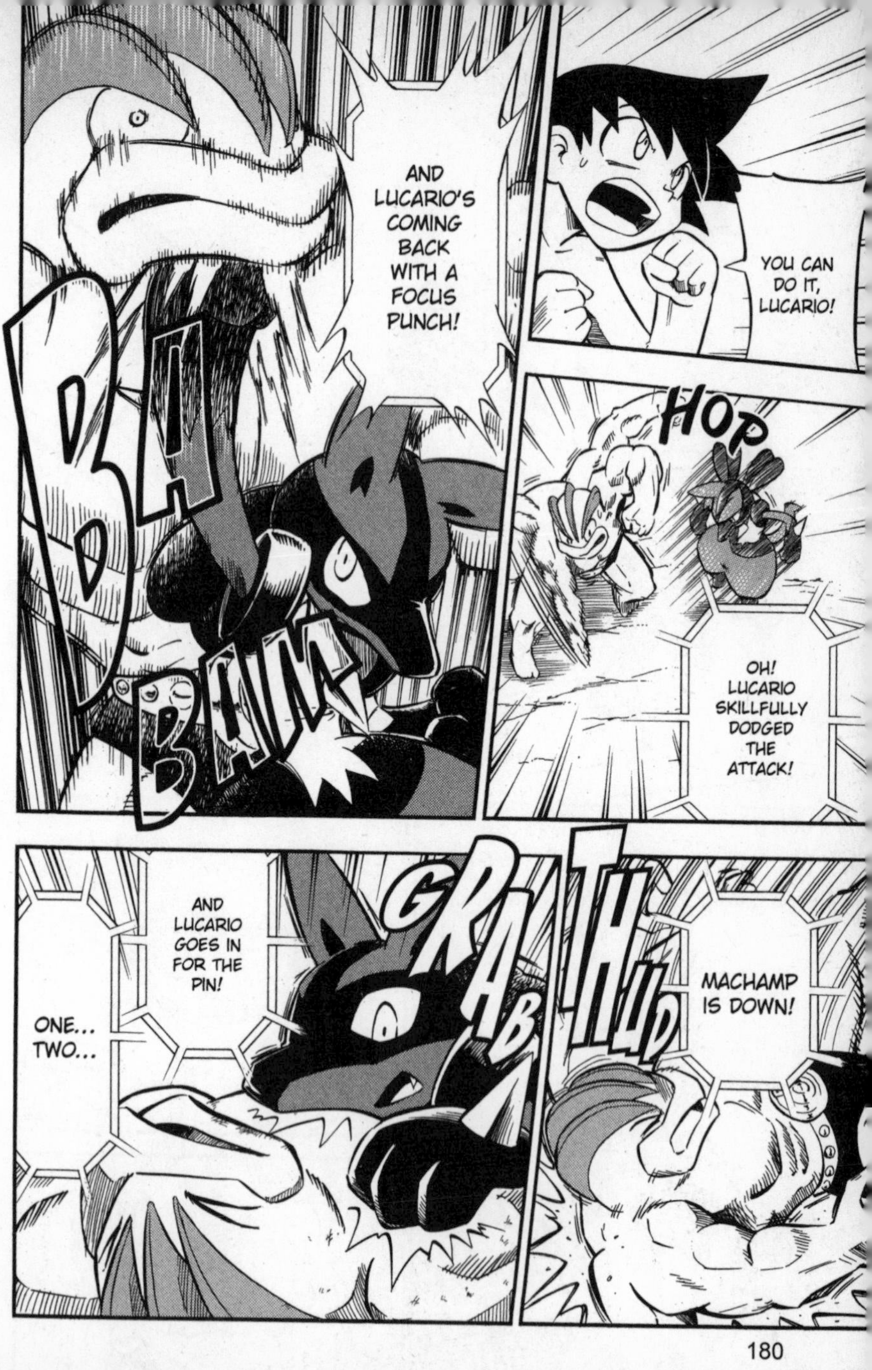
YOU CAN DO IT, LUCARIO!
HOP
OH! LUCARIO SKILLFULLY DODGED THE ATTACK!
AND LUCARIO'S COMING BACK WITH A FOCUS PUNCH!
BAM
THUD
MACHAMP IS DOWN!
GRAB
AND LUCARIO GOES IN FOR THE PIN!
ONE... TWO...

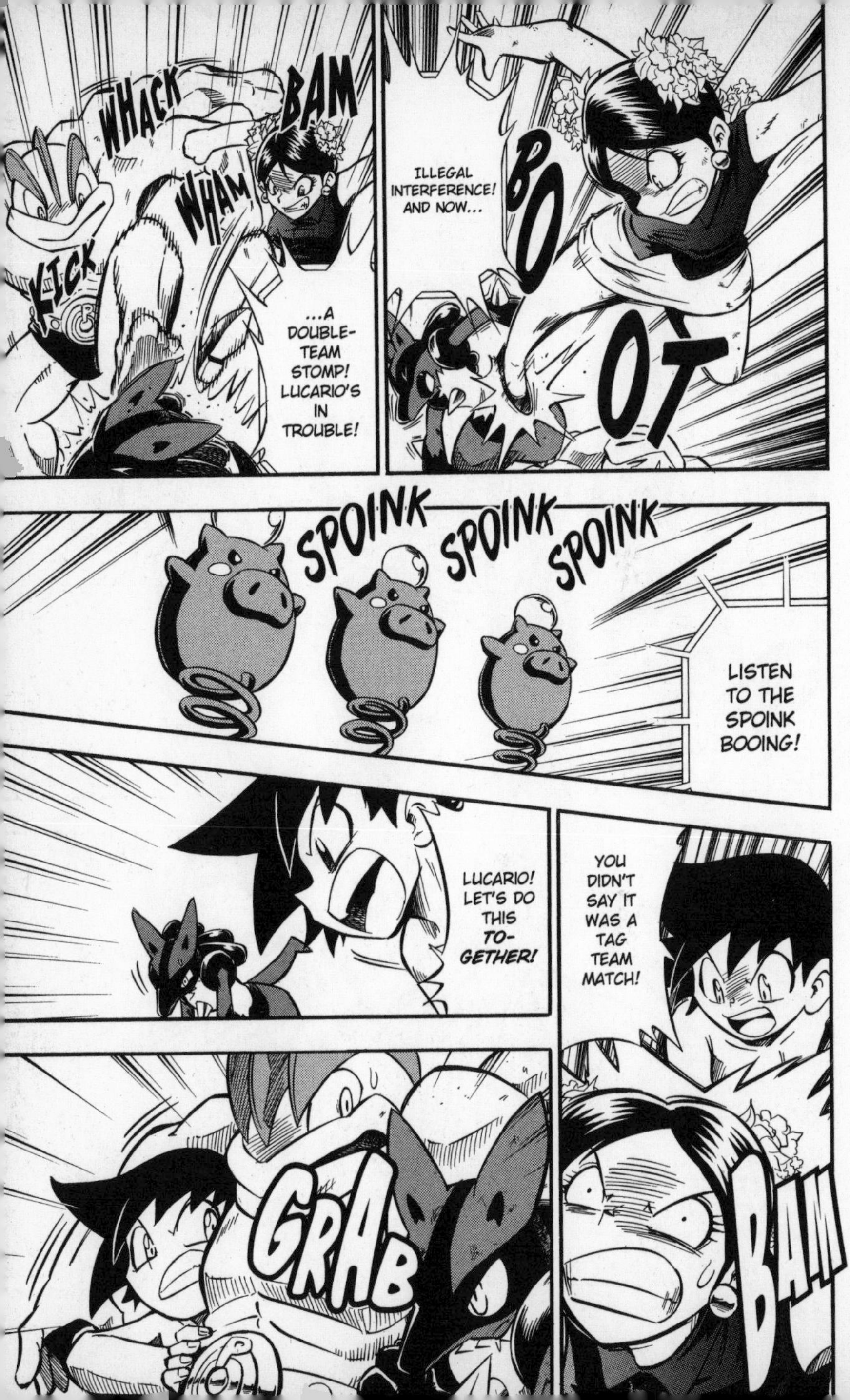
ILLEGAL INTERFERENCE! AND NOW...
BOOT
WHACK
BAM
WHAM
KICK
...A DOUBLE-TEAM STOMP! LUCARIO'S IN TROUBLE!
SPOINK
SPOINK
SPOINK
LISTEN TO THE SPOINK BOOING!
YOU DIDN'T SAY IT WAS A TAG TEAM MATCH!
LUCARIO! LET'S DO THIS *TO-GETHER!*
BAM
GRAB

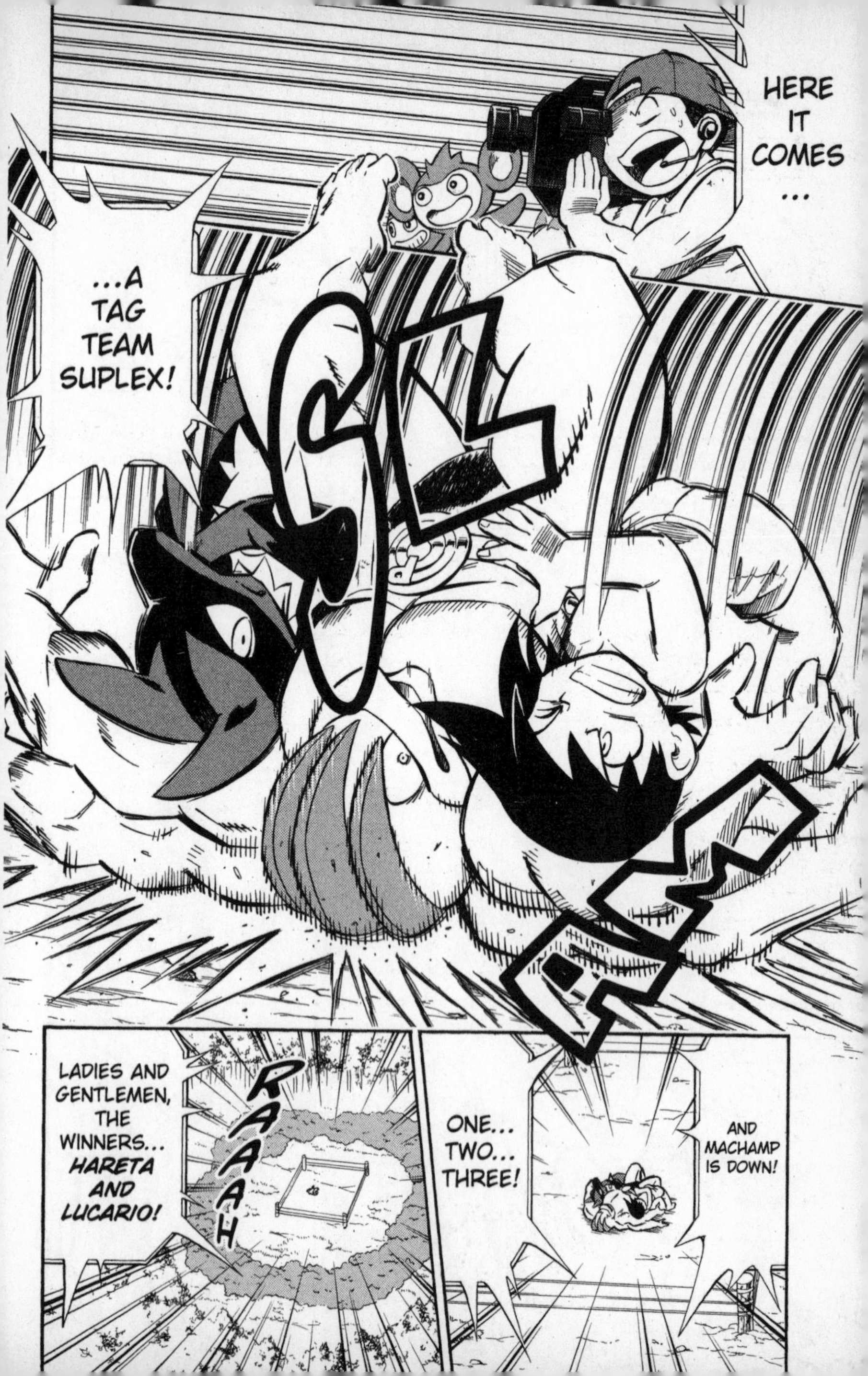
HERE IT COMES...
...A TAG TEAM SUPLEX!
AND MACHAMP IS DOWN!
ONE... TWO... THREE!
LADIES AND GENTLEMEN, THE WINNERS... *HARETA AND LUCARIO!*
RAAAAH

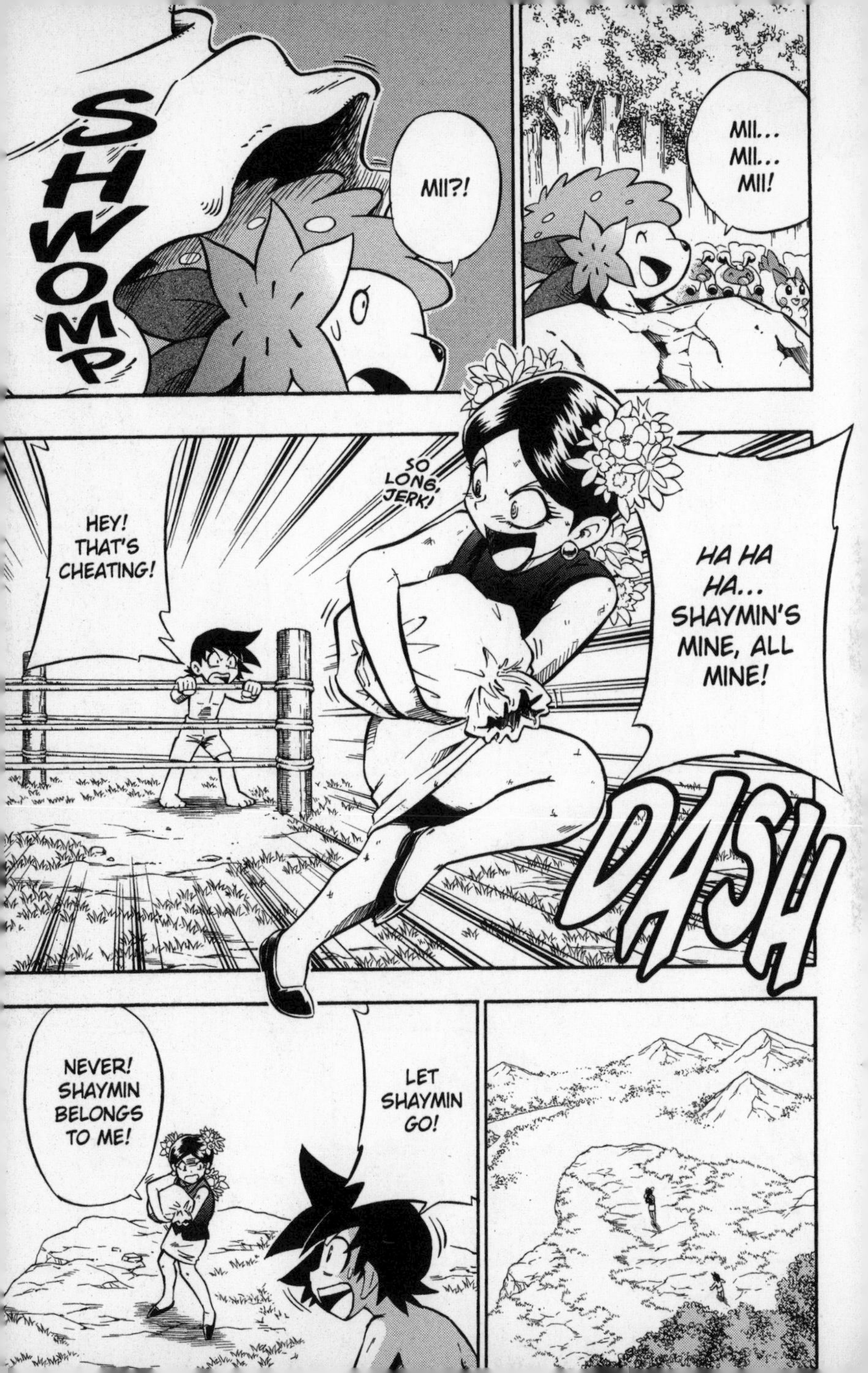
MII... MII... MII!
SHWOMP
MII?!
HA HA HA... SHAYMIN'S MINE, ALL MINE!
SO LONG, JERK!
HEY! THAT'S CHEATING!
DASH
LET SHAYMIN GO!
NEVER! SHAYMIN BELONGS TO ME!

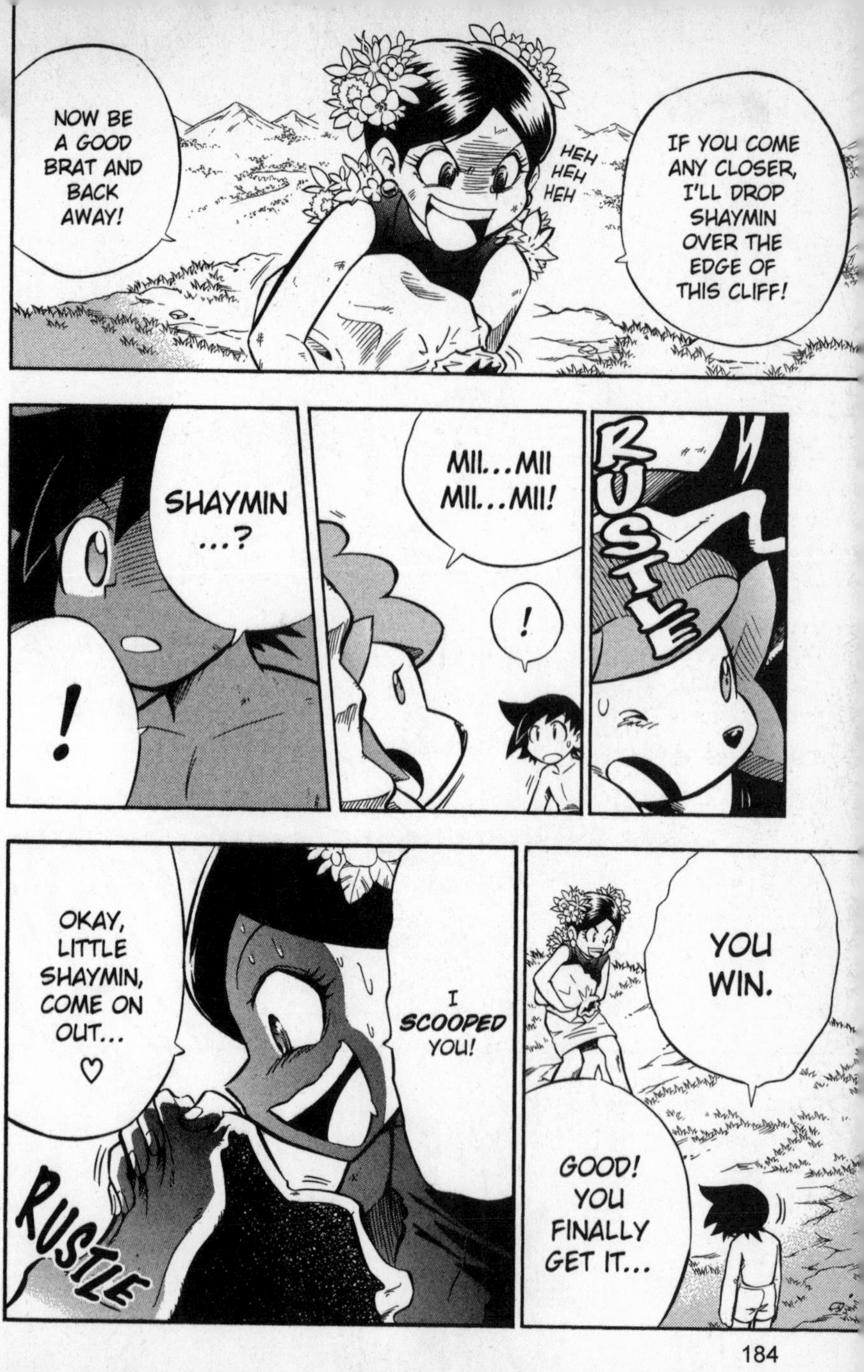
IF YOU COME ANY CLOSER, I'LL DROP SHAYMIN OVER THE EDGE OF THIS CLIFF!
HEH HEH HEH
NOW BE A GOOD BRAT AND BACK AWAY!
RUSTLE
MII...MII MII...MII!
!
SHAYMIN ...?
!
YOU WIN.
GOOD! YOU FINALLY GET IT...
I SCOOPED YOU!
OKAY, LITTLE SHAYMIN, COME ON OUT... ♡
RUSTLE

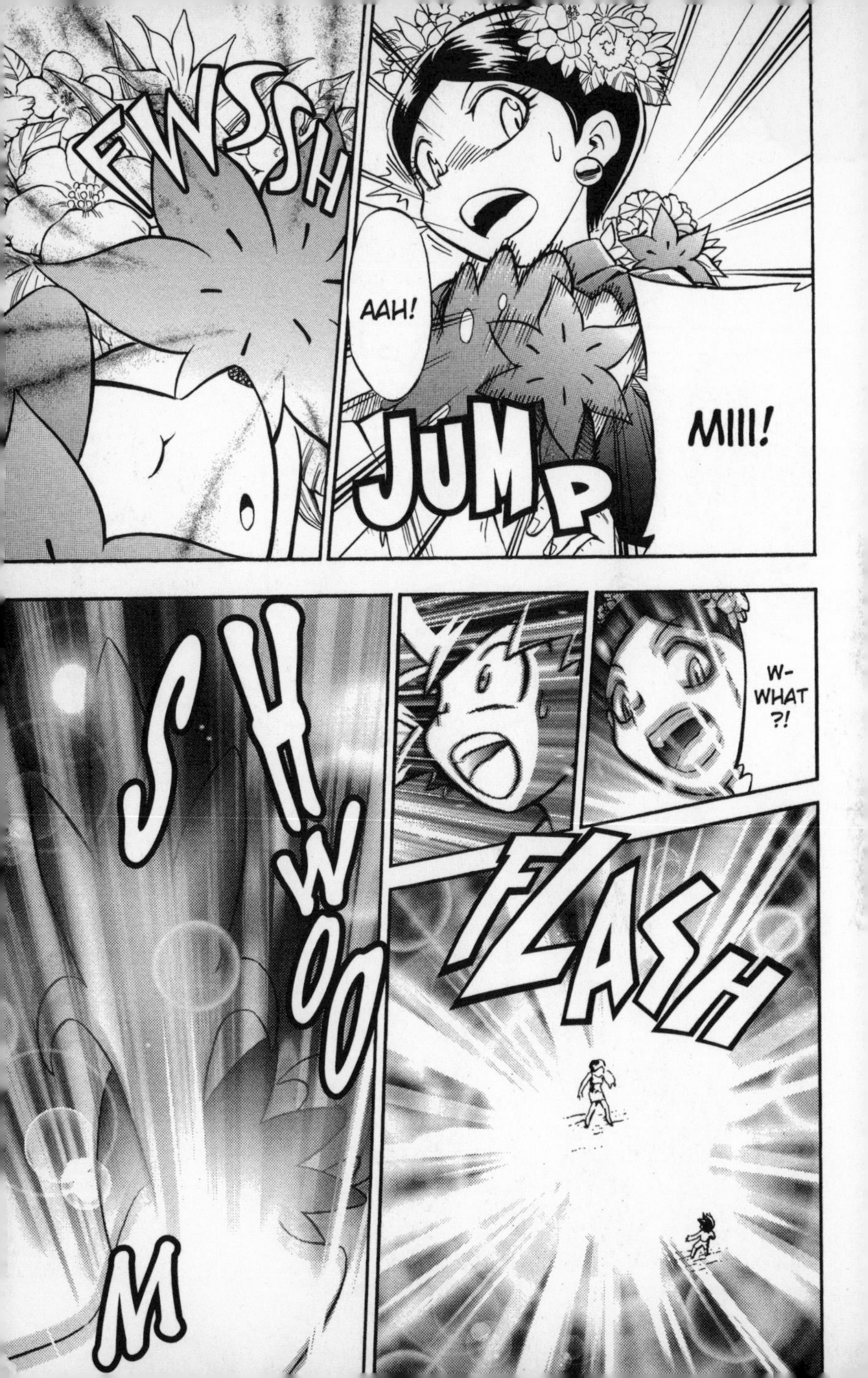
AAH!
MIII!
JUMP
FWSSH
W-WHAT?!
FLASH
SHWOOM

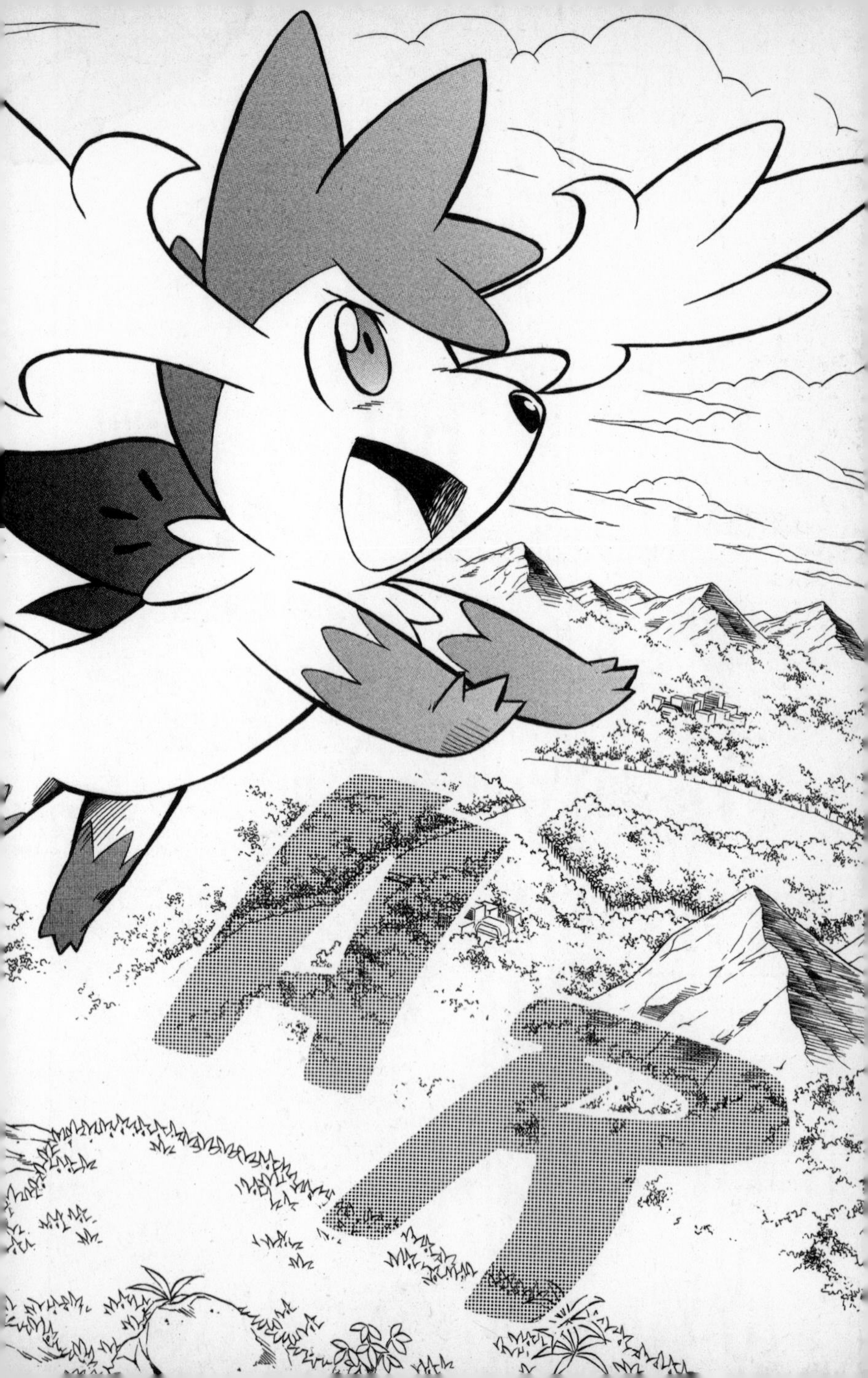

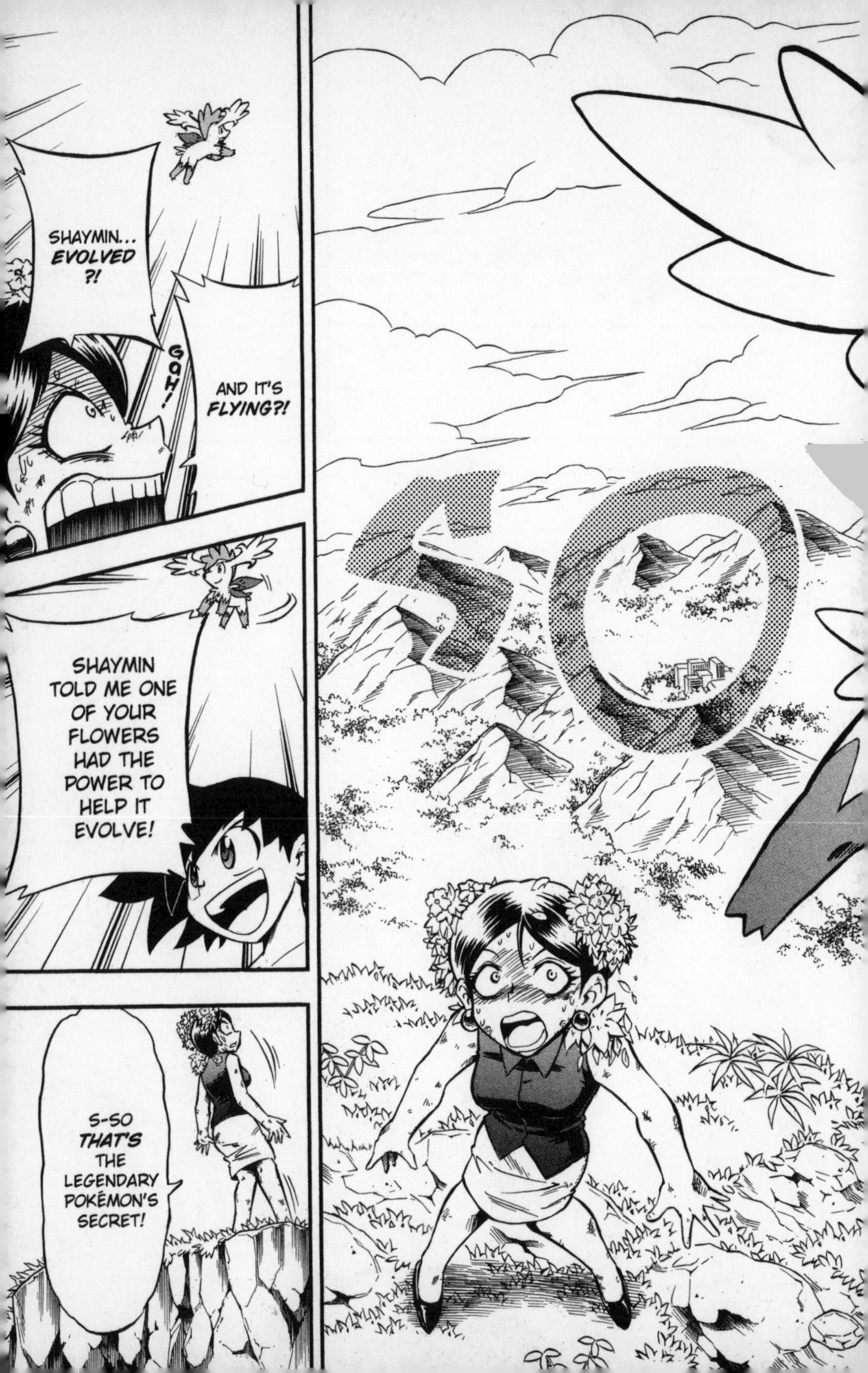
SO
SHAYMIN... EVOLVED ?!
GAH!
AND IT'S FLYING?!
SHAYMIN TOLD ME ONE OF YOUR FLOWERS HAD THE POWER TO HELP IT EVOLVE!
S-SO THAT'S THE LEGENDARY POKÉMON'S SECRET!

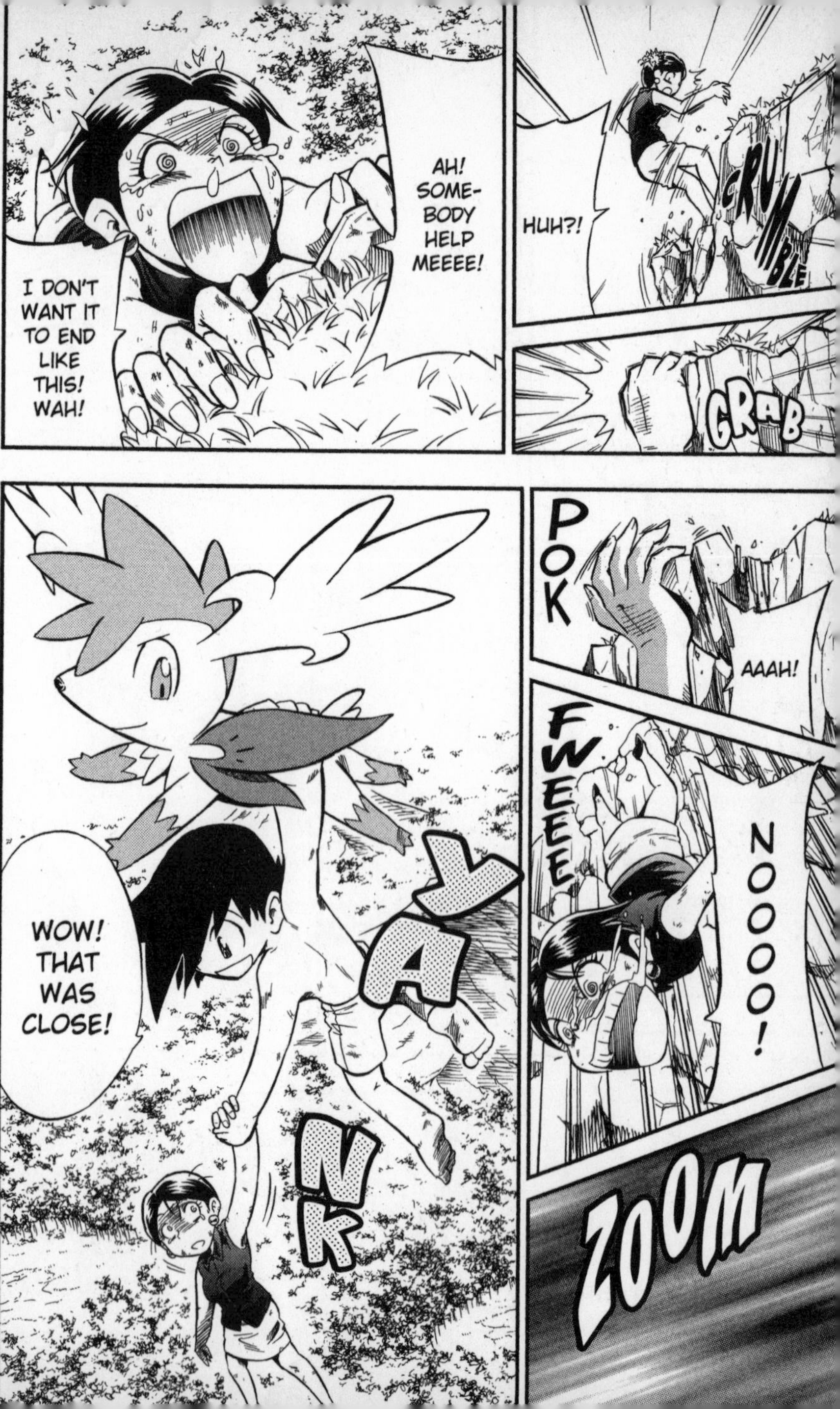
HUH?!
CRUMBLE
GRAB
AH! SOMEBODY HELP MEEEE!
I DON'T WANT IT TO END LIKE THIS! WAH!
POK
AAAH!
NOOOO!
FWEEEE
ZOOM
YANK
WOW! THAT WAS CLOSE!

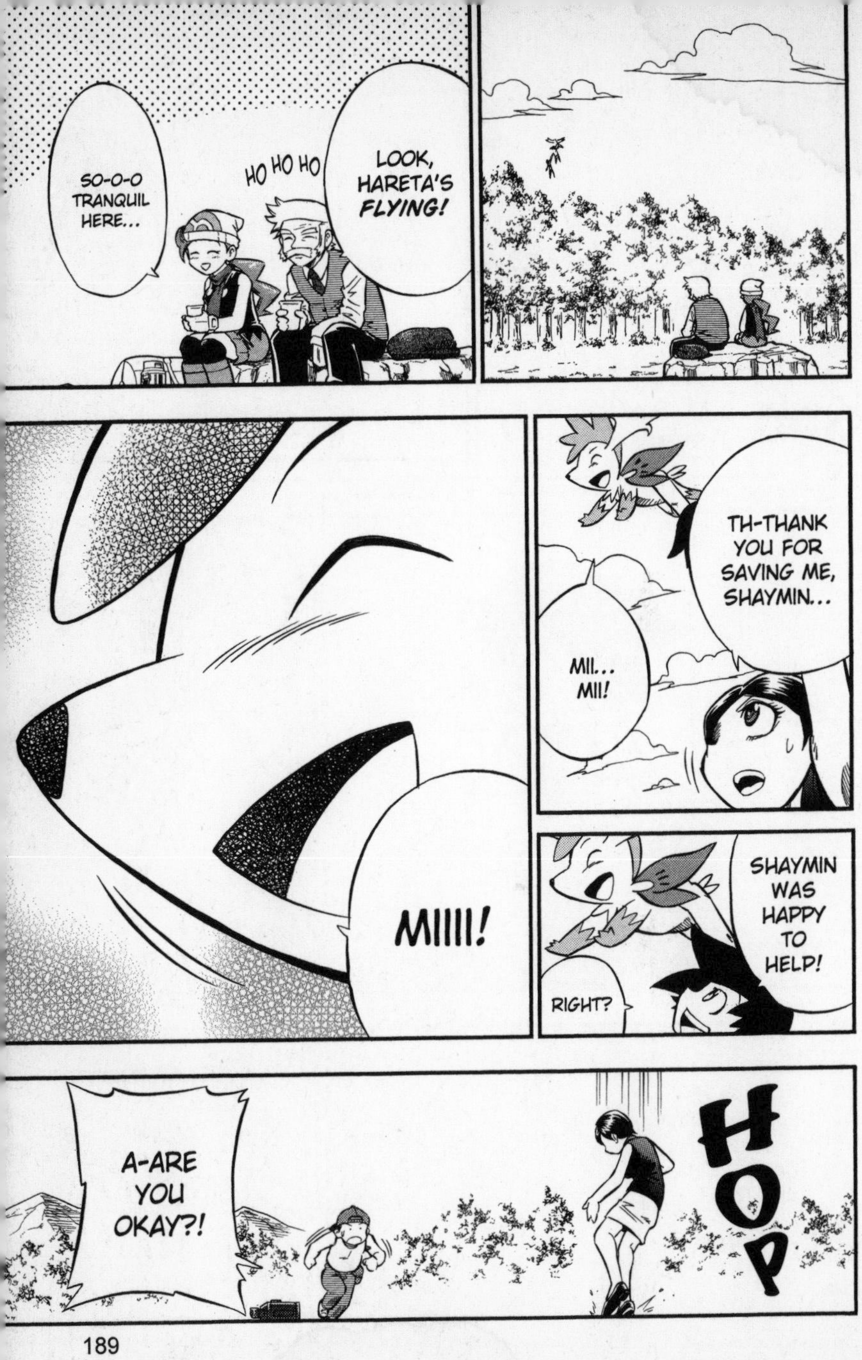
LOOK, HARETA'S *FLYING!*
HO HO HO
SO-O-O TRANQUIL HERE...
TH-THANK YOU FOR SAVING ME, SHAYMIN...
MII... MII!
SHAYMIN WAS HAPPY TO HELP!
RIGHT?
MIIII!
HOP
A-ARE YOU OKAY?!

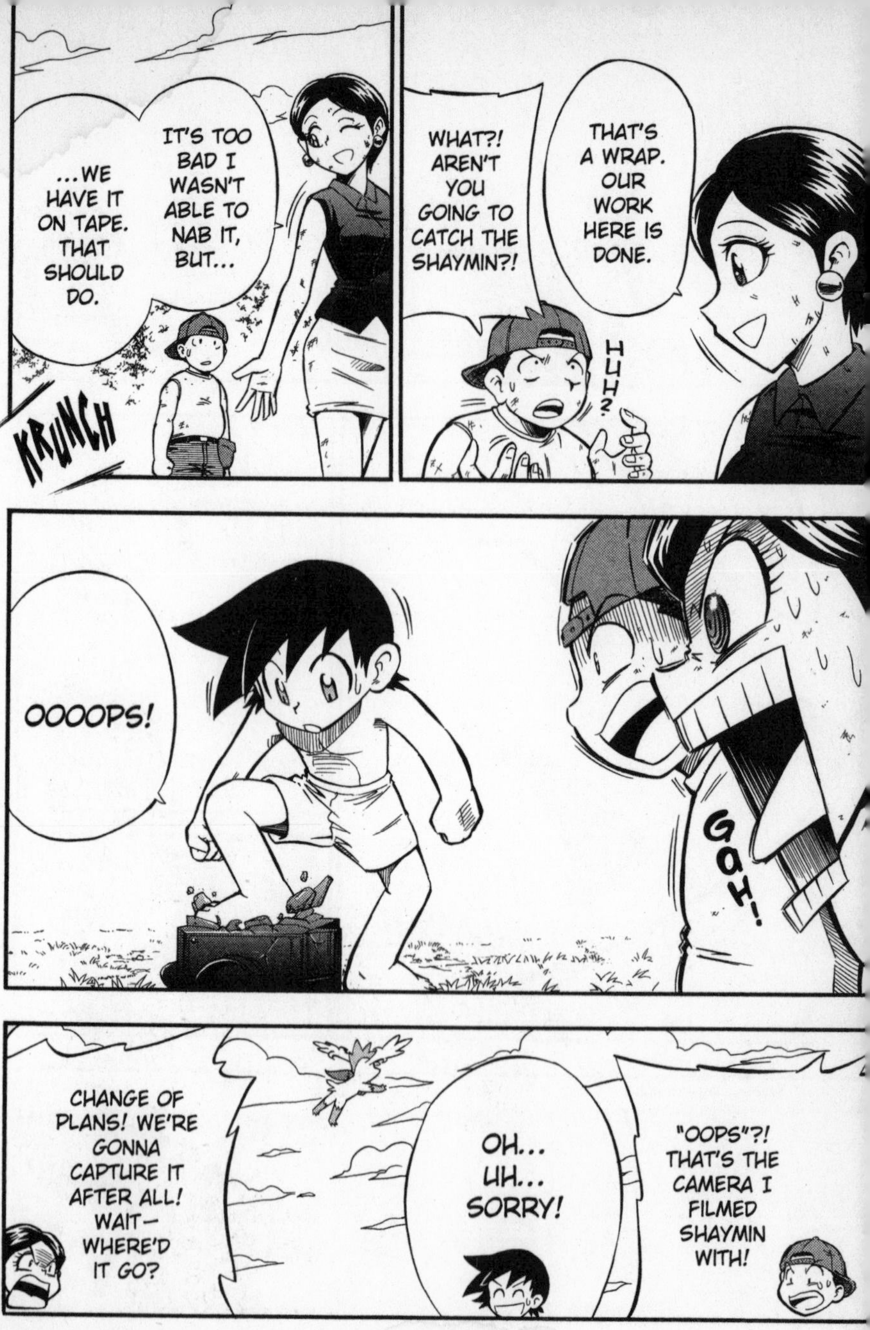
THAT'S A WRAP. OUR WORK HERE IS DONE.
WHAT?! AREN'T YOU GOING TO CATCH THE SHAYMIN?!
HUH?
IT'S TOO BAD I WASN'T ABLE TO NAB IT, BUT...
...WE HAVE IT ON TAPE. THAT SHOULD DO.
KRUNCH
OOOOPS!
GAH!
"OOPS"?! THAT'S THE CAMERA I FILMED SHAYMIN WITH!
OH... UH... SORRY!
CHANGE OF PLANS! WE'RE GONNA CAPTURE IT AFTER ALL! WAIT—WHERE'D IT GO?

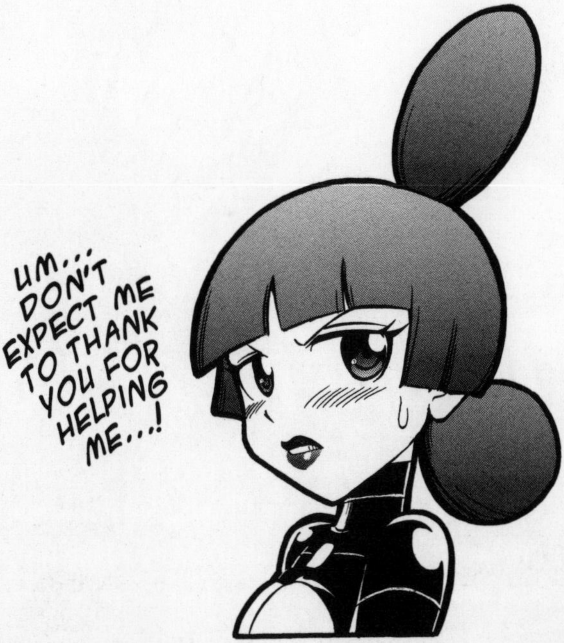
UM... DON'T EXPECT ME TO THANK YOU FOR HELPING ME...!

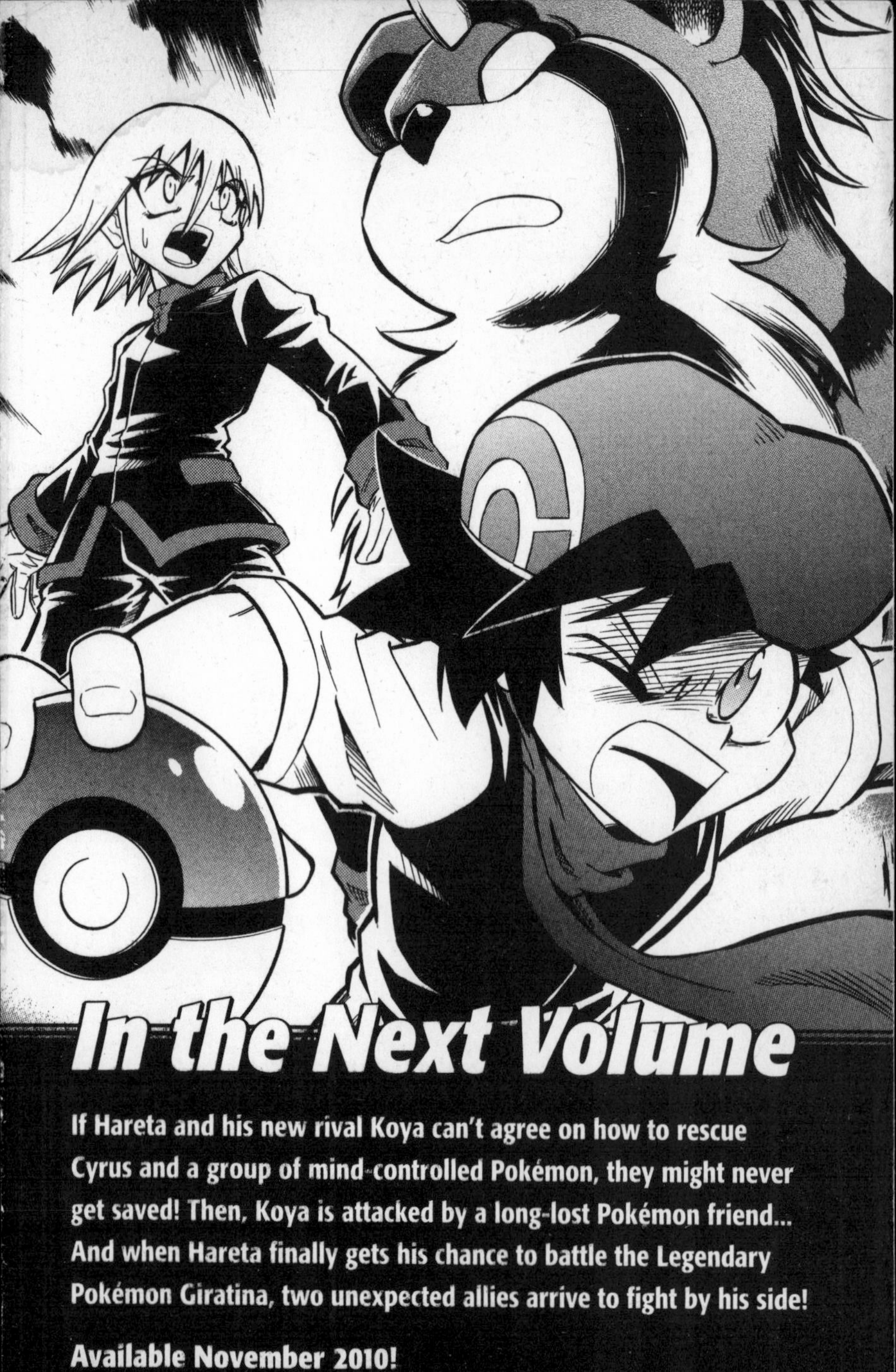

In the Next Volume

If Hareta and his new rival Koya can't agree on how to rescue Cyrus and a group of mind-controlled Pokémon, they might never get saved! Then, Koya is attacked by a long-lost Pokémon friend... And when Hareta finally gets his chance to battle the Legendary Pokémon Giratina, two unexpected allies arrive to fight by his side!

Available November 2010!